Praise for MACROLIFE

"It is a very impressive book, not only because it is so well written but, most especially, because of its imaginative scope. It takes courage, confidence, and real ability to tackle these magnificent Stapledonian expanses of space and time, to confront the Universe in all its ever-changing majesty, and to dream of the infinite variety in which it can challenge man and change him (or make him change himself).

"That, of course, is the challenge of the science fiction field, and at a time when too much SF is trying to reduce the vastness and wonders among which we and our world live to mere backdrops for teenage suspense plots, it is refreshing and encouraging to have someone tackle the greater scheme and do it so splendidly. I hope there will be more books where *Macrolife* came from."
—Reginald Bretnor

"It's been years since I was so impressed. *Macrolife* manages an extraordinary balance between the personal and cosmic elements. Altogether a worthy successor to Olaf Stapledon's *Star Maker*. . . .

"I'm confident that George's book is so good it doesn't need any recommendation from me. You can quote that!

"One of the few books I intend to read again."
—Arthur C. Clarke

"A work of sweeping imagination, exploring the fascinating implications of humanity's breakout to the era of space colonies. Zebrowski addresses the deepest of questions: what is the human destiny? I read this book with great enjoyment."
—Gerard K. O'Neill

"*Macrolife* is the sort of novel that is not often seen in science fiction. It is thoughtful and deeply textured, somewhat reminiscent of Le Guin but on a much larger canvas; its scope alone should fascinate many readers, though its underlying philosophy is equally attractive."
—Chelsea Quinn Yarbro

"With the publication of *Macrolife*, George Zebrowski takes his place next to H. G. Wells, Olaf Stapledon, and Arthur C. Clarke as a novelist of ideas on a cosmic scale. It is one of the most intellectually adventurous science fiction novels of all time.

"I am especially moved by Zebrowski's success in striking a balance between the demands of thought and art . . . a splendidly wrought novel . . . much more than a book about space colonies, it presents a comprehensive vision of human destiny. *Macrolife* is magnificent."

—W. Warren Wagar

"*Macrolife* is a thoughtful and detailed extrapolation of a staggering concept: the survival of our species in extraplanetary habitats. In rich, meticulous prose Zebrowski examines the emotional and philosophical ramifications of this concept, and in the novel's powerful finale—the section entitled 'The Dream of Time'—he creates a farsighted and poetic coda that is absolutely lovely. An important book."

—Michael Bishop

"The first writer since Stapledon to get the Stapledonian flavor-vistas, perspectives, a kind of distant, serene motion. I think it's a book that will last, if only for its first statement of an emerging, probably inevitable vision. The novel oscillates nicely between long view and close focus, capturing a mood and feeling that few even attempt in this field, and at the conclusion there is a genuine vast perspective evoked. The prose is very good—smooth, evocative, adroit—a solid work that will have a following of the best sort."

—Gregory Benford

"What Zebrowski has tried in *Macrolife* is beyond the abilities of most writers in the field. He has shown the sweep of time, and the future evolution of mankind. Indeed, he has shown the future of all living things, from microbes to sun systems. And this on a canvas which stretches from now to Forever."

—Howard Waldrop

"George Zebrowski's ambitious novel *Macrolife* is constructed on a scale completely different from that of most science fiction being written today, so much of which is too conservative in its outlook. *Macrolife* —with its graphs, charts, illustrations, and interludes of theory—is as striking in form as it is imaginative in content. The book is in the best utopian tradition of Wells and Stapledon."

—Curtis C. Smith

"Impressive . . . *Macrolife* theme beautifully and convincingly developed: all based on credible cosmic technology. A history of eternity, done with grace and optimism. The last section, 'The Dream of Time,' with its serial universes and macrolives, has melodies and cadences reminiscent of Elizabethan sonnets. For contrapuntal contrast, the destruction of Earth is the best I ever read. It should satisfy even John, writing on Patmos. This, we agree, is the Way of Last Things."

—Charles L. Harness

"Its sheer sweep, its grandeur of concept, its daring, integrity, and rational intelligence put to shame those science fictioneers who can only fill up the next hundred billion years with space wars and other high jinks orchestrated by heroes who are only giant dwarfs, fantasy projections of our as-yet rather primitive selves.

"Integrity, yes, and honesty. Here is a piece of fiction which may well be more than fiction, which demanded to be written, and to be written in its own terms. *Macrolife* is a work of grandeur and intelligence. With it, George Zebrowski's career as mature prophetic writer really commenced. . . ."

—Ian Watson

"The Utimate Utopia. There's a lot of wonder in this book."
—Richard E. Geis, *Science Fiction Review*

"A truly *sui generis* book . . . a massive intellectual achievement, a work that will be discussed and debated for years."

—Thomas N. Scortia

"No higher praise could be offered than to say that *Macrolife* is almost Stapledonian in its approach to the subject of man in the galaxy."

—Brian W. Aldiss, *Trillion Year Spree*

"A very plausible cosmology . . . Zebrowski has plotted and executed a fascinating story . . . superlative 'hard science fiction.' . . ."

—United Press International

"An intellectual tour de force of great imagination and reverence for mankind's potential."

—Dean Ing

"Reminiscent of Stapledon's future history in its breathtaking scope, and Blish's *Cities in Flight* tetralogy in its grand theme."

—*Publishers Weekly*

". . . the gradual evolution of human society in the artificial worlds develops richly. The novel will probably be remembered rather longer than swifter, more superficial works."

—*Science Fiction & Fantasy Book Review*

"*Macrolife* has acquired a cult following."

—Stephen Baxter, *Vector*

MACROLIFE

MACROLIFE

A MOBILE UTOPIA

GEORGE ZEBROWSKI

an imprint of **Prometheus Books**
Amherst, NY

Published 2006 by PYR™, an imprint of Prometheus Books

Inquiries should be addressed to
PYR
Editorial Department
Prometheus Books
59 John Glenn Drive
Amherst, New York 14228–2197
VOICE: 716–691–0133, ext. 207
FAX: 716–564–2711
WWW.PYRSF.COM

10 09 08 07 06   5 4 3 2 1

Library of Congress Cataloging-in-Publication Data

Zebrowski, Geoerge, 1945–
    Macrolife : a mobile utopia / George Zebrowski.
        p. cm.
    Originally published: New York : Harper & Row, 1979.
    ISBN 1–59102–340–8 (hardcover : alk. paper)
    ISBN 1–59102–341–6 (paperback : alk. paper)
    I. Title.

PS3576.E35M33 2006
813'.54—dc22

2005027866

Printed in the United States on acid-free paper

To *Pam*

for the beginning,
for the years after,
for the friendship and love,
these words

INTRODUCTION
TO THE NEW EDITION

ncreasingly, and sadly, American science fiction continues to be dominated by what George Zebrowski has referred to as "print television": by books conceived and written as if they are TV films rather than works that challenge and enhance the emotions and the intellect of the reader, examples of "the precious life-blood of a master spirit, embalmed and treasured up on purpose to a life beyond life."

George Zebrowski's *Macrolife* is the latter kind of book, and that definition of a good book is almost three hundred and fifty years old. It comes from the pen of the poet John Milton, in his long political pamphlet *Areopagitica*, which is also one of the masterpieces of English prose. Subtitled *A Speech for the Liberty of Unlicensed Printing*, this pamphlet of the year 1644 attacked state censorship, which was implemented by requiring official approval for the products of a printing press.

Nowadays works of science fiction—a literature of such potential to liberate the imagination and the mind—are censored *commercially* by a virtual conspiracy of publishers, editors, voters for prestigious awards, and, alas, by authors themselves. In many respects the pressures of commercial censorship are far worse than anything against which the author of *Paradise Lost* protested, because today's pressures train readers to think and to respond shallowly, to consume the intellectual equivalent of fast food while convinced that they are feasting on fine cuisine. Which average reader nowadays—the audience for Milton's polemic in *his* day—would get far beyond the title of that eloquent, finely wrought pamphlet? Even the title seems a bit of a mouthful.

George Zebrowski's *Macrolife* certainly isn't fast food.

"Print television" doesn't simply refer to the flood of zippy, slick adventure fiction on the book racks, clones of previous SF, clones of *Star Wars*, clones of clones. The phenomenon is more insidious than that. For adventure fiction merely represents the low-level consensus of escapist entertainment. There also exists a high-level consensus consisting of literary work that is finely crafted, replete with a care for words and narrative tone and interactive dialogue that is both snappy yet unvulgar, populated with properly rounded characters, equipped with significant themes, laced with emotional concern, and with tasteful daring, and with a banner-waving show of insight and responsibility. Much of this work is also a sham, a confection. Too many budding writers write in order to see a well-wrought book in print with their name upon it, rather than to affect the consciousness of readers and even to change their lives in some minor or even major way (which, to me at least, is a principal reason for writing). Pretty soon those writers who do succeed become authorities on writing SF.

"Show but don't tell," aspiring authors are advised. Learn how to sugar the pill until the pill is buried deep, lost in a cyst of saccharine. Endless workshops—which are commercial as much as literary since they are guiding the evolution of new authors toward survival and success in the consensus marketplace—and "How to Do It" articles by professional authors who have adapted to this ecological niche advise the young hopefuls how to cast narrative hooks like an angler fooling the fish and the best way to slip exposition of ideas painlessly into a tale without clunky chunks of facts or ideas interrupting the smooth momentum of the story. A major crime is to let one's grasp on the reader slip for a moment or to hold up the onward rush of events. Thou shalt not discomfort the readers by making them slow down in the reading and actually *think*. They must simply experience the cunning, superficial semblance of deep feeling and intellection. Thus readers are conditioned not to think, so that ultimately they will not be readers of fiction but viewers. Thus writers are trained to think carefully about avoiding the appearance of rigorous thought.

George Zebrowski is an author who will make the reader think; and the ideas, the experience of his work, will not, therefore, slip away afterward like some phantom of thought, some illusion that the "viewing" of some subsequent book will presently eclipse.

This is why Arthur C. Clarke described *Macrolife* as "one of the few books I intend to read again," adding that "it's been years since I was so impressed. *Macrolife* manages an extraordinary balance between the personal and the cosmic elements. Altogether a worthy successor to Olaf Stapledon's *Star Maker*."

Spurred on by peer fame in the form of Nebula and Hugo nominations and inclusion in "Best of the Year" anthologies as well as by inflated advances for "long awaited" first novels or sequels to previous, much-loved confections, the concept of the award-worthy piece of fiction—one which possesses the magic ingredients of balance, artistry, characterization, significance, et cetera—exists as a kind of abstract idol that now tends to condition, even if unconsciously, the kind of stories and novels that authors will write and how they will go about writing these. This system trains writers not to attempt other things or even to believe that those other ways could be valid. And editors punish deviancy as being "uncommercial," which is tragic for authors, for readers, and for science fiction itself insofar as American science fiction commercially dominates world markets. To many people in America, consensus science fiction seems the only conceivable kind.

Thank God, then, for George Zebrowski.

Or should we, perversely, thank that madman Hitler? For Zebrowski, child of displaced Polish slave-workers, only came to America courtesy of the Nazi cataclysm, bringing with him a European tradition of literature, philosophy, and science that distinguishes him from most of his peers. He himself has commented that "Platonic dialogue, the symphonies of Mahler, utopian fiction and Wellsian prophecy . . . these are the personal and technical sources of *Macrolife*." Brian Stableford, reviewing *Macrolife* on its first appearance, was moved to wonder what possible future there could be in the science fiction field for a writer like Zebrowski. *Macrolife* was far more worthy "than a dozen sickly novels of the species that currently dominate the American SF scene," yet the book seemed to Stableford to be a literary mule, something that just ought not to have been a novel. How deeply the divide has grown between fiction and nonfiction—even though historically this schism is of fairly recent origin and was irrelevant, as Stableford points out, to "the most ambitious works of the seventeenth century."

Macrolife is certainly an ambitious book, if any book is, yet though it is rooted in an older tradition of passionate thought, its own ambitions aren't those of the past at all. They are of the future, of the furthest futures conceivable.

If any book is a treasure in Milton's sense, here indeed is one, in a world where so many contemporary "masterpieces" are like doughnuts, fresh sugary hot sellers today, stale and discarded by tomorrow. The first edition of *Macrolife* nonplussed several reviewers, but favorable opinion has prevailed, for instance, in most major critical reference works and in *Library Journal*'s must-read list. *Macrolife* is one of Easton Press's Masterpieces of Science Fiction.

In Stableford's view there is simply no way that a vision such as Zebrowski's can be presented using the narrative techniques of the novel, since—to take a couple of examples—these compel Zebrowski to have his characters lecture one another or require the protagonist to read a book of commentary "in order that we can read it over his shoulder." For the novel has become preoccupied with character and narrative whereas Zebrowski is concerned with future sociology.

Isn't it curious that one of the great classics of the twentieth century was George Orwell's *Nineteen Eighty-Four* in which O'Brien lectures Winston Smith at length and in which Smith reads page after page of *The Theory and Practice of Oligarchical Collectivism*, quotations from which occupy almost exactly *one-tenth* of the whole novel?

Yet Stableford's criticism is correct, if reformulated to express precisely what is wrong with much American SF, namely, its betrayal of its own content in favor of novelistic tricks. Time and again, philosophical problems—of sociology, cosmology, the nature of existence, all of which are of the essence of science fiction—are presented but then hastily sublimated into mere story. One opens so many SF novels with such high hopes only to find that the science—in the broadest sense, of *knowledge*—is the merest pretext for a fictional adventure.

Zebrowski, for his part, has diagnosed a fundamental anti-intellectualism in American SF. In his view too many of its authors believe that they are sages, full of wise opinions, whereas the truth is that they have never thought rigorously enough as part of their basic existence.

On the contrary, they have schooled themselves to conjure up a mirage, an illusion of intellectual rigor. Zebrowski himself studied philosophy at the State University of New York and might have become an academic philosopher. The best teacher in that college (in his opinion), one Robert Neidorf, was a philosopher of science, but also a science fiction reader. The two strands *could* combine. "There should be more people," Zebrowski has stated, "who are moved by the ideals and examples of science, and who understand its sociology and history, its importance to human aspirations and survival. Most workaday scientists rarely think about these things either."

Its importance to survival. To a life beyond life, to quote Milton again. Survival, the triumph over powerlessness, and life beyond life

are indeed the themes of *Macrolife*. Just as the writings of its character
Richard Bulero are harked back to by subsequent characters, as rational
visions of the future of life in the cosmos, so, too, may this novel of
Zebrowski's be harked back to aboard some space habitation out
among the stars in the year 3000 as one of the founding texts, when
other SF authors of today are as much remembered as medieval French
court poets. If the future does follow a certain path, away from planetary surfaces into free space—as Zebrowski argues with a fierce convic-
tion that it must—then he may well be regarded as a true literary seer.
Few other writers are in the running for this sort of reputation.

    Macrolife is a major vision of social intelligence transforming the
cosmos. It is in three sections. The first focuses upon events in the year
2021 when the disintegration of the "miracle" all-purpose building
material Bulerite destroys civilization on Earth. The events that are set
in motion propel the first kernel of macrolife free of the solar system.
The second and longest section deals with more mature macrolife of
the year 3000. The star-faring habitat visits a degraded dirtworld to
obtain raw materials with which to reproduce itself, then it returns
with its new twin to Earthspace, where the first contact with alien
macrolife occurs. The human race is accepted into the cosmic circle
because people have learned how to link with artificial intelligence,
thus overcoming—or at least taming—the instinctive passions inherited from dirtworld evolution. The final section begins a hundred billion years later when macrolife has filled the universe but the universe
is beginning to wind down back toward the point of final collapse.

    The Bulerite calamity renders the Earth dramatically uninhabit-
able. Earth's very crust is cracked, recriminations trigger an all-out
nuclear war, and to trump the doom the Earth and Moon are engulfed
in a bizarre, other-dimensional bubble. At first glance this may seem a
rather histrionic and arbitrary plot device to compel macrolife to set out
on its journey of growth; almost a deus ex machina at the very outset of
the novel. If it requires such a far-out set of circumstances to launch

macrolife, then macrolife cannot be such an inevitable future, can it? Could it be, also, that Zebrowski deliberately lays on the apocalyptic action with a trowel so as to refresh the reader after some rather lengthy and serious philosophical conversations in Platonic dialogue mode?

A problem of substance? And a problem of style?

Zebrowski's concern with rebirth from out of cataclysm reflects his own background as a member of a mutilated nation. "I feel the force of memory that pushes out from my parents," he has written; "it's always there, a shadow cast by a world gone insane." His past was "brutal, cruel, and stupid . . . created by people . . . who didn't want me to be born." Dirtworlds are also brutal, cruel, and stupid as environments; and the escape to a space habitat, which is free from the shocks to which planetary flesh is heir, may be emotionally patterned upon Zebrowski's own escape as a child from war-torn Europe to America. This, plus a subsequent pattern, which segued with his discovery of science fiction. For though he was an adoptive New Yorker, a temporary move to Florida from the gang-haunted, refugee-packed, decaying South Bronx presented him with warmth, cleanliness, light, and a white marble public library, "a place out of Clarke's *Against the Fall of Night*" (or something in the meadows of a macroworld) where he discovered endless shelves of early hardback volumes from Fantasy Press, Gnome Press, Shasta, and Doubleday.

Thus there is an emotional pattern in Zebrowski, of salvation from apocalypse—not for everyone but only for the fortunate ones. There is an intellectual argument, too. The Bulerite disaster is appropriate because it is an example (this particular one mixing natural calamity with human folly) of a whole range of disasters that can very easily overtake natural planetary life when all the eggs are in one basket. The very escape route from ravaged Earth—aboard the hollowed asteroid, Asterome—is a reminder of another possible disaster that was narrowly averted. Until diverted and moored at a libration point in the Earth-Moon system, this same asteroid had once been on a collision course with Earth. Nothing in our present day prevents a similar asteroid or comet from impacting with our planet at any time, as has happened repeatedly during geological history. Such an impact, releasing the equivalent power of thousands of hydrogen bombs, would destroy civilization and probably cause a mass extinction of species, our own included. A planet-bound culture is also threatened by any instability in its sun, by the climate flipping into a new ice age, and it is challenged by its own success in the form of chemical and thermal pollution, as witnessed by the ozone holes and global warming.

At the moment we only have one single planetary egg with only a finite amount of nourishing yolk in the shape of resources, and only a finite ability to tolerate the stresses of the growing chicken of civilization within itself before it cracks wide open, killing the chicken because nowhere else is available. The crack in the Earth's crust is a telling symbol. Likewise is Bulerite, that super-strong substance that allows lattice-cities to be built and the Empire State Building to disappear underneath layers of new New York.

Bulerite seems to strengthen the frail shell of the egg. But this proves untrue. Bulerite is unstable and highly destructive when it releases its locked-up energies. Its exploitation by eager capitalism, which neglects to pursue the fundamental research work of its discoverer, is a complacent strategy, and complacent strategies are potentially lethal ones.

Bulerite will find its rightful uses later on, in connection with other scientific advances that permit space-warp travel. Thereby it is further integrated into this well-designed, cleanly dovetailed book, not only as an instance of the false buttressing of the frail shell that is the Earth, but also as an appropriate example of future science—in this case, exotic states of matter and their applications.

Zebrowski does not allow his free-enterprise Bulero family simply to build higher and higher until they reach the stars. What sets macrolife on course is the failure by those exploiters of the wonder substance fully to investigate it, in other words their treachery. Through the trauma of their "crime" the Buleros are able to liberate themselves and a segment of the human race, leaving the solar system behind. A realist ever, Zebrowski acknowledges that even a millennium later the Buleros would be viewed by many people as renegades. The dramatic argument is a complex one, with no simple black versus white.

Nor are there easy black/white solutions to the possible sociological problems of space habitations. In various permutations Zebrowski explores not only the inevitable conflicts of interest between planetary and nonplanetary dwellers but also the unavoidable conflicts within a macroworld itself, which must somehow be channeled so that internal rebellion expresses itself as reproduction by consent. This was all some way removed from the rose-tinted optimism of many advocates of space colonies with their vision of geriatric joggers happily trotting around the bent meadows of the profitable paradise in the sky, at L-5, where everyone is blissfully of accord.

And a problem of style?

Zebrowski has remarked that *Macrolife* is a meditative book and should be read meditatively. Space stations may explode, cities may collapse, the Earth itself may convulse; however, the prose is meditative, just as the long-lived inhabitants of a future macroworld would be. "Their minds are still, waiting for every ripple of space-time to register," Zebrowski has commented. We are mayflies now, but they are not. Despite scenes of action and even violence, and notwithstanding limpidly beautiful descriptions, this is a book of thought, its pages turning with a measured sureness. For Zebrowski, the ideal reader is a "performer," not a "slave." Himself a child of slaves whose Nazi masters wished to stamp their ideology upon the face of Europe, Zebrowski perhaps detects an analogy with those addicts of junk SF who expect an author to insert a cassette of thrills into their heads. For the *performing* reader, by contrast, "the novel is a series of opportunities for thought, understanding, and empathy."

Macrolife is an excellent novel to perform with.

Stylistically, much of the time a solemn, neutral mode of speech prevails. People don't swear or crack jokes or use slang. This isn't so much because a lot of the conversation is expository as simply that this is the chosen tone (with emphatics provided by occasional, italicized internal dialogue). Reviewers criticized the novelist Morris West for his neutral-sounding dialogue, to which West replied in an interview with a British newspaper some years ago: "Listen, love, it is all deliberate. My dialogue is sedulously designed, not as real speech but as a cerebral vehicle for ideas in the novel. I want dialogue to be understood at once in every Anglo-Saxon country and to translate easily into the major European languages. . . . I elected this style."

Likewise with Zebrowski. Yet there is a further reason beyond the aspiration to an international (and even interstellar) style. This crops up in miniature early on when three of the characters discuss macrolife over a Chinese meal and a bottle of brandy. One of them, Sam, fades out of the discussion. Afterward: "'. . . I hope you followed some of what we said.' 'I really did, Orton. Inside I'm sober, really.' *How can frail beings like us think of doing the things Richard and Orton described?*" Certainly somebody can drift off into a brandy haze, yet in most novels they would become tipsily involved in the discussion. Sam does end up knocking over the brandy bottle, yet he never knocks over the conversation. The point is that our irrational heritage from the evolutionary jungle of rape and murder—"nature's agriculture of death"—must be opposed by rational intelligence if we are to survive and transcend ourselves. The style of *Macrolife* reflects its firm adherence to reason and to the power of rational persuasion.

It isn't the case that it would be vulgar to have the characters joking, swearing, and "slanging" each other. Rather, the mood of the dialogue is the mood of the book's deepest beliefs, beliefs that are sincerely held rather than merely being adopted as a pretext to write a momentarily vivid but forgettable yarn.

Much trivia occurs in novels, a lot of it concerned with so-called character-building. Zebrowski's characters aren't flat; they are complex and imperfect, especially John Bulero in Part 2, no superhero but a study in failure who manages in the end to transcend his somewhat self-indulgent angst. Yet trivia as such are absent. Perhaps this reflects Zebrowski's relations as a child with his own parents. The Nazi war, and the sufferings of his parents and his people, "cast its shadow over everything," he confesses, "preventing my problems from just being my own. I had no right to have lesser problems." Personal trivia were as nothing.

In Part 2, "Macrolife: 3000," the cloned John Bulero is an old-style human being among a space-faring community of genetically enhanced specimens of humanity-plus—who link with the presiding artificial intelligence and are now part way toward the larger mind-fusion to come. John's compulsive, if shy, adventuring upon the dirt-world Lea, which becomes increasingly bound up with his own erotic mesmerism by the planet-born young woman Anulka, comes to grief finally through failure of forethought on his part followed by a failure of rationality. Being ruled by the old drives—such as plain savage revenge and the habit of pulling the wool over one's eyes—John may seem in some respects a more "real" character than others who are genetically akin to him in the "Sunspace: 2021" section. Yet he is, in fact, exactly as they were. It is only by comparison with the transhumans now surrounding him that he seems more familiar *to us*. This is actually an illusion, a product of our mesmerism by the old emotional drives and of our consequent expectations as to how "real" characters ought to behave, namely, to fly into rages, to sulk, to fight, to agonize, to act irrationally. Just as the personal must eventually be superseded and integrated, so "personalities" should not be valued too grossly.

At the same time, John's errors—and the errors represented by the dirtworld—forcefully illustrate an important fact about evolution in any species, namely, that individuals and species alike must not aspire to a wholly perfect state where they can no longer make errors from which to learn.

Macrolife first appeared in 1979. Just over a decade earlier another believer in the transmutation of humanity, Alexei Panshin, won a

Nebula Award for his novel *Rite of Passage*, detailing the twenty-seven-thousand-strong society of another macroworld, an asteroid starship commuting around the dirtworlds that were seeded before nuclear cataclysm destroyed the Earth due to overpressure in the egg. Zebrowski's "factual" sources for *Macrolife* were such as J. D. Bernal and Dandridge Cole, but it's illuminating to examine the fictional evolution of the idea between *Rite of Passage* and the later book.

Panshin's society, like that of Zebrowski's original Asterome, is a two-tiered democracy with an executive council and the option of universal plebiscites. However, Panshin's macroworlders are quite rigidly conservative and opposed to change, and a power ethic prevails. In *Macrolife*, when the UN commander Nakamura attempts a coup to seize control and force Asterome to remain in the solar system to aid in reconstruction, we witness the misuse of conservative power. The moral is that conscious life must be willing to take giant risks, to engage in acts of wild faith such as the departure of Asterome and the consequent birth of macrolife.

Zebrowski adds spacious shells to the argument, just as Asterome itself builds shell upon shell of additional space. Panshin's macroworld remains a rock with the hard ideology of a rock. Thus its own population must be culled in Darwinian fashion by the rites of passage of the title: the dumping of well-prepared youngsters upon dirtworlds to see whether they can survive the experience. Many do not survive, to a large extent on account of the hatred and contempt of the "mudeaters," locked up on their hardship worlds, for the privileged star-commuters who control the void-spanning hives of human knowledge, wealth, and skill. Heroine Mia is helped to survive by an old radical of a mudeater who opens her eyes somewhat, though it is to a fellow macroworlder that she opens her legs on the planet, by contrast with John Bulero's sexual infatuation for a native. In the end the whole world of Tintera is destroyed by the peeved macroworlders, who have lost more juniors than desired during the rite of passage there.

Zebrowski's macrolifers do hate the past and what a dirtworld stands for—a chain upon the human spirit—but they are by no means so dogmatic, and John's voluntary rite of passage upon the surface is at once more lightly undertaken and more ambiguous in its lessons. The macrolifers wish to be neither philanthropists nor destroyers of worlds. The attitude they aspire to is one of empathy without overt altruism. Life must remain open-ended, all possibilities available. The macrolifers aspire to immortality—to life beyond life—whereas Panshin's elite merely live longer lives than ours, and basically their society and their mind-set are closed. Certainly Zebrowski's macrolifers do not inhabit a perfect utopia. Boredom and suicide are rather too common for comfort. However, there is enough challenge to shake them up and spur them to continue on the royal road toward multivalent, cosmic intelligence.

In the third section of Zebrowski's novel, "The Dream of Time," macrolife must reconjugate the unmodified John Bulero from out of the collective higher mentality of which he has become part, because by this late date only such as he can decide on the error-liable risk of trying to survive the collapse of the universe through into the next cycle. Like the original founders of macrolife, he can make a blind decision of transcendent potential.

Bound up with this essential feature of the importance of error and of the capacity for error is the strange fact that the universe is both capable of being known yet eludes being known in its entirety. The universe possesses a built-in incompleteness. Were it wholly knowable, thought and life would become static. Consequently, those macrolifers who survive the collapse of the cosmos at last meet earlier, wiser macrolifers from a previous cycle of creation who suspect, for their part, that even higher, earlier entities exist. There are shells beyond shells.

If this is the case, surely macrolife must already exist in our universe. Surely the universe today must be teeming with macrolife. Why, then, is there no sign of it? When human macrolife first encounters alien macrolife in Part 2 of the novel, that more mature civilization is already a million years old, adept at concealment until it chooses to reveal itself.

In cosmic terms, even a million-year-old civilization is almost contemporary with us. As human and alien macrolife fuse and evolve, so do the old suns burn out and so are new stars formed, with new planets where new life-forms can arise and in their turn develop intelligence, master space, and give rise to new macrolife. Our universe is very large, and time is long. Successive hierarchies, shells, are possible. This may equally be true of the succession of universes themselves.

This final, remarkable section—with its dialogue between the reconjugated ancient man and metalife falling apart under stress, with its triumph over time—is the most moving, sustained, and poetic sequence in the novel (always with a *lucid* poetry). It opens up whole cycles of possibility, just as the hundred-billion-year "gap" in the book's chronology leaves riches yet to be explored in subsequent, varied macrolife novels that Zebrowski plans.

Cave of Stars appeared in 1999, a fascinating and deeply thoughtful account of a giant habitat's fatal encounter with a dirtworld. Actually, to say "giant" belies the reality, since a habitat a hundred kilometres long, constructed of concentric shells around an original asteroid core, contains more internal space than the entire surface of a planet, space enough for numerous alternative worlds such as an entire sea-world especially tailored for adapted humans with gills who have opted for an aquatic existence.

Other citizens exercise their freedom of choice by entering virtual realities; or they may need to enter these temporarily for medical reasons. Whichever the case, VR tends to become addictive, posing a subtle threat to such a habitat, namely, that not enough citizens may remain in the real world to continue guiding its destiny and make vital choices. Lotus-eating and virtual adventures may occupy all their attention. Indeed, certain philosophers aboard this particular habitat speculate that it in itself may be a virtual reality, a sophistical argument soon refuted by events—with all the brusqueness of Dr. Johnson kicking a big stone to refute by demonstration Bishop Berkeley's notion of the nonexistence of matter. Overconfidence in superior technology makes this habitat vulnerable to destruction by one bigoted dirtworlder, who also holds keys of power, for he is the pope of a conservative Catholic Church which has survived upon that world, determined to prevent progress.

Arthur Clarke has variously observed that religion is a form of psychopathology—a neurological disorder—that within a few centuries from now all the old religions will accordingly have been discredited, and that civilization and religion are incompatible. In this sense a disciple of Clarke, Zebrowski destroys the last redoubt of Catholicism in spectacular fashion in *Cave of Stars*, although not before the last pope has committed an ultimate atrocity.

Cave of Stars contains a neat definition of what macrolife is: "a mobile . . . organism comprised of human and human-derived intelligences. It's an organism because it reproduces, with its human and other elements, moves and reacts on the scale of the Galaxy." It is larger inside "than the surface of a planet. And larger still within its minds."

Macrolife itself, the feature-length pilot novel (naughtily to adopt a TV category), already spans the whole of time from the present to the end of the universe and beyond. Its sheer sweep, its grandeur of concept, its daring, integrity, and rational intelligence put to shame those science fictioneers who can only fill up the next hundred billion years with space wars and other high jinks orchestrated by heroes who are only giant dwarfs, fantasy projections of our as-yet rather primitive selves.

Integrity, yes, and honesty. Here is a piece of fiction that may well be more than fiction, which demanded to be written, and to be written in its own terms. *Macrolife* is a work of grandeur and intelligence. With it, George Zebrowski's career as a mature prophetic writer really commenced, just as the real career of the human race may be only now commencing, just as we are still in the early youth of the universe itself. In times that sometimes seem trashy, yet are pregnant with glory, a book like *Macrolife* keeps our vision bright.

—Ian Watson

SEQUENCE

I. SUNSPACE: 2021

This concept of a new life form which I call Macro Life and Isaac Asimov calls "multi-organismic life" serves as a convenient shorthand whereby the whole collection of social, political, and biological problems facing the future space colonist may be represented with two-word symbols. It also communicates quickly an appreciation for the similar problems which are rapidly descending on the whole human race. Macro Life can be defined as "life squared per cell." Taking man as representative of multicelled life we can say that man is the mean proportional between Macro Life and the cell, or Macro Life is to man as man is to the cell. Macro Life is a new life form of gigantic size which has for its cells, individual human beings, plants, animals, and machines.

. . . society can be said to be pregnant with a mutant creature which will be at the same time an extraterrestrial colony of human beings and a new large scale life form.

—DANDRIDGE COLE,
"The Ultimate Human Society," 1961

One day there will arise an experimental community that works much more efficiently than the polyglot, rubbery, hand-patched society we are living in. A viable alternative will then be before us.

—CARL SAGAN,
The Cosmic Connection, 1973

Among the first forms of macrolife were earth's latticework tier cities of the late twentieth and early twenty-first centuries. They were preceded by the historical city-state, and followed by small organized communities on the moon, Mars, the various space bases, and by Asterome, the hollowed-out asteroid that became the core of the first macroworld. . . .

The tier cities were made possible by the application of advanced structural materials. The building of these cities led to the radical reorganization of urban earth society, the stabilization of population at 12 billion, and a decrease in the frequency of disorderly political change (this last change was helped by the influx of psychosocially trained designers and engineers into politics and planning). The planet was partially macroformed, and the grosser industrial processes, among them solar and fusion power systems, were moved into space. . . .

The start of the century saw the sustained widening of the world's industrial base through the exploitation of the solar system's huge reserves of energy (the sun), raw materials (the asteroids, moon, and planets), and off-planet manufacturing conditions (where pollution could never be a problem); earth's isolation was over, the finitude of its resources no longer a liability. The new economic-industrial base not only created nearly full employment; it gave earth its first chance at creating a Type II civilization.

—RICHARD BULERO,
The History of Macrolife, vol. 1, *Asterome*,
Sigma Draconis Star System, 2041

From the vantage point of several decades in the future, I believe that our children will judge the most important benefits of space colonization to have been not physical or economic, but the opening of new human options, the possibility of a new degree of freedom, not only for the human body, but much more important, for the human spirit and sense of aspiration.

—GERARD K. O'NEILL,
The High Frontier, 1976

We are in the teen-age period of explosive growth and acquisition of knowledge. We are achieving control over our environment and our destinies, and even the power and responsibility for determining the time of our own deaths. We have secured weapons with which we can kill ourselves if we choose, and we have now achieved the first sign of biological maturity—we can reproduce. We can send out colonies to other parts of the universe which can take root, grow, and establish themselves as new civilizations. . . .

The next step in evolution is from man—as the most highly organized example of multicellular life—to Macrolife.

. . . we should not be surprised if the race on earth ceases to proliferate its "cells," achieves maturity, reproduces, continues its growth in other "individuals" (space colonies), and the "individual" remaining behind on Earth, ages through hundreds of thousands of years and finally dies.

—DANDRIDGE COLE,
Beyond Tomorrow, 1965

Each of our cells contains dozens of tiny factories called mitochondria that combine our food with molecular oxygen to extract energy in convenient form. Recent evidence suggests that billions of years ago, the mitochondria were free-living organisms that have slowly evolved into a mutually dependent relationship with the cell. When many-celled organisms arose, the arrangement was retained. In a very real sense, then, we are not a single organism but an array of about ten trillion beings and not all of the same kind.

—CARL SAGAN, 1978

1. Lives

The earth pulled him down, tugging at him like a burdensome friend. Richard Bulero felt trapped as he looked up at the stars, cut off from the openness of space. Earth's turbulent ocean of air was the cloudy lens of a giant eye, sun-blinded by day, astigmatic by night. Even here in the desert, the stars lacked the brilliance he had come to know on the moon.

The planet was nervously alive around him, enveloping his body in an aura of sounds, smells, and dust, pushing against his skin, trying to make him fit in again. The physical adjustments of coming home were a nuisance; his adaptation to Luna's gentle pull conflicted with his muscle-memory of earth's stronger attraction, even though he had kept in shape through exercise.

He missed the moon's stillness. A year at Plato University had made him a stranger on the home world, and at home.

He had not come back to New Mexico just to attend this evening's party for his father and Bulero Enterprises. Margot had been first in his plans, and he was anxious to get away from the celebration as soon as possible. He had not seen her for over six months, ever since she had completed her field work on the moon and had returned to Princeton to continue her studies in biology.

He was looking forward to personal talks with his uncle Sam and with Orton Blackfriar; they would at least notice his progress. Sam's courses in philosophy had been the brightest part of his first two years at Princeton, opening his mind to problems beyond those of family and self-concern. Sam and Orton would be in New York during the next two weeks, and he had a dinner date with them. He would stay with Margot until then, and return to the moon by the first of May.

He was impatient for the party to be over. Richard turned away from the terrace railing and hesitated. There was no point in going back inside; his parents were monopolizing Sam and Orton, and he had lost his taste for starting pointless conversations with strangers. He was tired of playing the promising son of a man who had not spoken to him for most of the evening and whose presence seemed to destroy the possibility of genuine conversation.

Richard took a deep breath of the night air. He stretched, feeling a pleasant ache as his muscles adjusted to the earth's pull. It was like coming back to life. Nevertheless, the dry, starry silence of the walled lunar plain at Plato made possible a clarity of thought which was missing here. There he could look out into the vast cave of stars with a measured emotion, with a sense of the future, while here on earth his thoughts longed for sunlight and warm water, and lovemaking. There the lunar shadows were sharp, eliciting clear distinctions in his mind, cutting away the jungle growth of his emotions; here his feelings grew in a jumble, obscuring his goals, weakening him.

He missed the spirit of consensus among Plato's scientists and teachers, as well as the cooperativeness of the lunar colonists; it was the same, he had been told, among the L-5 colonists of Asterome, and on Mars and Ganymede. The colonies were a new branch of humanity, joined to their environment through a problem-solving struggle which demanded of them the resolve to work through disagreements to the

best possible conclusion, whatever that might turn out to be; the openness of free space was matched by the openness of inquiring minds.
Failure in maintaining this attitude could result in costly disasters and
loss of life.

Those who lived permanently on the moon, Mars, or Ganymede,
could never return to the high gravity of earth without powered
external support harnesses or wheelchairs; much of this growing population had no desire ever to visit earth. Asterome maintained an
earthlike gravity, but even so the colonists had more in common with
sunspace humanity than with earth. He wondered if he and Margot
could cut themselves off from earth, begin a new life elsewhere in the
solar system's growing family of environments; he wondered if he
could ever cut himself off from the fact of his family name.

How will I ever introduce Margot? he asked himself as he started
toward the terrace door. He stopped again, startled by the thought that
he did not know what his parents were like within themselves. He
knew their faces, the gaze of their eyes, their manner of speech and
dress; but he did not know them as he knew Margot. He had never
known anyone as he knew Margot. He knew Sam; Orton was easy to
understand.

Margot was lucky not to have her parents; her past was gone,
leaving her free to grow in her own way, without having to measure
herself by it constantly. The past was not conspiring to enlist her in its
service; his was waiting to swallow him with its complexities of money
and responsibility. He knew that he might never be able to accomplish
anything to match the wealth of his family or its corporate power. His
intellectual and scientific achievements would be respected only if they
resulted in practical consequences; a treatise, or a theory, would not be
enough. Even his mother, who missed him genuinely, took little notice
of his work in philosophy and science.

There had been a time, only a few years ago, when he and Sam
could still get above their lives in discussion; they could stand off,

independent and all knowing, from the family's affairs, and talk about the dangers to personal happiness and achievement posed by the past. Sam Bulero had taken the most painful path, selling his shares in the company after setting up an annuity. His brother, Jack, made constant fun of him for this, even though the annuity provided Sam with less than what Princeton paid him. Sam's work, however, was real, and a source of enduring fame. Jack Bulero was an elaborate fake, but known as such only to family and close associates. *My father*, Richard thought. *Not an evil man, just someone who's not what he claims to be.*

How long before I put my hand in to take a share? In time Richard Bulero would become a device for the servicing and preservation of Bulero Enterprises; his needs and desires would be met in return. He would be able to help Margot, show her the world, and much more; he would like that, he admitted, hating himself. If his work in physics and the philosophy of science came to nothing, he would have no choice but to try and accomplish something within the company; and if he failed at that, he thought bitterly, the cushion would be there to catch him again, for the last time.

What else could there be for him? He envied the space colonists; they had real work to do. On Asterome they were looking forward to a society that would be free of planets. Somewhere there had to be something for him to give himself to—an enterprise that would combine his love of knowing with flesh-and-blood concerns, with issues and human needs that would put as much love and caring into his life as he felt toward Margot.

His family was pulling him down more strongly than the earth, and he wondered if he could ever break free for long. *I've got to get moving. I'm twenty years old and just beginning to wake up. I've got to escape, permanently, into my own kind of world.* He looked up at the Bulero Orbital Factory as it passed overhead. Three hundred miles out, with a period of two hours, it was the brightest object in the sky. As he watched its familiar, lazy passage, the sudden feeling came over him that he was too late, that all the forces necessary to crush his hopes were already in motion, advancing toward him out of a distant past, and that he had somehow missed the moment that would have resolved his problems.

He took another deep breath, set his face into a mask, and went inside.

Smoke, billowing, churning gray and black; protean shapes fleeing through the thickening flux; russet masses constrained within a contorted internal space; swelling densities struggling to escape through narrowing fissures in the earth. It was cold in the dream. She struggled to open her eyes. . . .

A glow spread through the cumulus, revealing for a moment the titanic shoulders and limbs of something fighting to be born.

She saw dashes of light—measured electrical activity in the deepest layers of her brain—dreams seen from outside. . . .

She opened her eyes. The sun burned in an abyss, waiting for her to fall in. . . .

A misshapen finger of lightning pierced the ground. The sky darkened and a giant moon cast its indifferent white light through a cancerous opening in the clouds, only to be covered by a black shape gliding toward the dawn, where the sun crouched below the storm, a beast ready to lash out at the world with a scorching tongue.

The rain whispered and fell in a rush of crystalline droplets which still held starlight in their structures. The fissures drank the flood, and dead things floated to the surface. The flapping sound of a large bird came up behind her; sharp talons entered her neck and a ragged beak dipped to drink her blood. . . .

The universe collapsed into a throbbing point inside her head.

A hammer blow struck stone. She cried out. . . .

Pieces of the dream echoed within her as she stood on the stone terrace. The sky was strewn with searingly bright stars, the ones she had come to love as a girl. Here in New Mexico, she had escaped the cotton fog of cities; the clouds had broken to reveal these stars—a universe coming into being, a new immensity for her thoughts; in twenty-five years, she had not tired of its sanctuary.

She reached out across the cathedral of space-time to those hopelessly distant candle-furnaces, where all the material elements had been forged again and again inside the generation of suns, where alien sunspaces were certain to contain other humanities, however different, and she wondered if someone there might be her friend.

The cold air made her shiver, as if in reply, and she turned to go back into the house. The door slid open and she stepped inside.

I'm alone, Janet Bulero thought. She stepped forward and grasped the bulerite railing that circled the pit of the sunken living room, where the aftermath of the party was still alive.

Her only child was a man now. Richard was sitting alone on the sofa in the center of the room. She had watched him grow, become graceful and serious, a quieter version of his father. Sometimes she had worried that his loyalty would go to Jack, but Richard had always been too independent for that to happen; Jack had not tried to win him over, and Richard had not seemed to care.

Behind the huge felt sofa, a slightly drunk Jack Bulero stood with a drink in his left hand. His brother Sam nodded lazily as Jack waved his free hand. Janet recognized the old arguments and self-justifications, wishing that Sam would learn not to be baited into a discussion.

There was still a considerable pride in Jack's six-foot frame, more than he needed or deserved. His tan and his loose-fitting blue suit were hiding overweight and bad posture. His eyes looked up at the ceiling as he spoke, as if he were struggling to look up into his head; his lips tightened and relaxed as he stooped to hear his brother. Janet felt a moment of superiority.

Samuel Bulero's tan reflected a genuine vitality, she told herself, examining him as if he were a stranger. Why had she encouraged this stocky and muscular man, she wondered as she looked at his streaked brown hair and bushy eyebrows. *Was it just another way to hang on to Jack?*

At her left, halfway around the raised level, Orton Blackfriar sat puffing on a Cuban cigar as he listened to the Beethoven quartet floating out of the high-backed chair's hidden speakers. As she observed his large, familiar shape, the entire mood of coming in from the clear, quiet night was shattered. She looked at Jack. Their formal marriage contract had expired five years before, bringing the informal option into effect; that last link would expire today. As her one-time lawyer, Orton knew the significance of the evening, but had made no comment yet.

For a wild instant this morning, she had dreamed that Jack would send her a confidential record of his declaration as a surprise. She turned from the rail and walked toward Orton.

"I'm thinking of all the work on my desk," he said, shifting as she came near. *He's trying to avoid the subject.* She sat down on the cushion at his right and listened to the music.

Orton was too good to be governor, she thought. He had not assumed the job from any of the usual motives, but he did it well. He had taken all the wretched cases during his law practice, finding it difficult to blame anyone but the powerful for social problems; as governor he tried to use the public trust of wealth and power to make a difference in individual lives. There were limits to that, he had found.

"You didn't have to do this," Orton said.

She looked up at him. "I'm not really disappointed."

"He did come, after all."

"To reinforce his own view of himself," she said. "To have it reported that he was present at the anniversary celebration of Carlos Bulero's gift to the world."

She had once toyed with the idea of writing down the truth about Jack, especially after she had learned how little could be proved about the Buleros. The documentary broadcast viewed by the guests earlier tonight had been at least one-third fiction. She had found it difficult to remind herself of the truth after the telecast. *That's because I'm part of the lie.*

It was Carlos Bulero, son of a country doctor from a small village in Ecuador, who had made the family rich through his discovery of bulerite—*the family element*, she thought, *common to us all*. Carlos had been a major physicist; his son, Jack, had only dabbled in physics, a businessman taking credit for the work of his employed scientists. It was not known outside the family that Jack had altered his father's records to give himself a large share in the discovery of bulerite and all the credit for the structural applications of the building material. Since all the records were in computer storage, even that much could not be proved, unless Jack produced the written records, but he denied their existence; only Sam had claimed, privately, to know what was in them. Carlos had not cared much for publishing his results.

In recent years, control of the Bulero multinational had begun to slip away from Jack, but he did not seem to care as long as he was not deprived of his wealth, fame, and influence. She looked at Jack's face, noticing the sudden loss of confidence, as if Sam had said something cutting. Gone was the smugness that she had seen at the financial meeting, where she had given her annual report as internal-program auditor. He looked up, noticed her scrutiny, and turned his back as he answered Sam, producing a dead spot in her feelings. To reveal the truth about Jack would make no difference, except as a matter of curiosity; the Bulero stock might dip a point, Jack would issue a denial, and the incident would be forgotten.

There was not much that Jack could do to her; her share of the wealth was safe. No one would object if she chose to do nothing for the rest of her life; with new interests coming into the company, she doubted if she would be missed. She was good at her job, but others were just as good. As Jack was fond of saying, the Buleros had done their bit for the world and should be permitted to live as they pleased.

She had never thought of it in overly dramatic terms, but in a very real sense the skeleton and much of the sinew of the present world had been born in a Bulero brain; that much of the documentary had been true. In the final years of the last century, amid famine and ecocrises, the world had been rebuilt; not perfectly, not completely, but well enough for a new start. The richer nations had divided themselves into ecologically manageable provinces and had built new cities—upward. The open towers, cubes, and pyramids were shelflike latticeworks, into which the remains of the old cities had been moved, preserving the best of the older architectures. She liked to think that there was something of ancient Inca strength in bulerite. Among the superstitious rich, the dream substance had long ago replaced copper and bronze as a material for bracelets and chains.

Every major human settlement in sunspace—on earth, on the moon, Mars, the satellites of Jupiter and Saturn—was built up with the virtually indestructible material, which could be prefabricated into parts of any shape and size, and fitted together permanently on contact.

Abandoning the two-dimensional spread of twentieth-century cities, arcologies housed up to a million people comfortably on a thousand-acre base, in varied structures rising more than a mile into the sky, leaving the countryside to renew itself. Waste was removed through giant vertical chutes, letting the passive action of gravity do the work of carrying it to underground processing plants; these were now fusion torches, vaporizing everything into atoms of pure elements, the ultimate in the recycling of nonrenewable raw materials, while providing clean energy at the same time. Planet-scarring activities such as strip mining, forestry, coal mining, and oil drilling had been cut down to sane proportions. Every decade saw the building of fusion-powered arcologies in the world's needy areas. Janet knew the whole success story; no one in Bulero Enterprises was ever permitted to forget it.

But still, the world belonged to North America, EuroSov, and Japan. They continued to keep AfroAsia and South America down to mid-twentieth-century levels, as much as that was possible. Properly developed, this other world could easily become their equal. The documentary had avoided this point, ignoring the inevitable, even desirable, conclusion as to the world's direction. The lines had been drawn and redrawn throughout her life, always to include more of the world in the center of influence, always modifying the dominant cultural styles. As the world's wealth had increased, the inducements to be destructively greedy had grown weaker. The old middle was now the bottom; the old top was now the middle; and the top might one day, with luck, be the whole future. Only power was still hoarded, subtly, with a few traces of wisdom, she thought.

Nevertheless, she could not help feeling pride. It was the peace of the West that had made the world stable, the culture of the West that had led to science and the ideals of democracy (though not yet to democracy itself); it was the West that had given out its riches, however reluctantly, and was now drawing the world into an economic involvement which would lead to an energy-rich sunspace by the end of the century. Perhaps by then the national pride she felt would be harmless, and power without accomplishment meaningless.

Mike Basil, the research chief of Bulero Enterprises, entered the room below. He went up to Jack and whispered something in his ear. Jack waved him away impatiently. Basil walked around the sofa and sat down next to Richard.

Her son would have been a prince in another time, she thought, noting the look of deference in Mike's face as he tried to make conversation.

There was a grim expression on Sam's face, the look of a university professor who had failed to convey his view of things to a student. Sam was usually content with personal rewards, the satisfactions of his theoretical work, with seeing those he had taught go on to success in the world. She felt the strain between the two brothers, who had been talking for two hours behind the sofa and for an hour before in the kitchen. They rarely met outside of family occasions. Sam had never visited the company headquarters, and Jack avoided meeting Sam at Princeton. *They're each other's judges*, she thought, *and they accept it.*

She could no longer feel what Jack was like inside. The last time she had been able to do so had been at Christmas twelve years ago; and before that when he had been a young man. The thought turned into fear, and then into a quiet panic. She wanted him to run up the stairs to her and say anything to show that he was still the person she had known. *"It's still me inside, Janet,"* she imagined him saying. *"Don't you know me?"*

But Jack was opaque, vague, a scarecrow making fragmented gestures. She stared at him carefully now, almost with an astonished good humor, and still he would not look up. For a moment she believed that he could make all his pretenses real, simulate anything, appear in any way he wished; there was no safe way to expose him.

Wealth held the family together and freed them all from one another. It was easy to be polite and cheerful at a distance. Suddenly looking back, she trembled on the edge of hatred; the world was a dungeon around her, with walls of family and fear.

She looked up at the haze of blue smoke hanging over Orton. The circulating air was slowly whipping the top of the cloud away as the Beethoven quartet rushed toward a frenzied finale.

Jack Bulero finished his drink and put the glass down on the server. "Go on."

Sam looked up at him. "Who in Bulero is doing any research into bulerite? I've read about dozens of theories for its properties—all published by outsiders. Carlos died a curious man, Jack, and you've done nothing to carry on his basic research."

Sam had not called him by his first name in a long time. "The theory is good enough to work—we're doing fine."

"But the work is unfinished," Sam said. "The whole scientific community agrees that the theory is inadequate, and it's not just the difficulty of the problem that is stopping you. What worries me is that a working-results approach will quickly use up Bulero's store of knowledge and leave the company with nowhere to go. It's an approach that belongs to the chaotic growth of the last century."

"The working-results approach," Jack said, "also produced solutions to the problems created by chaotic growth. It's never penetrated to you that we needed the twentieth century's chaos, its urgent momentum."

"But the work Carlos left unfinished. . . ."

"Look—you want me to say it: I'm not the physicist our father was."

"Maybe you could have been."

"It's irrelevant. My interest was in doing what Carlos didn't do. Bulero Enterprises helped reshape the earth. We linked all the human outposts throughout sunspace with fast space haulers made of bulerite. We organized the magnetic-boost train system for the entire hemisphere, as well as making heavy investments in the zero-g manufacturing plants out in space, so we could feed industry with bulerite and basic products. What use would the moon and asteroid resources have been without those factories? Even laser fusion reactors need bulerite casings. At the moment we cannot create the conditions needed to experiment with bulerite. It's not a research toy any more. Do you know what it would cost?"

"No."

"We would need a whole community of scientists far out in space, where the work would pose no danger. To study bulerite's properties requires the control of extreme states of matter, and that takes vast amounts of energy. It's all we can do just to make the stuff."

Twenty years out of my life, he thought. The present world would have been delayed by decades if he had not decided to apply bulerite on an industrial scale. He deserved the power and privacy of his life, and he resented his younger brother for provoking these self-justifications. Sam was a withdrawn university type, despite his fame in philosophy—a powerless man who knew nothing of industry and business. *He can't intimidate me*, Jack thought.

"The technology of bulerite," Sam said, "hasn't been around long enough. It makes me uneasy to see the ignorance in which we run our world."

"You're so damn sure of yourself—sorry we can't tidy up all the books for you."

"It's easy to see that you're whistling in the dark."

"You want perfect theories and comprehensive explanations—."

"Come off it, Jack. Sure, we can't be omniscient overnight, but we can do more basic research, worry more about the dangers in our technologies, distinguish more between what we can do without understanding and what we can do with understanding."

"What dangers? We've cleaned up our technology, or haven't you heard?"

"How many industrial deaths in Bulero last year?"

There was a sudden quiet between them.

Jack laughed. "Sam—reading about the problems of the last century has scared the crap out of you. Maybe the world is safer because we're doing fewer new things, because we're developing a long-considered technology. You're the one who wants new things."

"No. I don't mind a slower pace of innovation and application. I'm calling for a better understanding in the one area of application where it is obviously lacking."

"Only one?"

"The greater the complexity of our technology, the more pervasive our applications without a sound theory, the greater will be the collapse if something goes wrong. Just consider the air and water processing plants we needed, the cost of dismantling the fission plants. . . ."

"They patched us through until we got fusion and solar sources," Jack said. "Take the cry over the finiteness of earth's resources—we blew that problem away when we moved out into space and changed over to an energy currency. Earth will now get more than it needs in energy. Everyone will get a chance at a decent life, and the point of world affluence comes long before the moment when we'll be putting too much generated heat into the biosphere. You're not going to throw that old bone at me?"

Jack felt the void between them, the years of unexpressed disdain and false goodwill. Sam and Janet seemed to share a snide solidarity against him. He felt his own hatred of them, seeing its shabbiness at the same time; it was a trembling thing inside him, and he was afraid of it.

"Are you feeling well?" Sam was looking at him. Jack stood up straighter. He was not going to show weakness in front of the bastard.

"I'm fine." He forced a smile. *I'm an intruder*, he thought as he glanced around the room. He peered up at Janet, but she did not notice him as she looked down at her son. *She doesn't even remember that today is the end.*

Jack leaned over and tapped Mike Basil on the shoulder. The executive turned and gazed up at him earnestly.

"Good-bye, Sam," Jack said. He sought out Janet again, but she was not looking at him.

Richard was saying good-bye to him distantly. Jack turned unsteadily and walked out into the kitchen and out the back door. Basil was behind him, rushing to keep up.

The night air was cool and dry. The hovercraft was a huge insect waiting for him on the lawn, menacing him with its lights. He almost expected it to rear up and tear him to pieces like some huge mantis.

He walked across the dark grass and climbed into the creature's belly. Basil followed him, sitting down on the facing seat as the door slid shut.

Jack closed his eyes and leaned back. In the morning he would be on his yacht, far away from the family he had outgrown.

The charade is over again, Orton Blackfriar thought. He took a long pull on his cigar and let the smoke out. Richard was alone on the sofa. Sam was finally mixing himself a drink at the bar by the far wall. Jack had been too much for him. Janet sat on the cushion next to him, her thoughts painfully evident.

Richard got up. His expression was one of contained exasperation as he turned and went out through the side door.

Sam turned, toasted the air, and gulped down half his drink. Janet rose and leaned over the railing. "He panicked this time," she shouted.

"May he enjoy the company of his flunkies," Sam said, and finished his drink.

Janet still managed to fill her jumpsuit quite well, Orton noted. At another time he might have loved her, but no one could ever replace Evelyn. "There are concerns more important than personal ones," she had often said. He felt closer to her when actively following her advice.

There were a number of worthy dreams searching for workers. The interstellar group had contacted him more than once. Despite the disappearance of the Centauri sublight starship more than twelve years ago, the dream of exploring beyond sunspace had not died. The optimists still believed that the expedition was merely late. His reputation as a state governor had attracted the group's interest, but they had been delighted to discover that he was a gifted administrator and lawyer who shared their dreams. He would not be at a loss when his last term ran out.

He wondered for a moment why Janet was so cautious with Sam, why they did not live together openly. She was cautious, perhaps, for no reason other than that Sam was Jack's brother. Suddenly he inhaled some smoke and started coughing.

"Silly," Janet said as she turned around and looked at him with her large brown eyes. She took the cigar from him and dropped it in the floor slot. "Orton, have you replaced that old heart yet?"

"Works well enough for a loveless man."

Her smile turned to a look of concern. "I'm serious—retire that tin lizzie."

The idea of growing a clone of his heart made him uneasy. The col-

lagen enzyme treatments that cleaned out his aging, hard-boiled proteins were not so bad, but the replacement of his organs by using cells
from embryonic twins disturbed him at times. Material drawn from
his embryonic clone would be injected into him, slowly replacing him,
until a complete cell change of his body was finished, continuing a
process that stops in the body after a certain age; the unborn clone, of
course, would die. He might double his life span, as many were already
doing. The procedure was as objectionable as abortion had been in the
last century, and for that reason he would be happier when individual
organs could be grown without embryos; still, the process had eliminated the heartbreak of waiting for suitable donors, as well as the
problem of tissue rejection. One day, the risks of cloning from existing
body cells would be eliminated. The DNA code for an individual
would be read directly, and the cells made fresh out of raw materials,
for use in growing replacement parts or for growing a whole individual
as an alternate method of reproduction.

"A natural heart wouldn't work hard enough," he said, "to support
my large frame and eating habits. I'd wear the poor critter out, just
like the last one. This old atomic will do well enough, even though it's
not as subtle as the organic one—it goes a shade too fast when I get
excited, and too slow at times, and it makes my face red when I look
at you. Besides, I'm waiting for better techniques."

She laughed and leaned back against the rail. "You've lost weight."

"I'd better get back to my desk," he said, rising. "One more year
of office is still a lot of work."

She stepped toward him, stood up on her toes, and kissed him. He
almost started to hold her. In a moment she would reduce him to a
schoolboy, startled by his good luck.

"My cane—I don't know where I left it," he said, trying to blot out
the sudden vision of Evelyn in the automated car as it stopped without
warning, throwing her forward to break her neck. The route input had
sent a garbled signal, killing a dozen people that week. . . .

"Take care," Sam shouted. "We'll see you."

Janet got his cane from behind the chair. He turned away from her and confronted the terrace door. It slid open to release him, but she hurried ahead into the night and kissed him again when he stopped at the top of the steps leading down to the front of the house.

As he packed his bag, Richard felt anger rising. He stopped suddenly, sat down on the edge of the bed, and punched Margot's number. She appeared on the small screen.

"Hello," he said. "I should be at the old family house in Princeton by morning. Can you meet me?"

"What is it?"

"I just can't take it here any more. I've been away too long to be blind. The party is almost over; I'll slip out when they watch the news."

He looked at her, admiring the slight tilt of her almond eyes as she smiled up at him from the screen.

"You like to make me . . . nervous," she said.

"Is that what you call it when you're excited?"

"I miss you," she said shyly.

"I miss you, too. How's school?"

"They were glad to have me back," she said, "but I miss the people at Plato."

"I'd better get going," he said. She broke the connection.

He picked up his bag, went out into the hall, and walked toward the door that opened under the terrace. It seemed to take an eternity to reach it, but finally it slid open and he slipped out into the shadows.

He stopped and waited as a car pulled away, then walked quickly across the driveway toward his own vehicle.

The door opened and he climbed inside. He looked back through the clear bubble, expecting to see dark shapes watching him from the terrace; but there was no one and he felt relieved.

He touched the keys for Santa Fe, attached his seat belt, and sat back. The car moved down the long driveway toward the semiautomated road. In the rear-view mirror, the house slipped behind dark trees, its light a fire in the night.

When the car stopped, he snapped the wheel out from the panel and drove the mile to the freeway. *Jack didn't even say good-bye*, he thought, *and he said only two words to me all evening.* Everyone had behaved differently in his father's presence. *The son of a bitch doesn't care about anyone.*

Central injected the car into the high-speed flow, and he released the wheel as the surge shot him across the starry desert toward the airport.

Samuel Bulero leaned back into the sofa's cushions. He felt uneasy, disappointed. There was no point in thinking about Jack, he told himself. His brother's attitudes got him through the only kind of life he knew; the time for choices was long past. There was no way that he could tell Jack about his disappointment. Jack's neglect of bulerite was also his neglect of himself. Sam hated him for what he had done to Richard and Janet; he hated him for continuing the coldness that stood between them. This evening had been mild compared to others of the last twenty years.

He tried to think of hopeful things. His position at Princeton was secure. Although he was without wife, daughter, or son, he was not without family, love, or achievement. Janet cheered him, but he wondered about the slowness of their relationship. Was he afraid of taking his brother's ex-wife?

He tried to think of things outside himself. AfroAsia and South America, especially Brazil, were rising influences, their economies fueled by pollution-free hydrogen, made from sea water, stored in bulerite tanks, and piped as natural gas had been in the last century. The older powers were using more advanced energy systems, but the world's regions were moving toward economic equality, if not one of cultural-scientific influence and military power; even the smallest nation could now obtain enough energy for a better life.

He thought of all the arcologies—giant human organisms attached to the earth. The countryside and atmosphere were still in traction; the sunsets were blood red from all the dirt. People felt freer, no longer living as if catastrophe was inevitable. An indefinite peace prevailed in the garden. His personal discontents were minor; it was good to be alive, he told himself, wondering if he was a happy idiot.

Janet came into the room, sat down, and put her head on his shoulder. He put his arm around her and hugged her, afraid that she might fade from reality at any moment. She kissed him lightly on the lips.

He reached around, took her small hands, and compared them to his rougher, hairy ones. "How about Jack?" he asked. "How did he seem to you?"

"Nothing. It was dead a long time ago. I think he was bored with all of us. I don't want to talk about it, Sam. I'm really fine—let's forget it." She tried to kiss him passionately, but he held back and she broke away. "Don't treat me like a small girl, Sam."

"What's the matter?"

She sighed, "Old—don't you feel it?" She poked him in the ribs.

He stretched his arms out on the back of the sofa. "My doctor's team says I'm good for a hundred or more, and he's not joking—but I'm an old man with my students. I'll be forgotten when I go."

"I'm counting on it."

"On what?"

"On a whole lot of time left for us." She turned away from him. "I want enough time to forget everything. It would be another lifetime, Sam—like the ones from one to twenty-five and to forty—the longest and best. . . ."

He reached for her. "Janet, dear Janet, come here." She turned around, tucked her legs under her, and buried her face in his shoulder. "A long time," he whispered, holding her.

The lights in the room dimmed.

"It's the one AM news," she said. "Someone preset it."

The holo appeared in the air above them, revealing a three-dimensional long shot of the earth-moon in space, then pulling back to show the sun. Sam remembered the old CBS colophon, earthrise on Mars, which had been retired at the turn of the century. The current logo was closer to the full-earth-above-the-moonscape scene of the 1960s. The Martian settlers had been right to look upon earthrise over Mars as a symbol of earth's supremacy; every Martian schoolchild knew that earth was the green star in their sky—sometimes it was blue-green, but never the size shown on the media link.

"Let's watch," Janet said. "I feel like news."

The standing figure of a newscaster whirled in like a propeller blade from a background of stars, growing larger until the figure stopped upright and lifesize. The brown-haired man was dressed in the artificial one-piece tweed, gray with tunic collar, popular in the great cities.

"Good morning. This is Frank Eiseley." Suddenly he was floating against the red globe of Mars. "The cargo hauler *Poseidon* has blown up during its approach to the Deimos docks around Mars." The figure of the reporter whirled toward the potato-shaped Martian moon. "Mars City officials report that very little debris has been observed by the rescue tugs. All one hundred and three crew members are believed dead." A model of the sluglike vessel appeared against the stars, with the reporter projected to appear as if he were standing on the hull. "*Poseidon* was the second-largest interplanetary hauler, next to *Scorpio*, which is nearly a kilometer in length. Both vessels were built almost twelve years ago, completing the bulerite fleet of fifteen ships." The reporter seemed to be walking on the polished hull. "The UN Sunspace Commerce Commission and the government of the North Americas Region will conduct an investigation."

The three-dimensional view pulled back, suddenly dwarfing the reporter to convey a sense of the ship's size. "Informed sources are speculating that the vessel may have had hidden defects in its nuclear propulsion units. As a precaution, the third-largest hauler, *Atlas*, has been ordered to moor at the nearest port for inspection."

An image of the sun flashed on and off, and was replaced by the reporter's head hanging in space. "A bulletin: *Atlas* has also been destroyed, while delivering supplies to the Solar Science City on Mercury."

"My God," Janet said.

The view switched to a sun-blasted plain covered with debris and small crushed hulls. "Apparently," the voice said, "a few tugs which had attached themselves to the ship as it came in to moor at the orbital station were also brought down." The tugs lay like dead gnats under the stars, but there was no sign of the big ship.

A vertical view appeared, showing a huge black hole in the plain below. The shadows were sharply painted by the low angle of light from the big sun offscreen. The shadow darkness inside the blast crater was a black mirror turned to the stars.

2. The Funeral

Blue daylight filled the hoveryacht's decktop suite; sunlight flooded in through the skylight, its brilliance made bearable by the tinted dome. Jack turned his head on the bed and looked out over the sea-green Gulf. Sea birds cried as they dived for their lunch; green islands floated on the water near the horizon.

Erica had gone to her cabin to prepare for his day, leaving him to dodge his thoughts. He reached back, grasped the large bed's bulerite posts, and stretched. Straining, he tried to touch the toes of the Promethean figures at the top of each post, but it was too far; he let his arms fall and relaxed.

He could almost hear what went on in Sam's mind. *No real dedication to science . . . all surface, nothing like his father. Carlos was a scientist, technologist, administrator, and teacher. Jack is not even one of those things . . . flashy intelligence, more concerned with being somebody. He'll endow a Bulero Prize. . . .*

He was surprised at how many remarks he remembered. They stuck in his brain, irritating and painful because they had been made by someone close to him.

He thought of Orton Blackfriar. A lame-duck politician and bleeding-heart lawyer, seeking to be near the mighty; he had been doing that all his life, under the guise of noble ideals. Janet must have invited him to the party.

He hated them all. They were all pushing their fingers into the Bulero brain, greedy for the wealth and power which was not theirs.

Jack closed his eyes and tried to enjoy the sunlight on his face and unclad body. . . .

He sat up suddenly, wakened by a flash of light in the sunny field of his closed eyelids. *A strange dream,* he told himself, remembering when years before he had heard a girl screaming faintly in the center of his head. . . .

He stood by the bed and stretched, thinking of the warm waters around him. The yacht would be here until noon, before heading back to his island in the Bahamas. He would have enough time to swim and forget everything.

He sat down on the bed, thinking of the great bulerite rod sunk deep in the earth's hot core, an indestructible tap drawing enough heat to light a continent. He had made it possible, just as he had sought out the market for all bulerite's applications. No one could take that away from him. Others were welcome to play with Carlos's theories later.

He stood up and wandered over to the open window, remembering the blue bikini that Janet had worn at Cocoa Beach when they had first met. He had been grateful for the encouragement of her hello. The sky, sand, and sea had been so much more impressive than the callow boy on vacation from college.

He had been full of admiration for his father, filling her with talk of a career in physics. History had been coiled up inside him; but even then he had known that he would somehow disappoint her. She was still punishing him for not being like Carlos.

Jack took a deep breath of the salty air. The warm breeze touching his face made him feel secure. Then he was shaking suddenly, shivering throughout his whole body. It was the exposure to the sea air, he told himself, releasing the tension he had built up at the party.

He should not have gone to the house in New Mexico; that part of his life had been over a long time ago. His family was a strangely backward group of strangers, unable to see him in any way other than the personal. Janet was clever enough to be useful to the company; Sam was supported by institutional fools who understood only credentials; Richard, like all young people, had too many legal rights—he ignored his mother, but listened to Sam. Was Sam a father figure, or was Richard really interested in Sam's philosophical work?

I don't need any of them. By evening he would be well over the irritation of the party.

For a moment he remembered Janet's youthful, shy embrace, her softness, the delicacy of her arms and shoulders, her black hair in his face. He wondered what she would be like now under her expensive clothes. However beautiful Erica was, he realized, she could never be Janet. Erica was timid, not as intelligent, easily made happy, or so it seemed; he had no doubt that she loved him. He was careful never to show her that he did not love her; it would be unbearable to be without her. Janet was free now, and he would never ask for her again, even if Sam were not part of it. Why is it, he wondered, that so much happiness is lost when we break with those who started in life with us? What kind of special imprinting leads us to live as if they were watching? Why are we so dependent, forever compelled to desire their approval, their envy, even their hatred? It was all nonsense, he told himself, feeling his calm returning.

He looked out over the sunny water and his eye caught the white underwing of a bird as it wheeled crying across the sky. The explosion tore through him from behind, throwing him out onto the sun deck, where he lay breathing heavily and holding his arms around his torso in a futile act of containment. His right eye stared into the blazing sun; his left eye was blind. His pained consciousness flickered through his body, appalled at the ruin. "Janet," he whispered as the next explosion hurled him—

It was a bright day, unreal in its transparent clarity. Richard watched the five other funeral hovercraft floating slowly ahead of the one he shared with Janet and Sam. Sunlight yellowed the grassy aisle between the trees; wind fluttered the oak leaves. The day seemed to reveal itself to him, hiding nothing.

Six fliers, resembling old-style black limousines with curtained windows and leather seats, carried friends and relatives to the family plot in the park just south of Princeton. His father's coffin rode in the first hovercraft, alone except for the chauffeur. The casket was a bulerite capsule which Jack had ordered for himself twelve years before.

The fliers were spaced one hundred feet apart as they continued their stately drift. At his right, Janet sat with her hands folded in her lap; Sam was staring down at his feet. The only sound was the soft whisper of the lift fan from below the floor. The wind was rushing through the trees in the afternoon outside, but Richard could not hear it; the sun moved slowly behind the crowns, slanting its shafts to strike the lens of the window at his left.

"I remember how happy he was when he built the yacht," Janet said.

Richard turned his head and looked at her, as if at a stranger. She was dressed in a plain black skirt which came to below her knees, a white long-sleeved blouse with ruffles, and a black vest. She seemed calm, but her hand was cold when he touched it. *All this has not really happened*, her eyes seemed to say.

"I wish I'd talked to him more that night," she said.

"Don't think like that," Sam said.

Sixty feet of water. Seven bodies brought up by the divers. Margot and he had just come in from the pool when the fax screen flashed the news. She had not wanted to attend the funeral, so he had left her alone at the Princeton house.

The police were still checking on Erica's friends, hoping to find a motive for murder; but the explosion had been too big for any kind of bomb.

"I'm all right," Janet said, biting her lip to stifle the signs of crying.

Jack would have liked the funeral, Richard thought. Elaborate, it would seem worthy to the public that had known him as a Nobel Peace Prize recipient.

Richard saw the lead hovercraft rise and wobble, as if the wind were going to flip it over. A strange light shone from the rear windows. The rest of the fliers slowed and sat down on the grass. The lead vehicle continued forward erratically.

Five hundred yards ahead, the hovercraft burst into white brilliance and settled, withering the grass.

Richard opened his door and jumped out. The distant hovercraft was now a yellow mass inside the white, pulsating radiance. Warm air pushed against his face. The chauffeurs and some of the mourners were getting out to watch. The pulsations quickened and the mass brightened into a painful glare.

The explosion threw him on his back.

A strong wind passed over him; the trees strained at their roots and the leaves rustled like insects. Even with his eyes closed, the afterimage was vivid.

In a moment the air was still. He got up and looked around. The others were getting up; no one seemed hurt.

Richard climbed back inside the cab and closed the door. Janet's face was a pale mask, her eyes full of fear. He took a deep breath and sat back, grateful for the quiet inside the cab.

"That was not a bomb," Sam said.

The flier lifted from the grass and turned around; the others were also lifting and turning to leave the park. The grassy aisle started to rush by as the hovercraft accelerated. Richard thought of blackbirds scattering from a shotgun blast.

"Were they trying to get me, too?" Janet asked.

Sam looked at her as they sat in his apartment on the twentieth floor of Princeton's faculty housing complex. The picture window provided a southerly view over the central park of the campus. The greenery was bright in the late afternoon sun. He did not want to tell her his suspicions, not when it was obvious that she was struggling to get past what had happened. There was a normal life for her, for both of them, up ahead somewhere, where Jack's death would be a remote thing; yet he knew that she had once loved Jack and that something of that love still lived, buried deep within her, bound up horribly with guilt and pain.

"Who will run Bulero?" he asked to change the subject.

"Mike will. It's in Jack's papers, and Mike is on the board. Sam, what kind of explosion could blow out a bulerite hull, and what could destroy a bulerite coffin, turn it into ashes?"

"I don't know," he said.

She said nothing for a while.

"You can stay here as long as you like," he said, feeling that he was going to lose her forever.

"I'm going home, Sam, for a long time. I've got to sort myself out, and you've got a semester to finish."

They both stood up. She put her arms around him wearily. "Call Richard at the old house and tell him. He wants the place to himself with Margot." She kissed him and he held her for a long time.

The light of afternoon was fading. He could see dark patches in the trees below. "Later, Sam," she said. "Come to me later." And he held her as she withdrew into herself.

3. Undercity

The sky over old Manhattan was made of concrete-gray bulerite, a ceiling studded with electric stars and huge, sunlike fluorescent disks. Sam often imagined that he was seeing an overcast sky through circles of glass; it was his way, he knew, of wishing away the city that pressed down on Old New York. The great ventilators could never eliminate the dusty smell of the old streets. He thought of the tomb blackness of Harlem, farther uptown in the basement city, buried now for almost forty years beneath a mile of New City.

But much of the Old City had endured, as had London and Paris, Tokyo, Rome, and major areas of Moscow and Peking—subterranean haunts tucked away in the world's memory like dear, unwanted relations.

The indoor climate of the upper levels was perfect, and the tiers gave an open view of land, ocean, and sky; but it would be a long time before the New City acquired the sense of tradition belonging to the original ground level.

The elevators from the skyport had grown more utilitarian as he had neared the undercity, until he had emerged from the shaft that stood in the square on East Broadway, Old Chinatown.

It was almost ten in the evening as he walked across the empty square and down the street toward the restaurant. As long as there were people willing to live or do business down here, the Old Cities would continue, links to the past that would live as long as the earth endured.

The door was made of wood and glass. Sam paused as three electrical maintenance workers came out. He nodded to them and went inside, saying hello to the owner who sat behind the desk register. A young Chinese waiter showed him to a large table set for two.

Sam sat down, noticing himself in the wall of mirrors at his right. They made the room look larger. His one-piece black evening suit was a bit out of style, and his gray turtleneck was slightly soiled. His hair was getting long around the edges. For a moment he thought he saw something of his youthful self peering at him. He looked up at the Chinese lantern hanging from the ceiling. The waiter brought him a glass of tea. Sam put some sugar in it, took a sip, and looked around at the unoccupied linen-covered tables, speculating about their age. He heard voices behind the Oriental screen in front of the kitchen door and wondered at the efficiency of people who could produce almost two hundred dishes in such small quarters. He thought of the levels above him, open to the sky; the undercity would never see sunlight again, unless the very bedrock of Manhattan were split open. He thought of the magnetic boost-train tunnels, airless arteries as black as interstellar space, running to the terminals in the rock below him.

Jack is gone, he thought, realizing that he had not reminded himself of the fact for a whole day.

Orton Blackfriar came in and dropped his cane into the rack. He was wearing an old-fashioned tweed blazer, gold sports shirt, slacks from another era, and silver glasses which made mirrors of his eyes, giving him the appearance of a well-to-do panda. He walked into the dining area, stooping gracelessly to avoid hitting his head on the partition.

The wooden chair creaked as he sat down opposite Sam. He took off his glasses and put them in his jacket pocket. "How is Janet?" he asked quietly.

"I haven't seen her since the funeral." Sam paused. "They got some ashes from the coffin and buried them as Jack's remains. The chauffeur's family and the hearse company are suing Bulero."

"I asked Richard to join us," Orton said. "He should be here in a moment. Any more news?"

Sam shrugged. "The investigations are going on as quietly as possible. Bulero is making its own investigation. Things don't look promising for the company. Space shipping is at a standstill. They still haven't found out what went wrong with the haulers."

"Can the losses be absorbed?"

"If nothing else goes wrong," Sam said.

Richard came in and sat down in the chair facing the mirror.

"Go on," he said. "Don't let me stop you."

"Janet is doing a good job with the company," Sam said. "She took care of the transition period after the will was read. Everybody looks to her, even Mike Basil. She knows now that she's needed and that Jack did not keep her on out of charity. I think she feels closer to him now than when he was alive."

"I've been taking care of things on the East Coast," Richard said. "It's eating into my time. I don't know when I'll get back to my studies."

"Janet is really good with the accounting computers," Sam continued. "I'm told that her diagnostic programs are very clever, very useful to the regional directors."

"Do you resent having to involve yourself in the company, Richard?" Orton asked.

The waiter interrupted them.

Sam ordered first. Wonton soup, sweet and sour pork—all of it made from meat and vegetable culture stock, an industry which was finally competing with animal husbandry and plant farming. Orton spoke Chinese to the waiter, ordering wonton and beef lo mein for Richard and himself.

"I do resent it," Richard said when the waiter left. "I'd rather be back on the moon, finishing my work. Margot and I would prefer to live on Asterome, where we can have access to facilities for our work. The bio-isolation labs are really fine out there."

Sam noted Richard's nervousness.

They ate their soup in silence. As they waited for the main course, Sam asked, "Have you decided what to do after your term is over, Orton?"

Orton took a sip of tea. "I think I'll take the offer to help run Asterome. There's room to grow out there. I've been reading a lot, talking to people, dreaming."

"In dreams begin new responsibilities. Watch out."

"You wouldn't believe the dreams that were shelved by the research priority boards of the last century."

"Tell me about it," Sam said, hoping to take some of the lethargy out of himself through stimulating conversation.

"The food will get here before I can finish."

"Go ahead, Orton," Richard said. "You know I'm convinced."

"I can still take an interest in things outside my personal troubles," Sam said. "So what have you two been talking about?"

The waiter arrived with a large tray. They traded portions of one another's dishes. Sam savored the crisp, factory-grown vegetables. The tea was strong and aromatic. He remembered when Richard had been his student at Princeton, studying philosophy and getting excited about creativity in the sciences; it had been inevitable, looking back, that he would go into physics. Sam sensed that still newer concerns were developing in Richard, and that Orton was somehow involved.

After the meal was finished, Orton took out a cigar, prepared it with a small century-old penknife, lit it with a gold lighter, and took a few puffs.

"It took thousands of dollars to make this great bulk of mine," he said as he sat back, "which supports a dreaming brain. So I'll dream as well as I possibly can." The chair creaked as he leaned back. "Of course, any reality made from a dream will sober up a bit. . . ."

"What are you talking about?" Sam asked.

"Let him tell it his way," Richard said.

Sam watched the cloud of blue smoke forming around Orton, making him look like a demon sitting in mists. "I don't think that planets are the best places for a civilization. They're not necessarily the best we can do at all."

"You suggest that we all pack up and leave?" Sam said.

"Not at all. I want to sketch a long-term development leading to another way of life, one that will institutionalize the pursuit of ambitious goals for humankind. Part of human life is the need to reassure ourselves about the future that we may never live to see, rather than fool ourselves, as many did in the last century, that there won't be any future and they might as well lie down and die." The waiter stopped by the table and Orton told him to bring a small bottle of brandy.

"The earth is a biological crib," Blackfriar continued, "rocked back and forth by the sun—but we've got to grow up, start walking around, or rot. What I want to tell you about is a new kind of human society, one that may become a permanent form of culture." He was puffing heavily on his cigar. "Picture this: a mobile space colony, supporting more than a million people. No, not a colony, but an organism which can move and grow as long as it can obtain resources and maintain a food supply within its ecology. It's a living organism because it can respond to stimuli through its optical and sensory nervous system. It thinks with the intellects of its human and cybernetic intelligences. And it can reproduce, which is what we expect from a living organism. Its reproduction would be asexual, in part. The mobile world would undergo mitosis, the result of construction by human-directed machines of a complete new mobile container, and duplication of the human, animal, and plant cells by the usual means. If, for example, fifty years is the period for doubling the life of the mobile, then a new vehicle would be built during that time."

"The new social container," Richard said, "could be built as an outer shell, only slightly larger than the original, and when completed it would be removed from around the original and its interior work finished. Or the original could expand in size, shell after shell, to the limit of practicality. I suppose it could grow to be as large as a planet."

"But we're already out in sunspace," Sam said, "and developing it quite well, as far as I see. Asterome is pretty much the kind of colony you describe."

Orton flicked a long ash into his ashtray and leaned back, creaking the chair dangerously. "That's not the kind of thoroughgoing development I'm talking about, just as travel within the solar system is not real space travel. Interstellar travel is real space travel. The solar system is our backyard, our Wild West. I'm talking about using the resources of sunspace to create a new kind of social system, free of planets, free of the accidents of nature."

"The asteroid hollow of Asterome has a completely controlled environment," Sam said.

"It's only a start," Richard said. "The organism we're talking about would be a continuation of biosocial evolution on a large scale. It would possess the sum total of human culture and knowledge in its memory banks, much as the cell carries DNA information. Its capacity for expanding human perception, range of experience, and creativity would be limited only by the most basic natural limits."

"I take it," Sam said, "that Asterome's interstellar group has something to do with this?"

"Yes," Orton said. "They've been looking into this prospect for many years. Now, given time, the number of these societal containers would increase. A dozen could be in sun orbit within fifty years. You wouldn't believe the amount of basic research going on now on Asterome into communications, gravity and experimental relativity, methods of achieving near light speeds, and maybe even trans-light speeds. The reason for such research is that it would make it possible to send a mobile world out into the galaxy, to reproduce itself over and over again, growing step by step as population increased."

"The space colony ideas of the twentieth century," Richard said, "will not reach fruition until Asterome becomes mobile and reproduces. To really take full advantage of the possibilities, the only instance of macrolife must stop behaving like an extension of a planetary civilization."

"It would be just as well," Blackfriar said, "to send a few macroworlds out of sunspace as to have them circle the sun."

"It seems to me," Sam said, "that the vicinity of the sun has room for . . . millions of such worlds. There's more space here than we could ever use."

"That's right," Richard said. "You see the potential. But macrolife is a form of life, and macroworlds are highly complex seeds which we could scatter into the spiral arms of the galaxy, ensuring the survival of human culture—a permanent, open-ended, mature culture. It's something we've never done in our history, a really novel development."

"All the components exist," Orton said. "We can use solar and fusion power sources efficiently, and we know how to build powerful nuclear propulsion systems. There's no end to the number of nickel-iron asteroids that we can heat and blow up into hollow containers."

"It would take a great upheaval to drive us out to the stars on the scale you both suggest," Sam said.

"I'm talking about a few hundred thousand men and women," Orton said, "only those who want to participate. I'm talking about branching humanity, something like what's happening to people on the moon and Mars. The humanity I have in mind would remake itself after leaving the solar system, by creating a second nature, maybe even a new kind of human being to live in it."

"Look at it this way," Richard said. "Eventually we'll have to open the bigger sky or perish."

"Not soon," Sam said. "Maybe millions of years from now."

Richard shook his head. "Not true. Sun studies on Mercury have shown for some time now that the sun is not the stable star we thought it was. Have you forgotten how close we came to being struck by a large asteroid in the 1980s? Macrolife would be an independent society, retaining its basic, social-container-like form while permitting mobility and a great variety of social systems. With no limits to growth, it would permit a better development of man's freedom and inner resources. A planetbound culture repeatedly reaches a volatile point and attempts to organize itself after the point of greatest danger and difficulty. We're still such a culture."

"We don't seem to be doing badly at last," Sam said.

Blackfriar grunted. "True—but consider how much of our success is made possible by that portion of humanity that lives and works off the planet. We may be coming out of industrial adolescence, but I still don't feel safe about human survival. The earth is too fluid, too vulnerable in the perspective of geology, ultimately too limiting. In time it will become completely dependent on offworld industries, countryside to the urban space habitats, providing nothing they need except maybe nostalgia."

"We need a nature of our devising," Richard said, "one where the natural realm is only a garden. The man-nature alliance on a planet leads to an anesthetic equilibrium, since planets are physically limiting."

"You mean the small-is-beautiful movements of the last century," Sam said, "the zero-growth ideas. But we won't have the static society you're afraid of, since we've left the planet."

"But twelve billion people still live in a halfway house between nature and the nature we can make for ourselves. We could slide back."

"A mature society, like a mature individual," Orton said, "reaches the age of reproduction. Macrolife will be our viable offspring. Any number of social experiments can be made within its framework— we've never experimented with social forms on a large scale in our history—and each one will have enough mobility never to come into conflict with anyone. Here on earth, cultures have tended to exclude each other. Macrolife is a class which can include all others, all subcultures."

"Consider," Richard said, "that organismic life grows out of a tiny speck into an organism such as man. So macrolife will grow outward from earth and its sunspace, using the units of previous biological and social structures to form larger multiorganismic units. These will grow into the universe, achieving a scale of existence to match the scale of the universe."

"And you see our three-dimensional cities, and Asterome, as steps along the way?" Sam smiled. "I think, Orton, that you have it in you to be a founding father, and it's rubbing off on Richard."

"What idiot would dream small if he was going to dream at all," Orton asked, "or be content only with dreams? These things we've been talking about involve basic reexaminations of life and living."

"That's a big subject."

"The point of life," Richard said suddenly, "is to do more than repeat things. On the other hand, novelty for its own sake is chaotic. What are needed are unifying procedures that will allow novelty to be linked with past achievements. The retained past would become the basis for the emergence of significant innovations. Carried out on a reliable basis, this would be real progress, Sam."

"Go on, it sounds interesting."

"Progress is a tension between the notion of perfection and the notion that striving, not finding, is important. Macrolife embodies both ideas, but eliminates the tyranny of striving after material security, destroying that ancient activity's conflict with the search for personal satisfactions. The universe is very rich, so we should not be poor."

"Poverty prevents us from thinking on the true scale of reality," Orton added.

"You think we're poor?" Sam asked.

"A trillion-dollar GNP for North America was poor for 1975, and ten times that is poor now, because it is not enough to undertake what is really possible. It's a relative matter."

"Let me finish my thought," Richard said. "The conflict between scarcity and personal growth has led to the disruption of civil order by revolutionaries."

"Tell me," Sam said, "how would you deal with the boredom of the well-to-do?"

"Macrolife would permit adventure and intensity of any kind, but without that kind of creative disruption coming into conflict with the economic container. Malcontents could always found their own macroworld. Natural worlds might also draw a fair number of disaffected."

"I'll grant the constructive nature of the idea of progress," Sam said, "but it seems to me that the overall pattern or direction of progress for macrolife would remain unfathomable."

"True," Richard said, "but the human life span winks on and off too quickly to detect any pattern. All of recorded history is too little."

"Both human and social life spans must increase," Orton said.

"Perhaps," Sam said, enjoying the novelty of the conversation, the way in which their egos were taking a back seat to issues, "but what also worries me is individuality. You seem to be suggesting a mass organism." In a philosophy department seminar, the rivalries would all be just under the surface, driving the nature of the argument.

"Macrolife is the individual's needs written large," Richard said. "I think it was a commentator on Stapledon who said that the most advanced communities place as high a value upon individual personality as upon the group."

"An individual insight or innovation," Orton said, "might easily sweep the group, determining its overall character. Individuals are sources."

"Symbiotic links develop," Richard continued, "between individuals and between the community and the world. The community moves toward pan-sentience of self and world."

"In a sense," Orton said, "we do belong to a collective mind, since we share physical origin and structure, and in language we share a mental space. Our individual abilities belong at once to the society which recognizes them. We can only be individuals in distinction from others. Individuality is only a problem in societies which value a certain type of individuality above others. I think this is long beyond dispute."

The waiter brought the brandy and glasses, poured the liquid, and left. Sam picked up his glass and sipped.

"Rudimentary forms of macrolife exist today," Orton said. "Besides Asterome, there are the mining settlements in the asteroids, various observatories and research stations, the settlements on Mars and Ganymede—anyplace where human beings live in highly structured man-made ecological systems. It was easy to see such systems working in a small spaceship, but on earth we couldn't see the walls for a long time, and some of us can't see beyond them."

Sam poured himself another drink.

What Orton and Richard were envisioning, he thought, was a historical birth—it would have to be called that—with the earth and sun as parents. One had to think in terms of centuries to see the point, in terms of creative social engineering, a humanity to replace the half-hearted technological humanity of the last two centuries, a humankind that would consolidate its place in reality, to create the first civilization that would have any chance of standing against the eventual certainty of species extinction. Macrolife would be a permanent civilization. "I like the idea of an uncoercive, open-ended culture," Sam said.

"Think," Orton said. "A civilization which might see its millionth birthday."

"Of course, most of humanity can't see any of this," Sam said. "How large is the group you'll be working with, Orton?"

"There's Japan, hundreds of private fortunes, some heavy-industry backing—including Bulero, I found out. The macrolife group has been gathering all the other space colonization groups to itself during the last decade. Asterome is the prime mover for all this."

They were silent for a few moments, sipping their brandy.

"Just think of how much there would be to work for," Richard said. "There would be little that macrolife could not undertake in time. With its exploratory mobility and access to special research conditions, its presence on the galactic stage would place it in a position to contact other intelligent life, perhaps hybridize its culture. The citizens of a macroworld would achieve life for as long as they wanted it—practical immortality would be theirs in the same way that the ancient city-states offered their citizens various cultural benefits. Death is the ultimate insecurity to a conscious being, the break that takes away all productivity and vitality, the meaning of all further growth. Even if there will be those who choose to end their lives after a long period, they will know that macrolife will be virtually immortal."

"I tend to think," Orton said, "that we will want to live longer if our vitality continues. It's possible that in time a kind of natural selection will see only the most intense and creative types choosing the long-range life, one that might even last into the old age of the universe. . . . I wonder what that kind of consciousness would be like."

The City of God, Sam thought, only half listening now. The brandy had made him sleepy. How many attempts had there been to raise humanity up to the level of its better self? He thought of Jack, the stuff of his body strewn by incomprehensible forces, the pattern of his consciousness dispersed, dissolving the compact of matter and physical laws, and whatever else, never to be repeated. Death was an infinite cruelty. Where Orton's and Richard's words opposed death, the sorrow of it seemed to recede. Regret mingled with his lifelong disappointment in Jack. There was nothing to be done about it. *Except to take his wife and be a father to his son, who no longer needs a father. Replace him, finish his life for him. . . .*

"Macrolife," Orton was saying, "was first described, using that term, by Dandridge Cole, who died in 1965. The word is a shorthand for the whole range of humanity's social and biological problems. Our spaceborne peoples have already faced them in the industrialization of sunspace. Macrolife is life squared per cell. Man the multicelled organism stands between macrolife and the cell. Macrolife is to man as man is to the cell. Macrolife, Cole wrote, is a new life-form of gigantic size which has for its cells individual human beings, plants, animals, and machines. Civilizations have had this same structure, except that macrolife is mobile, and it can reproduce. . . . Sam?"

"The brandy . . ."

"Sam, do you want to help?" Richard asked, looking at him with Jack's brown eyes.

"What could I do?"

Blackfriar looked at his watch. "It's twelve-thirty, Sam. Want to come up top for some air? It'll clear your head. You look like a lazy rhino."

Richard stood up. "I've got to get back. Sam, I'll see you in Santa Fe next month. Orton, thanks for helping with the legal side of those firings at the Chicago complex. I'll call you—there's more I can use you for." Sam felt his nephew's hand on his shoulder. He looked up sleepily, but Richard was already on his way out.

"It's elevators all the way up, Sam," Blackfriar said. Sam watched him rise, walk over to the old man at the register, and pay the bill. The terminal chimed as it recorded Orton's credit.

Sam got up and knocked over the brandy bottle.

The lights in the undercity seemed brighter. Orton held him up by the arm. "I can make it now," Sam said.

"You never needed much. Puts you away like milk. I hope you followed something of what we said."

"I really did, Orton. Inside I'm sober, really." *How can frail beings like us think of doing the things Richard and Orton described?*

They walked across the square to the elevator shaft and stepped into the empty lift.

Two minutes later they got off on the first tier of the New City; from there they took the elevator to tier two, one thousand feet above the Old Empire State Building, which stood like an arthritic giant supported by the braces of the New City. A shiny new elevator shot them up to one of the six observation decks rising from the partially complete third tier.

Sam followed Blackfriar up a rampwalk, through the large open portal, onto the huge flat area. Orton was moving quickly toward the transparent barrier at the edge.

Sam came up next to him, and they stood looking down at the lighted canyons which cut through the layers of the city. There were sections still under construction directly below, lit by flashing work lights. New City was a diamond-studded latticework, a leviathan standing on the base of Manhattan, Bronx, Brooklyn, and Queens. New York harbor was under the great structure, together with the East River, part of the Hudson, the rebuilt Statue of Liberty, lighted entirely by artificial sources, hidden from sun and stars, open only to the ocean.

The Atlantic was dark in the east. Sam looked up at the sky. He felt a chill breeze; the stars twinkled. For a moment the spell of Richard's and Orton's ideas took hold of him and he wished that Janet were here to feel what he felt.

His head began to clear in the night air.

"In the Amazon," Orton said, "there are places where they've never heard of a spaceship, or oceangoing cities, or that men make a life for themselves on a moon of Jupiter."

"The present is never the present," Sam said. "It's layered with persistent pasts."

Orton was peering at the glowing dial of his watch. "Can you get home without me? I've got to be in Santa Fe by morning to sign some things."

"I'll stay a while," Sam said.

He shook hands with the big man and watched him disappear into the lighted mouth of the exit ramp, which seemed for a moment to become the fiery maw of some huge beast crouched under the stars. Then he turned to look out again over the billion lights scattered at his feet.

How did Janet really regard him? Was he just a brother-in-law, a friendly benevolence? Suddenly it seemed absurd that he should be her lover, that she should have any interest in him at all. Orton was perhaps more her type. Orton was passionate about life and seemed to be preparing for some new effort which would redirect his life.

Orton and Richard had stirred something in him tonight, a sense of possible renewal.

The wind grew stronger and colder. He imagined the dawn moving across the continent to strike the windows of Janet's bedroom, lighting up the desert and brightening the snow into blinding white-ness atop the mountains that held up the sky.

A part of him was dead, he realized, the piece of him that had been joined to his brother.

4. The Shatterer

There was little sense of speed as the car moved across the desert under the stars. Sam leaned back and stared up at the moonless June night. The green light glowed on the panel near the bottom of his vision, signaling that the manual controls were locked until Santa Fe Central released him from the road. Only the sudden passing of a sign or cactus reminded him that he was moving at two hundred miles an hour, but that was slow compared to the boost train that had brought him across the continent in less that five hours; the fractional-orbit shuttle would have delivered him in an hour, but like Orton, he liked to think about where he was going before he got there.

Night was an iron bell containing all space-time, the vault of an empty cathedral whose bright lights had been left burning. He imagined the unseen center of the galaxy, the distant altar, where, it was said, lay a massive black hole, a dark exit from the known universe. There suns and dusty clouds circled the eye of the galactic maelstrom, radiating lost energy as they were drawn in.

He thought of his own death, the death of all those he knew, the passing of humanity through historical time. *What are we?* he thought. *What is left? Everything is hidden from us, as if deliberately.*

The car slowed, and two other cars whipped by him in the far right lane. It pulled off at exit 99 and came to a stop at the end of a luminous yellow line.

The seat came up with him as he sat up. He pulled the steering wheel out, locked it, and eased the car forward.

He drove two miles down the old paved road and turned off onto the driveway. As he came along the gravel way between the planted trees, he remembered that long ago he had thought of the house as Jack's, later as Janet's; he would never feel that it was his own.

He halted in front of the terrace, turned off the power, got out, and walked over to the night entrance under the terrace. He pressed his palm on the key surface; it glowed and the door opened.

He stepped into the hallway and went through into the night-lit living room as the door slid shut behind him. At the bar he took a small container of orange juice from the cooler, tore off the top, and drank the juice down.

He resisted the impulse to waken Janet. Everything seemed at once to be balanced on a brink, their lives frail, pitiable things, poised in the morning stillness.

He waited in the stillness, thinking of Janet, admitting that he wanted her, without question. There would be a life for them, quiet, personal; he would write new books, revise the old ones, make them definitive. Richard would go his own way, like a son.

Poor Orton, Sam thought. *He has no one. . . .*

"Sam," Janet was saying from far away. "You crept in and didn't wake me."

He opened his eyes. Daylight flooded the guest room and Janet was sitting on the edge of the bed in a red robe. He found himself ignoring the lines in her face, the slightly crushed look of sleep. "I must have fallen asleep," he said, wondering how he looked to her.

"Sam . . ." He rose up and embraced her. They fell back and he kissed her for a long time.

She sat up again. "I look a mess. Who would want to kiss me like this?"

"An old fool like me." He began to tug at her arm.

"I don't care how old you are," she said.

"I'm fifty-six."

"Don't be old-fashioned. Fifty-six is what forty was half a century ago."

"Anything new from the investigations?"

"Richard may know something when he gets here."

"How's the company doing?"

"Well enough," she said with a shrug. "Mike has got things in hand, with help from Richard and Orton, and myself. Bulero goes on without Jack. Richard coming in has helped keep the shares stable, but I know he resents the interruption of his life. I'm sure that's why I haven't met Margot yet—I don't think she likes me."

"I'd like to know why Jack died."

"There are stories," she said, "about something in the yacht's power plant, and that the coffin was Jack's own kind of crazy joke, to cremate himself in public, but we know that Jack wanted to be put in suspension, if there was anything left to freeze. There's more to this than we know." She seemed to brighten, but with some effort. "Come on, we'll get some breakfast."

"Where are you?" Richard shouted.

"Here in the study!" Janet called back.

Sam looked at her from behind the ebony desk. She sat in the old easy chair, facing him. Her black hair was piled on top of her head, and she was wearing white slacks with a sleeveless turtleneck. The silvery bulerite medallion which Jack had given out for the family to wear many years ago hung around her neck. Sam admired the deep tan and silky texture of her bare arms. She sat secure in his gaze, her long legs set out casually in front of her.

Richard came into the study and stopped with a nervous, catlike grace. He appeared taller to Sam and his light brown hair seemed darker.

"What happened? Look at your clothes," Janet said. His collarless blue shirt and side-creased slacks were covered with dust, Sam noticed.

"We've got to get out of this house," Richard said.

"What is it?" Janet asked.

"I'll explain later. We've got to go."

"I want to know now—tell us," Janet demanded.

Richard ran a hand through his hair. "The Bulero Complex outside Chicago is falling apart. All three tiers are—well, glowing strangely, as if burning inside."

"The whole three-thousand-foot pyramid?" Sam asked, trying to imagine the event.

"Yes. There are a lot of electromagnetic phenomena. There's smoke. Everyone has been evacuated." Richard took an unsteady step forward.

"It must be on the evening news," Sam said, looking around for the remote control.

"No! Listen—we don't have time. It's the bulerite—it's unstable. When our two ore haulers were destroyed in space . . . we found the same kind of ash in Jack's yacht and around his disintegrated coffin. When they refloated what was left of the yacht, the bulerite statuettes of Prometheus were gone, together with all the bulerite on the vessel."

Sam saw fear in Richard's tired eyes, as if something of Jack had taken possession of him.

Jack killed himself, Sam thought, feeling a guilty satisfaction.

"Earth-moon," Richard said softly, "it's all built up with bulerite. All our major cities and hundreds of lesser ones, sea-bed communities, the magma and geothermal taps—patients walking around with bulerite hearts and bones." He looked at Sam with despair. "Even if we could take it all apart by tearing it loose at the adherence joints, which we don't know how to do easily, what could we do with the stuff? It would take years to ferry it off-planet."

"You're here to warn us about the bulerite in the house," Janet said. She sounded composed, resigned, but Sam saw the frightened look on her face.

"We've got to leave," Richard said. "This house is old enough to be in danger. Don't stop to take anything."

He turned and went through the living room out into the bright desert night. Sam and Janet followed. Halfway across the driveway,

Richard looked back and pointed at Janet. "Your medallion—you'd better get rid of it."

Janet took off the bulerite jewelry and threw it toward the house.

Sam got into the driver's seat of Richard's large rented car. Richard and Janet got in next to him. They sat still suddenly, looking at the house.

Sam had never felt comfortable in it; now the house was an open threat, and he expected it to strike out at any moment.

He pulled the wheel out from the panel. The car started and he drove away, glancing back nervously every few seconds. When he reached the road, Sam stopped the car, and they all gazed at the house among its trees, lights blazing in the darkness.

"Get us out of here," Richard said.

Sam accelerated.

There was a bright flash of light somewhere overhead.

"The orbital factory," Richard said.

The brightness faded. Sam peered up through the windshield at the band of stars arching across the sky and down behind the snowy peaks on the horizon. Where the bright, man-made star should have been moving toward the mountains, there was nothing now.

"Did they get away?" Janet asked.

"I don't know," Richard answered. "The evacuation had started."

Sam regarded Janet. She sat next to him, looking down, her hands together in her lap.

He drove until he reached the automated highway, and then he braked.

Again they turned to look at the house. It was completely hidden by trees now, but its lights shone through like ghosts congregating on high ground.

"It will happen," Richard said.

"I don't want to see it," Janet said.

Sam put the car on automatic and let the road take it.

As the vehicle shot across the desert, Sam sat back and tried to think. Where could they go?

"What's the worst that can happen?" Sam asked.

"Only the worst can happen," Richard said. "The world's urban areas will go from any of the variations of bulerite's instability. The oldest bulerite structures will go first—all the city mayors have known that since last week. But that will be nothing compared to the magma tap that transmits heat energy to the Caribbean power stations. When that goes, there may be earthquakes and volcanic activity, and a steam cloud that might affect the world's weather. The survivors will have decades of ruination to look forward to, until the last piece of bulerite is gone."

Sam tried to imagine the political strife during that time.

"Let's hope that this is all bulerite can do," Richard added, "and that there won't be any more surprises."

"One thing is sure," Janet said.

"What's that?" Sam asked.

"Buleros are not going to be liked very much."

"We may be in danger," Richard said. "I think it might be prudent for us to get off the earth, maybe to the moon, where some of the cities are not built up with bulerite. Besides, a lot of the stuff there is younger and may take longer to fall apart. Maybe Blackfriar and I can arrange for us to stay on Asterome."

"As long as only a few people know the truth," Janet said, "things can still be arranged."

We'll be criminals, Sam thought, noting the bitterness in Janet's voice. He wondered about Mars, Ganymede City, the outposts. Would life be any better there?

"I think we might be safe at the old house in Ecuador," Richard said. "It's outside the earthquake zone."

"What kind of heart does Orton have?" Janet asked suddenly.

Sam looked at her. "Why, I don't know. It might be bulerite, or older. We'll call him."

"The phone in this car is out of order," Richard said. "We'll have to stop at the first booth we see."

Janet began to check the roadmap screen for the nearest drive-in phone. She pushed a few buttons, programming the car to pull off the road when the time came.

Could we have foreseen all this? Sam asked himself. *Jack could have done more.* There was nothing to be done now except help himself, and those close to him, to survive. He looked up and saw two falling stars whisper across the sky and fade. He noticed an earthwatch satellite, which circled the earth every ninety minutes, climbing toward the zenith. It was also made of bulerite, growing heavy with the forces that would soon tear it apart.

Traffic outside Santa Fe was growing heavier. There were a dozen cars on either side of them, floating backward and forward as Central adjusted the road flow.

"Richard," Sam asked, "can any of this be an exaggeration?"

"The longer we ran the computer simulations, the worse things looked."

5. Doomwatch

The house sat among sparse trees, high in the stony foothills above the valley; behind it the mountains reached skyward, their summits lost in a haze of blue-white clouds. Sam turned and leaned over the stone wall of the terrace, remembering when he and Jack had last gazed out at the green Andean valley; it had been summer, more than thirty years before, but the view was unchanged. He took a deep breath of the thin, cool air, marveling at the clarity of the morning view.

In the sturdy houses of the village below, men and women who did not belong to the twenty-first century were already up and readying to start their farm work on the slopes. Many of them did not belong to the twentieth century, much less the twenty-first; a few had been born in the late eighteen hundreds. The longevity of Vilcabamba's people was a gift of heredity, diet, and way of life. The outside world's achievement of extended life through other means, however, had come too late to save the exiles, Sam's grandfather, Juan Bulero, and Carlos. Even now, Sam knew, he was not as strong as men his own age living here.

A hundred yards below the house, the copter sat on its landing block, a giant dragonfly with knife-blade wings; it was an obsolete model, with a simple-minded landing and takeoff program, but its manual controls were good.

The morning sun grew hotter on Sam's face. He thought of Juan standing here before going down among the villagers to practice his folk medicine, together with the remedies of the northern doctors he had outlived. He saw Juan returning to the lights of the house, where Isabel Samuels, the impatient American woman who loved him, was planning to make Juan leave the valley. Sam and Jack had visited their grandfather Juan long after he had come back here. He had looked like

Carlos, except bald and bearded, standing perfectly straight until he died—five years after his son's private jet slammed into a Canadian glacier. Juan had taken the news quietly, accepting a new companion into his life, expressing grief to no one; that would have been a defeat, a betrayal of Carlos, Juan had thought. Sam remembered his stern face at the funeral.

Sam closed his eyes and tried to see his mother, a large-boned woman with large black eyes, whom he had seen twice in his childhood. Carlos had told his sons the whole truth as soon as they were old enough to understand. Sam remembered his father's nervousness that summer, here by the wall, as he had explained his life. "I came back and married Ricardina to please Juan, mostly. I stayed for two years, doing theoretical work while you were born, my sons, but I was anxious to return to my experimental work in physics. My youth was slipping away. I took both of you with me, because I did not want you to grow up buried here in the valley. Ricardina refused to come along, sensing that I would be ashamed of her. It became easier to keep you with me when I became wealthy and forgot the past. By the time I returned to do something for Ricardina here, she had died of pneumonia. I could not really have given her anything from the outside anyway. . . ."

Carlos had cried in front of them. "I visited her only two or three times in ten years, and always she refused to come to Chicago with me."

Sam wondered if he and Jack might have been happier here, living a simpler life with their mother; certainly the world would have been better off if Carlos had stayed home with his bride. . . .

It was a sturdy stone house with a wooden floor. The handmade furniture would last forever. Sam had turned on the generator and stocked the kitchen for two months. The hydrogen tanks would provide heat and electricity for six months, with care.

Orton and Richard would arrive by noon, bringing Margot with them. Richard had insisted on taking her under the family's protection, and Janet had not objected. *It was not my place to offer an opinion,*

Sam thought. A vertical lander would drop them in the village, and Janet would pick them up with the copter. It was an hour's walk up from the village otherwise.

Looking across the valley, Sam tried to fill the great space under the sky and fell back into himself, content with having tried to encompass it. The sun was more than an hour past sunrise. He turned and went back up into the house.

The fire was almost out. He crossed the large room and opened the bedroom door. Sunlight spilled over the textures of the floor and bed, brightening the colorful quilt covering Janet. He went to the window and opened the other shutter, flooding the rest of the room with light. Then he knelt by the large wooden bed, reached under the quilt, and stroked Janet's stomach. She smiled and took a deep breath. He remembered the chilly night of their arrival and how they had huddled together in the old bed.

"Can't be safe in my own bed." She stretched and opened her large brown eyes.

"You'd better get up. It's well past sunrise and they may be early. You're sure you don't want me to go with you?"

"I want to meet her first." She was quiet for a moment, looking up at him anxiously. "Is there any news . . . from outside?"

"I haven't gotten the old tube out to see."

"Don't, until after we've all met."

He remembered Janet's conversation with Richard. She had asked him whether he loved Margot. *Why her?* Sam had asked himself. *Why not any stranger who might need help?* Margot was very lucky—they were all lucky to have a place to hide.

"I do love her," Richard had said vehemently.

"I'm glad," Janet had said, seeing a potential friend, if not the daughter she had always wanted.

"I don't care what I have to do to help her."

But would you save her if you did not love her? Sam had asked himself.

"I would keep her with me even if I didn't love her," Richard had said. "She's my friend—how could I live with myself?"

Janet motioned for Sam to sit down on the bed.

"Are you afraid you won't like her?" he asked.

She sat up. "Sam, what are we going to do? We can't live here forever."

"One thing at a time."

"I'm sorry, Sam, for what's happening."

"We'll know more later." He smiled, knowing that it was an obvious, uninspired smile. "Get dressed while I see about that tube." The bed creaked as he stood up.

He went out into the main room, knowing that she would have liked company while dressing, but he was afraid that she would sense his fears.

He went to the small alcove in the corner and opened the door to the basement. Turning on the lights, he slowly descended the stone steps. *A day at a time*, he told himself. The stairs went deep into the earth, into the empty wine cellar. A day at a time; there was no other way.

Sam hung the old picture-frame screen on the wall and plugged the cord into the socket by the bedroom door. He turned the set on and fine-tuned to World Channel 1, picking up the signal from the synchronous station above the Western Hemisphere. He heard the copter landing outside and hurried with the adjustments.

The color picture was quite good, despite the age of the receiver. The program was a rerun of *Fantasia*. He turned up the sound and recognized Stravinsky's music blaring from the small, inadequate stereo speakers. Newer sets were receiving the program on full three-dimensional holo rechanneling or on large wall screens, but the forty-inch picture would be enough to serve as their link with the outside world. He turned the sound off and faced Janet as she came in the front door. She seemed nervous.

A shy-looking girl stepped into the room, followed by Orton, who looked winded from the walk up from the copter block. They all stood a bit awkwardly, dark outlines in the daylight from the curtained windows.

"Sam, this is Margot Toren," Janet said, putting her arm around the young woman's shoulders. Sam looked at her carefully as she took his hand and held it. Her hair seemed black in the daylight; her eyes were brown with slivers of gold. She smiled as she took her hand away. Sam noticed an Asian slant to her eyes, realizing that she had a sub-dued beauty which would surprise the eye even after long familiarity.

"I'm very happy to meet you," she said.

Sam smiled at her, afraid that she would take his scrutiny to be unfavorable.

Orton stepped forward and Sam shook hands with him. The tele-vision speakers crackled with static. Sam turned around and saw that the *Sorcerer's Apprentice* sequence was in full swing, the brooms marching silently.

"I hope I'm welcome," Orton said.

"I'm sorry, Orton," Sam said. "I was fiddling with that set."

Janet walked over to the front entrance and switched on the over-head light. Suddenly the daylight silhouettes were gone, and Sam was looking at distinct faces. Margot seemed even more exotic in the glare of the old incandescent bulb.

Sam surveyed the room. "Where's Richard?" he asked, looking to Janet.

"He went back to Chicago," Orton said, "to find Carlos's records. Basil thinks there may be some old cassettes—"

"We can't raise him on the copter radio," Janet said. "I tried to patch through on the way here."

"He'll follow as soon as he can," Margot said.

No one spoke for a few moments.

"Is there any danger?" Sam asked.

"He didn't think so," Orton said. Janet turned away to the window.

As it grew dark outside, a few lonely lights appeared in the valley below. Sam stood with Orton by the window. Janet had gone to the copter radio half a dozen times, but there was still no word from Richard.

She expects him to die, Sam thought, sensing that she was preparing for the possibility.

"It's not good to retreat like this," Orton said.

"What can we do? We may be here a long time. By the way, what about your heart?"

"It was not a bulerite implant," Orton said. "The new one was cloned without a full embryo, I'm told. I feel fine."

Sam turned and looked at Janet, who was sitting with Margot on the old wooden bench. Both women had grown very nervous toward evening. It was obvious that Janet liked Margot, but Margot seemed to be holding back.

"News time, I think," Sam said.

Janet got up and turned on the set. Sam motioned Orton to the two wicker chairs. The picture brightened as Janet returned to her seat. Orton pulled his chair back a little and sat down. Sam remained standing when he saw the red letters appear on the screen:

NEW YORK EMERGENCY
PLEASE STAND BY

A commentator appeared, seated behind a plain desk in an empty room. "The bulerite supports of New York have collapsed," he said. "That report has been confirmed."

Air monitoring showed smoke rising for miles into the sky. The three levels were caved in at the center.

"No official explanation has been released. We have no reports of conditions at the old street level. . . ."

Sam felt the room grow warm and unreal.

"Millions are certainly dead. . . ." The reporter's eyes showed dismay.

A new scene appeared, revealing a huge artificial island slowly sinking into the sea.

"The pylons of Atlantic Arco One have failed, leaving the island of two million people to sink off the coast of North Carolina. . . ."

Farewell, Atlantic City, Sam thought, remembering when the old town's remains had been moved aboard at the turn of the century.

"Ships are picking up thousands of refugees, but two disasters of this size at once are too much for East Coast rescue operations. . . ."

The screen failed suddenly, leaving only the audio.

Janet got up and hit the set, but with no result. She sat down quickly.

Sam listened, conjuring up in his mind a terrifying vision of what was happening.

". . . without warning at seven AM. There—another section is collapsing into what has become a huge crater. Thousands of structures, some of them hundreds of years old, preserved with love in the shelf tiers, are gone. . . . A dream is dying. . . . The smoke is making it hard to see. Moments ago the Empire State Building became exposed for the first time in decades. . . ."

Sam thought of a broken bone jutting out of the dying leviathan of New York.

The sound went dead. Sam's stomach knotted. Janet got up and hit the set again, again with no result. She hesitated for a moment, then went into the bedroom and closed the door. Margot followed her, pausing to knock at the door. There was a faint answer and Margot went inside.

The television blared static and voices for a moment.

"We should prepare to leave," Orton said. "It's worse than I thought. If the magma tap goes, the whole hemisphere will feel the shocks. They'll never draw it out in time, I'm afraid."

"You saw how Janet feels. She feels responsible."

"We've got to get out, Sam. People still don't know what's going on. When they do it's going to become a political mess on earth, in addition to the physical dangers. Money and power may not help us."

"You're right, of course."

"You'll have to get Janet not to think about it. Assigning responsibility is for future historians."

Sam thought of the mountains outside. The house was solid, secure. He could not imagine any danger here.

"Janet would say that we have an unfair advantage in knowing about the danger." He thought of the people in the valley.

"It was hard to see this coming," Orton said.

"I guess. We were making the earth over," Sam said with tears in his eyes, "and we were doing fairly well."

Blackfriar was silent.

"What about Margot's parents?" Sam asked, composing himself.

"Richard told me a little, and Margot told us the rest on the way here. Her father was from Eastern Europe, a scholarly man, expert in the history of science and alchemy. Margot was born late in his life. He disappeared when she came to college in California, but he left her some money. Her mother was a Hawaiian. She walked out early. Margot is convinced they're both dead and doesn't seem to care. She's strong."

"I like her," Sam said, "and I think Janet likes her."

"Governor Alard will take us in on Asterome," Orton said. "Besides, Bulero has offices and facilities at L-5. You can be sure that the Bulero people on the colony have told Alard about the danger. If I know him, he's stripping the asteroid of what little bulerite he has right now."

"We'll go there for now," Sam said. "It's a free state, where we have some rights, as you say."

•   •   •

Sam got up in the darkness and put on his robe. When he was sure that he had not disturbed Janet, he went out into the main room. Margot was asleep on the air mattress in front of the fireplace. Orton was sprawled across two mattresses in the alcove next to the basement door. Moving quietly, Sam stepped outside.

The village was a dark abyss. A night wind swept from the mountain behind him. The snow on the peaks across the valley was bright in the starlight. Suddenly he knew that the security of the valley was an illusion; the immensity of these mountains was an illusion. Only the stars would endure, shining even when the earth was gone. The stay in the valley was a doomwatch, nothing more.

He went inside quietly, lay down next to Janet, and tried to sleep as he listened to the wind.

But the earth moved under him, gently at first, then shaking the house, conspiring with the wind to drive them off the earth.

They dressed quickly, and Sam led the way to the helicopter.

The blades started nervously, but finally Janet was able to coax the overburdened craft up from the shaking block. With luck, Sam thought, they would reach the Machala airstrip before morning, long before the fuel ran out. From there it was only an hour to the equatorial earthport at Quito.

He thought about Richard.

6. A Mobile Utopia

Asterome was a settlement in space, circling the earth at Libration Point 5, a quarter of a million miles behind the moon's position, equidistant from earth and moon. The tourist screen at the end of the shuttle aisle showed a diagram:

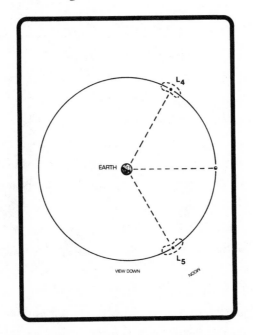

The screen switched to an occasional view of earth, stars, or moon, always returning to the diagram as if to a test pattern.

Sam turned and looked at Janet; she ignored him, staring ahead, hands clasped in her lap. She had failed to reach Richard from Quito, and it had been difficult to get her on the shuttle. Margot had taken her side, but after some discussion both women had been convinced to board the moonbus. Sam was not happy about leaving, either, but

Orton had insisted that Richard would follow with Mike Basil. All four of them now understood that there was very little they could have done by staying behind, whether Richard followed or not. For the moment, Sam told himself, there was no reason to think that Richard was in danger.

He turned and glanced at Orton and Margot in the seat behind his and Janet's. They were asleep, floating gently against their seat belts.

There were no familiar faces among the other ninety-six passengers; it was obvious that they were well-to-do skilled people on their way to Asterome and the moon, probably to replace people who had left, to continue their professional experience and studies, or to fill new positions.

The twenty-four-hour passage had grown oppressive. As the shuttle maneuvered for the final approach, Sam tried to relieve his worries by recalling something of the history of Asterome. He had been relatively ignorant of the community, he admitted, until Richard had gone to study on the moon and had written letters home about the place. Even now, Asterome was difficult to imagine. Nothing, Richard had written, can replace the experience. *I'm more used to ideas than to experience*, Sam thought. *Even experience is a concept for me.* Emotionally he was not convinced that he was out in space. The viewscreen did not seem real; after all, stars, the moon, and space were not like streams and trees, or stones that one could touch. He remembered his grandfather's view of space travel and the notion of space habitats: walls . . . glass and metal, cramped cabins, a starry, desolate darkness outside . . . no life for a human being. . . .

Asterome was an arcology, much like the tier cities of earth-moon, a societal container housing a new branch of humankind. Once it had been a minor planet, a chunk of nickel-iron and rock ten miles long and five wide, roughly ovoid in shape, moving in an orbit that would have brought it into collision with earth five years after its discovery. In the late 1980s, the Japanese had sent out an engineering team to land on it, using a modified atomic version of a Type III American space shuttle.

The group had brought supplies to set up housekeeping, as well as a nuclear rocket engine, industrial atomic explosives, and sunsails. After laying a solar-powered mass driver track along the length of the asteroid, and attaching the atomic engine for attitude correction, they had diverted the asteroid into the relatively stable L-5 position.

Sam imagined the moment when the mass driver had begun to move the asteroid by accelerating bits of rock off the surface opposite to the direction of travel, using the asteroid's own material and electrical power from the sun to change its orbit slowly. That must have been a moment without equal in the lives of the engineers, who had spent years in space to save earth from a great catastrophe.

The danger of collision had played into the hands of the International Asteroid Mining Lobby, which also ran the two equatorial earthports on a commercial basis. The lobby had argued that the energy expenditure to avert world catastrophe would show a good return on investment as Asterome grew to be self-sufficient; it would be silly to bring the giant rock into L-5 and do nothing with it. No one had doubted that an ocean strike by the asteroid would have permanently altered the earth's climate, plunging humanity into an ice age. Once the investment snowball had started, nothing could stop it; but it had taken a near disaster to start the development of the greater solar system. *It always takes a crisis to wake us up*, Sam thought.

The mining of the asteroid belt between Mars and Jupiter began even as the inside of Asterome was being hollowed out. Both ends were opened with nuclear charges, permitting the mining of the rich nickel and iron ore. When the interior space had been cleared, the ends were closed by installing recycling plants and multiple docking locks. The pumping in of a pressurized atmosphere and the arrival of colonist workers had signaled the birth of the first genuine macrolife settlement, capable of self-reproduction and mobility. The population had grown to a hundred thousand by the turn of the century, but the three hundred square miles of interior real estate could easily support a million.

Asterome was the shielded residential area of a growing industrial and scientific complex at L-5. Six large manufacturing structures used the space environment's cheap solar energy and unlimited heat and waste sink. Metals mined on the moon and in the asteroid belt were refined and cast with the high precision made possible by zero-g facilities, the use of controlled acceleration and gravity gradients, the high-quality vacuum, and other conditions available on earth only at high cost, if at all. The list of industrial processes continued to grow, even after a quarter of a century; many earthbound industries no longer bothered to make basic products; it was cheaper to import from free space. . . .

Sam closed his eyes. Impersonal concerns had always been a comfort to him during bad times. Janet might be right about Richard, though she would not say it. *What could have happened?* Sam wondered. There were many things that might have delayed him; death was too extreme an explanation; Janet was almost certainly wrong. . . .

Besides being a way station, Asterome provided space-rescue capability that could reach to any part of sunspace. The settlement's maintenance crews regularly serviced the solar energy collectors in near-earth orbit. The UN Space Fleet's dockyards were on the moon, where many of the ships were in mothballs, but the hired specialists from Asterome kept the vessels operational.

Richard's letters from Plato University contained a wealth of detail about life away from earth, more than Sam had cared to know at the time; but now something of Janet's foreboding took hold of him, and he was surprised at how much he remembered. The letters revealed, he realized, Richard's growing commitment to a new kind of life.

Asterome's best efforts went into basic research, following Daniel Bell's well-known description of a postindustrial society as one in which the organization of theoretical knowledge is central to innovation, a society in which intellectual institutions are the heart of the social structure. This was also true, to a degree, of societies on earth, but Asterome

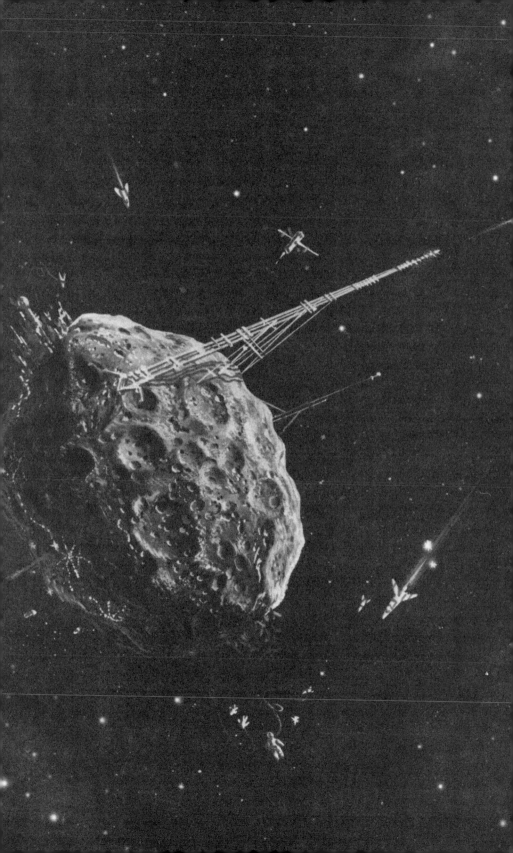

had the potential of becoming genuinely open-ended and self-shaping, creatively incomplete on the model of science and art, without having to live with the historical brake of economic insufficiency.

In physics, gravity research, sun studies, the various astronomies and cosmologies, Asterome continued at a competitive pace with earth-moon, excelling in applied physics, especially in the improvement of solar and fusion power systems; in basic research, Asterome's forays into aspects of gravity wave generation led the field. In biology and medicine, Asterome dominated both research and applications, producing thousands of export drugs in special conditions, as well as providing safe areas for the more dangerous forms of biological research which had been banned from earth's biosphere by the various safety boards.

Sam thought of Laputa, Swift's fictional island in the sky, where all kinds of seemingly useless scientific research was carried out in the name of knowledge. Swift would have considered most of Asterome's activities inexplicable, unless he had radically altered his outlook. Richard had exhibited such a change in his letters from the moon, and Sam found himself approving the change. Richard had prepared him for Orton's visions; but they were not Orton's property; a large group of people shared them. Sam wondered how he would have tolerated these views in a colleague, rather than in a nephew and a friend.

The colonies on Mars and on the moons of Jupiter and Saturn could not have been founded without Asterome's support. Asterome had helped earth-moon corporations invest in exploration and development. It had built the Bulero Orbital Factory for the manufacture of bulerium, in addition to a half-dozen other Bulero spacegoing facilities. Ganymede City could not have been built in Jupiter's radiation zone without the shielding for the construction crews provided by Asterome. The asteroid's ties were strong with every human settlement in sunspace, Sam noted; it had even helped with the first efforts at exploration beyond sunspace. Yet Asterome managed to remain independent, despite its ties, despite successive efforts by earth-moon multinationals to buy up control of its stock.

Asterome's governors had been mostly Japanese, except for a few Chinese in the late 1990s. Their stewardship of a thriving crossroads community had revived Asia's self-respect and sense of legitimacy in world affairs, especially after the Russian civil war had left the USSR as two associated republics. The six-month war had destroyed a quarter of China's industrial capacity; Moscow had termed it a preventive strike, made to discourage China from taking advantage of the civil emergency. The close call with full-scale nuclear war had finally brought a UN Nuclear Arms Control Treaty, beginning a process that might one day have resulted in a total ban.

Sam thought again of the initial act of daring that had resulted in the building of Asterome, in the gathering of skills and investment for the industrial development of the asteroid belt, in the opening of the solar system's vast wealth for human use. A huddling humanity had needed to grow beyond the limits set by a century which had been learning to be a miser in a universe of plenty. . . .

The earth eclipsed the sun on the screen. The view changed and Asterome's docking chutes gaped at him as the shuttle made its approach, slowly correcting its forward drift.

"We're almost there," he said, floating gently against his seat belt.

The screen went blank as the craft docked; through the port at Janet's right, Sam caught a glimpse of a metal plain and a close, ragged horizon of slag and rock. His stomach felt queasy as his mind produced an illusion: The shuttle had landed nose first and "down" was directly ahead; at any moment he would fall forward and shatter the screen.

Janet grasped his hand. The perspective disappeared as the vessel was drawn inside, covering the port.

A voice spoke from the screen, warning passengers to be careful when they released their seat belts.

"We're still at zero gravity," Sam said, "because the docks are along Asterome's long rotational axis. Gravity will return as we move off that axis."

"No kidding," Janet said as she floated over him into the aisle. She was making an effort, he knew, to appear cheerful.

"I was trying to explain," he said, "but maybe I should have started with the difference between centrifugal and gravitational forces."

Orton and Margot were gliding toward the nose exit. Janet pushed after them. Sam waited until the other passengers had drifted out, then followed; he floated to the exit, passed through a long curving tunnel, and emerged into a small green room, where Janet, Margot, and Orton were waiting. At once his feet drifted down to touch the floor, and his stomach noted the change.

The walls seemed recently painted. There was a rack with a dozen spacesuits and a small screen next to a portal leading into another long tunnel. Sam walked over carefully and looked into the dimly lit passageway.

"The place is honeycombed with rooms like this. I guess it's a reception area," Margot said.

"Is someone meeting us?" Janet asked.

Sam saw a man's head in the passageway; shoulders became visible, then a torso and feet. The figure was obviously coming around a curve. In a moment the man stepped into the room.

"I'm Governor Amadis Alard," he said, smiling. He was dressed in green shorts and sneakers, his black chest bare. His hair was closely cropped, resembling a black skullcap; touches of gray were visible.

"Samuel Bulero?" he asked, squinting at him. "Orton, we meet in the flesh at last. And Janet Bulero."

"This is Margot Toren," Janet said.

"How do you do. My helpers will show you to your housing. I'm very busy, as you may guess, so you will excuse me if I leave suddenly. This is the first time in decades that the Bulero family has asked to use its privileges on Asterome. You are welcome." He spoke in a rich bass voice. Sam saw the uneasiness in Janet's face; Margot was not looking directly at the governor. "Where is Richard Bulero?" Alard asked.

"He'll arrive later," Orton replied.

"We will go the way I came," Alard said. "This spiral will take us farther away from the axis. You will note a gradual increase in centrifugal, or pseudo-gravitational, pull. But let me show you a view first." He stepped over to the screen and turned it on.

Suddenly they were looking across the length of Asterome, as if from a high mountain, except that green countryside, bodies of water, houses, and roads were visible in every direction.

"I wanted to prepare you. Follow me, please."

Alard stepped into the passage. Sam followed first, grasping the handrail as he walked through the nautilus-like curve, which slowly turned uphill toward an exit.

Sam stepped out into sunlight and stood next to Alard. One by one, the others came out and were silent before the view.

In the contained space of the sky, the triple beams of the linear sun marked the long axis of the hollow world. The light, Sam knew, was caught by the giant sun mirror on the outside of the asteroid, more than ten miles away, entering through a series of focusing devices and filters. The three beams, Sam saw, were projected across the hollow to another focusing and reflecting device, somewhere below where they stood. The air glowed between the beams; the distant light terminal was a circle of sunlight. A giant lake circled the world's equator without spilling, reminding Sam of water in a whirling bucket.

"This way," Alard said. He led them to a downhill path. "Please watch your step. There are idiosyncrasies in centrifugal pull: it will increase to only three-quarters earth normal, but watch your added strength, and do not jump. You may not come down in the same place."

A trolley-like vehicle waited for them at the end of the path. They climbed in and took seats behind Alard. The car left its dead-end terminal slowly. "It runs downhill on this track," the governor said as he turned to face them, "then climbs to the high country at the other end, where we also have docking facilities."

Sam felt his weight increase as the car rushed down into Asterome's heartland. His stomach was still upset, as if he were on a ship at sea; part of it, Sam knew, was his worry about Richard, nagging at him, making him anxious to confront the truth, whatever it might be. Maybe he was one of those rare individuals who could never get used to centrifugal gravity; yet he remembered getting his sea legs, so perhaps he would get his space legs.

"We should arrive in a few minutes," Alard said loudly over the sound of rushing air. "Everything is ready for you."

Sam nodded, wondering how much faster the car would go.

Alard suddenly pointed upward through the canopy. "There's an automated line like this one on the sky side," he shouted, "but we also have a subway in the service level below the land. That line fans out to reach more branch stations."

Sam nodded and smiled. Alard finally noted his distress and smiled in sympathy.

The car was coming to a small town just before the central lake. Sam took a deep breath, enjoying the smell of flowers and grass. The land was flattening out; his legs touched the floor more firmly now, and that quieted his stomach.

The car sped into town and slowed to a crawl. Sam looked around at the buildings, handsome widely spaced single and multistoried structures from every period of the last century and a half, terrace after terrace climbing on each side of the roadway in the curve of the world.

The car pulled up to a platform and stopped. "Please be careful," Alard said as he got out.

Sam stepped down and stood next to the governor. As the others emerged, a man came along the sidewalk and stopped next to Alard.

"This is my assistant, Soong Weng Ling," Alard said. "He will show you to your quarters." Before Sam could thank him, Alard turned and walked away down the street.

"You will forgive the governor," the assistant said, "but he is a busy man in troubled times. Please follow me."

Soong Weng Ling led them down the sidewalk of what appeared to be the main street, which ran at right angles to the trolley line. The lake was at their left, and for a moment the street suggested an interior latitude line, sloping gently upward before them. It occurred to Sam that here one had to go "below" to see the stars, that Asterome's observatories, its maintenance and docking facilities, were in the world's basement.

They followed Soong Weng Ling across the street. Sam paused before the rotating doors of the Hotel Asterome-Hilton and waited for the others to catch up.

"Mr. Soong," Sam started to say.

"You may call me Weng Ling."

"Weng Ling, how extensive is the level below us?"

"One day it will equal the inner surface, but with less overhead space, of course. We excavate as we need more space for industrial and scientific facilities, but only a quarter of the available limit has been used."

Sam found himself liking the young Chinese; his answer had been full of hope, like something Richard would say.

"I count three towns," Margot said while looking up.

Sam glanced upward. The tribeam was warm on his face, a captive sun shining by stolen light in a garden world that seemed to exist outside human history.

"Shall we go in?" Janet asked.

Orton and Margot stopped their sightseeing. Soong led the way through the spinning doors into the lobby. A very ordinary-looking desk clerk gave Sam the register.

"I will take them up myself," Soong said after they had all punched in their names. He led the way to the elevator.

Their suite was on the top floor of the ten-story structure and consisted of a large solarium—living room common area and four bedrooms. A large screen showed the earth from twenty-five thousand miles out, looking like a painting on the wall opposite the solarium windows.

The light filtering in through the orange curtains created a warm, peaceful glow, inviting forgetfulness, but the magnified image of earth was a direct link to all his fears. Sam thought of the students and colleagues he had left behind.

"There's a good Chinese and Japanese dining room down the street," Soong said. "I will be back later to see if you have any needs."

He turned and went out, closing the door carefully behind him.

Janet stared at the screen. Orton and Margot sat on the sofa. Sam approached the screen and examined the controls. He touched the highest setting and the earth drew nearer.

"At that magnification," Margot said, "you can tell time by which cities are visible."

Sam looked closely, but clouds hid the Western Hemisphere. He imagined thick smoke rising from New York and drifting out over the ocean.

The linear sun went out at six, dimming slowly. Streetlamps came on and filled the darkened hollow with a firefly glow. The evening air was dark as Sam and Janet led the way back to the hotel. Strolling people filled the streets; couples sat in the open cafes and small groups stood talking at the corners.

Sam looked up across the world, at the lights scattered like stars across the green country; the overhead towns were galaxies of concentrated light; the ends of the world were black, as if open to the void.

Suddenly a holo of the full earth appeared in the night overhead. Janet cried out; the crowd in the street grow silent. The sunlit globe seemed terrifyingly close under high magnification.

Silently, bright flashes appeared; dark blotches covered the daylight, marring the blues, greens, browns, and whites of the home world. Alard's voice spoke over the public address system, seeming to fill the hollow with the utterance of a quiet god.

"A massive earthquake in the Caribbean has created a running crack in the earth's crust, moving east and south. Radio transmissions from Washington, Moscow, London, and Peking are filled with debate and accusations concerning responsibility for what is happening. The remains of New York continue to be wrapped in fire and strange electromagnetic storms. . . ."

Sam saw the look of dismay on the faces of Janet and Margot. Orton was tapping the pavement with his cane. The magma tap was gone, Sam knew, and a new Bulero monster was wandering across the face of the planet, swallowing even more lives.

The image of earth faded from the skyspace.

Soong was waiting for them in the lobby. They entered the lounge and sat down in the air-filled furniture that formed a broken circle in one corner of the paneled room.

"You know what is happening on earth?" Soong asked.

"Yes, we do," Sam answered.

"It was relatively easy, though costly," Soong said, "to remove what little bulerite we had. The governor and I mean no offense to the Bulero family—"

"That's not important," Sam said. "The question now is what can Asterome do to help earth?"

"You think it will be very bad," Soong said.

"There will be those," Blackfriar said, "who will try to gain political advantage if the major powers weaken."

"Can Asterome go on by itself?" Margot asked. It was the kind of question Richard would ask, Sam realized.

Soong nodded. "We produce everything we need, but our capacity for receiving refugees is limited. There is a limit, also, on how many people can be evacuated from earth, if that becomes necessary. We can take everyone from the various earth-moon zone space installations and a certain number from earth, but the moon, Mars, and Ganymede City must look after their own. Ganymede City should have the least problem because much of it was built of nonbulerite materials; most of what they have is in their space vessels. Mars and the moon will have a lot of damage, but many will survive to rebuild. Earth is a different matter, however."

The large screen on the far wall lit up, showing the face of Governor Alard. "There's a first-strike missile barrage coming up from Africa and South America, moving toward North America and Europe. I don't see much intercept response yet. You'd better get over here, Soong." The face faded, leaving the image of earth. Soong stood and hurried out of the room.

Sam got up and approached the screen, searching earth's cloudy face; the signs of disaster would be small at this distance, difficult to connect with what the mind knew was happening.

The relay angle changed to show earth half in darkness. Sparks played on the dark side—invisible, radiant, dark again, luminous stones sinking into a dark lake; it was impossible to tell ground hits from intercepts. Sam almost expected the planet to shudder visibly; the earth was shaking, he knew, shocks were flowing through the crust, and the final ruin would be greater than anything man could muster.

He thought of the house in New Mexico, wondering if the desert sands would begin to glow, draining the life out of the cacti as the bulerite grew more indeterminate, catching fire from within, like some primordial substance from which universes are made, finally dying into an eternal blackness, where even the starlight would be trapped. . . .

The fools didn't know that the bulerite alone was enough.

Janet came and stood next to him. The magnification increased, framing the entire Northern Hemisphere. Huge areas of smoke filled the daylight portion, slowly being pulled apart into delicate strands by the winds of the upper atmosphere; the fireflies multiplied rapidly, reminding Sam of the flickerings on a computer panel.

"They're not stopping," Janet said.

"Return strikes have been made at every possible target," Alard's hushed, quavering voice said over the picture.

The cities glowed in the night, refusing to fade after multiple hits.

Sam wondered if any missiles had been fired toward Asterome; they would reach the colony long after it was all over on earth. The bulerite would continue, however, second-best destroyer.

I'll never see another sunrise on earth, he thought as he put his arm around Janet. Orton and Richard had wanted something that would present humankind with the choice of a shovel for its grave or the stars; immortality or death. *Either to wait for the sun to die and the cold of space to take us, or to go when we are still able and aware of what we can become.* Was he grasping at the words to make this all bearable? Civilizations have died before, he reminded himself, and new ones have grown to take their place.

Margot came and stood next to Janet. "All the people," she said, "all the friends I knew in school, dying. Now we'll have to survive out here."

"Richard," Janet whispered, and pressed her face into Sam's shoulder.

Sam heard a breaking sound and turned in time to see Orton drop the two pieces of his cane, get up with a grunt, and walk out of the lounge.

As Sam looked back to the earth, he felt a rushing in his head, spreading outward from the terror lodged in the center of his brain. His imagination conjured up what his eyes could not see, his ears could not hear. All those who knew him, whose relationship to him gave him his identity and career, would soon be gone; his past was dying, and with it the planet's history. This island in space would certainly not survive the earth by more than a few days; a warhead could reach the settlement in one day.

"Look—there in the Caribbean," Margot said.

He saw a glowing red spot where the warm blood of the earth was spilling up into the sea from the magma tap. Steam clouds were rising, marking the crack's progress through the crust.

Sam held Janet close and looked at Margot. She seemed in control of herself, despite the terror in her eyes.

"He can't be dead," she said, "he just can't be. Excuse me." She turned and left the room. Janet pulled away from Sam and went after her.

Sam watched the screen, welcoming the painful rigidity in his neck muscles. A long time ago, it seemed, the plans had all been made, the world's problems identified; humanity had started remaking the future. Nothing so obvious as the rivalries of the last century would have led to a thermonuclear exchange; the way had been complex, hiding the result until too late. If the war continued for another hour or two, the earth would not recover for a century; longer if the bombs being used were of older design.

What would he live for if Asterome survived? Could Janet and he make a life for themselves off the earth? Suddenly he was afraid that he would never again feel useful or needed. He was worried about Janet; she might react very badly to the news of Richard's death.

Then he realized that there might be no way for the news to reach her, that no one would ever know who was alive or dead in the ruins of earth.

7. The Cage of Life

Richard gripped the cassette case and looked through the milky transparency of the floor, down toward the base of the three-thousand-foot pyramid. Silent bursts of light passed between the bulerite floors, strange fish swimming through what should have been solid matter. The entire Bulero Complex seemed dreamlike, about to dissolve.

He hurried to the elevator, knowing that he might not reach the lobby before the building disintegrated. As he passed a giant window, he glimpsed the vast burning ruin of Chicago, its tiers caved in as in New York, the strange glow of anomalous forces becoming visible in the blue twilight.

Thanks, Jack, he said silently. *You killed yourself, but you haven't got me yet.* He thought of the frenzy of the last week, feeling grateful that it had been possible to evacuate all the employees to nonbulerite areas.

Miraculously, the elevator doors opened. *A small kindness.* He might never reach the shuttle, even if he got down to the lobby and out of the complex. He stepped inside and the doors closed, leaving him in darkness as the world fell away and he clasped Carlos Bulero's records to himself. *They had better be worth it.* The future would have to redeem the past. It had taken him many hours to find them among Jack's records, misfiled where only he could have found them easily; and there was no guarantee that they were not Jack's carefully edited copies of the original papers.

Richard's weight increased as the elevator slowed to a stop. The doors opened, revealing a floor of white light. A dark figure was coming toward the elevator, gun in hand. *A looter.*

"Wait!" Mike Basil shouted as Richard stepped out and turned right quickly. "I've got the car."

Richard stopped as Basil walked up to him. "What are you doing here, Mike? You should be at the shuttleport. Did the rest of our people get out of the area?"

"I'm glad I found you. There's not much time."

"Why should you care?"

Mike noticed the cassette case. "I was Jack's friend, as much as that was possible."

"Let's get out of here before his handiwork ends our friendship," Richard said.

Mike smiled, then turned and led the way out through the main entrance to the waiting car, where he got into the driver's seat. Richard threw the cassette case into the back seat and got in next to him.

The vehicle moved down the driveway leading out of the thousand-acre world headquarters of Bulero Enterprises. The tree-lined road was empty.

Mike did not release the car when they reached the automated road. "It goes out intermittently," he said. "No use taking a chance."

He turned right and the car gained speed.

"Do you think we'll have enough power at the launch laser?" Richard asked.

"We should, since it's powered by our own fusion plant. That's bulerite-enclosed, but there have been no signs of instability yet."

"How about the shuttle itself?"

"Its bulerite is too young to go; it'll last long enough."

The Bulero Industrial Spaceport appeared in the distance. Richard saw the launch pad, a brightly lit cut-off cone against the darkening sky. As the car drew closer, a shuttle went up, riding a thick column of ruby red laser light; in a moment the roar grew very loud, dying away slowly as the vehicle disappeared overhead. The beam followed for a minute, imparting the last of its heat energy to the fuel mixture in the ship's reaction chamber, then winked out.

Another minute later, Richard saw the last shuttle coming into vertical position on the pad.

A mob of people pressed in around the main gate, while guards struggled to clear the way. The car came to a stop at the edge of the crowd.

A voice boomed over the public address system: *"Please proceed to the airport, or to boost-train terminals. We have no way to evacuate you here. This is an earth-to-orbit line only."*

"We'll have to go around them," Mike said.

They opened their doors and got out. Richard reached into the back seat and grabbed the black case.

"Let's go," Basil said. Richard remembered that Mike was armed.

Basil started to lead the way around the crowd. The crowd was oblivious to them, shouting at the guards. They reached the fence easily and started to push through toward the gate.

A pair of hands shoved Richard against the fence. "Who do you think you are?" a voiced demanded.

"Another bigshot," a second voice answered as Richard held himself up against the fence. A hand reached for the case.

"Where are you going, bigshot?" the first voice asked.

A roar went up from the crowd, signaling some new response from the guards. Richard pulled the case away and held it close.

"Come on!" Mike whispered, and helped him along.

"Watch it!" a voice shouted. Richard took a deep breath of the summer air, expecting to be shoved again.

"Mr. Basil!" one of the uniformed men said, and opened a way past the line of guards.

Mike pushed Richard through and followed. Another cry went up from the mob.

"There's no way to avoid angering them," Mike said inside the gate.

Richard stopped and looked back. The guards were retreating inside and closing the gate.

"Come on!" Mike shouted.

"The fence may be bulerite," Richard said, "but the ground it's standing in isn't. The crowd can still press it flat."

The mass of people was now pushing against the gate.

"Even if we took a few with us," Mike said, "the rest would mob the facility and prevent us from taking off. We can't risk damage to the laser controls."

The gate seemed to move; the floodlights flickered. Richard hesitated. People clambered onto the gate.

"Come on!" Mike repeated.

The guards fired tear gas grenades, but a few figures reached the top and jumped inside.

Richard turned and ran after Basil, catching up with him as the other reached an empty port car.

They got in and Basil pulled away, heading for the launch pad. As he looked back, Richard noticed that the guards seemed to have quieted the crowd.

"Another bunch will be back later," Mike said.

The address system crackled, then a voice said: "*Attention all personnel. This is a nuclear alert. Repeat: This is a nuclear alert. Please go to your shelters. Warheads will reach us within twenty minutes. This is not a drill.*"

Mike pulled up to the pad as the warning was repeated. The shuttle towered a hundred and fifty feet above them, bright and silvery in the floodlights.

"The crowd's broken through the fence," Mike said. He jumped out and ran toward the lift cage. Richard stuffed the case into his shirt and followed. "Sada will wait for us," Mike said as the elevator door closed.

"But will the laser work if the city is struck?" Richard asked.

"We only need it for a few minutes," Mike said.

The cage opened. Toshiro Sada, the shuttle pilot, was standing on the ramp, motioning for them to board.

Basil pushed Richard ahead. "Thanks," Richard heard Mike say to Sada as they went up the ramp into the shuttle's midsection.

Inside, most of the seats were full. Richard climbed up the floor rungs and approached the first pair of empty seats. Mike struggled along next to him and they strapped in, facing straight up.

Richard looked out through the port at his right. *How can this be happening?* He turned and looked into Mike's face, which was close to his in the cramped seats.

"Somebody has decided to cut himself a piece of the world," Mike said quietly.

"Do you think we'll respond?"

There was a look of resignation in Mike's blue eyes. "I don't see how we can avoid it. Some of the warheads are bound to get through. The best we can hope for is a measured, target-by-target response— but if the war doesn't finish us, the bulerite will."

We might have had a chance with the war alone.

Richard felt a vibration. Below him, he knew, the laser beam had come to life, nursing the shuttle with heat energy. The shuttle started to rise slowly, gaining speed as it fed on the awesome power of the beam, which would follow the craft until it reached escape velocity.

Bulero Port fell away; clouds rushed by the porthole. In a minute stars appeared on the horizon. The acceleration pinned Richard to his seat, squeezing a few tears out of his eyes. He tried to breathe more deeply, knowing that he would have a bruise from the case in his shirt.

The shuttle shook a little; then the acceleration cut off and the weight was lifted from him. He saw the western curve of the earth at his right, where the sun was being prevented from setting by the shuttle's climb. The Pacific came into view on the blue-violet horizon.

Two flashes appeared, false suns rising and suddenly fading.

"Los Angeles and San Francisco," Mike said. "Chicago is probably gone below us."

The shuttle continued its climb into the west, tipping over into a horizontal position as it made orbit. The rungs retracted into what was now the floor, creating an aisle.

The stars grew numerous over the dying earth. *Thanks, Jack,* Richard thought. *The planet might have destroyed itself without you, but you helped eradicate my world, where I might have made my mark.* Yet a part of him looked away, telling him that he would have gone from the cage of earth as he had gone from home, that the bulerite disaster had only delayed him. If it had not been for Margot's return to earth, and the lingering help that he had given Bulero Enterprises, he would have been on the moon when all this happened. Now the war was quickening his departure, and he felt guilty.

A new fear crept into his mind. "Do you think Asterome might become a target?"

"Depends," Mike said, "on who started the war, and who they think Asterome will side with."

"Is Asterome armed?" He thought of Margot and his family.

"I don't know, but there would be enough time for Alard to send out a crew to trigger or disarm the warheads some ways off. One might get through."

He and Mike might reach Asterome just before it died.

"Sada will know if missiles are headed for Asterome," Mike said. "They'll be on radar before we enter a trajectory for L-5. Let's go sit up front."

The Bulero passengers were watching the war as Richard and Basil drifted out of their seats into the aisle.

"Mr. Bulero, remember me?"

Richard looked toward a redheaded man in the seat ahead.

"I fixed your intercom in the office last week."

"Oh—yes, how are you?"

"My wife and kid didn't get out of New York."

"I'm sorry, Hank."

"The way I see it is that the rest of us have to go on." Hank stared fixedly at Richard for a moment, looking for a confirmation; there was terror in the man's green eyes.

"I think so, Hank," Richard said as he turned away and drifted forward.

When they reached the bulkhead, Richard caught a glimpse of nuclear flashes through the port at his right; he tried not to look.

8. The World Swallower

"Janet?"

Sam came into the hotel room and sat down on the bed. She lay on her stomach with her face in the pillow. He touched her shoulder. "Richard is safe—we've had a radio message. A few Bulero shuttles will reach us within a day." He rubbed her shoulder. She turned over slowly and looked at him.

"People will be coming up from earth," she said, as if to show him that she was in control of herself. He knew that she had been waiting for bad news. "Can the moon handle all the refugees?"

"I don't think there will be more than we can handle," Sam said. "It won't be possible for large numbers to escape. The moon has well-developed communities. Asterome and the moon will help each other."

"It's horrible," Janet said. "We're responsible, the Buleros."

"The war is over," he said, realizing that he had never thought of himself as a real Bulero, or privileged; the thought startled him, confronting him with the degree of his alienation from Jack. "The big defense control centers are gone," he continued, "including a few no one knew existed until they showed their teeth. The big cities are gone, and the surface temperature is rising. Magma is still spilling out, but the ocean crack seems to have stopped for now."

"How can you talk about it?"

He looked at her carefully. "I try to understand what is happening, because it helps me to live, as it always has. It's all I can do now." *It's all I've ever done.*

She reached up suddenly and pulled him down to her. He was quiet as she held him, and all her fears seemed to drain into him. He stayed with her until she fell asleep.

• • •

Orton sat in the low-gravity waiting room. Richard's shuttle—the last one from the Bulero Complex—would arrive in a few minutes. Refugees from earth, and from the smaller, supply-dependent near-earth stations within the radius of geosynchronous orbit, were being given the choice of remaining on Asterome or of going on to the moon. About a third of the arrivals were accepting Alard's offer, but the rest held back, still loyal to the Earth-Moon UN Authority, refusing to believe that this disaster would not right itself in time. Of course, Asterome would have to close its doors after a while.

Orton knew that he would become a part of Asterome; he had wanted it before, and now it was the only place for him. "Natural planets are too big," Alard had told him a few hours before, "too big to run properly, given the variables of our history. It's always been a bad start—never a world government that works properly, not even good local ones. If the earth's population had always been small, then maybe we could have worked up to a large democracy. Sure, we've had some peace and a lot of creativity and production, policed by large powers. But the smaller nation—gangs start a war at the first sign of weakness among the police. I've had it, planets have too much room to hide nasty schemes. Humanity can do better with worlds like this. We'll reproduce, keep a loose association, scatter across the galaxy, ensuring both survival and human diversity."

Orton felt close to the man, and he knew that Richard would also respond. Alard made him grasp after dreams in a practical way. Most important, they both saw the danger in the scattered power centers left in the solar system. After it was clear that earth would not recover for a long time, these might begin to work against one another, depending on their previous loyalties.

Asterome would be a valuable piece in this game. Its computer libraries, manufacturing facilities, and skilled personnel would be decisive wherever it went. Alard's feeling was that the moon could take care of itself, but that Mars, Ganymede, and the asteroids might need help. He was planning to shift Asterome's position to the Jovian system in order to keep a balance between the various sunspace sectors. *Maybe we'll turn out to be bloody fools also*, Orton thought. He knew that the dream of an interstellar macrolife would have been better served with a whole earth behind it. Now the view back from the stars would be a bitter one; migrant humanity would know that the small yellow sun carried a corpse through space; the inner stains would never be washed away for those who had lived through the end.

A sense of helplessness came over him, and he felt that he understood Janet's withdrawal, Sam's stunned passivity, and Margot's quiet rage.

"Hello, Orton," Richard said as he stepped carefully into the room.

Orton stood up. Suddenly dreams seemed to be the most urgent things he knew. They shook hands. Richard seemed tired, but well. There was a look in his face, Orton saw, an ethereal, longing gaze, capable of peering across the dark light-years of an entire galaxy without flinching.

Just a little while ago it had seemed that all the waiting in her life was over; that within a reasonable set of compromises things would be the way she wanted them, with no more subtle threats, no more tedious striving for appearances, no more unexpected irritations.

"But can you get the Bulero outposts to listen to you?" Orton was asking from the lounge chair at her right.

Janet looked at the orange curtains as they moved in the slight breeze coming into the solarium from the hollow. "We've got to pull what's left of the company together," she said. "I know all the division heads by phone, and I met the chiefs of the centers on the moon, Mars, and Ganymede, when they first went out to their jobs. They'll listen to me, but the question is what to tell them." She looked at Sam sitting across from her in the sofa. "Should they stay where they are, or come to Asterome with their families?"

"Alard wants to take Asterome out to Mars, then to Ganymede," Orton said.

She thought of Richard and Margot, sleeping in the nearby bedroom. Alard would like to go farther than that, she suspected, out of sunspace completely, especially if things got any worse. Orton, together with Richard and Margot, was sympathetic to the idea. They were taking a long view, but it was the short-term possibilities that pained her most.

"What did Soong learn from his conference on the moon?" she asked.

"They're asking that Alard send out all his shuttles to earth, to help bring out survivors," Orton said, "primarily friends and families of those on the moon. Fewer large ships are making it to Luna. Alard agreed to send as many shuttles as possible."

"But they've got a whole fleet in mothballs," Sam said.

"Those are deep-space vessels," Orton said, "incapable of landing on a large planet. Some will be sent, but the most they can do is stand off in earth orbit and wait for survivors to come up."

"Technical and skilled people," Sam said, "may be the only ones in a practical position to be rescued. And they are the ones most needed, if civilization is to recover. We've lost most of the engineering and scientific community, as well as those who could train a new generation."

She felt her expression harden as she looked at Sam. "Everyone deserves a chance," she said.

"But even with all the cooperation possible down there," Orton said, "and with our best efforts here, we can only save a few hundred thousand at most. That sounds like a lot, but it's a handful—and time is growing short. After a while it will not be possible to go to earth at all. The decontamination alone. . . ."

We're guilty, she thought as she listened to them trying to break her ties with those who were dying. She felt her own tendency to turn cold, to protect herself; it frightened her. Their words were a tyranny of reason and facts, as oppressive to them as to her. She had helped sign the execution order for a world, hundreds of times, with her name and Jack's on Bulero work orders. There was no way to deny that.

She sat in the hotel lounge and watched the turning discus of the old American space station on the screen. The station turned slowly on its axis, four hundred miles above the Pacific. Suddenly she remembered that almost a month had passed since her conversation with Sam and Orton in the solarium.

The screen view shifted to show two old moonships hanging like toys near the wheel. The wine-bottle shapes seemed so small, capable of carrying away only a few lives. Orton was with Alard, she knew, planning and discussing; Sam, Richard, and Margot went daily to the docks, to help receive the refugees. *I'm not doing anything*, a voice said within her, but it was so far away that she could ignore it.

She felt helpless as she struggled with herself. *The great majority left behind had more right to be called humanity than we do*, the voice continued. *There are so few of us, yet we have all the advantage.*

Her heart beat faster and a weakening fear spread through her body; her eyes opened wide and she felt the muscles in her face tighten; she was a stranger in her own body, trapped, looking out through frozen eyes.

The main conference and communications hall of Asterome was a large drum space with a polished black floor and twelve screens running around the ribbon of wall. The ceiling was a solid circle of white light. A giant desk console dominated the center of the room, surrounded by a dozen chairs.

Governor Alard sat behind the desk, Soong at his right. Sam, Richard, Margot, and Orton sat in a semicircle, facing Alard.

Sam looked around at the screens. Four showed a full quarter of earth in close-up; two showed entire hemispheres from relays in geosynchronous orbit; one pictured the entire day side, another the night face; and four contained views of earth-moon space and the moon itself.

Orton coughed, creating an echo in the hard-surfaced chamber.

Alard leaned forward and said, "You can see that the earth's atmosphere has taken on a strange glow."

The yellow-white effulgence had appeared suddenly less than twenty-four hours earlier, varying in intensity, pulsating into white, then back to yellow.

If I had taken more of an interest in Jack, Sam told himself, *then I might have convinced him to look into the problem of bulerite. I might have saved his life.*

"Radio contact is now gone completely," Alard said. "This shroud is clearly not a result of the nuclear war. We've measured its balloon-like expansion. Something has affected earth's normal electromagnetic and gravitational fields to generate this anomaly."

This, too, Sam suspected, was caused by bulerite's presence.

He heard steps behind him. Mike Basil sat down next to him.

"Mr. Basil has been doing some checking," Alard said. "Do you have anything to tell us?"

Mike ran a hand through his thinning brown hair and sat back.

"Look at that!" Orton said just as Basil was about to speak.

The membrane around earth was now clearly larger than the planet's atmosphere. Stars shone through the edge of the radiance—streaks, as if someone had smeared them.

Alard opened the audio channels with earth, releasing the machine-metal roar of a million gears into the room for a moment before breaking the link.

"Radio is still out," he said.

Suddenly Sam saw a clear view of the earth on all the screens. The field had become transparent, leaving only a silvery glow in the atmosphere. Surface features, however, seemed distorted, enlarged, as if seen through a warped glass.

The earth was stately, silent in its prison.

A huge spark erupted across North America and disappeared into the arctic tundra; others appeared intermittently. Within a half hour, as they watched, the globe was crisscrossed by an awesome system of electrical arteries, glowing brilliantly inside the optical distortion of the shroud.

"There is a measurable increase in rotation," Alard said as he looked at his computer display screen.

With a sinking feeling, Sam realized that this was the end of all rescue operations on earth.

The screen room came to dominate Sam's life during the next month, because it was from there that Asterome confronted every new development of the crisis. Sam was there with Orton, Richard, and Margot, observing and commenting, together with the countless officials and spokesmen who came through the hall daily in search of solutions to myriad problems. The chamber was screen-linked to every human outpost in sunspace, receiving a storm of feedback. Ultimately this information passed through Asterome's computers and was acted on by Alard and Soong when a course of action became clear. When a problem was ambiguous, more information was sought until a resolution was found; and if this failed, the problem would be shelved for discussion by a larger body of citizens. Asterome's constitution provided for checks and balances among judicial, legislative, and executive branches of government, except that a high level of interest and expertise was demanded of the citizenry; every person from the age of fifteen could enter a discussion or, through the communications system, record an opinion into the community computers, where it would be compared and weighed against what was known, what was desired, and what was possible. Policymaking, Sam realized, had not escaped the hazards of human error, ethical failure, or power-seeking; these failures were present in subtler ways, but in a context that permitted them to be more easily exposed.

Janet came with him only occasionally, preferring to spend her time walking around Asterome. In the evenings she would tell him about the shops, the arts, and the landscaping skills of the people who lived in the towns of the hollow. Sam felt that contact with their well-ordered life would help Janet, and he encouraged her to tell him about what she had seen. He needed it as much for himself as for her, to set against the tragedy of the last few months, knowing that it would take a commitment to a new life, a resolve greater than any he had made in the past, to enable him to hope again.

"I went up to the lake," she had said one night as they lay in bed, "where the refugees have set up a tent city. A boy was fishing in the lake. His father came by and told him to stop, then he took a look at me and asked if I was Janet Bulero. When I said yes, he came up to me and pushed me, saying that it was because of people like me that he had lost everything. He thought that the Bulero family had started the war, Sam." She had turned and sought to hide her tears in the pillow. "I tried to tell him that we were refugees also, but he cursed at me and walked away."

"You had better not go out by yourself," he had told her. It would take some time, he knew, to sort out who had started the war, but the bulerite disaster had certainly contributed. Placing blame, however, was a matter of degree, involving primary and secondary responsibility, he told himself, knowing that he was in agreement with the man who had accosted Janet; the ugly side of the problem was that in all likelihood the people singled out for blame were the proud possessors of tendencies belonging to all humankind. *Wonderful*, Sam thought. *Next I'll blame the victims for their own deaths.*

"You think he was right, don't you?" Janet had asked.

He had not answered. Later he had realized that he should have said something, no matter how harsh; a free exchange was better than a crushing silence.

Meanwhile Alard's physicists, together with Richard, were trying to make sense of the anomaly that was swallowing the earth. Sam imagined strange electrical storms dancing across a grotesque night sky, ragged survivors crouching in ruins, terrified by the shaking earth and the mad heavens. Something had swallowed the planet as a frog swallows a fly. Earth was now in the bowels of another universe. . . .

And the bubble was expanding, forcing Alard to prepare for moving Asterome into a sun orbit.

"We suspected what was happening," Richard said, "just before I left." He cleared his throat and looked around at the gathering. There were about fifty people scattered across the hall, Sam estimated. Most of the chairs were empty; for some reason attendance always fell off toward the end of the week.

"Could you review what we know to date for us?" Alard asked.

"Bulerite obeys its own laws," Richard said loudly. "We thought that we had made a stable substance." Sam was startled by the "we," since Richard had played no part in the development or manufacture of the family element. "We knew that there had to be a lot of energy locked up in it to give it its strength, but we failed to see that the stuff was a process, until it reached its limits." As Sam listened to the familiar explanation, he found himself caught up again in its implications. "We now believe," Richard continued, "that bulerite is strong because it absorbs energy. Any kind—kinetic in the form of air molecules striking it, earth tremors, sunlight, cosmic rays, any kind of radiation. You hit it with your hand and it will accept the blow as a contribution to its equilibrium. But it doesn't always need energy. It was stable when it left our factories. In physical terms its binding is a kind of extended quark binding—a force that increases with distance of separation and can be made to do this over the atomic scales. Thus bulerite is dense and arrayed in a tight lattice, unlike any other solid. But the force can in a certain density regime extend over larger and larger distances, so once a certain amount of energy is absorbed by the lattice, which converts some of it into mass and achieves even higher density, the stuff starts to grow—among other things—unevenly, creating striations in the exotic lattice, destroying the material. It took a while for it to drift from stability and become chaotic. Until then only

minute absorptions of energy were enough to keep it stable, apparently. If it had been an obvious energy sink, then a chunk of it sitting
in a room would have made the room cold and we would have known."

"The time element hid the problem," Alard said.

"Right. Bulerite absorbs energy slowly for years, then goes wild. It
may then grow to become super-dense in ways we don't understand."

Sam thought of Antaeus, the giant who renewed his strength
whenever he was thrown to the ground, turning the energy used
against him to his advantage.

"Can't we make it stable?" Alard asked.

Richard shook his head. "We don't know how. I'm not even very
sure of the explanations I've given, except that something like this must
be true. Look at it this way: matter is locked-up energy, solid to our way
of perceiving things. Bulerite is a way of freezing energy into an untried
state of matter. Basic realities may be involved—the realm below the
Wheeler-Planck unit of length, ten to the minus thirty-third centime-
ters smaller than atomic structures, where the statistical regularities of
our scale of nature may not hold. What if these effects spill into our
larger scale of things whenever a sample of bulerite loses its stability
and goes into flux?" He paused, waved his hand, and shook his head.
"We thought we'd left behind the problems of metal fatigue, structural
flaws, and materials limitations, believing we could build with a virtually permanent material. But bulerite is an intruder. It belongs perhaps
to an untried possibility of the universe. Our natural elements range
from simplicity to complex instability, but bulerite seems to belong to
a completely different periodic table, beyond our island of stable elements. Maybe zones of chaos separate the endless series of possible periodic tables. We bridged one such zone and brought a new material into
our realm of experience, where we saw it as being orderly according to
our mode of perception, in the way our senses slice time. Somewhere,
universes will begin differently than our own, and in one of them
bulerite will be a normal element—but not here."

Richard was silent, as if he had cast a spell over himself.

"What about this new thing?" Alard asked. "What is it?"

"We don't know. Forces we don't understand have been set in motion, distorting space-time around earth. Physical laws may be . . . inconsistent inside."

"Can't you tell us anything?" Alard asked.

"The bubble, whatever it is, may expand until it reaches the limit of bulerite's capacity to cast the field. If it is a field. There's no science for this, I'm just speculating . . ."

"How big can it get?"

Richard shook his head and looked up at the ceiling. "Maybe as far as the moon . . . maybe the entire sunspace." He shifted his gaze to Sam. "Maybe there's no limit. Maybe the fault we've opened in the fabric of space is permanent." Richard sat down stiffly, like a mannequin whose limbs were being bent to fit the chair. Margot leaned close to him as Alard started to ask another question.

Janet sat by the window in the bedroom, eyeing the empty street ten stories below. The dispersion of the tribeam was down to resemble moonlight. She peered to her left and followed the curving ground upward, until she was looking at the continuation of Main Street miles overhead in the clear night. The lack of a horizon always startled her. Here the stars were underground, literally beneath one's feet, and the land closed around its store of humanity like the protective husk of a spore. Richard would say that it *was* a spore, the core center of a new world.

The hollow planetoid was slowly moving out of L-5, she had been told, into a powered sun orbit that would put it near Mars within six months; once it was there, a decision would be made whether to go on to Ganymede or not.

She was calm in the stillness. Sam was asleep in the bed behind her. The plan to depart from earth-moon space had settled his mind, despite the harrowing difficulties with the lunar communities. Asterome was already overloaded with refugees from earth; now more people were coming up from the moon as it became certain that the bubble would expand to touch earth's satellite. Alard had agreed to admit another hundred thousand, most of the lunar population—there was nothing else to do—but with the proviso that Asterome would act as a ferry to Mars, where all the refugees, including most of those from earth, would have to disembark. Asterome had also agreed to evacuate the remaining lunar population if no other means were found for them to reach Mars. These were mostly technicians, scientists, and engineers, who were anxious to salvage resources that might be needed by humankind later—hardware, cultural artifacts, and the old Space Navy, which was being reconditioned rapidly.

She looked down at the closed shops across the street, remembering the people she had watched go by during the day, especially those who had spilled in from the tent villages. She had watched vehicles running around the ribbon of road, the toylike trolleys that ran overhead and around the inner equator; but she no longer went out to talk to people, afraid of their reactions. Only a little while ago, she thought, Asterome had been a place untouched by recent events, free of the past, a place for her to rest; she sympathized with some of the citizens, who felt that a prolonged stay by the refugees would inevitably change the worldlet.

Maybe her roommate from college was among the tent dwellers, or the boy who had first made love to her in high school; she could not imagine them as grown people. Would they also reproach her for having driven them from their homes?

She would never again see her parents' graves in Vermont or the town in Maine where she had attended grade school . . .

She thought of the strange bubble around the earth. *A cancerous something.* A few hours ago she had watched the giant transparent cell eclipse the sun; the earth had been a dark nucleus floating inside.

She got up from the window and turned to look at Sam. He was sleeping on his stomach, his hair a mask looking at her in the pale light. Suddenly she wanted to turn him over and strike his face—to tell him that she had looked ahead to see what kind of life was waiting for them and that it would not be worth living. . . .

"Is it certain that the moon will be engulfed?" Sam asked in the screen room. "Maybe it won't reach that far."

Richard shrugged from behind Alard's desk. "As certain as practical people need to have it." Sam was surprised at how easily Richard was able to fill a few of Alard's functions.

The screen chamber was almost deserted in the early morning hours, with only a half dozen people keeping vigil.

"Can it grow large enough to enclose all of sunspace?" Orton asked.

Richard threw up his hands, sat back, and sighed. "I don't know. It's growing slowly, but steadily. It might stop. Maybe it will shrink and disappear out of our space-time." He reached over to the controls on his desk and turned on the screens.

Earth was wrapped in a shimmering albumen. Bright points of light were bursting inside with clockwork regularity.

"The increase in diameter," Richard said, "can be measured easily from day to day."

"God damn," Orton whispered next to Sam, and crumpled up an empty pack of cigarettes. "The last Gauloises anyone will ever see again."

"The moon will be nudged in a matter of weeks," Richard said. "I hope the remaining personnel leave themselves enough time to get away."

"Don't you think they will?" Sam asked.

"They should be able to—but remember, they're staying behind to save what they can. They'll skeleton-crew every last ship after they've packed everything they can aboard, and they'll be using the mass driver catapults to launch Mars-bound containers into unpowered orbits. We'll be picking up stuff near Mars for years. I hope that in their zeal they don't forget to leave themselves enough time or that they don't spread themselves too thin."

Sam thought of Janet, alone up in the room. He would have to bring her meals to her again today. Her appetite was not good. He felt her fears inside him, adding to his own sense of loss. He would never again see the places he had known as a child, or visit all the places he had meant to see; no one else he knew would visit them, either. The sunlight on Mars would be cooler; the countryside on Ganymede would be dark and stony; only Asterome offered a semblance of earth. . . .

The bubble shimmered on the screens. The earth swam silently inside, unmindful of the destruction raging on its surface, where an age of order was ending and one of chaos beginning.

We will not come alive again, Sam thought. *Those of us who survive will become moribund, our existence marginal, unless we begin to dream, and soon enough to do some good.* He looked at Richard, wondering if there were any effective dreamers left, or any good dreams.

Richard sat alone in the darkened screen room, viewing the magnified image of the moon. Its cities were diamonds in the rough terrain, the bright lights of an old house on the night when the inhabitants are preparing to leave.

Slowly, steadily, Asterome's velocity was increasing, as the hard-shelled societal container moved along the powered orbit that would bring it into a more distant sun orbit, for a rendezvous with Mars in six months.

He looked at the huge, glistening field of force that imprisoned the earth. Occasionally a surface feature would become visible, greatly enlarged by the random distortions of the shroud: a ghostly view of ocean; a field of arctic snow; a half-glimpsed shadow of a ruined city; the red glow of a new volcano streaming a river of red. A whole world transfigured in a crystal paperweight . . .

He almost hoped that the anomaly would expand without limit, swallowing the sun and all its planets, driving mankind away from its sun-filled cradle.

Alard, Margot, and Orton shared his view, as did the interstellar group; but this was not the time to discuss it openly. For the moment it was enough that certain types of research were going on, and succeeding; the time would come when more people would care, if humanity survived. It remained to find out what kind of leadership was present on Mars, in the asteroids, and on Ganymede. The research teams and facilities at Ganymede City were especially important to have intact. But if cooperation became impossible, for one reason or another, he knew that Asterome would have to make its own decisions.

Margot came into the room, and he watched her as she crossed the empty hall toward the desk.

"I know I'm early for my shift," she said, "but I couldn't sleep, so you might as well get some."

He started to get up. "How's Janet?"

"Not too good—and Sam's too wrapped up with her problems to care for anything else."

Powered by the giant communications transmitter at the Lunar University at Plato, the continuous laser beam was streaming the world's accumulated wisdom across space to data storage on Asterome. No human mind could ever hope to master even a small portion of what was being received every second, Sam thought, but it would all be there—the literature, the science and engineering, the records of unfinished research, in all the languages of history, indexed and accessible through any terminal. He wondered how much new work had been lost, because it had not yet been recorded.

The last ships were readying to leave the moon. Sam was grateful that so much rescue of knowledge and culture had been possible. The loss of the library at Alexandria would not be repeated on a grand scale.

"The transmission is over," Alard said.

"I wonder," Sam said as he paced back and forth on the black floor, "how much of it is useless knowledge." He was alone with Alard and

Orton in the screen room. "How much of it will seem like so much dark-age groping a thousand years from now—if we survive."

"You're tired," Blackfriar said, sounding irritated.

"The index is coming through now," Alard said.

Sam looked around at the screens. The bubble now covered the entire field of vision, and only the most distant pickups could frame the entire anomaly. It was difficult to shake off the mood of cynicism and doubt. Sam imagined Asterome's laser receptors pointing back toward the moon, listening, the attentive ears of a child trying to hear the words of a dying parent.

At eight o'clock in the evening, four weeks out from L-5, a large crowd gathered to watch the end of the moon.

Richard watched them fill the screen room. Throughout the worldlet, people were gathering in homes and public places; but these were the settlement's leaders—biologists, electricians, agricultural specialists, builders, engineers, academicians, area leaders, generalists, mathematicians, and troubleshooters; they were Russians and Japanese, Africans and Indians, Americans and Polynesians, Englishmen and Europeans—the mix of two generations born away from earth. The community worked, Richard had come to realize, because its people carried around in their minds a picture of their society, the same vision of macrolife that had so affected Orton, a knowledge of who they were and what they wished to accomplish; their world was humanity's other basket of life and dreams, now more important than ever. *It might not have happened*, he thought, *and we would be dying with the earth*.

He was becoming part of this world very quickly. Alard was not merely allowing Orton, Margot, and him to help; he was allowing them to learn how to manage a world. Orton was already convinced that he would cast his lot with Asterome, wherever it might go; the skills that he would contribute would be his tie to the future, he had said, in place of his unborn children.

Alard stood behind the desk. Richard saw a different man for a moment; as he looked at the mixture of Asian and African features, he saw a kind of satisfaction. Alard seemed to lack the charisma of powerful leaders; perhaps the look of satisfaction came from an unpretentious self-respect. As the switching center for the ideas and demands of his community, Alard was the eye of the storm, where a thousand differing demands were reconciled and prepared for implementation; any kind of posturing beyond simple pride-in-work would impair Alard's unspecialized receptivity, especially his ability to grasp relationships among blocks of information from areas in which he was not a specialist. In his capacity for assessment, he could integrate technical-scientific ideas with psychosocial issues—using information-processing systems, both human and artificial—with a sureness undreamed of by the last century's futurists; yet he was not unique, since this kind of information handling was a basic part of Asterome's educational system, whether or not an individual went into social management. Alard's individual contribution came from the harnessing of his imagination, in his way of demanding, and getting, things that more specialized innovators would not ask of themselves.

A lesser man would have been flattered by the attention of such a talented group, but Alard was unimpressed. He waited until everyone was seated, then he sat down behind the desk. He seemed to grow smaller as he welcomed them with a few subdued words.

Sam, Orton, and Margot came in and sat down next to Richard in the front row. Margot looked at him, and her eyes told him that there was no improvement in Janet's nervous condition.

At nine o'clock the last ships left the moon. All the screens were on, showing earth-moon sunspace. The swarm of ships looked like fireflies as they boosted from the pocked surface, becoming almost invisible when their rockets cut off; some were launched from catapults, with brief bursts of correcting thrust. Only a few ships had enough power to catch up with Asterome; most would reach Mars in unpowered orbits, sometime during the next year.

The view pulled back suddenly, revealing the rogue field, a huge man-of-war blister growing from minute to minute; earth was lost within the milkiness, visible only during brief fluctuations.

By ten o'clock the edge neared the moon. Luna's shape became distorted as the space around her began to glow; silvery streamers reached out to the satellite and caressed it.

The moon protruded into normal space, half submerged, sinking into a shining lake.

It was gone by a quarter past the hour.

Our moon, Richard thought in the silence, the moon of dreaming ages—shield for lovers, puller of tides, timepiece for uncounted generations—gone to swim in a strange sea, with a stranger earth below it.

9. The Minor System

Alone in the hotel suite, Janet watched the approach to Jupiter on the screen. Galileo had described the gas giant as the center of a miniature solar system, with the moons as planets, unaware that his analogy had any literal truth in it. Jupiter was not a sun, but the giant planet was all that remained of the sun's unborn companion, a protostar which had failed to burst into prominence for lack of mass.

The stillborn image persisted in her mind.

The Galilean moons were circling wolves.

The stars watched.

The plain below Sam was cut in two by a dirt roadway leading to the landing area three kilometers away, where six tugs squatted against the background of ragged hills. Each vehicle was being unloaded by a stocky, waldo-armed surface module. The cartons were placed on the open platforms of balloon-wheeled vehicles, which ran in a steady flow to the base of the main dome in which he stood.

The main dome of Ganymede City covered three square kilometers of the moon's surface. Here on the top level, the observation screens covered the interior of the dome; they could be turned on individually or en masse to show a panorama of sky and surrounding terrain. A direct view would have left the observation level with too little shielding against the leakage of solar radiation trapped by Jupiter's magnetic field; even though Ganymede City sat in the moon's radiation shadow, the aboveground portion was protected, as an added precaution, by meters of water in the outer shell, piped in from the nearby ice field. Natives called Ganymede City "the big igloo," because of the liquid that was kept frozen in its insulating space. In addition to the physical shielding against stray radiation and occasional meteors, the laser-fed fusion reactor powered the super conducting units which cast a magnetic shield over the domes.

Ganymede plowed through a sea of death; but despite this, ships had visited all the Galilean satellites by 2015. Built at the Martian space docks on Phobos and Deimos, the water—and magnetically shielded tin cans, as the ships came to be called—had penetrated into Jupiter's radiation belts, setting up research bases on Callisto and Ganymede, as well as temporary facilities on a few of the close-in rocks whipping around the edges of the gas giant's atmosphere.

To make power for building the first underground living quarters, the tin cans had deployed a giant sun mirror. The collector was no more than a few molecules thick, but its huge size and focusing capacity made up for the fact that the sun's intensity was only about four percent of what it was in the vicinity of earth.

While Ganymede City's first levels were being built, a mass driver track had been constructed beyond what was now the tug port. Using the three-kilometers-per-second escape velocity from the Jovian moon, the track began to toss copper ingots toward Jupiter, whose escape velocity was twenty times greater; this large energy difference was expressed in the form of eddy currents of electricity forming in the copper as it rushed through Jupiter's powerful magnetic field; these were lased back to Ganymede by a small disposable unit, continuing right up to the moment when the ingot hit the atmosphere for a final, dramatic surge of electricity. Current flow was evened out by storage facilities at the receiving station on Ganymede.

As a result of this and other systems, Ganymede became one of the energy-self-sufficient places for science, attracting research and development from earth. The solar mirror was still working; the lofter still threw ingots into Jove's face; and a second fusion LFR had recently been completed.

Ironically, Sam thought, success on Ganymede had slowed the

building of facilities on Saturn's moons, as well as delaying development of the larger asteroids such as Ceres. A whole system of worlds waited to come alive out here, offering conditions for industry and research, room for a civilization to grow. He understood why the Bulero chiefs had convinced Jack to invest in such a large facility here; they had, of course, played on his guilt about basic research, but the purely factual merits of the case were also strong.

In any case, valuable work was continuing, despite the psychological blow of losing earth. Janet's visits to the various projects had cheered the scientists and their families, even though nothing could ever cushion the fact that they would never see home again.

Earth is not there, he told himself, at least not the earth that he had known. He had tried to occupy himself with an interest in the history of life here, to shut out what had happened nearer the sun. A lot of human history, he was learning, had been made out here also.

Jupiter was a color-streaked colossus in the black sky, a sphere of solid marble held up by the ragged mountains. As Sam watched the reverse eclipse cast Ganymede's moving shadow across Jove's full face, he found it hard to think of today as Saturday morning.

He reached down to a control terminal and turned up the magnification on one of the higher screens. Asterome appeared, circling Jupiter within Ganymede's orbit, its sun mirror drawing strength from the distant sun. The stubble of sensors and communications equipment reminded him of a strange metallic moss. Slowly the ovoid spun on its ten-mile axis. The worldlet was a long way from home, but for more than a third of surviving humanity it was the only homeland left. Curious, he thought as he searched the rocky outer shell of the spaceborne community, that he could not see the nuclear engines that had pushed it into the Martian sun orbit.

The rendezvous with Mars had been an unpleasant experience, especially for Janet; by the time Asterome matched the orbital speed of Mars, it was well known that Buleros were aboard. Alard and Richard received all the cautious and angry words in the screen room.

The Martian officials had been sympathetic, but they did not wish to divide their own leadership further; refugees would be received as agreed, but no members of the Bulero family would be permitted to land. The population—a million or more, counting the refugees—was angry; a garbled version of the bulerite disaster had reached Mars, resulting in riots; Bulero executives and employees had been beaten and murdered. The arrival of new refugees had only made the situation worse. Janet even felt unwelcome on Asterome, where angry words were not frequent.

Alard had broadcast a speech to Mars, explaining his understanding of the war on earth. Sam remembered Alard's voice thundering on the screens, the holo of his face hovering in the hollow as he argued for understanding and courage. The speech had stopped some of the more hysterical criticism from Mars, but the sense of doubt remained, reflected in the occasional hostile stares; not even Alard could change the facts.

Richard had been impressed with the restraint of the UN military presence on Mars. He had introduced Sam to Commander Alberta Mason, a gray-haired, blue-eyed woman of immense charm who seemed deeply concerned about the strife that might yet develop between the surviving communities of sunspace.

"We should not set a precedent for violent solutions," she had said during her visit to Asterome, "yet some level of force might become necessary to keep what peace we have left."

With Asterome's departure for Ganymede, Janet's spirits had risen; there, it seemed, the atmosphere would be more neutral. Once again she looked forward to pulling together the remains of Bulero Enterprises.

Bulero authority, as it turned out, was still recognized, at least tacitly; Greg Michaels and many of the old employees seemed friendly. Richard and Janet had been given a tour by the research chief and had reported that loyalty among the small group of scientists was genuine.

General Kiichi Nakamura, a Hawaiian, was the UN authority on Ganymede. He was governing under emergency rules, but it was not clear what his relationship would be with authorities on Mars and Asterome. Sam thought of him as a man with an irritating dullness of manner; he had greeted them with too many words, making Janet anxious during the introductions.

Sam and Janet had taken an apartment on the first underground floor of Ganymede City's main dome; Orton, Richard, and Margot had stayed on Asterome, visiting regularly at first, then infrequently.

Sam and Janet had busied themselves with helping Greg Michaels, but it soon became obvious that the research community did not need them, except for busy work that did not have to be done on a schedule. After a few weeks, Janet isolated herself in the apartment.

Margot, sensing that a strain was developing between Richard and his mother, came and stayed with her as often as possible, but Janet began to feel guilty about keeping her away from Richard and their new life; slowly Margot realized how troubled Janet had become.

Sam felt out of place. The unpacking outside reminded him of the movers who had brought his cartons of books when he had moved into his instructor's quarters at Princeton. The view was a relief from the windowless apartment he shared with Janet.

There had been talk of setting up a college faculty for the younger people, and he had been asked to join; almost no one wanted to abandon the community in order to join Asterome. In time, many argued, Ganymede might be terraformed—a heat trap of some kind could be cast around the moon, one that would hold in an atmosphere warmed by the sun; but this was still very speculative and full of problems.

There was comfort in watching Jupiter. After a month, Sam could picture Ganymede's motion around the big planet. Ganymede, cupbearer of the gods, circled Jove once every week, always keeping one side toward the giant as his face changed from crescent to full phase. On Monday the sun would rise and Jupiter would be in half phase. The sun was such a small thing, less than a fifth of its size on earth. On Tuesday the sun would move behind Jupiter, making it glow around the edges for up to three hours. The stars would be brilliant during the eclipse. After three and a half days, the sun would set, making Jupiter's other moons more prominent; at one point in its orbit between Ganymede and the giant, Europa would grow as large as earth's moon. He had watched Europa and Io chase each other's shadows across Jove's clouds. By the weekend the planet was in full phase, its colors becoming brightest when the sun was down. The great red spot was a crimson wound twenty thousand miles across, yet small when compared to the planet's nearly ninety-thousand-mile diameter. As he watched, Ganymede's crisp circle of shadow crept across the face of colors six hundred thousand miles away; a mere speck, yet it took a three-thousand-mile diameter to make it. By Monday the sun would rise, Jove would be in half phase, and the cycle would repeat itself as the gas giant carried its system of minor planets around the sun every twelve years.

Jupiter's ring was an eighteen-mile-thick band of meter-sized boulders only thirty-six thousand miles out. More a belt than a ring, it could be glimpsed during crescent phase, near the terminator. Callisto was larger than Luna and Mercury; Europa was as big as Luna. In addition to the thirteen moons of various sizes, there were countless fragments, ranging from a few feet in diameter to miles across. Richard had mentioned the possibility of using the larger ones to build Asterome-type habitats. Humanity would not lack for space to grow. If Ganymede were given an atmosphere, it would disperse the sunlight to give earthlike daylight, as far as the human eye could tell.

The Bulero Research Center was on the floor below the observation deck. Sam would go there frequently to escape his constant sense of uselessness. There was usually some kind of discussion going on among the scientists and technicians about the earth anomaly, the future, about what could be done. Alard held brainstorming sessions via screen link, which Sam was often invited to join. He wished that Janet would reconsider going back to Asterome, but she wouldn't even discuss it. It was as if she were exiling herself from useful work, believing that she had lost all right to hope; Asterome was for Richard and Margot, not for her.

Today, before coming up to the observation floor, Sam had listened to a discussion of Jupiter as an undersized companion to the sun, stillborn for lack of mass, hovering between being a planet or a star, but like a star giving off more energy than it received, in the form of heat and radio energy; Jupiter was most like a faint M-type star, a sun just hot enough to burn hydrogen. He had tried to interest Janet in what he had learned, hoping to distract her, but she had screamed for him to leave the room. . . .

Like Asterome, Ganymede City had been built just when bulerite was coming into wide use, and what small amounts were present had been comparatively easy to remove; it had been ferried up to an unmanned barge and kicked into an orbit that would slowly take it out of sunspace.

Sam thought about Alard's plans to take Asterome out of the solar system. Could anyone stop him? Did the remaining UN authorities have any jurisdiction over Asterome? From a practical viewpoint, the surviving localities were answerable only to their local leaders. The pre-bulerite UN Space Navy was in orbit around Mars; it seemed doubtful that it would be needed to enforce order; the ships had done their job in bringing survivors out of earthspace. Their most likely role would be as a physical link between Mars, Ganymede, the belt outposts, and Asterome.

Sam touched the terminal and picked up earth on the electronic telescope. The rogue field was now more than a quarter million miles across; it had slowed its pace of expansion and seemed to be stopping. Soon the earth's motion would carry it to the far side of the sun, where it would be difficult to see.

The sight reminded him of a huge effulgence on a photographic plate, the sun's light brightening the inside into whiteness. A month ago it had been possible to see stars through the membrane; now the anomaly suggested a bloated creature washed up from a strange sea beyond space-time.

Sam wiped the image away and sat down in the nearest inflatable chair. He tried to cheer himself; everything that could be done was being done. Richard and Margot had transferred Asterome's complete computer memory into the computers at the Bulero Center; they had done the same during the Mars stopover. That memory, shouted into space from the dying moon, was the birthright of every human being, living and to be born.

Another lien on the future had been established in the form of a frozen cell bank, distributed from Asterome's stores to the medical facilities on Mars and Ganymede. The banks now included animal cells, plant cells, human egg and sperm deposits, contributed by Asterome's population to increase the previous holdings. All of them, except Janet, had contributed. Blackfriar had advocated that the restrictions on human cloning should be lifted, arguing that all forms of human reproduction possible should be made available to ensure a variety of human types, especially after so many billions had died.

Sam thought of the past. All research into earth's historical and natural past would now be limited by the amount of stored information and materials; all roads leading back would now end more abruptly than ever; the interpretive and observational cleverness of investigators would be tested to the limit.

Richard, Alard, and Blackfriar, he knew, were looking beyond sunspace, to the nearer stars. Asterome's engineers wanted to add an outer urban shell, thus making the hollow the basis of a larger structure as the population increased. Alard was recruiting skilled people from Ganymede; it was an open thing, and no one had objected yet.

Create a new society, Richard said, reach beyond sunspace into the greater world of the galaxy—into the real world. *It seems like running away*, Sam thought, realizing suddenly that this was perhaps the reason for Janet's coolness toward her son; maybe she saw his ambitions as another form of the irresponsibility Jack had exhibited; but it might also be that she was afraid of losing him forever.

News came from Mars in a steady flow. Venus had been abandoned. All the remaining orbital installations had been fitted with nuclear propulsion units and were moving toward Mars. The Martian population was expected to grow by a third; Ganymede's had leveled off at slightly more than fifty thousand after the outlying bases had been closed down. An inventory of skilled persons, fusion power capacity, and food production was being made.

The Bulero Research Center continued with its previous projects. Among them were laser scanners, steps toward the dream of materials synthesis—the creation of anything out of basic materials and information; bulerite was being reevaluated, to see whether its instabilities could be avoided; work was being done on improved deflector shields for starships attempting significant fractions of light speed. Many of the engineers thought that the failure of the previous type of energy shield was responsible for the disappearance of the first interstellar expedition; a bulerite shield might protect a starship from bombardment by particles at high velocity, if a stable form was possible, perhaps together with a conventional repelling field. The anomaly might yet make it necessary for us to get out of sunspace fast, Orton had said a few days ago.

At times Sam felt that he could almost look outward with Richard, Margot, and Orton; but was it fair to think of leaving? Asterome would take the skilled and useful, the youngest. The ones most needed at home would go; he could not see how the truth of the objection might be circumvented.

It was easy to see why Alard had brought Asterome into Jupiter's space; the work being done here was consistent with Asterome's long-range plans. Circling Jupiter in a close orbit was a kilometer-long chunk of nickel-iron, where Bulero had built a facility for the study of ultradense matter. A small black hole, less than one gram in size, was being driven with an electric field, converting electrical power into gravitational waves; such an engine could accelerate an object the size of Asterome to any fraction of light speed, given enough power. Sam had been surprised to learn that a similar innovation, rather than a fusion-powered torch engine, had pushed Asterome out of the inner solar system, but the fact had been kept quiet. Asterome was planning to attach the experimental facility near Jupiter to one end of Asterome. Richard had given the official Bulero permission. Alard, Richard had also told him, was massing creative workers, encouraging them to speculate radically on such topics as the elasticity and solidity of space, the control of inertia, in the hope of forcing a solution which he felt would be needed very soon.

Janet, Sam thought. The very thought of her was a burden. She spoke to no one. She ate as if rationing herself, fearful of using more than her share. He would try to talk to her in the darkness of the bedroom; she only listened. Occasionally she talked in her sleep. When he woke up in the morning, she would be sitting in her chair, looking at him without expression.

"Do you want to come with me today?" he would ask.

No answer.

"They ask about you at Bulero. They've worked for . . . us all their lives, some of them, like ascetics when things were more primitive out here. They're trying to help, you know. It would help them if they saw you there occasionally. It's why you wanted to come."

No answer.

He knew that it was a kind of verbal pap which he said to her each day. He would dress, kiss her on the forehead, and leave for the day, knowing that he should stay—except that it was better to be active. He would do small jobs, run errands, take care of children, supplement the grade school teaching machines; it was better to have the illusion of useful work.

Richard and Margot would be visiting soon anyway; they had promised.

•   •   •

The shadows spoke to her.

Janet sat in a metal chair. The soft lights and lack of strong gravity were a comfort. She thought of the huge dome above her, with its levels, elevators, and people. She thought of the barren, rocky surface, the cold stars . . . and something near the sun. It had stopped growing and was waiting for her to come up and look at it; it was waiting for her to help it grow with her fear.

She would never go to the surface; she would never look at it; she would not help it, even if she had to die. She would die soon, free Sam, and stop its growing. There was a cold lump in her stomach and dryness in her throat.

Sam looked up to see Margot come out of the hospital room. She came to the air-filled sofa in the waiting area and sat between him and Richard.

"She's asleep now, so you'll have to come back when she's awake."

"I'll wait," Sam said.

"She'll recover?" Richard asked.

"Definitely. As soon as she's better they'll put her into sleep therapy."

Sam was still shaken by Janet's suicide attempt.

"Don't blame yourself," Margot said. "There have been a lot of breakdowns. It would have been strange—"

"I should have stayed with her."

"There was not much you could have done, Sam. You're probably the smallest part of her problem."

"We'll wait a while with you," Richard said.

Janet smiled at Sam when he was finally let in. She reached out to hold his hand as he sat down by the bed.

"Richard and Margot are outside."

"Now don't worry, Sam—women have children all the time."

His breath caught in his throat, but he tried not to show his distress. She seemed so calm and beautiful, her face as pale as the bandages around her wrists; her black hair was combed out on the pillow.

"You're strong," he managed to say, knowing that he would have to be what she wanted him to be. He smiled, feeling grotesque and unreal.

He wanted desperately to say a few healing words that would waken her from her delusion; but in the strange silence between them, he saw that she was an uncomprehending child, and he should not try to explain anything to her.

Sam turned and saw the nurse motioning to him. As he stood up to see what she wanted, Janet closed her eyes. The sedative had taken effect.

When he came out into the waiting room, Sam saw General Nakamura standing with Margot and Richard. His gray UN coverall was stiff and perfectly clean, as usual. Sam noticed the three stars on his cap as the general turned to greet him.

"Mr. Bulero, you are under arrest. You are to go to your apartment. A guard is posted at the door. He will accompany you when you wish to visit your mistress—at appointed times." Nakamura's eyes were direct and stern.

"Why? Please explain."

Nakamura's forehead became knitted, distorting his thick eyebrows; he smiled in a show of composure. "Frankly, Mr. Bulero, I'm shocked by your friends and relations. If I were you, I would be ashamed of them."

"What are you talking about?"

Nakamura shrugged. "Perhaps . . . it's possible that you do not know. Let me explain. Asterome is subject to UN law, which I administer in this part of sunspace. Also, we are under emergency conditions—"

"It's a power grab, Sam," Richard said.

"Kindly be quiet," Nakamura said. "Your friends," he continued, "are behaving like brigands, a pack of adventurers who wish to squander humanity's last resources. You understand the value of Asterome for our recovery, don't you?"

"Of course."

"A few hours ago, Governor Alard altered the course of our research satellite and attached it to Asterome—"

"The drive, Sam," Richard said. "It works! They've moved the whole thing."

"Please be quiet," Nakamura repeated.

"You'll never get away with it, General," Richard said.

"In a few days," Nakamura said, "a military vessel will arrive from Mars to help me enforce the law. Asterome makes a big target. I'm sure that Alard will see reason by then."

"He wants to control Asterome in a takeover of Mars," Margot said. "He's got cronies there who are setting up a coup."

"Come with me," Nakamura said.

He led the way past the hospital desk and into the open elevator. The lift took them below the surface level, where they stepped out into the green corridor of the housing complex.

Sam saw a guard by the door to his apartment.

"He is very effective," Nakamura said. "The entire dome is under martial law."

The door slid open. Margot and Richard went in first, and Sam followed after a moment. There was no point in discussing anything more with the general.

"Are you here alone?" Sam asked when the door slid shut.

"No," Margot said.

Suddenly the door slid open. Soong stumbled into the room and caught his balance against Sam.

10. The Struggle

"We are hostages," Soong said.

"Nakamura spoke of a ship from Mars," Sam said, "coming to support him here. You don't suppose Commander Mason is in with him?"

"It's possible," Richard said.

"I don't think so," Margot said. "Alard was talking to her about something this morning."

"Nakamura doesn't recognize Bulero property," Richard said. "There has always been friction between him and the research center, from the day he came here. Greg Michaels has never gotten along with him."

"Governor Alard has been expecting trouble," Soong said, "but not over a piece of Bulero property, and not this soon."

"But won't they question a ship's departure on Mars?" Sam asked.

"Not if Nakamura's bunch has already taken over," Richard said.

"There's not much we can do here." Margot sat down in the middle of the sofa.

Sam started to pace back and forth. "Why did Alard want the black hole facility, when he already has a gravitational wave generator?"

"It's a larger and more efficient unit," Richard answered, "and Asterome has a lot of electricity to feed it from its fusion reactors. I wanted Asterome to have it. It's none of Nakamura's damn business."

The door slid open and the guard entered. "Please come with me," he said, and waited for them all to go ahead into the hall.

When they were in the elevator, the guard stepped in and faced them. The lift rose to ground level, where Sam walked out behind the guard and followed the pistol-armed figure down a long, green-tiled hall to a set of double doors at the end. The doors slid open and they entered a large rectangular communications room.

Sam noticed the guards by the door as he went in. Three communications technicians sat in front of the main screen ahead, which covered the ten-foot-high wall.

Greg Michaels and Mike Basil stood in the center of the room, handcuffed to each other. A feeling of guilt and failure passed through Sam as he looked around the bare room.

Richard went up to Mike and touched his shoulder. Sam heard the doors slide open and turned in time to see Nakamura come in. Ignoring his prisoners, Nakamura went to the screen, which now showed the landing area.

On it, slightly magnified, squatted an older military spacecraft, atomic torch, vintage 1998—three hundred feet of dark ovoid body resting on four sturdy shocks—pre-bulerite, designed to land in any accessible place in the solar system.

The sun was drifting toward Jupiter and would slip behind it in a few hours. The ship cast a sharp shadow.

Sam turned and looked at his companions. Richard was angry, but Margot seemed angrier. Soong appeared patient and graceful, as always. Greg Michaels stooped a bit to accommodate Mike. The tall, white-haired research chief seemed resigned.

A man's face filled the large screen, leaving the ship as a small insert in the left-hand corner. "General, the ship that followed us here will arrive in about an hour. She still does not answer calls."

"It may be that their communications are out of order," Nakamura said. "These are all old vessels. In any case, we can handle one ship."

"I think so, General."

"Thank you, Captain Scorto."

Nakamura turned from the screen as Scorto's face faded. "I regret these tactics," he said, looking at Soong, "but they are in the interests of humanity. I may have very little time, but perhaps further extremes will be unnecessary."

Sam could feel that Richard was struggling to restrain himself.

"Mr. Soong," Nakamura continued, "in a few moments you will address Governor Alard, and you will suggest that he step down from office and recognize UN authority, as represented by my government here on Ganymede. Tell him that there will be a place for him later, after consolidation is complete."

The vagueness of Nakamura's words was precise. The force of their persuasiveness lay elsewhere. *He has us all*, Sam thought, *and he has Janet.*

"Why don't you tell him yourself?" Richard said.

Nakamura's face went rigid. Sam noticed that the general was wearing a pistol now.

Governor Alard's face appeared on the screen, again leaving the ship as a small insert.

"Hold the sound back," Nakamura said. He turned back to Soong. "Your lives depend on what you say." Nakamura raised his arm and the sound came on.

Alard blinked and seemed to be peering around the room.

Sam swallowed. The threat to Janet's safety was a terrible anxiety spreading outward from his knotted stomach. He had failed to help her as her condition had grown worse; and now he could not help her at all. He clenched his fists at his sides; his jaw muscles tightened as he struggled to hide his feelings.

"Well, General," Alard said, "I can see for myself. Get on with it."

Nakamura looked at Soong.

"Governor, he demands that you step down and turn control over to him," Soong said.

"By what authority?"

"The new government of Mars-Ganymede," Nakamura announced, "which speaks for all surviving humanity. The official declaration will be made soon."

"Excuse me for a moment, General," Alard said softly, and walked away from the screen.

Sam's arms trembled slightly.

Alard reappeared and looked at Nakamura. Sam had a sudden vision of his larger-than-life figure crawling in through the window of the screen and crushing Nakamura into a bloody pulp. His mind was looking for a way out, Sam knew, even if it had to loosen the bonds of the real world to do the impossible.

"There is no such government," Alard said.

"You are mistaken," Nakamura replied. "I have declared martial law. If you do not resign, you will be dealt with as a criminal."

"A self-appointed dictator," Margot whispered.

"Excuse me again, General," Alard said politely. The screen went blank.

"UN law is all the law we have left," Richard said, "but you are not its representative."

"I am not aware that I have been relieved of command."

Richard shrugged. "A technicality."

Sam looked at Richard. Surely he knew enough to see that he was putting them all in further danger.

"You are criminals!" Nakamura shouted. "Adventurers who would betray humanity. The new government speaks for reconstruction and conservation of resources. Asterome is part of those resources and now directly under our jurisdiction."

"Asterome has always been a free state," Richard said.

"You will comply."

"General, you claim to be a reasonable man." Richard took a step toward him. "Exactly why do you think that Asterome will not do its share in the job of reconstruction? We've been duplicating all our resources, on Mars and now here."

A long silence followed.

"I have gathered that Asterome plans to leave sunspace," the general said at last.

"We're planning for the long-term future of human life," Richard said.

"A very irresponsible idea, cloaked in idealism."

"I don't think that you are interested in honest disagreement, General, but in personal power. There is not much more to you than that."

"I can force Asterome to comply with emergency regulations. We can disable and board it."

"Where's Alard?" Sam whispered to Margot and Soong.

"Playing for time," Margot answered.

Unlike Richard, Sam thought, Alard was being careful of their safety.

"Governor Alard!" Nakamura shouted. "I know that you are receiving. Kindly return the visual link." The general unfastened the covering of his holster and drew out a shiny black automatic.

Alard reappeared and looked around the room. His face was without expression as he waited for Nakamura to speak.

"In a few moments," the general said, "my warship will fire a missile at your sun mirror, perhaps at one of your fusion plants. Where will your Asterome be without them?"

Sam noticed the sweat stains on the general's back and under his armpits. Alard did not answer.

Nakamura turned around and Sam was looking into the black hole of the automatic.

"He will die first, Alard. Can you afford this life?"

He'll shoot me as a throwaway example, Sam thought, *because I'm unimportant.* The gun shook slightly in Nakarnura's hand; the barrel moved in a lazy circle.

"Ship approaching fast," one of the communications officers said.

An insert appeared in the lower-right-hand corner of the screen, showing a telescopic view of a military vessel identical to the one in the left-hand insert.

Nakamura stepped up to Sam and raised the gun. Sam closed his eyes and clenched his teeth as the cold barrel touched his temple for a moment. Opening his eyes, he saw Soong leap at Nakamura from the side.

The general turned and fired; the shot hit Soong in the forehead and he fell backward slowly. Blood streamed from his head as he hit the floor.

"General!" Alard shouted.

"No answer from the ship," the com officer said.

Nakamura shifted and held the gun near Sam's face. "It's another one of ours," he said calmly.

Sam looked past the gun to Soong's body on the floor. Then he regarded the man who was oppressing him. What had he ever done to him? He hardly knew him. Nakamura returned his gaze without blinking.

"General—voice link," the communications officer said.

Sam looked at the insert; the incoming ship was larger now. A third insert appeared in the top left corner, a woman's face, middle-aged, with handsomely groomed short gray hair.

"This is Commander Alberta Mason, UN Forces. General Nakamura, you are relieved of command. Place yourself in immediate custody under military or civilian personnel at Ganymede City."

Nakamura surveyed the room. No one moved. Sam expected that at any moment the general would point the gun at Richard or Margot. *It's what I would do.* The thought surprised Sam.

"Surrender," Mason said. "The coup is over. It's been over for a while."

Nakamura grew rigid. He lowered the gun, but kept it pointed in Sam's direction. Slowly the general reached up with his left hand, took off his military cap, and threw it to the floor. "So much for UN rank." He ran his fingers across his wet forehead and back through his hair.

"Surrender," Mason said, "or I will open fire on your ship. Do you hear me also, Captain Scorto?"

"I hear you."

"Land your ship and prepare to be boarded," Nakamura replied, "or I will kill these hostages before your eyes."

Sam was grateful that Janet was not in immediate reach.

"Scorto—open fire on Asterome and the Mars vessel when I give the command."

Sam felt the gun press against his temple. The floor seemed to shift slightly as he tried to keep his eyes on the screen.

"Mason, you can't fight a triple threat!"

"I will not bargain with you, General."

The gun pushed Sam's head sideways. With one eye he peered at the lower-left insert, where Nakamura's ship was suddenly coming apart, its center glowing cherry red, turning white until the hull was lost in a bright flash. The concussion shook the floor. Sam faced the screen as Nakamura moved the gun away. Gas and debris filled the insert, clearing slowly to show a crater where the ship had stood.

"I regret the loss of misguided lives," Mason said. "They and the ship might have served us better."

"How?" Nakamura asked as he stepped back from Sam. "You're too far away."

"A simple destruct sequence code. The civilian governments that gathered the taxes to build these old ships kept that much insurance against them. Of course, such a safeguard is only effective when not too many people know about it."

Sam looked at Nakamura, aware that the general would take the explanation as an insult, since it implied that he was not important enough to have known.

"I can still kill the hostages," Nakamura said.

Sam gazed into the man's eyes. There was frustrated hatred behind the gun now. *Trapped animals*, Sam thought. The nearness of the gun made him angry. He looked at Richard and Margot, at Mike and Greg. If *Nakamura loses interest in me, he'll kill them all. The gun must stay on me.*

"You're beaten," Richard shouted. "What can you gain now?"

Sam knew. An enraged puppeteer's hand entered his body. His arm came up and knocked the gun out of Nakamura's hand. The weapon coughed unimpressively, floated toward the floor, bounced with a clatter, and lay still. Sam seized Nakamura by the throat and tried to close his fist. A distant part of Sam watched, startled by his disregard for his own life.

The general sputtered and punched at him. Sam pushed Nakamura and tumbled down on top of him, feeling an anger that he had almost forgotten existed. Nakamura pulled the hand away from his throat, but Sam punched him in the right eye; the general howled. Sam hit him in the jaw; Nakamura's head went back against the floor. He lay still, staring up at Sam with one eye.

A pair of booted feet approached. "That's enough, Mr. Bulero," the guard said. "We'll take him now." The other guard was removing the handcuffs from Mike Basil and Greg Michaels. Sam rose and looked down at Nakamura. The general was everything that he had wanted to strike out at since they had abandoned earth. Sam shifted his gaze to Soong's body nearby. He might have saved him if he had acted earlier, if he had been stronger. *Nakamura did not expect me to act.*

Margot knelt and felt Soong's pulse, shaking her head as she looked up at Sam. Suddenly Sam stepped closer to Nakamura and kicked him in the ribs. The general groaned.

Richard took Sam's arm to hold him back. Sam stood still, staring at the gun on the floor, as if all the mysteries of creation were somehow contained in the weapon. He had acted because he had sensed weakness, in himself and in Nakamura; and for once his mind was in complete accord with his deepest feelings. The narrow aims of the general's coup had suddenly clarified Sam's view of recent events. He had struck out on behalf of a future in which survival would not be as precarious as it had been in the past. Macrolife was about to take its first step out of the cradle of sunspace; humankind was about to gain a larger lease on life; yet it might so easily have become impossible, for lack of men with vision and goodwill. Nakamura's objections were mere excuses in his bid for power; Asterome's presence was not absolutely essential, since its facilities were duplicated here and on Mars; Sam realized with a chill that he and Janet might have accepted Nakamura's views, if he had concealed his motives.

Sam regarded Richard and Margot, knowing that he had also acted out of love for them—children becoming adults, looking away not so much from the physical as from the psychological ruins of sol.

He stooped and picked up the gun.

On the screen, Orton was lighting a cigar next to Alard. There was a hole in Orton's left eye, where the stray bullet from Nakamura's gun had pierced the screen.

Richard and Margot embraced, and for a moment Sam saw something of the boy he had known long ago.

Alard scowled into the room.

The sun slid slowly behind Jupiter, leaving a stream of red light at the planet's edge.

Nakamura stirred. The two guards helped him to his feet.

"Hold him," Mason said. Sam noted the strain in her face. "We'll have to take him back to Mars for trial with the others. Mr. Bulero—Sam, you'll be in charge."

Sam made sure that the safety was on the pistol and put it in his pocket.

Nakamura stared at the floor as he was led toward the door.

"One moment," Mason said. The guards paused and Nakamura looked back at the screen. "We expected this kind of thing, Kiichi. Alard and I discussed it during his Mars stopover, and we picked the places where it might happen. A false announcement of your exposure unmasked your cohorts on Mars, forcing them to cooperate with us to keep you in the dark. Some of them are reasonable people—"

"You're not better than I am," Nakamura said contemptuously. His hands shook as he struggled to control himself.

"General—I may still call you that until the court-martial—we are what remains of the UN. Your betrayal of its laws was not motivated by any honest criticism of policy. We may not be better than you, but our laws and ideals are. You did not learn to do what you did at Luna Academy, though I remember you had your hand up often in History 15. Take him away." Mason's insert winked out, cheating Nakamura of any further reply. Sam was sure that Mason had wanted to say more, but it would have been pointless.

The images of Alard and Orton disappeared, leaving only the view of Ganymede's surface, where the blast crater was still obscured by floating dust.

Nakamura looked back at Sam as the door slid open. Sam's hand closed on the gun in his pocket. More than threatening all the lives of those closest to him, Sam thought as the door closed, Nakamura had threatened humanity's high hopes; he would have denied Orton his new dream, Richard and Margot their future; humanity would not deserve to survive if there were too many of his kind still around. Again Sam was surprised at how his mind came to the support of his feelings. He wondered if this was something new within him or if he had simply not noticed it before.

Mike Basil, Greg Michaels, Richard, and Margot came and stood around him.

"Good going," Richard said. Basil nodded at him. Michaels shook his hand. Margot kissed him on the cheek.

"You're shaking," she said. "Are you okay?"

Sam nodded.

One of the com technicians was covering Soong's body with a piece of plastic. *Janet might have died*, Sam thought.

The radio noise from Jupiter crackled on the screen's open channel.

11. Shares of Glory

After a seeming eternity of sleep, Janet opened her eyes. The lights on the ceiling were clear, ordinary objects, a relief after the dreams.

She remembered a lost dream self, cowering from something in the sky. . . .

Turning her head, she saw Sam, Richard and Margot, and Orton.

"It's okay," Sam said. "You'll be up soon."

You're so kind, she thought, remembering why she was here. *It might not be okay for long.* She tried to smile, but she was tired again, and sleep began to press her into a calm oblivion.

"She needs weeks of rest," Margot said. "I'll stay with her."

She's my friend, Janet thought.

They sat in a circle of chairs on the huge black floor of the observation level—Sam, Richard and Margot, Janet, Orton, Alard, Commander Mason, Greg Michaels, and Mike Basil. All the dome screens were on, creating the illusion of an open night sky.

Sam looked at Janet next to him; a new independence had taken hold of her, making her mysterious and desirable. He would still wake up from dreaming that for some inexplicable reason she had died, only to find her warmly next to him, surprising him with her presence; he had fallen in love again.

All their faces were half in starlight, half in the amber glow of Jupiter's full phase. As they spoke, they would look up at the giant hanging above the distant mountains. Callisto was a silvery disk; Europa and Io were oranges about to chase each other across Jove's streaked face.

Sam was beginning to feel at home. On the map, Ganymede City was a cluster of domes and underground warrens in the northeast, only a few hundred kilometers from the moon's north pole. To the south lay lava plains and mountains, glaciers and deep valleys which held occasional mists.

"After you take Asterome out," Mason was saying, "certainly in this century, after we've begun our economic recovery, we'll probably send out smaller ships in various directions from the sun. Phobos and Deimos might make the beginnings of additional macroworlds. I'm sure that the asteroid dwellers will develop in this direction. We'll need all the insurance we can afford. Maybe the anomaly around earth won't grow any larger; maybe it will fade and we can go back for a look."

And twenty worlds circle Jupiter and Saturn, Sam thought, *worlds we might want to work into something people can live on. Mars and Venus can be terraformed. . . .*

Orton grunted at his right. He had been out of cigars and cigarettes for weeks and had been unable to locate even a small cache.

Mason got up from her chair next to Orton and stretched. "Back home on Mars they're saying the universe is a queer place and we should not overstep ourselves. Our survivors are the most educated and skilled human beings of all time, and still they're superstitious."

"The war—" Alard started to say.

"There's risk in everything," Richard said. "What may result from our holocaust may yet be good."

"That good and bad will happen is inevitable," Janet said. Sam noted a coldness in her voice, as if she were speaking to a stranger.

"Inevitable," Sam said. "It is a strange universe."

"Sam, Janet—last call," Alard said.

"No," Janet answered before Sam could reply. "Our place is here, where we failed, where we have to pick up the pieces."

We don't deserve to go, Sam thought.

Alard tried to make the best of it. "Ganymede has a new governor, and he's getting the feel of useful work again—right, Sam?"

Sam nodded. Janet would never show Richard and Margot how

much she would miss them. They would have a new start. She was letting go as she had let go of Jack; perhaps now she would have a chance to be herself; that would be the Janet, Sam knew, who could love him. Sunspace had to let go of its child now; macrolife had to be born as an act of wild faith or not at all. Richard and Margot had to leave before they became overimpressed with humankind's capacity for cruelty and failure; they would have enough failures of their own.

"When is departure?" Sam asked.

"When we've finished testing the gravitic pusher units," Richard answered. "They still produce pretty weak gravitic shortwaves for the power we put in. We have to be sure of one g acceleration for indefinite periods."

Orton was going, of course. If anyone were to try and stop him now, he would tear Ganymede City down piece by prefabricated piece. Sam wondered what kind of societies would develop when Asterome grew and reproduced.

"We'll miss you," Margot said, looking at Janet.

Janet would go back into organizing what was left of Bulero Enterprises on Mars and Ganymede, assembling all the records, plans of projects, and memories into two central facilities. Sam knew that he would have to teach as well as govern; he had a lot to learn. Suddenly he realized that he might well be the last living professional philosopher anywhere; the implacable unknown had given him another chance, after all.

He looked up and saw Europa's and Io's shadows moving across Jupiter's clouds. . . .

He was alone, yet it seemed that those who had gone were still sitting here with him under the stars. Jupiter hid the sun. Sam waited, thinking of those last moments here, more than two years ago. . . .

There had been embraces and handshaking, clumsy words and averted eyes; the effort to get through to the other person had been desperate. Margot and Janet went off to be alone; Orton and he forgave each other's sins a dozen times. The final conversation with Richard had been impersonal—about the undesirability of deciding the future in advance; it had ended with Richard pleading with him to come along, almost ordering him to convince Janet. "There's got to be an end to Bulero guilt," Richard had said. *But not yet.* Sam remembered Margot's passionate kiss, so freely given.

The empty chairs sat with him one day, and all those people he had known were somehow contained in the bright star that was rushing toward Jupiter in half phase, to steal some of its gravitational energy for the outward push to the stars.

Somewhere out there, Asterome was moving at a considerable fraction of light speed. He imagined its shield of force, a birthing shroud repelling gas and dust from the newborn creature coming out of the trillion-mile whirlpool of sunspace.

Biological time was slowing for Richard, Margot, and Orton, while he and Janet grew older. Recent communications were becoming unreliable.

He thought of Kiichi Nakamura. The Hawaiian had recently committed suicide in the Martian prison. Janet had urged Sam to visit the general before he was removed to Mars.

"What do you want from me?" the general had asked from the corner of his cell.

"Janet suggested that I see you."

"Oh—she feels sorry for me." He tried to smooth back his black hair.

"You need a barber."

Sam had stood in the center of the cell until the general spoke again. "I suppose, Mr. Bulero—"

"Sam, please."

"I suppose that I am to explain myself."

"If you want to." What had shaken Sam was the way the man had suddenly looked up at him.

"You think me a villain and a fool?"

"I think I do," Sam said, feeling guilty.

"You think yourself a perceptive man."

"What was I to see? Tell me."

"I saw Asterome as a source of recovery, while Alard——"

"But Asterome is helping."

"It remains independent when we need everything."

"I see your point, but I think we'll manage. Centralization is a debatable virtue. Asterome is not the only source of recovery left, and there are greater things to consider—but that's not it. Your methods set lawless precedents for later strife—your means pollute what may be reasonable ends. Our future is dirty enough from what we have to carry around inside. Asterome will have its chance and we'll have ours, for what it's worth."

"I believed the situation called for desperate measures."

"What can I say? You may have been well meaning—but you were wrong. A lot of history was against you. Asterome left us what it had to give. You fail to see that it had to leave, to begin the proliferation of macrolife. That's the long-range goal for which it was built."

"What? What are you talking about?"

Sam had tried to explain, but Nakamura had shaken his head in disagreement. "All you Buleros are a pack of dreamers! Your bulerium destroyed the world, my family, and whatever career I might have had." Then he had looked down at the floor, refusing to speak further.

"You might have contributed your talents, but you're still thinking in terms of personal glory."

But you might be right about other things, Sam said to himself, remembering the desolation of the broken man in the cell. *Only future time will justify Asterome's leaving, but not for us. For us there is the consolation that humanity no longer has its eggs in one basket. If we are to die, it will be from internal failures, from the ungovernable dark places of the mind—the scaffolding left over from evolution's bloody building program—not from a lack of vision. Apocalypse is the eye of a needle, through which we pass into a different world. Whitehead had once said that it was the business of the future to be dangerous, that the major advances in civilization were processes that all but wrecked the societies in which they occurred.* It was as close as he would ever come to a statement of faith. It begged the question, of course, saying no more than that there are things which cannot be decided in advance.

He smiled, knowing that he would not have let a student get away with such talk, yet it had involved a man's life and the future of a whole branch of humanity. Deliberate, deductive reason was such a conservative, clockwork thing, best used on known quantities, not on creative acts, which are always a mix of known and unknown. It was almost as if the universe had been designed to be knowable but not exhaustible . . . an involving creation, one that would not be boring or statically perfect for its inhabitants, but always presenting new things and people. *The best of all possible worlds, or a shell game?* He resented the lurking, layered, Troy-like nature of the human mind, where old impulses lingered in the shadow of reason, going about their subterranean business in a billion-year-old maze. *I could have easily killed Nakamura. . . .*

A river of light carried the sun out from behind Jove's face, beginning the week. High in its orbit, the solar mirror brightened into life and Sam thought of Soong.

It was getting on toward the spring of 2026, the spring that would have been on earth, but Sam sensed the coming of spring here also, despite Jupiter and the dark mountains. Ganymede only appeared to be sleeping under its glaciers, with humanity hibernating in its dark crannies; the spring here was one of waiting to live again, while listening for the stars to speak with the voices of humankind's children.

Suddenly Sam realized that even if earth were to be miraculously returned to them, people now living on Mars or Ganymede could not go back; they would be unused to the higher gravity. Only Asterome had people living in three-quarters earth normal. By the time earth became habitable again—and that might be never—there would be no humans in sunspace who could live on the home planet without mechanical aids. A struggling colony would have to readapt to earth by giving birth to a new generation, for which earth gravity would again be the norm. The great human summer of time to come, he realized, would be lived out of the cradle, in free space, around the sun in space habitats, and out among the stars.

Janet and he had given their germ plasm to a host mother, and the three of them would have a child by Christmas. Sam often wondered in what ways their banked genetic materials would be used on Asterome. Alard had joked about cloning them all someday, but in the time since Asterome's departure, the idea had acquired some reality for Janet and himself; perhaps there would be a braver Samuel Bulero or a happier Janet. He imagined the eyes that would someday look at a starry sky somewhere far away, and perhaps recognize the sun, and wonder about the earth from which they had come. He thought about the fragile, spontaneous nature of beginnings, the agonizing uncertainties of things new and complex; a crisis point approaches and the new entity must crystallize, become whole and stable, or the light will flicker and die within it, and it will be passed by in time, perhaps to reappear later, or never again. Somewhere in a clear midnight, human consciousness had been born in this way, out of physical complexities, wending its way upward past the watchdogs of instinct into self-recognition. And if the new thing survives its beginnings, it thrives; the uncertainty of its contingent, miraculous start is obliterated; the past becomes a black hole of mysteries. . . .

Last week a faint message had announced that Asterome's engineers were ready to test the new drive. If successful, the large-scale quantum effect would permit the bridging of space-time on the parsec level; a side benefit might be the development of an instantaneous communications system; but the experiment had to be tried at a substantial fraction of light speed. It had already failed or succeeded by the time the message had arrived. With such a drive, Asterome might return in the near future.

As Sam stood looking out over Ganymede's surface, the dark yet comforting landscape of his new life, he hoped that here in the ruins of the solar system unreason would now sleep for a time, giving wounds time to heal and love a chance to grow.

No matter how often he sent his thoughts after those who had gone, no matter how far his mind reached or how long his body endured, he would die and others would be born to move through the shadow play of phenomena around him; those who had left sunspace would also die, and others would take their place, until such time when humankind became more than human. He saw all those living on Mars and Ganymede, all those close to him, as ghostly stuff that would fade into nothingness. It outraged him to think it; life was longer than it had been, but nowhere long enough.

I'll die here.

"Sam, how long have you been here today? You let your class out early, didn't you?"

He turned and saw her dark shape near the elevator pylon. She came forward and he saw a pencil behind her ear; her hair was tied up on top of her head and the look on her face was there for him. *For me, finally.*

She handed him a piece of paper.

"From Alard."

He read the words in the starlight:

ACCELERATING NEARER LIGHT SPEED BEFORE
STARTING EXPERIMENT. IF SUCCESSFUL YOU
MAY NOT HEAR FROM US. FAREWELL.

This message was also more than a year old. He looked at Janet. Her face was calm, and he knew that she was ready to have no further word in her lifetime. They might not be seen or heard from again, and that possibility was closest to death; the darkness between the stars had swallowed them.

Alard and Richard had not been content with the sublight gravitic pushers, which could have taken Asterome to any of the hundred stars within thirty light-years of the sun in reasonable earth and ship times; instead, the macroworld had elected to take the next step in mobility as soon as possible.

Sam pictured Alard's engineers working to harness the wave effects of dense masses, feeding them with vast electrical forces, as the macroworld's acceleration shortened light waves fore and lengthened those arriving aft, darkening the universe to human eyes, except for a narrow band of yellow stars circling at right angles to the course. What other distortions of space-time were being created by the contained quantities of unstable bulerite as the universe prepared to black out?

It had already happened. More than one light-year out from the sun, the drive had been cut in—perhaps throwing the macroform into far spaces, from where it could never return. He tried not to dwell on the possibility of complete disaster.

"They're brave," Janet said, "to risk everything."

She's let go.

He turned and looked out beyond the superconducting power station, where the catapult had just lofted another ingot toward Jupiter, an offering to a god in exchange for energy.

Janet came and embraced him. He kissed her and she held on to him. *Farewell,* he thought, realizing that the share of glory given him would have to be enough.

Richard tried not to waken Margot as he got up and went out into the solarium; there he turned on the screen for a view of the distant, reddening sun. As he looked at the fading star, he knew that he had what he wanted—something other than the past to give himself to completely—and that he would have to live with the choice, make it work, because it had come to him at great cost, paid for by all humanity; he would not have the right to be unhappy. This fact, as true and deserving to be heard as it was, dragged him down, reminding him again of the past's ever-present ability to spill into the present and spoil the future.

Planetary history is one long dark age, he thought, *an evolving slaughterhouse.* He wondered what kind of civilization, if any, would now develop in the home sunspace.

He reached out and changed the view, mentally turning his back on the dwindling darkening sun, and looked outward across the cave of stars.

After a moment, he turned from the diamond-strewn abyss and walked over to the hotel window. He pulled back the curtains and saw that daylight was young in the hollow outside. The town was going about its business as the tribeams slowly grew brighter, fed now by internal sources, not by the sun. He slid open a window and leaned out to look to his distant right, where the trolley was climbing out of the central regions, toward the mountainous ends of the world.

II. MACROLIFE: 3000

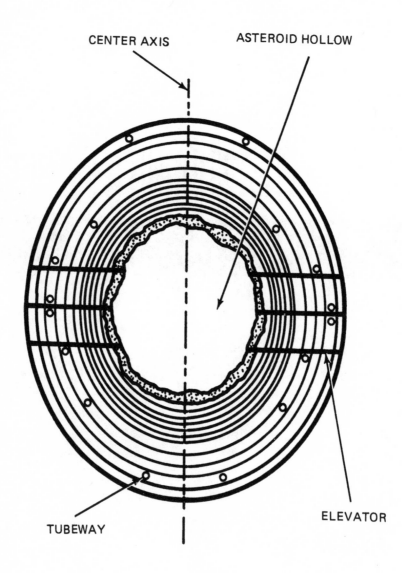

CENTER AXIS

ASTEROID HOLLOW

ELEVATOR

TUBEWAY

The most perfect example of macrolife . . . is the {deep space}
extraterrestrial colony.
                                        —DANDRIDGE COLE, 1961

Macrolife, as we know it, was made possible by the develop-
ment of fusion power systems, gravitic technology, and the per-
fection of bulerite and derivative materials. The under-
standing of bulerite's instabilities, especially its tendency to
distort space-time at subatomic quantum levels, led to the
development of reasonably fast star drives which did not vio-
late the structure of physical theory. Research into the proper-
ties of ultra-dense matter was carried out on Asterome as it
left the solar system in late 2023, and in 2024. The
resulting theory linked the gravitational force with the strong
nuclear force, expressing the binding force inside the nucleus as
being supergravitational; the experimental result was a star
drive which could be cut in at near optic speeds. The discovery
was eventually transmitted back to sunspace. . . .

At Centauri in 2050, Asterome became the core founda-
tion of the first large macrolife societal container. A second
world was begun at Procyon in 2075, from materials
contributed by the Asterome biosphere, and from materials
mined in the Procyon system.

Design description. *These first two macroworlds grew to*
be three-hundred-kilometer-long ovoid shapes, with one hun-
dred and fifty urban shells enclosing the original asteroid
hollow. The meadows and towns of the inner countryside
remained relatively unchanged during the thousand years of
shell building. To reach the urban levels from the core was a
matter of traveling down, since one's head always pointed
toward the center; this arrangement dated back to the time when
the asteroid required a spin to produce pseudo-gravitation

through centrifugal force on the inner surface. Asterome, with two hundred shells, measured three hundred kilometers from end to end, and one hundred fifty kilometers across the middle. Gravitic elevators went up and down across the short diameters, and tubeways made the six-hundred-kilometer circuit on every tenth level. The outer level, just under the vacuum insulation layer and deflection shield blanket, was a network of engineering facilities—laboratories, observation stations, heat control and dissipation centers, small-craft docks, raw material ingestion locks, and emergency backup installations. The total land area of the one hundred fifty levels was almost 100,000,000 square miles, or twice the usable land area of earth. This area could be doubled by building one additional level between each two existing levels, which would still leave half a kilometer, or one-third of a mile, between levels—more than enough to produce the illusion of open sky, where desired. The macroworld could reproduce in a number of ways: by moving out of its outermost shell and building up the empty interior; by adding levels between levels to the practical limit; by adding outer shells.

Throughout the millennium following Asterome's departure from sunspace, Mars-Ganymede may have released as many as a dozen macroworlds into the galaxy. However, the nostalgic desire to find earthlike planets, rather than take up macrolife, persisted. It is believed that as many as fifty smaller starships were used to colonize sunspaces within a hundred light-years of earth.

Many of these colony ships were equipped with defective drives and faulty shielding systems. Historical-cultural evidence suggests that ships may have been thrown to any point in the galaxy within a thousand-light-year radius of earth. . . .

The division of humanity into macroworlders and planet-dwellers stems from this period, and is the precondition for understanding the conflicts that followed—conflicts within the macroworlds themselves, as well as conflicts between macrolife and natural worlds. . . .

—RICHARD BULERO ET AL.,
The History of Macrolife, 10th ed.,
Revised and Updated, vol. 9, Sol, 3025

I recommend that we do not interfere with colony planets. We can't trust ourselves. Consider examples from earth history. The West trained, armed and supported dictatorships in Asia, Africa and South America. It would be difficult not to support authoritarian elements, out of self-interest, and because backward planets have few genuinely inner-directed individuals who have their own people's interests at heart. A society must be left to grow out of its ways; it cannot be directed from outside, lest these means toward a well-meant end damage the potential for self-determination. Violent revolutions always destroy their own ends. Take the example of India's partition. Even with a nonviolent, well-meaning leader, conflict could not be controlled; it had to run its course. . . .

The old idea of humankind settling earthlike planets in an endless expansion is absurd; if an earthlike world does not already have its own intelligent life, then it will very likely develop such life in the future. We would be committing a form of genocide by interfering with the nursery world's course of development. Even if we were to find earthlike worlds likely to remain free of intelligent life, we are still faced with the usual objections to life on natural worlds. . . .

Looking through history, we can easily see the dangers of power. Clearly, a good society must have recourse against itself, in the planned struggle between its institutions and public sectors, as well as through the civil action of one individual against another. A good society enlists the divided nature of man to sustain itself, producing for itself and its individual citizens a variety of avenues of appeal. . . .

If Vico was right and the social world is certainly the work of men, then macrolife is a journey into the possible, a move that will create an endless series of differing social containers for the human imagination to inhabit. . . .

I may be wrong, but the successful forms of macrolife will retain the capacity for self-criticism, an area of independence for the individual. . . . They will succeed to the degree that consensus or forced participation is avoided, to the degree that the society retains its ability to leave people alone. . . .

—RICHARD BULERO,
Notebooks

Theories of progress have been many. There was the simplistic idea of unlimited progress; cyclical theories saying that there is nothing new under the sun. Yet it can be shown that progress does occur; but when a thing is accomplished, we are no longer as impressed by it as when it was lacking. Progress eliminates yesterday's problems, and creates today's and tomorrow's. We can be optimists as we look into the future out of what will become a historical ruin; but to the future new problems will be important. This has always been the case; the fact that old problems have been solved, especially social problems, is little cause for joy to a present whose expectations have risen. Utopias, then, are what we see looking into future possibility, possibilities which would be unlikely unless progress had already occurred. Progress occurs, make no mistake about it—utopias are real places (any person coming out of a prior condition would attest to that, at least for a while); but the solution of even the gravest problems cannot close the future to newer problems. I would not want it any other way; the relativity of progress is the source of our continuing discontent, and the necessary precondition for continuing satisfaction.

—RICHARD BULERO,
"The Relativity of Progress," speech before the
First Session of the Projex Council, 2041

. . . modern man suffers from unfulfilling religious, educational, familial and work institutions. Humane institutions make people human; that is why Socrates called the laws of Athens his "parents." Enveloping, shaping, restraining institutions free people from enslavement to anarchic passions.

—GEORGE F. WILL,
Newsweek, October 31, 1977

The common idea that success spoils people by making them vain, egotistic, and self-complacent is erroneous; on the contrary it makes them, for the most part, humble, tolerant, and kind. Failure makes people bitter and cruel.

—W. SOMERSET MAUGHAM

The State is for Individuals, the law is for freedoms, the world is for experiment, experience, and change: these are the fundamental beliefs upon which a modern Utopia must go.

. . . it is certainly the fate of all Utopias to be more or less misread.

—H. G. WELLS,
A Modern Utopia, 1905

12. Transhumanity

John Bulero had waited all his life to see a natural world.

He had seen sunspaces during the gathering of raw materials, but none of them had contained an earthlike planet. He remembered the gas giants, the airless worlds of nickel, iron, and rock, naked before the tides of cosmic dust and sunstorms, worlds of ice, desert worlds, planets shattered into asteroid belts around their suns. A world with an outside surface was dangerous, even with an aura of atmosphere for protection; yet the inescapable fact was that humanity had originated on such a world.

The approach to the system had stirred something within him, quickening his anticipation into an eagerness he had never before known. The stars of Praesepe, the open cluster in Cancer, had flickered longer than usual as the macroworld had come out of jumpspace. He had never fully accepted the idea of his entire world phasing itself in and out of the wave structure of familiar space-time, appearing and disappearing like a ghostly needle stitching through the folds of a fabric; tachyon transfer sometimes produced a sense of unreality, it had been claimed, but the data were too fleeting to prove much.

Emerging from the complex spatial variability of superspace, the biosphere had become continuous at ninety-five percent of light speed, one light-year into the cluster, with velocity dropping to five percent of light within three months. The protective deflector shield had been turned off after the orbit of the system's tenth planet was crossed; deceleration was continuing until the world entered orbit in the equatorial plane of the double star, to match the position of the fifth planet at a distance of one million kilometers on its sunward side.

The doors slid open and he stepped into the drum of the vertical shuttle. He touched the control surface and thought of Margaret as the lift rushed toward the world's center. *I've put off breaking with her too long*, he told himself. *It's time to move on.*

The doors opened, releasing him on the level below the old hollow. He went down the long passage toward the lockers, thinking how unbearable his exemplar had become. *I can't stand her looking into me any more.*

He walked into the equipment room and took his wings down from the wall rack. He put them on over his bare shoulders, fastening the straps. Then he stepped onto the lift surface in the center of the room.

As he was carried upward, he wondered how many people his female exemplar had taught during her eighty years and if any of the males had been like him. A portion of the ceiling slid back and he felt gravity decrease as the platform delivered him outside.

He opened his wings in a green world, a memento of human origins, a jewel set inside the urban shells; here nature was an ally, no longer an enemy or a victim.

With a few strong strokes, he rose from the platform, beginning his climb into the vast open space. It was an easy ascent in the minimal gravity. Taking a deep breath, he pulled toward the central region, where the gravity was zero. There white clouds were allowed to gather, and only an occasional wind was permitted to disperse them when they grew too thick.

As he gained altitude, his gaze swept across the tall trees below,

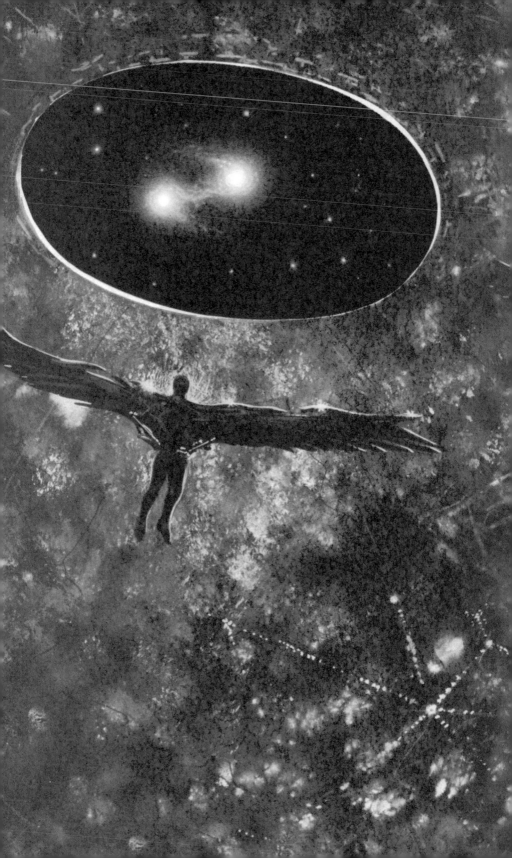

taking in the black ribbon of road winding its way between them to the village on the shore of Central Lake, five kilometers away. The lake trickled small streams around the inward curve of the core, feeding the land with moisture recycled for a thousand years.

He looked up at the town four kilometers above him. A winged couple moved across it, passing to his left high above him. He waved but they did not notice.

He stopped moving his wings and his momentum carried him into the zero-g region. He turned once to look at the whole expanse of the interior. Then he looked eight kilometers forward along the axis of the hollow to the light plate.

The giant disk stood in the narrow forwards, lighting the land with soft daylight. John waited motionlessly for what he had come to see, forgetting his resentment toward Margaret. Slowly the kilometer-wide sun plate grew dark, and stars appeared in its field of view. The yellow-white double star appeared, a main-sequence contact binary flooding the core with light. He looked at the strangeness around him. The greenery seemed to grow fresher; the air took on a bluer glow; the lake became a pool of fire, the streams arteries of something living, the trees a thick moss spotted with yellow.

He thought of his ancestral twin, Samuel Bulero, from whose banked cells he had been cloned. When Samuel had walked inside this world a thousand years ago, there had been no urban shells, only the hollow rock; there had been no gravitic control, only the crude spin. Asterome had been dependent on the solar system for its resources, unable to seek on its own. Material synthesis and duplication had been a far-off dream. Macrolife had been a child, still unable to walk.

Why had Samuel Bulero chosen to stay behind? How could he have made such a decision in the face of so much possibility, especially when there had been no earth to return to? The questions made him even more impatient to see a livable planet. There were probably thousands of civilizations in the galaxy, thriving on worlds of air, dirt, water, and growing things, worlds with all their insides out under the stars, open to all the radiation of their parent suns, helpless before the shiftings of the planetary crusts, unable to control winds and storms; on those worlds intelligent life died by the thousands every day and would disappear when its star died.

But he wanted to test for himself what he had been taught—that macrolife was the safest and most durable way of life. Seven other worlds had been modeled after this one, seven children scattered into the galaxy to grow and differ and make others after their own kind. Each could support whatever society it chose to contain within the permanent, self-reproducing framework; each world was immortal, a hyperpersonal organism in which each individuality flowered to enrich the whole.

He floated quietly as he looked at the double star, wondering if he dared go see for himself. Margaret would probably oppose him: Rob Wheeler, his male exemplar, would probably think it was a good idea. He would have to take his chance now, while the planet was being searched for signs of a colony ship which had been lost in the cluster centuries ago; otherwise he would have to wait decades for another earthlike world. Between the search for the colony and the floating up of raw materials from the planet, he would have more than enough time to explore.

Moving a wing, he turned himself to feel the warmth of the new suns on his face. If he were living on the planet, a slight change in the radiation of these suns would alter the genes of his descendants, for better or worse. Life warred with itself on natural worlds, and the direction of evolution's war was always an adaptation to the status quo, whatever that might be at the moment.

He wondered if he would find something to do with his life. Was it true that some people took most of a century to decide? What if he never found anything? What could he ever achieve that would make him a fit exemplar? What would he be able to say to someone like himself? It wasn't so much the pressure of Margaret's prodding, but the lack of something specific; sometimes he wished that his exemplars would simply tell him what to do, instead of making endless suggestions and offering countless alternatives. Wheeler would always tell him to be patient and attentive, that in time he would discover what he wanted. Macrolife had been bought with the dedication of all those who had left the solar system. Its resources were his birthright, to be used in creative ventures. *What's wrong with me?* he asked himself. "No one will tell you what to do," Wheeler had told him. "You'll have to figure things out for yourself, mistakes and all. That's the difference between science and faith, dogma and freedom." Freedom was an open nothingness before him, oppressive and terrifying.

Soon he would be twenty-six earth years old—and still he was a mystery to himself, living in a larger mystery. *I'm a mistake*, he thought. *What was it in Samuel Bulero that they want to see in me?*

Sometimes he wished that he had been born like the more modified citizens, who seemed to have better control over their feelings, whose brain chemistry had been designed for better concentration; he wished that he could read body language as well as Margaret could. He thought of the link, and it seemed that he would never be ready for it. *I don't belong here; everyone is different from me.*

He looked longingly at the yellow-white suns. Some of their light was being cut down by filters, but he could see that the stars shared atmospheres. They were joined by a river of plasma which flowed back and forth in magnetic channels, a fiery umbilical stretched across a distance of less than one diameter.

John wondered about Lea, the fifth planet. What would he have been if he had grown up there? Then with two powerful strokes of his wings, he pushed himself out of weightlessness. In a moment he was gliding forward across the world, the wind singing in his ears as he plunged closer to the huge sunscreen, drawn by the awesome splendor of the double star.

13. Exemplar

The door slid open and John Bulero stepped into the brightly lit workroom of his exemplar. Rob Wheeler was not in the large circular chamber, but the workscreen on the center desk was on, displaying a dozen mathematical functions. John went past the various Humanity II terminals to the door of the observatory. The door opened and he stepped into darkness.

His eyes adjusted as the door closed behind him, and he saw Rob leaning over a horizontal screen in the center of the room. Only two of the twenty-five screens ringing the observatory were on, showing magnified starfields; the projection space overhead was dark.

Wheeler turned a pale, white-haired profile to John and motioned for him to come closer.

Silently they looked down at the planet on the map screen: a full disk veiled in swirling white clouds, dark blue oceans, brown wrinkles of mountainous land, stretches of desert and greenery, and polar caps, dazzlingly white in the sunlight.

"I haven't seen a truly beautiful planet for over a century," Rob said. "The last was when I was two hundred and three."

"Beautiful and dangerous," John said, remembering what he had been taught, "filled with disease and unpredictable processes." He remembered when at the age of ten he had played in the forest near the lake in the hollow, pretending that he was lost on some far planet half a galaxy away. As he looked down now at the black grid covering the view of Lea, he thought of the glass windows he had seen in the images of old books.

Suddenly the planet was gone, and a column of light was streaming up into the dark observatory from the filtered brightness of the two suns.

"Do you know anything about this planet's history?" Wheeler asked.

"Only the name."

"We're less than a hundred and fifty parsecs from earth's sunspace."

"And you think there are earth colonists here?"

"We know the planet's name from scouts who have been here at various times during the last two centuries. We know something of what happened after the sacking and destruction of the partially completed macroworld at Tau Ceti IV in 2331. Evidence suggests that what was left of the destroyed world was used to build a makeshift starship, which disappeared into the Praesepe cluster carrying a few thousand people. Blackfriar has evidence that a relative of his was the captain of that ship. Most of the documents we have from Tau Ceti and Centauri show that the names of Blackfriar and Bulero play important roles in the developing schisms over whether to settle natural worlds or build mobiles. There were Blackfriars and Buleros on both sides, apparently. I don't know what we can find out down there after seven hundred years."

"I hope we don't anger them by taking the resources we need."

"The culture here is almost nonexistent," Rob said. "There may be no one alive."

John was silent.

Wheeler stood up and turned to face him. "What do you think about it?"

"I don't know what to think. I'm not sure I want to join the building of the new macroworld or go with it when it's ready. What I really want is to go down and see the planet. I've waited a long time."

"Go and observe by yourself. I'm glad you're interested."

"Why?"

"You'll get some firsthand experience concerning an old problem, one we've never resolved."

Wheeler had taught him everything he knew about the nature of inquiry, acquainting him with the rich spectrum of the sciences, with the basic questions of scientific philosophy, especially with problems in stellar evolution and comparative cosmology. Rob had taught him the concerns which should belong in every life, stressing the ethical procedures implicit in the honest gathering of knowledge.

Rob had been the first to discuss Samuel Bulero with him, helping him to better accept his own identity. As a clone, John Bulero was simply the twin brother of an earlier individual, no more, no less, free to follow his own path. Cloning was only one of a variety of reproductive methods available to macroworlders. Nevertheless, someone had wanted to give these Bulero genes another try. "That's true," Wheeler had said to him a decade ago, "but the rest will be up to you." The Buleros and Blackfriars had helped create macrolife; and they had seen to it that when a world reproduced itself, it would have a bank of genetic material from earth to draw on, as a complement to normal sexual reproduction. All the people who had dreamed of a new kind of life in those final days of earth were still alive; somewhere each of them had a twin, an individual who had been called up to live his or her permutation of the original. As Samuel Bulero was his historical brother, so he had other brothers on distant macroworlds.

"Are you interested in the solar system?" John asked.

"The star still shines, and I can't see any signs of the anomaly at this distance."

"You want to go there, don't you?"

"I do, but I'll have to convince the Projex Council. As long as our drive systems move us at a hundred light-years a week, they'll be prudent about the energy we spend on movement. We need smaller and more efficient power sources. Even a thousandfold increase of power for our drive will only move us a small fraction of a parsec faster. We have the means in exotic forms of matter, but the engineering is a million times more difficult than fusion was a thousand years ago."

"Do you think civilization survives in the solar system?"

"I suspect that the anomaly might have receded."

"Do you think life has survived on earth itself?"

"Possibly." John thought of how easily this man could inspire him about impersonal things. "If we help any natural world, it should be earth," Wheeler said. "Does this interest you?"

"It seems worth doing."

John followed him out into the bright workroom. Wheeler sat down behind his desk. John seated himself at one of the terminals and turned the chair around to face him.

"If you like," Rob said, "we can work together on making a case for a return to the solar system in the near future."

"I'd like to see Lea first," John said.

"I'll help arrange it for you."

"I don't want Margaret to know until I'm gone."

"It's your business entirely. Not everyone will think you strange for wanting to see a dirtworld. We have our provincialisms, but we try not to enforce their observance. It will be mostly those who are your own age who will look down their noses at you."

"While the older citizens will merely tolerate my odd taste."

"We have to. It's our youth who are conservative. Don't worry, frivolity is said to return at about age five hundred."

John laughed.

"You know," Wheeler continued, "extended life was once regarded as a continuing old age. All kinds of dire predictions were made about the adverse effects of long life on the human mind. Few thought that creativity and vitality would increase to match the new scale of time."

"Not everyone achieves a dynamic longevity," John said.

"And not everyone could live a successful century before, or even a productive decade or two. Failure can't be eliminated by guarantee. It's still up to the individual, no matter how much help is given."

That's me, John thought. "It's a wonder humanity developed any foresight at all."

"On earth old men became jesters, "Wheeler said. "There may be such men on Lea. I don't know what else has survived. There are no standard forms of communication that we can detect, not even radio. That by itself signals trouble; there's seven hundred years of history down there. . . ."

John got up, feeling uneasy. "I've got to meet Margaret at the link training center."

"But you won't—you haven't been there at all today, have you?"

"No."

"Don't be too hard on Margaret. She's not like you. You're a healthy, relatively unmodified type. Her behavioral range was developed for long attention span, logic, a minute grasp of body language and sexuality, and emotional control. Try to understand her difficulty—in you she faces a very unpredictable person."

"She has no imagination. I'll be glad when we go our own ways. I can't stand her impatience. She talks at me, not to me."

"You'll be friends when you're a hundred," Rob said. "But if you're that unhappy, go on your own, do without exemplars." Wheeler's bushy eyebrows went up toward his white hair. John looked directly into the wide blue eyes, and for a moment the person he knew was gone. The being who confronted him was alien, projecting what seemed to be an amused empathy toward a lesser creature. John thought of the man who worked on dozens of undiscussed projects, his brain enormously magnified through the Humanity II intelligences who ordered the world for their human partners, as once nature's gods had ruled earth. John wondered why unchanged types like himself had been permitted to persist. Was it to keep a tie with natural worlds?

Rob smiled, releasing him from his gaze, and John knew how the exemplar would answer his question. Initial types, as well as innovative ones, had to be preserved as a matter of law. The worth of human adaptability and creativity could not be predicted. His life was his own, his own burden, to do with as he pleased. But what could he ever do to please or benefit the world around him? He felt a general, shapeless hunger in himself, a vague devotion which seemed directed at nothing more than itself; there were answers to questions which he could not even put into words.

He turned and the door opened for him. He stepped out into the passageway, feeling ignorant and afraid.

14. Discontent

Level six was dark as he neared the apartment. Half the sky was alive with the bright stars of Praesepe, half with the glow of more distant suns. The curving plain of spaced dwelling columns held up the night sky. Sturdy oaks and white birches from earth rustled in the gentle breeze.

He passed three olive-skinned males sitting on a bench near the column entrance. He did not know them, but they glanced at him with their large brown eyes. He felt hostility toward them as he went through the archway. Tall, black-haired, graceful, they were the true macroworlders. He was an intruder from the past, and not even a copy of a pioneer, but a shadow of one who had stayed behind.

He turned left and walked around the curve to his apartment at the end. The door slid open and he stepped inside.

Margaret Toren-Bulero stood in the center of the living room. He stopped and looked at her as if she were a stranger. They had shared this apartment for more than a year now, ever since he had left the dorms on level five. He remembered their closeness of six months before as he looked at the bundle of her long black hair tied up on the back of her head. Her skin had a tendency to lose its tan and become very soft and white. She was not a clone of one person, but a mixture of materials from Janet Bulero and Margot Toren, with modifications. She looked back at him without blinking.

"You were to meet me," she said.

"I didn't want to." He resented the view of him which her age gave her.

"You've neglected your Humanity II seminars."

"That's my business, isn't it?"

"You'll fall behind."

"I don't care, right now. Can't you leave me alone?"

She did not react for a moment. "Let's make love. It will relax you."

He shook his head. "I'm going down to Lea."

She stepped nearer and looked directly at him. She was thin and graceful, making him feel crude in his stockiness.

"Whatever for?" she asked.

"To see . . . how they live, what it's like."

"You really don't know why you want to go, do you?"

"I want to see a natural world."

"They're creatures. Life is an endless war. Do you want to see that?"

"I have a right to go."

"I don't recommend it. You're easily impressed."

"I won't get another chance very soon."

"You'll handle it better later, not now."

He remembered how much he had needed her once, how happy he had been when she had taken him from the loneliness of the dorms.

"I wish to dissolve our bond," he said.

"You're upset. Think about it later." She tried to embrace him.

He pushed her away and turned to leave, knowing that he could never live in this apartment again. Margaret was a manager, leaving him nothing for himself; she meant well, but she could not understand what he wanted, especially if he himself did not know. It would not be fair to stay with her.

She was silent as he went out the door.

The nearest watch held only a dozen people, though it could accommodate three hundred. Lea swam in the darkness on the screen. John sat alone in the front row.

The view changed and he was looking into a conference pit. Franklyn Blackfriar, a clone of Orton Blackfriar, sat between councilmen Stav Rees and Miklos Anastasian. The four-hundred-year-old first councilman scratched the black stubble of hair on his scalp and waited for the report to begin. John knew him as the most respected first councilman who had ever held the office. He would retire for decades, but something would always draw him back into public planning.

Rees and Anastasian were scarcely half Blackfriar's age, but he liked to pick younger people for his administrations. John knew them both from the engineering school, where they had been his instructors. Both were at the head of the action to build a new mobile.

Rees summarized the resource-gathering procedures, already in progress. It was easier to bring materials up from Lea than to send out foraging vessels to hook and bring back asteroid fragments; before the advent of large-scale gravitics, the task of bringing up resources from a planet would have been too large even for atomic boosters, but now entire mountains could be floated off using a portable generator, while smaller loads of scarcer materials would be brought up by shuttle haulers.

Miklos Anastasian said a few words about security precautions. As long as the macroworld stayed in a sunward parallel orbit, directly in line with the planet, an undetected boarding attempt would be impossible. The accidental transfer of an unknown disease would be minimized through strict procedures, but preliminary investigations had revealed nothing dangerous. The first scouts had concluded that there was little possiblity of any danger from Lea's surface. Its human population was made up of scattered tribes, too backward to have an opinion about the macroworld's presence; few, if any, would even understand what it was that had come into their sky.

"When will the two outer shells be ready?" Blackfriar asked.

"We can separate the two outer shells almost immediately," Rees said.

"Where will you go when all is ready?" Blackfriar asked. He seemed to have little interest in the project, but he would go through all the public hearings and administrative functions connected with the process of world reproduction.

Rees started to answer again, but Anastasian cut in. "Maybe one of the globular clusters, assuming we have a faster drive soon. Planetary civilizations might have developed favorably there, easily spanning the closer spaces between the suns to achieve an optimum distribution of population. We may find a great diversity in a small space. I think the isolation of cultures in the spiral arms may be a grave handicap to their progress. A culture must limit energy consumption and population at its most productive stage of development, when the momentum of cumulative innovation is just beginning to produce decisive break-throughs; the culture must reach beyond its planet or die."

"Or fall into a marginal existence, like Lea," Rees added.

John decided not to hear the rest. He had expected Blackfriar to contribute more to the discussion. What would the councilman think of his desire to visit Lea? Their meetings had always made John feel that Blackfriar was taking a personal interest in him, that the way to friendship was always open.

He felt a growing sense of hope as he left the hall. He would go see Blackfriar and make his own arrangements to visit Lea. Maybe Black-friar would understand what he felt.

"Go," Franklyn Blackfriar said. "Go right away."

John stood in front of the first councilman's huge desk.

"Well, sit down. I've been waiting for you to come and see me." Blackfriar rapped his desk with his knuckles as John sat down. "Old earth teak. There's nothing like it, not even mirrored bulerite." He paused. "Why do you want to go?"

"I can't give a reason—I just want to see."

"You realize," Blackfriar said, leaning back, "that a macroworlder is a powerful individual on any dirtworld? We lose a lot if we lose one of our own. Afraid?"

"I don't think this world is a threat to us."

"You've got an idea about helping out down there?"

"I don't know—I don't know anything. I want to see."

"Good. What does Margaret think?"

"We're dissolving our bond."

Blackfriar shrugged. "Nothing unusual. Maybe one day your experience may be useful. So few of us have any direct experience of natural worlds."

John looked directly at him. To be accepted so casually was disturbing.

"Have you talked with Wheeler?" John asked.

Blackfriar smiled and leaned forward. "Of course I have. You're going—but see the medics. There are a number of tricky things you should know about dirtworlds."

"I will." Blackfriar's breezy sympathy had disoriented him.

"I know that look, John, I've worn it myself. You're distrustful of me. Don't bother answering. I don't need to confirm what I know. Let me tell you what it means to live a long time. It's the younger people who are most rigid, because they ask that things go one way—their way and no other, according to some idea of proper development which they think just. They exclude and exclude, concentrating all their skills on their desire, whatever that may be. And they often get what they want. That's more true in our social system, but it happened surprisingly often in past cultures. Nothing can stand forever against that kind of patience and persistence, because when the one chance for success comes along, the youth is there and waiting, ready to seize it. And he was there all the other times when the chance was not there. That one time is all the time he needs. That's why youth has a historical reputation for innovation and change."

"What's your point?"

"Don't you see? Youth's approach is narrow. The older you get, the more innovative you will become, at least in our way of life. You'll begin to see how long it takes to do anything really well, and you'll know that you have the time, if you're patient. You'll take the time to do more than one thing well. On dirtworlds young and old were rigid. The young person had only one thing to add; the old, one thing to preserve—the things he learned when he was young. There was no time to do more, no energy. So the generations struggled hand over hand, unaware of their closeness, blind for lack of life and vitality. They could not have what we have, what still lies before you."

"I know all that," John said.

Blackfriar got up from behind his desk and stretched his huge frame. Then he came around into the center of the room. John stood up. Blackfriar paused and looked down at him. "John, what you want is vague enough to intrigue me. You want to go and poke around in places. Go see Miklos Anastasian; he'll help you get down. Rees will be supervising the final separation of our outer shells, but Miklos will be going dirtside. I think you and he will get along. Eventually an investigative team will go down and make some sort of historical report. I have a lot of interest in that. But for the moment we'll send you." He smiled again. "Right now I have to go and resolve a bitter feud in the outer levels. Seems the new world is carrying off equipment they're not supposed to have. Maybe someday research will stop complaining to me and produce some of the dreams I've been ordering for more than a century."

"What dreams?"

"Walk out with me part way and I'll tell you," Blackfriar said as he led the way out of the office.

15. Wayside World

The map screen was a large oval well in the control room. John looked down into the planet's ocean of air. Three haulers drifted nearby, slugs readying to descend from low orbit, fill their bellies with ore, and depart. Each was a kilometer of hull with a detachable passenger module in front, a cargo hold in the middle, and a gravitic workhorse in the back.

"Thirty percent of the surface," Miklos Anastasian was saying, "is two continents joined by a narrow land bridge. The northern mass extends to within thirty degrees of the pole, the southern reaches the south pole. The sea between the continents is warm and shallow. The land bridge is part of the western mountain chain running up across both continents. There are deserts and grasslands east of the range, then wooded mountains and the eastern coastal plain. The coast itself is cliff rock, with hundreds of offshore islands, once part of the mainland."

John sensed amusement in the wiry man's voice. A hundred-fifty-year-old researcher in planetary geologies, Miklos belonged to the middle range of modified citizens. Stronger than most of the populace, he was able to run at better than twenty kilometers per hour, and he needed one-third less sleep; implanted in his bare head was the usual Humanity II link. His dark eyebrows seemed to be made of solid material in the light streaming up from the screen.

"What about settlements?" John asked.

Miklos extended a muscular arm over the screen. "There seem to be cities in the northeast near the coast. There's a big city some thirty kilometers north of the shallow sea. Everything is very quiet." He leaned over the screen intently, as if preparing to scrape his bony fingers through the wrinkles of land in search of life.

"What about climate?"

"Be prepared for changes during the day, something you're not used to. The north is tundra, changing through temperate to tropical as you go south. Vegetation and animals are hybrids of earth-derived and local. It will be hard to separate the kinds. Gravity is eighty-seven percent earth. It's the fifth planet out of ten, orbiting the double star at one point four astronomical units. A stormy place."

Miklos stood up and looked down at John. "I'll fill you in on as much as I can before we land. The suns are slightly smaller than sol. You'll see them taking up about twenty-five minutes of arc in the sky. They're within ten percent of each other in size; one is brighter than the other, but you won't notice that because your eye is not sensitive enough to differences between very bright sources."

And yours is, John thought.

"During day you'll see only a spread-out mass of light when you glance up, not two disks. By the way, don't look directly at them, you'll harm your eyes. The suns circle each other in nine hours, producing eclipses every four and one-half hours. The amount of light is then cut down, depending on which sun is eclipsing which at what time and position, and where you are on the planet. It's a twenty-nine-hour day. When the suns are side by side, it gets warmer in the afternoon. On a clear day you may see two shadows of yourself. At sunset you'll see that the suns are elongated, flattened at the poles, sharing stellar material across the distance between them. Watch out for winds and storms. Auroras are intense at night."

"What about intelligent life, besides the colonists?"

Miklos shook his head and a sad look came into his gray eyes. "I suspect there aren't many left. Something has been very wrong down there for a long time. We've located the dead hulk of the starship in orbit. I doubt anyone we'll run into will know who we are. We may not run into anyone, native or colonist."

"You mean they're all dead?"

"A few individuals might find the mountain valley where we'll be mining, but it's a big world and few people. We'll see more animals than intelligent life. It may be too early in the planet's history for intelligent life, or it never developed for some reason."

John imagined large beasts creeping through thick vegetation, breathing shapes covered with hide and hair, eyes filled with madness.

"I'll find them," John said.

"That's up to you," Miklos said, the tone of amusement returning to his low voice. "What are you looking for?"

John looked into the well of the screen instead of answering. The angle of view was changing rapidly. The shuttle was in the atmosphere, coming down fast. Cloudy material rushed by; filaments of white and dark wispiness gathered and were torn apart by the shuttle's passage. The view cleared to show mountains only a few kilometers below. Jagged peaks stretched to the horizon, a line of sharp rocks ripped out of the ground by some titanic plow. The shuttle dropped lower, revealing snow on the cloud-wrapped summits; green valleys nestled like moss.

"There's a pass ahead," Miklos said, "and our base is in the valley."

Slowly the shuttle passed between two mountains and entered the valley. The vertical screen went on. John looked up and saw a stream cutting through mossy vegetation as the shuttle landed.

"We can go right out," Miklos said. "Don't worry. You've been protected against possible disease. The open space above is something you're not used to, but it's not so different that you'll be disoriented."

Anastasian turned and went down the ramp leading from the observation area to the airlock area below.

John lingered before following. He looked out at the stream, the sky and clouds, the snow on the peaks, and he felt that to go out there would change him forever. Anastasian's indirect jibes had nothing to do with it.

He went down the ramp into the airlock chamber, determined to show Miklos that he was not afraid. Anastasian gave him a warm green jacket and a pair of boots. John dressed and followed him into the lock. The door slid shut behind them, and the outer door opened.

As John followed Miklos down the exit ramp, he noticed the wind blowing from his left, carrying unfamiliar smells and a sharp, watery freshness. The wind crept into the sleeves of his jacket, whispered in his ears, and slipped through his hair as if the planet were examining him before he stepped off the ramp. The suns were warm on his face, and he looked up briefly to see their massed light almost overhead. He noticed his shadow as he stepped onto the ground. The soil was soft and he could almost taste its smell. Worms and crawling things lived in it; he felt uneasy.

The shuttle hauler had landed near the stream that ran down the middle of the valley from the west. The three other shuttles had landed farther upstream. Miklos was walking toward the figures coming out of them.

The air was cool, despite the sunlight. John put his hands in his jacket pockets and started slowly toward the stream.

"Don't move around too fast until you're sure of your feet," Miklos shouted back at him, without stopping.

John ignored him, continuing toward the stream.

He came to the water and gazed into the flow. The air was chilly over the liquid. He looked at the sky, an inverted blue plain covered with clouds, hiding the stars as well as any artificial shroud.

Miklos was coming back toward him. Behind him, the three haulers suddenly seemed out of place. Anastasian stopped a few feet away and John saw that the man was grinning.

"Yes, I know," Miklos said. "If your tongue were thunder, you'd shake the planet to throw me off. I couldn't resist taking pokes at you. Forgive me. But you'll be more careful."

"Don't you have work to do?"

"First let me get you set." Miklos pointed. One of the larger hatches on the shuttle was open, and a small black flitter was rising out of the hold. When the craft was high enough, it glided toward them and settled to the ground.

"Blackfriar said you should have it."

The canopy in the center of the oval disk rose and two men got out. They were tall and dark, dressed in close-fitting green coveralls.

"Ibram and Aric are mining engineers. They're in charge of the mining camp in the range, between those peaks behind them."

John nodded in greeting. They turned and walked back toward the shuttle. As he watched them stride away, John again felt distant from their world. Their genetic heritage was continuous for more than a thousand years, combining and recombining in new and subtle ways, while he was a skipstone from the past, unchanged, living beyond his time. In one sense he was Samuel Bulero, but without his lost brother's memories. He was that exact throw of the genetic dice, the image of his other self, thrown into play again.

Clouds covered the suns. The wind died suddenly, as if the planet were holding its breath.

"It's an eclipse," Miklos said.

Slowly the light began to drain out of the world. The snow on the peaks took on a blue glow. The sky darkened as the larger sun covered its brighter companion.

"I measure a more than half drop in light," Miklos said.

John felt a breeze. He looked up at the clouds hiding the suns and saw one disk wheeling through gray ashes.

He turned to Miklos. "What's the flitter's range?"

"More than you'll need. Let me show you."

John followed him to the craft and up the footholds into the cabin under the canopy. He climbed down inside and sat next to Miklos in front of the controls.

"The automatic coordinates are set for this valley and for home, so the craft will bring you back quickly if you need it. Just press this area. But don't try leaving the planet on manual. You shouldn't have to.

This is the stick. Use it to maneuver or hover; accelerate by pressing on top. If you let go, automatic will take over. So if you can't do something yourself, let go, so the Humanity II routine can do its job for you. Any practical speed is possible in the atmosphere. You won't feel any acceleration in the gravitic field, and you won't be able to go faster than design limits. Good luck."

Suddenly Miklos was climbing out. It was becoming brighter outside as the eclipse ended. "The red is for the canopy emergency," Miklos shouted as he made his way to the ground.

Miklos stood and waved at him, but John was alone now, free to explore for as long as home was building its twin in the sky. For a moment he felt that he almost understood Blackfriar's trust in him, but the thought threatened to grow into complexity and he dismissed it. He would be the first to see the planet, before the survey teams went out to see what had happened to the colonists.

He took the stick in his hands. The canopy came down and the two seats came up even with the rim, giving him an unrestricted view. The landscape around him was slightly blue through the tinted canopy.

Imperceptibly the gravitic field enveloped the flitter, lifting it upward swiftly. A thousand meters up, he turned the craft into the southeast and started a shallow climb, moving slowly to get the feel of the controls. He pressed the speed control and the land below began to rush by in a blur. The mountains stood around him, powerless to keep him in the valley.

16. The City

Clouds covered the suns as the flitter rushed into the southeast. He climbed higher to keep their warmth on his face. At midafternoon the brighter sun eclipsed its larger companion, reducing Lea's illumination by slightly less than half. He caught a glimpse of the ocean just as the eclipse was ending. The water sparkled as if it were on fire.

A storm sat on the eastern horizon. As he flew lower over the plain, clouds obscured the suns again, turning the ocean dark blue. He turned the flitter eastward and dropped within a thousand meters of the beach, where powerful breakers crashed against the sand and rocks.

He was completely in control of the craft, sure of the freedom that it had given him. The afternoon's sights had helped him forget himself. It was enough that the planet was strange, enough that he was curious about what he might find; nothing else existed.

The small display map indicated that he was now more than two thousand kilometers southeast of the mining site. He eased the craft away from the beach, slightly toward the northeast, hoping to glimpse the large city that Miklos had mentioned.

Storm clouds now took up half the sky in front of him, gray and black cumulus illuminated by silent flashes of lightning. *The planet is alive*, he thought, *as much a system of living things as home.*

He saw the city, a dark mass of towers sitting under the thunderheads. The storm covered the whole sky as he flew closer and darted under the cloud ceiling. Rain began to hit the canopy. The lightning became more frequent, stabbing at the dark land below. The flitter cut through the rain without shaking, its gravitic field a vise holding it steady in relation to the planet's surface.

The city was a ragged black outline against the leaden sky, receiving the torrent without protest. As the lightning flashed, he imagined the city to be a huge black spider crouching ahead. He could almost reach out and touch it, though he knew that it was still kilometers away.

He turned on the outside audio for a moment and heard the wind howling; thunder rumbled and cracked and died. The craft slowed to a drift over the city.

The towers held up more than one level. Huge holes gaped at him, black pits into the lower levels. The wind whistled through the city's wounds. What suffering had been here? he wondered; the vast ruin was an external record of misery and decline.

He wafted toward a tower. A finger of lightning struck the top, hurling debris down into the ruin. He released the stick, leaving the flitter to hover while he cleared the map from the small screen to reveal the area directly below. In the moment of another flash, human figures ran across the wet surface.

He took the stick and landed the craft. For a moment he sat there, unsure of what to do next. Above him the clouds drove fast in the wind, covering the broken point of the tower. *Where have I come to? What am I doing here?* he asked himself.

As the rain lessened, he heard the aching groans of the city around him—metal grinding, slipping, breaking, and being pulled down somewhere below. It was a bass rumble in his stomach, the sound of dying things calling to him.

The canopy went up and he crawled out, making his way carefully down the footholds. The city shuddered as his feet touched the metallic surface. He took a deep breath of the damp air and looked up at the rushing clouds. Suddenly he felt a reversal of direction. For a moment the sky was down and the city was up; he was standing upside down on the outside of a round ball and at any moment the wind would blow him and the city away into the mists; but the moment passed and he steadied himself on his feet.

The rain was now a fine mist; the wind was losing its force. He wiped his face and walked toward the tower. There was a large hole in its side. Bracing himself, he looked inside; the darkness was impenetrable.

He turned and walked back toward the flitter. The sky was growing lighter as the storm passed. He looked to where the suns would be and saw only a patch of light. The wind was a cold breeze as he climbed into the flitter.

The sudden whistle of the communication link almost frightened him. He jumped into his seat and opened the line.

"John, this is Miklos. Just checking."

"I'm in the city, two thousand kilometers southeast, thirty north of the ocean. What a wreck this place is. There hasn't been a civil government here in ages. I've landed on the upper level near an old tower. There's been some rain."

"I know. Want to come home?"

"No. Is that all you called for?"

"Be careful," Miklos said. "We can die just like any living thing." He broke the connection.

John climbed out of the flitter, determined not to be frightened by Anastasian's warning. He jumped the last step and turned to look at the tower.

Three figures stood in front of the large hole. Their hair was long and wet, and they watched him with dark eyes.

Unchanged humans, he thought, *like me.*

Sunlight broke through behind him. He turned around and saw the misshapen red suns setting in the west, bathing the city in a rich vermilion light, two broken yolks spilling orange-red plasma between them. The storm was disappearing into the south.

He turned to the strangers again and took a step toward them. They drew back, but stopped.

Looking more carefully, he saw that the one in the middle was a girl. She was wearing a crude tunic of coarse material, stitched together with black cord. The tunic came down below her knees; her feet were covered with boots made from the same kind of material, animal skin of some kind. She seemed distressed by his gaze.

Both males were shorter than John. He sensed their protectiveness of the girl. He raised a hand and smiled.

Slowly the girl started to raise her hand. One of the men said something to her, but she smiled and kept her hand up. John took another step forward. Both men stepped in front of her suddenly, but she said something to them in an angry tone. She pushed between them and came forward.

She stopped and looked up at him with dark blue eyes. There was a green tint in her black hair. She pointed to the flitter behind him, at the sky, and then at him. He nodded, and it seemed to be the response she wanted. She pointed to herself and said, "Anulka."

"I'm John Bulero."

"Imjonbulero?"

"Anulka," he said, imitating her sound. She smiled at his effort, and for a moment he forgot her two companions.

Suddenly one of the men came up and tugged at her arm, while the other retreated toward the tower. Anulka pointed at the setting suns, then at the east, and at the place where she stood. He guessed that she wanted to meet here tomorrow, and nodded.

Then she turned and followed the two males. They climbed through the hole in the tower. He could go with them, he thought, but when he came and looked down into the breach, he saw her motioning for him not to follow. He watched as she made her way down the ladder on the inner wall. Her companions were lost in the darkness below her. In the moment before she disappeared, she looked up at him again, this time with a look of determination.

He tried to imagine what there might be for them at the bottom of the vertical passage. How did these people live, and what did they know about their origins? What had happened on this planet during the last thousand years? Why did the colony fail? Who was this girl? What was it like to live here? She seemed so vital and alive, as if she enjoyed her way of life. The confidence of her manner was not what he had expected.

He turned and walked toward the flitter. The suns were now flattened balloons filled with red light; the larger one was just beginning to eclipse its companion, hiding the vast spillage of plasma between them.

Around him the towers of the city cast black shadows across the blue metal surface. He took a deep breath, feeling open to the world, a sense of possibility mixed with uneasiness.

He climbed into the flitter and sat back. Stars began to appear in the darkening sky, until the east was ablaze with more than a hundred bright points of light. Lea's position just inside Praesepe gave it a night sky dominated by the stars of the cluster.

He turned down his seat and noted the food cupboard in the back of the cabin.

Can we help here? he asked himself as he lay back. *Maybe I can do something before we leave. We might be here for a decade. It would not be hard to do a few things.* He reached over and pulled a thermal blanket from its clip. Covering himself, he looked into the starry brightness overhead, feeling like an insect on a huge tabletop. The towers of the city were dark shapes around him, sentinels standing guard in the starlight.

The audio picked up noises from below, things just beneath his ability to hear; half-felt sensations came and went, moments of fear and excitement, and night sadness, all conspiring to keep him awake.

He fell asleep and woke up not knowing where he was; he was falling away from the unprotected outside of the planet, toward the suns. He opened his eyes, realizing that he was vulnerable under these quiet stars, but the thought of danger pleased him. In time he might want more than this new intensity, but for now the quickening of life's pulse was what he wanted most; for the moment he would compromise and give himself to opposing things. Unplanned opportunities waited for him on this world, and he would discover them for himself.

17. Relations

White clouds sailed across a bright blue sky. His eyes were open for an instant before he became fully awake. He lifted his head and it seemed that the suns were rising in an effort to catch up with the clouds. The city around him was silvery blue and charcoal black, reflecting sunlight, clouds, and blue sky from a million metallic scraps and shards. He lay back and closed his eyes again, lost in the strangeness of awakening here. He might have lived here all his life; home was a dream from which he had just awakened, and in a moment he would remember everything. . . .

He sat up and saw Anulka looking up at the flitter, hands on hips, smiling. She appeared older in daylight, more in control of herself.

The canopy lifted as he climbed out. In a moment he was standing in front of her.

"Hello," he said.

"Hel-lo?" she asked uncertainly, watching his face.

Feeling nervous, he looked around. Where the level was torn open, canyons opened into a daylit gloom. The metal plain of towers extended to the horizon in every direction except westward, where he saw some greenery. Slowly the colossus was toppling back into the soil; barring a major shift in the planet's crust, there would be nothing left above ground in a million years. Yet even without its power and population, the city had a kind of life.

Anulka was looking at him questioningly, but with confidence. He smiled at her. There was not much he could say until he acquired a log of their everyday words; he would have to make one trip home to compare notes at the language terminal and undergo imprinting. When he returned, it would be possible to ask her fairly complex questions. He could reach the proficiency terminals from the flitter, but imprinting required a direct link to Humanity II.

Looking at Anulka, he felt that she was older than Margaret, although he knew that this could not be true. Despite the decaying city, the planet seemed youthful, growing unplanned, turning through its seasons, renewing itself within its cocoon of air, passing through one life after another, always changing in the timeless light of its suns. The life of the planet was something different from the beggarly life of its human inhabitants. The suns were a pair of wastrels, negligent gods dissipating their power into space, energy so abundant that even a small fraction would be enough to transform this world.

Anulka turned and motioned for him to follow her. He hesitated, then walked after her to the tower. She climbed into the opening. He stepped in after her and started down the ladder. There was more light in the shaft during the day, and his eyes adjusted quickly.

He looked down and saw her growing smaller beneath his feet. He quickened his pace down the rungs.

After a while he called her name and she answered with a questioning sound.

"Nothing," he said. "I only wanted to hear your voice."

She laughed.

There was an earthy smell in the shaft, as if something were decaying at the bottom. After what seemed a long time, he stopped and looked down. He saw her dark shape moving in a circle of light. She had reached bottom and was pacing as she waited for him.

He hurried, but when he reached bottom she was already leading the way into a long tunnel. He followed, remembering when as a child he had played in the engineering labyrinth under countryside. He remembered watching mysterious adults doing their work, persons who had been old a century before his birth.

Anulka led him to another shaft. As he made his way down the rungs of the ladder, he remembered the first time he had seen the generators at home, massive objects containing the power of stars, surrounded by mushroom-like gravitics, ringed by feeders and converters. He imagined the internal fires of the planet below him and stopped; he looked down and could see no end to the shaft. *What am I doing here?* he asked himself as the possibility of danger became apparent. *I could die here and no one would ever find me.*

"Hel-looo!" she called up to him in a musical voice.

He continued, quickening his pace. It grew darker and the air became damp; he heard water running down the wall of the shaft. The rungs became sticky and cold. He slipped and landed on the next rung; the cold air hurt his lungs as he caught his breath.

He went down slowly, stepping carefully from rung to rung until his confidence returned. Reaching bottom, he stepped through a circular opening into a dimly lit room. Anulka was waiting for him. She turned and walked into another long passageway. He peered after her, saw the light at the end, and followed quickly.

They came out into daylight, onto ground covered with thick grass and tall weeds. John looked up and the sight startled him. He saw the sky through a massive breach in the city. A wedge had been cut out, exposing level after level on both sides. The area of open ground was at least two kilometers long and one kilometer wide, strewn with hundreds of pieces of glass, plastic junk, tiles, and large pieces of flooring. He looked up again at the open levels; beams and ragged platforms jutted into the air, threatening to break off and come crashing down.

Anulka was walking down a path through the weeds. He started after her. There was a fire and a tent ahead. People had once lived here, he thought, wondering how he would feel if home were somehow cut open like this city.

Anulka led him into the small camp and he recognized the two men sitting next to the fire; they had been with her on the previous night. There was a wooden table next to the tent. The surface was piled up with old books and canisters. Anulka motioned for him to sit by the fire. She went into the tent as he seated himself.

The man who came out with her was powerfully built, with white hair combed straight back and confined by a piece of cord. He wore a black shirt made of fine cloth; his pants were coarse and baggy, held up by a wide brown belt. He went to the fire and stepped into his brown boots, stomping hard on the ground to settle in. Then he turned and looked at John with a steady gaze. His face was lined and leathery, but there was someone familiar behind the dark tan.

Anulka pointed at the old giant and said, "Blakfar."

"Jonbulero," the big man said. He smiled and opened his palms toward John in greeting.

Sunlight came into the canyon, lighting up thousands of inner spaces on the right side of the cutaway, brightening the grass and weeds.

Blakfar lowered himself into the chair next to the table. "Old books," he said, pointing. "City library, starry." His Russo-Anglic was old, obviously acquired from reading. "Off-world?" he asked, pointing at the sky, then at John. It startled John to hear the language as a series of familiar sounds, triggering his imprinted memory of its structure and vocabulary.

John nodded, slowly accepting the idea that this was at least a relation of Blackfriar's, a planet-weathered descendant of the man who had brought a starship across the great dark from Tau Ceti. John felt that he had come upon an old friend who had not changed, despite the centuries and unimaginable forces working against him.

Anulka spread a blanket next to the chair, and Blakfar motioned for him to sit down. John obeyed, rehearsing the words of the simple question that he wanted Blakfar to understand.

John pointed to the city around them, at the sky. "What happened here?"

The gray-haired man nodded with a sad smile. There was pain in his eyes, the memory of pride and accomplishment, living now only in those who could stumble through the old words.

Anulka's two companions were looking at John suspiciously. *They're afraid of me*, he thought.

Blakfar said, "Skyship from Ceti . . . more than hundred fathers ago . . . we left the ship in the sky . . . we built cities . . . war, sickness . . ."

John listened, understanding the old man less and less, catching a word here and there, enough to know that the cities had been abandoned, scientific skills lost when the population declined. Those alive now were completely dependent on the natural ecology. John doubted if there could be more than a million human beings on the planet.

They had learned new ways, Blakfar said, but the line of his father lived to keep the old skills alive, for when they would be needed. Every spring he came to the city to learn what he could from the ruins. "I am Blakfar," he finished.

Throughout the chanted story, there had been a look of awe and reverence in the faces of Anulka and the two men by the fire. She sat cross-legged on the blanket with John, her gaze fixed on the old man. The flow of the sounds had affected John also, and it was a moment before he realized that Blakfar had finished.

"You . . ." Blakfar said, searching for a word.

John nodded. "I understand." Anulka smiled, as if taking pride in discovering him for the old man.

John thought of Franklyn Blackfriar. Would he want to help when he learned of this relation of his? John looked at Blakfar more closely. The family resemblance was clear, though he was certain that Blakfar was not a clone. These people could not have cloned anyone. His eyes were blue, while Frank's were gray; yet the look in them was the same, and the voices were similar.

John looked at Anulka, and she smiled at him. A long shadow cast by the western side of the canyon was creeping toward the camp. The suns went into eclipse, darkening the canyon, stripping the weeds and grass of their stolen colors.

John stood up and motioned that he had to leave. Anulka rose and took his hand. He was anxious to reach the flitter, so he could tell someone what he had found. Blakfar said something to Anulka, and she started to lead the way down the path. Then the old man got up, and John saw a look of loss come into his face. Blakfar wanted the offworlder to stay, John realized. The old man knew what it meant. Somewhere beyond the sky, the past of power and plenty was still real, not just in books and stories, but a living thing, and here was a visitor who might bring it all back. John saw that the big man was struggling to control his feelings; after all, he might never see the offworlder again. John felt a sense of duty mingling with the curiosity that had brought him to Lea.

"I'll be back, Blakfar," he said, and took the old man's hand, holding it for a moment to reassure him. When the look of desperation softened in the aged face, John turned to leave.

"Tomas Blakfar!" the old giant called after him, the syllables echoing in the ruins. John looked back and waved. The man was grinning at him. No, he would not forget the name. He turned away and almost tripped on a piece of rubble; then he felt a strange sensation in his nose and sneezed. Someone laughed behind him. He turned to see Blakfar glaring at the young men, who were still sitting by the fire. John felt their distrust as he turned to follow Anulka.

The upward climb was harder than coming down. He felt that Anulka was paying him more attention than before, even when she was not looking back to check. He was determined not to show her that he was afraid. She seemed to be laughing inwardly, as if she knew something he did not.

Finally, after what seemed an eternity of sweating and catching his breath, they climbed out of the tower at sky level. She walked ahead toward the flitter, stopped, and turned to face him, smiling as he came near. He stopped close to her and she looked at him very carefully; he found himself completely at ease as he looked back at her.

She touched his cheek with a sturdy, long-boned hand. Reaching around his neck, she pulled him to her and kissed him once quickly; then again more slowly; a third time with care and intensity. Each time he grew more familiar with her touch and more surprised by his own feelings. He drew her to him and held her, becoming aware of her odors, the taste of her mouth, the texture of her black hair, the unbroken skin of her face. She kissed him again, and the musky warmth of her excitement enveloped him. He knew that she did not bathe as he did at home, and she might be carrying disease; she was something wild from the wilderness around the city, and she was taking possession of him. As he kissed her, he could not tell whether she was his or he hers. The towers whirled and he fell down next to her on the sun-warmed metal, communicating with expression and gesture, and laughter, forgetting his fears.

"Do you want to go inside?" he asked, pointing to the flitter.

She shook her head no. He left her, climbed into the flitter, and brought out his blanket, spreading it next to her. She took off his clothes and her own, and it seemed that the warm light of the suns would be the only covering he would ever need. She lay on her back, eyes closed, and he wondered at her look of contentment.

Slowly she drew him onto her, caressing his thighs and stomach with her tanned fingers. Her breasts were firm, dark-nippled, rising and falling evenly. Her legs parted beneath him and he reached to touch her dark tangle. She opened her eyes and looked at him as he entered her, and her face darkened as the suns went into eclipse. A breeze blew across his back as he compared her vitality with Margaret's erotic calm. He was completely alive as he moved with her, open to every sound and smell of the city and surrounding land. Briefly, the eclipse at his back made him afraid, but her closed eyes calmed him.

She spent herself first, winding her legs around his back, opening her eyes and smiling at him. He looked into her, through her eyes, to the woman who welcomed him; the knot of pleasure opened within him, and he felt her strength containing him.

They struggled with each other for a long time. The brightness of the suns returned, warming them until their sweat mingled as they tried again and again to regain their first moment, and succeeded. An afternoon wind dried them with its coolness and they wrapped themselves in the blanket, exhausted. The wind whistled somewhere through broken places as he fell asleep next to her, thinking that it might have almost been a song.

It was twilight when he awoke. The suns were a red mass buried in gray cumulus on the horizon, casting a red-brown glow across the top of the city. Anulka was gone. There was a strong wind coming with the night, carrying a sea smell; the piping he had heard before was now a howl from below, as if some beast were trapped there, struggling to break free. He heard the tower creak and sat up.

Standing, he put on his coveralls, then sat down to pull on his boots. For a moment he thought that he understood Anulka and Blakfar. What better way to keep him here than through Anulka? He stood up and put on his jacket, shivering from the drop in temperature. He thought of Anulka's warmth and the luxurious curve of her hip and belly. He missed her so easily, so quickly, he noted.

He turned to the flitter and climbed inside. The call light was on. He did not remember hearing the whistle at all. Sitting down, he opened the link.

"John," Miklos said, "what happened? I had some free time, so I thought to check with you."

"I'm fine, just away from the flitter for a while. I met with some of the descendants of the colonists." John turned on the lights. The growing darkness outside caused him to think of the old starship.

"What's the matter, John?"

"Nothing." He sneezed.

"You'd better get to a medic."

"I'll take care of it." He paused. "What about the starship?"

"The crews are checking it now."

"Why didn't you tell me it would be so soon?"

"You were more interested in the planet. Anyway, some of the hulk seems to be functioning."

"Can I go up there in the flitter now?"

"I'd prefer it if you took the shuttle home first. What about your friends?"

"They're going west from here with Blakfar. I think there's a village near the mountains, in the chain that runs east, then south. They're a long way from home."

"Blakfar? What are you talking about?"

John told him what he had learned from Blakfar. "They're going to *walk* for about a month, until they get home. It seems they do this once a year."

"Why don't you help them out with the flitter?"

"I'll rejoin them after I see the starship. Expect me; I'm leaving now." He broke the link before Miklos could answer.

Turning off the cabin lights, he sat back and took the stick in his hands. The canopy came down and the flitter lifted from the dark tabletop.

He rose above the night clouds and released the craft for an automatic return to the mountain valley. The flitter rose higher, slowing the sunset for a few minutes. Below him was a gray-black plain of clouds, and the suns were a fire burning at the edge of the world. The flitter leveled off and continued northwest.

The moonless world grew dark, and stars appeared like stately marchers. He looked for home among them, then realized that it was below the horizon. He thought again of the old starship, circling in the dark through all these centuries. Anulka would miss him tomorrow, but it didn't matter. He would come to her out of the sky, in a few days at most.

He turned on the cabin lights, shutting out the view, turning the canopy into a black mirror for his thoughts. He pictured Anulka on the blanket, remembering his own uncontrollable commitment to her body. Margaret would say that he was a domesticated creature dazzled by the wild, mistaking it for something profound. It was all new, all strange to be on the outside of such a large world. He would need time to judge his experience of it; for the moment Lea was too vivid, too intense for him to believe that she wore a mask.

He turned off the cabin lights and the world expanded around him. Taking the stick, he increased the flitter's speed and altitude, until he saw the first range of mountains extending westward, massive shoulders huddling together on the planet, snowy summits aglow with starlight.

18. Macrogenesis

As the shuttle hauler approached home, John observed the progress of reproduction on the forward screen in the passenger module. Miklos had sent him up alone on the automatic return of an ore-filled hauler, refusing to let him use the flitter. During his absence, home had moved out of its two outer shells, reducing itself by about a kilometer over its entire surface. The new egg shape was a twin of the original, except for its three hundred kilometers of open interior. In time a large asteroid would be brought inside, to be mined and hollowed out; once braced at the center, it would provide additional surfaces. Construction would then proceed outward from its surface and inward from the two outer shells. The conic section which had been removed from the forward end of home would be put back to close the space of the new world.

It would take many years to complete the inner levels, but as soon as the human and cybernetic systems were active, the reproductive sequence would be essentially complete. A new macroworld would be born to roam the galaxy, to grow internally, and to reproduce itself when internal pressures became too great.

How many individuals had served macrolife across the centuries, their lives bound by decisions made for them by the founders? Many of the earliest citizens were still alive, precious resources conserved by a system which had given them a chance at immortality. Macrolife was committed to preserving its sparks of intelligence. Its body would reproduce endlessly, attempting all variations, gathering all knowledge, drawn forward by the fate of all things real; but the knowing mind, in whatever form, would always inhabit macrolife's center, seeking, understanding, while time lasted.

He thought of all the human flesh that would be born to fill the new world's innards; he saw all the cloned individuals from the past, alike yet different. The faces would be a living history; the eyes would gaze differently, the brain would perceive clearly and directly, unclouded by struggle, untroubled by defeat, living in a world where the very nature of rebellion had been altered.

Was this why he had gone down to Lea? To see the look of defeat, to taste something of its hardness, perhaps to wear its look in his own face? How could he argue with himself? The ruined city on Lea was an obvious failure. Lea, like all natural worlds, was the back country behind the growing urban culture of macrolife. He thought of roads leading into thick forests, winding around hillsides and down into hidden valleys, where suns were the only light. He was journeying back to the green worlds of humanity's beginnings, origins which were still present in every human being, and could not be denied without falsifying reality. Macrolife's break with planetary life was not a sharp historical discontinuity; it was a widening of nature, a birth from the complex organism of earth, a tumultuous but still legitimate birth. Space-time, with its endless resources and room to grow, was still nature; macrolife was a new kind of cellular life, multiplying in a realm as natural as the one inside the atmospheric membranes of planets.

Looking at the new shape, he wondered where the half-dozen other macroworlds were now and how different they were after a thousand years of isolation from one another. There were so many variables to consider. How many times had each world reproduced? How advanced were the individual propulsion systems? Advanced stardrives might have carried one or more of them out of the galaxy. A million years might pass before any two would meet. It was more likely that some kind of contact might be achieved through tachyon signaling, but that would require a more systematic scan of the heavens than had been attempted to date.

The parent, swimming before him in the black sea of space, seemed not at all diminished by its labor. As he drew nearer, it was almost impossible to see any differences in size. The offspring would inevitably strive to be faster, try to penetrate more deeply into unexplored regions, as it consolidated its rebellion.

He wondered where home would go next, and the thought convinced him that his loyalty was not with the childworld. Lea was suddenly a distant thought.

Home covered the screen and he saw the huge intake bay. Lights were on inside and he could make out the docking cradle. The hauler slipped in and came to rest.

"I came to meet you," Blackfriar said. "We're both going to see the old starship. The salvage team is about finished with it now."

John followed him down the corridor to the next dock, through a utility area, and into the open muzzle of a small shuttle. The lock closed behind them as they stepped up into the control area and sat down.

The shuttle pulled away, shrinking home until it was again visible next to its twin. The view changed automatically to show Lea.

After a short silence, Blackfriar said, "Tell me about my relative down there."

"He's a lot like you. Younger, but older . . . from another time. Maybe we'll learn more in the starship. Frank—they're all our people down there, what we would have been. . . ."

"Does he look like me?"

"Very much so. His name is Tomas. He says Blackfriar as Blakfar. He spends a part of each year exploring the ruins of a city, hoping to master what has been lost. His people are a mountain clan, he told me. It takes a lot of courage for him to leave the tribe and travel to the ruins."

"Sounds like what happens to a leader, a ship's captain, trying to keep up with the skills of his ancestors."

"A larger group lives on the plains, raiding the various mountain folk for women and supplies. I think the mountain people do some farming as well as hunting, preferring to stay in one area. Blakfar said that the nomads fight among one another, or they would have destroyed Blakfar's clan a long time ago."

"You sound as if you want to help them."

"How much can I help?"

"As much as you can convince Projex to back you."

"You already know that won't be much—why pretend? I have as much chance of support as Blakfar has in convincing his people that going to the city is a worthwhile activity."

"Yet he has people with him," Blackfriar said.

"I think the two men go for personal reasons, because they want to impress Anulka. The girl looks up to Blakfar, though. I think she believes in him, because he looks beyond the kind of life they all live."

Lea was growing larger on the screen. Blackfriar said, "Consider what you could do. You might want to unify the planet under some kind of benevolent rule. It's underpopulated, so it wouldn't be very hard to bring the scattered peoples together, if you could convince them. You might even succeed. . . . No, let me finish. Then you'd start teaching programs, engineering and medical projects. When would you leave off building a viable civilization? It might take our presence here for a half century to do it right. Do you want to be here that long? What if their particular obstacle course of development leads to a really original culture? Meddling with their development raises difficult ethical questions."

I could live here, John thought as he looked at the planet, *maybe even come to love it.*

"It's not even a growing culture," Blackfriar continued, "but one that has collapsed. I've seen it more than once."

John thought of Anulka.

"A vote of Projex might not even be enough," Blackfriar said. "It might take a referendum of our population to sanction such a chore. Working as closely as we would have to, we might even lose some of our own people—in accidents, and some would inevitably want to stay, if you're any indication."

"How about material aid?"

"That's easy to approve."

"How about accepting immigrants?"

"Possible, but you know the laws. Look, there it is!"

The ancient starship was a bright diamond riding in a high polar orbit around Lea. The vessel grew larger, until they saw a massive dumbbell attached to a sluglike hull.

"It's two kilometers long," Blackfriar said. "The thing up front is the deflector generator, to protect against hard radiation formed by collision with interstellar particles near light speed. There seem to be components missing from the ship."

"What kind of drive does it have?"

"I've been told it had two—the field-effect pusher to bring them to a significant fraction of light speed and maybe a primitive faster-than-light effect, though at near light alone they could have made it here twice during the last millennium."

The shuttle docked slowly with the modified lock.

"We can go in without suits," Blackfriar said. "Wheeler and the crew are inside. They've sealed the ship and restored the air supply. Rob didn't like drifting around in a suit when the ship was opened, but he was too curious to wait."

He's afraid for his safety, John thought.

"I'm more curious than afraid myself," Blackfriar said. "When you've lived more than a few lifetimes in safety, fear becomes a dear friend."

The log tape hissed and crackled from nearly a millennium of static deposits. A voice spoke in archaic English: ". . . One group after another is abandoning the ship, as fast as the shuttle can make the round trip. The world below is beautiful. The ship's confines have been too much for many of us. A ship is not the world home was. . . ."

"Who was he?" John asked.

"The captain, a Blackfriar," Rob Wheeler said.

John looked at Frank, who sat listening in the command station.

". . . The crew and I have the choice of taking the ship elsewhere or following the colonists down. If we go down, we'll have to take the computers and library to locate them on the surface for future generations. . . ." The ghostly hiss of time grew louder, the stifling sound of a universe which would always envy endurance.

Blackfriar floated around in his seat to look at Wheeler.

Rob nodded. "It's all gone. They ripped it out and ferried it down. But there was an accident; a portion of the ship lost pressure. We found a skeleton and some mummified bodies. We did not find the shuttle."

"Take me to this skeleton," Blackfriar said.

Frank pushed himself away from his seat and floated after Wheeler into the passageway. John followed Blackfriar into the darkness.

Wheeler led the way up the center of the vessel, the lamp on his safety helmet casting a bright beam ahead of them. John felt that he was floating upward out of a dark hole; and just as quickly he imagined that he was falling headfirst into a bottomless pit.

In a few moments the dark shapes of Frank and Rob were gone, and he saw light streaming out of the chamber they had entered. He floated to the entrance, looked inside, and pulled himself into what seemed to be an airlock antechamber.

There was an overhead light, attached with its own power pack. John noted the fresh seal on the small hole in the ship's side, but the repair had come centuries too late for the human skeleton which seemed to be attached to the gray metal of the floor.

Wheeler floated near the skull. He reached down and took the crew tag in his hand.

"This was James Blackfriar," he said, and released the tag to hover on its chain.

Blackfriar approached and floated over the bones, hands open, as if at any moment he would push himself away.

"There are others," Wheeler said.

"Could this," Blackfriar said, "have ever answered to the same name as my own?" He reached down and pulled on the chain. The skull loosened and floated up slowly, turning to stare at him. Blackfriar grasped it with both hands and placed it gently near the skeleton's shoulders. "Let's get out of here," he said. "Have the remains cleared, recorded, and destroyed."

As he followed Blackfriar and Wheeler back into the passage, John tried to forget the skeleton. Pulling himself along the way they had come, he thought of his own frame, the skull under his flesh, the brain which now tried to see death as a common event outside his world. The bones in the room behind him could not ever have been a real person; they seemed too unlikely for the fact of flesh. A man had died in that squalid corner of the starship, leaving his pitiable remains to wait there all these centuries.

Suddenly John stopped pushing himself forward on the handbar. The skeleton's frailty, and his own, astonished him. Floating in the darkness, he thought of all the accidents awaiting him if he returned to Lea.

"John!" Wheeler called from ahead. He grasped the rail and resumed his forward motion, filled with the sudden wonder of being alive at all.

19. The Village

John looked at his calloused hands. Everything in the village had to be done with the power of human hands. The endless streaming of energy from the twin suns passed, drastically diminished, into the plant and animal life of Lea, and only a pitiable portion of that natural wealth became the strength of human muscle. His palms, finger joints, and back still ached from working on the cabin he shared with Anulka. Six local months after his arrival, long after he had become conditioned to physical effort, the only sure way to get rid of his aches and pains was to move around and do more work, at least until the suns were high enough to warm him. The nights were cold; a fire heated only one side of a human body at a time; Anulka kicked him away from her at night. His only satisfaction was that he had taken a minimal amount of help from home, though it would have been easy to go and get a portable shelter instead of building a cabin.

He had grown used to bathing in the stream during the warmest part of the day. Most of the men shaved with long knives, and the rest grew beards. No one believed him about not having to shave; Anulka seemed to think that he went up to the flitter to do so, and nothing could change her mind. Those who wore beards found the disagreement very funny. Their repeated laughter at the mention of his hairlessness was growing tiresome. Hair, having children, and a certain capacity for violence were the signs of manhood here. Slowly the villagers were coming to regard him as a kind of visiting neuter, neither man nor woman, a kind of apprentice godling whose abilities seemed to be limited to flying through the air. *I'm an intruder*, he thought. *I'll never belong here because I know I can always leave.*

Below him, the village huddled inside a circle of massive rocks, thirty log cabins clinging to shelter like a colony of mushrooms, each rough-hewn tree trunk marking endless hours of hand fitting and sealing with mud. Trees and bushes pushed up between the rocks, adding a barrier of foliage. Fall would curl the triangular leaves into stiff rolls filled with sweet paste; these, together with meat stored in the smokehouse and the bread bush nuts, would provide enough food to get through winter. The villagers took great pride and comfort in this achievement; the last few winters had killed a third of the smaller children and half the older people.

He sat down with his feet over the edge of the huge flat rock, with the mountains at his back. The tree-clad foothills fell away from him toward the distant plains. Southeast across the dusty grassland lay the city where he had met Anulka more than six months before. Soon it would be most of a year since his world had entered Lea's sunspace to reproduce.

The suns eclipsed, marking noon; some of the late summer heat drained from the world. The lessening of light made him feel naked on the rock. Remembering the night, he shivered in the fur jacket which he wore over his coveralls; the thought of winter made him grateful for the rock's warmth.

The brute facts of life on Lea had created a nervous pressure in him, every small detail triggering a reaction. The fur jacket had belonged to Anulka's father; three of her brothers and one sister had died at birth; in a population of nearly two hundred, there were only a dozen children between the ages of five and ten; the eyes of children already held the look of their parents' acceptance of a world that would never change. One day he had wanted to take all the children home in the flitter, just to see the change in them after a few months of life offplanet.

Every couple in the village had come to examine the cabin when he had finished it; after the visits he had learned that he and Anulka were husband and wife, and the building and visiting had been the ceremony. Anulka's mother came to clean and cook during the day, leaving at night for her own cabin two doors away.

Time passed with a slow effort here, as if preparing to stop; winter would be a time of dead thoughts, a waiting for time to begin again. The ruined city was more than two weeks away; a month was a long time when measured by walking. It seemed an age since he had plucked Anulka from the plain.

Her future husband, Jerad, and her brother Konro had resented the flitter. After some coaxing, Anulka, Blakfar, and Konro had accepted the lift to the village; Jerad, the husband selected for Anulka by her dead father, had refused. A week after the flitter's arrival, Jerad had come into the village, cursing and kicking children out of his way. By then Anulka's mother had accepted her daughter's new choice, helped by Blakfar's approval.

Jerad had left, vowing that he would join the plains people rather than live with the humiliating loss of what was his by family promise; with Anulka's father dead, there was no one willing to enforce the old agreement or even to confirm that it had been made. No one would risk angering the man from beyond the sky; acceptance of him would ensure that he would help the village and not its enemies. John wondered if he would have felt better if Jerad had attacked him physically; clearly, Jerad had been afraid to fight with an offworlder.

I can leave, John thought, facing again the certainty that he would leave, that even a few years here would not be a life he could accept. He felt guilty about Jerad, whose commitment to Anulka would have involved the whole of his short life. *For me it's a stop on the way.* He had disrupted an older system for the preservation of life, one in which nature did not trust its intelligent organisms to do the work of life. Living bodies were joined through force or pleasurable attraction, and one body became the incubator for the new life; the mixing of genetic material was left to chance and the adaptive pressures of the environment. Here there was no real choice, except one between life and death; life always meant slavery.

He remembered the clustering of shy human forms around the

flitter on the day of his arrival, the stench of wastes and unwashed bodies, Anulka's mother, a toothless hag at less than twice her daughter's age, people without arms, legs, or eyes. It had shaken him to calculate that Anulka's mother was not much older than he was. Someone had died in the night four days after his arrival, had stopped breathing, had stopped thinking and dreaming in the next cabin. It had seemed impossible that such a thing could happen.

The suns had been a pyre in the noon sky, brothers to the bright fire consuming the body of Jerad's father. The mourners stood with bare heads bowed, hands clasped neighbor to neighbor in a ring of the living, men and women wrinkle-worn by a world where the look of youth passed quickly from the human face.

He noticed that the dead man's name was routinely avoided after the funeral. The ashes from the fire were spread into the dirt of the square by the old people. A visitor had come into the village and had left with a life. There was comfort in the sameness of hospitality toward death. . . .

The suns drifted apart, brightening the world and warming his face. His body had waited for the now familiar event; but no amount of time would free him of the vague uneasiness he felt before natural processes. At home everything was under intelligent control of one kind or another; human will prevailed. Here it was easy to imagine that some demented god ruled the visible world; proud, wasteful, and cruel, he drove all nature toward some distant shore of time, uncaring of the cost.

I will have only one chance to leave, when my world leaves this system. There was terror in the thought. Lea would be visited again, eventually; but was he prepared to wait that long—decades, a century? How long could he live without the med systems of home? If he stayed, he would have to persuade Projex to build a medical education station, as much for himself as for the villagers. "A little help is socially dangerous," Frank Blackfriar had said. "You'll have to spend time to make things work properly. Are you ready to do that? Go see for yourself what it's like on a planet—you'll find out who you really are."

John took a deep breath, tasting the smell of dusty sod grass coming from the plains with a wind that promised winter, mingling with the fresh green of the foothills. Nature was often an enemy here, at its best a powerful friend who still had to be watched. At home, planetary nature was something to be cared for, a bit of mind's past preserved for aesthetic reasons and deeply buried needs; uncontrolled nature was galactic space, the wheel of suns, gas, and debris onto whose scale of size and timelessness macrolife had recently entered.

He looked down at the winding trail that ascended to the rock and saw Anulka coming toward him. She glanced up, her blue eyes wide, black hair whipping in the rising wind. She walked with the grace of an animal, boots pushing firmly against the well-worn trail. Her coarse black body shirt was drawn together at the waist by a leather strap. He knew every muscle under that shirt, every detail of skin; he knew her smells and how she tasted when they kissed. She was as much a part of the landscape as the trees gripping the hills with their roots, the four-footed creatures prowling the forests and plains, the winged things riding the wind, mocking the high mountains. *I don't know her at all*, he told himself.

Her flesh had been nourished by the protein of living things, unlike his own, which had grown on perfect foods. His body had not struggled with the poisons of plant and animal, wearing out its systems transforming foreign materials into usable structures. All the foods of home were easily assimilated; his body would never have to work very hard and would last much longer than a natural worlder's, even without rejuvenation.

Anulka turned her face away from the wind and passed out of his sight behind a series of massive outcroppings. He would not see her until she came up behind him on the rock. He remembered how sick he had been after eating the roast meat she had prepared after his arrival. She had been horrified at his explanation, forcing him to invent a much simpler one for her benefit. The idea of chemical identity between the foodstuffs and flesh of macroworlders would have been interpreted by her as cannibalism.

Blackfriar had sent down a half year's provisions, which now covered one wall of the cabin. Anulka would look at the packages occasionally, but she would never taste anything; there was no way to dispel her idea that his food would make her ill because her food had affected him.

He heard her coming up the trail just behind the rock. He got to his feet and walked back to the center of the flat area. She came up to him and put her arms around his waist, pressing her face into the fur of his jacket.

"You will be going soon," she said without raising her head. The sounds of her earth-derived language seemed to vibrate against a black backdrop, giving her words the finality of a pronouncement. When he did not answer, she squeezed him roughly. Finally she let go and asked, "Why am I not with child?" She stepped back and looked up at him, humiliating him with her gaze. "You are preventing this from happening," she said. "I can feel it. There is so much you can do—this must be easy." He looked away from her eyes.

She put her fists on her hips and continued. "A child would bring us honor in the village, and if you left I would still have something. I gave up Jerad for you. If you leave and do not take me with you, I will be disgraced."

He looked into her face and saw fear. How could he leave her if she had a child? Could he take them both home with him? Suddenly he felt the power of her demand, its complete tyranny, the rigidity of the method that formed their relationship not for love or pleasure, but to ensure the transmittal of genetic information.

But there was no child, and never would be unless he chose; Anulka sensed that, and it made her angry because it threatened her position in the village. How could he explain to her? There could be no children for him unless he decided to become a parent-teacher, or exemplar, dedicated to raising persons different from himself. Here children were instruments of personal power and physical necessity; there could be no future without them, but they were born only to live the past.

Anulka smiled, took his hands, and sat down, forcing him to kneel; she let go and pulled the front of her loose tunic above her waist. *Dark shapes had entered the cabin during his first night with her, smiling hags leaning over to cover them with animal skins.* Anulka was pulling him down on top of her. She wants me to stay forever, he thought. *He had dreamed of his skeleton lying next to hers on the hot plain. He had tried to embrace her, but there was no flesh to move his arms.* He pulled free and staggered to his feet.

Anulka stood up suddenly, made a fist, and struck him across the face. He bit his tongue involuntarily. She raised her arms to guard against his reprisal, a pathetic animal waiting for the inevitable. He stepped back to show that he would not hit her.

She dropped her arms and spat at him. "You're a coward, afraid even to hit a woman!"

How little she thinks of herself. She was the physical focus for his guilt about dirtworlds. He had wanted to help through her, but to be effective he would always have to stand apart. Anulka had worked to draw him into the life of this world, but he knew now that he was not capable of giving that much of himself away. How could he explain his disappointment to her? How could he blame her for not being what he had wanted her to be? He had disappointed her completely, humiliating her in the eyes of the village.

She turned and marched away. He thought of those his own age and the new world they were building. He thought of the bones in the old starship. Lea had not grown to justify the sacrifice of those who had crossed space to settle here.

He watched Anulka going back down the path toward the village. He might have made love to her; it might have been kinder.

He walked to the boulder's edge, scrambled down the dirt incline, and walked into the forest, following the uphill path toward the clearing where he kept the flitter. He needed a talk with Blackfriar. Anulka had resented his coming up here to draw food from the supply dump, so he had ferried much of what he needed down to the cabin; but she was still suspicious of his going to talk with voices in the sky.

Once she had asked him if he had grown or killed the food he ate. She had been disappointed in his description of a food factory. She would have liked visions of a strange land on the other side of the sky, a geography of beasts and jungles and hunters riding steeds as tall as mountains. More than anything she wished for powerful figures who could redeem the harshness of her life. *We have solved the problems of planet life*, he thought, *only to become incomprehensible to those still living with those problems.*

He was sweating when he stepped into the clearing. The flitter sat in the grassy center next to a pile of supply crates, a black beetle bathing in a pool of sunlight rimmed by dark forest. He stopped to catch his breath, aware of the tanned roughness of his face, the dryness in his throat, and the weariness in his muscles. The planet was changing him, pulling him back into the past, where he could live only if he imported many of the features of his own world; anything less would be suicide.

He took a deep pull of the cool, clean air and looked up. The portion of open sky showed a mountain sparring with a wayward cloud drifting in to obscure the snowy summit.

He walked to the flitter and stepped into the boarding footholds. The canopy slid up and he climbed inside, settling into a familiar bit of home, shutting out Lea's sounds as the lift brought the bubble down and the dais of twin seats rose into the canopy. The craft sat on a slant and he was looking into the trees left of the path.

He tried to relax. Here the temperature was constant, the air free of dust and living things, and the light was filtered to a pleasant shade of blue; the silence was a space in which to think. *I can leave right now*, he thought. In a few moments he could reduce all this land to a few wrinkles in the vertical viewer, then shrink the planet into a glowing mote drifting in darkness. What would Anulka be then? A microbe yearning to reproduce?

John hesitated, unhappy with his thoughts, sad at their severity. At his left, the empty seat sat like a reproachful companion. *I need more reason to go*, he thought, *or a more attractive excuse.*

He touched his thumb to the laserlink, hoping that Frank would answer on his personal channel. As he waited he tried to resolve that he would ignore easy excuses and follow a reasonable path, whichever way it led.

"Blackfriar."

"Frank . . ."

"What's up, exile?"

"I needed to talk."

"Go ahead; I'm listening."

"I don't know if I can deal with life here any more."

"Why not?"

"I've gotten too involved, maybe."

"Leave, then."

"I can't, Frank, I just can't."

"To stay must mean that you have no doubts, and that you're ready to give everything."

"There must be more we can do. . . ."

"You're not being honest. What you want is for us to do something without abandoning you here. Look, have you tried to get others interested?"

"No. You know they're busy with their own world."

"Tell me what you think I can do. In my position I'm just a switch-

board. Sure, Humanity II tells us what is workable, but people make
all kinds of demands and I try to juggle them. You have no idea what
we're going through with the new world. It's an orderly rebellion,
that's what it is, but we're still having a lot of politics and bitterness
over how they're going to do things differently."

"I want Anulka with me, maybe some of the children here."

"Well—one or two people, that's up to you. You know the place to
find out about procedures. Just tap the memory."

"Frank, I don't even know how to talk about all this—is there
something wrong with me?"

"Not at all. Listen to me—you're struggling with the idea of how
to attach an underdeveloped culture to a more advanced one, in this
case a fallen culture. It's a good impulse. It gives you a sense of commitment, a sense of something to stand up for. Ages ago war drew
the same impulses from people, bringing out their courage, loyalty,
and constructive intelligence, as well as their sense of altruism, dis-
cipline, and sacrifice—not always to a good end, but bravery is real
even if the end is without value. It was important for people to have
their way against an enemy, against nature, against severe limits—
it's the mark of human free will. Later, moral equivalents for war
became possible."

"What does this have to do with me?"

"It's what you're looking for, but the process of attachment makes
a culture our dependent, an annexation, even if we limit our help to
material things. It's subtle, the way things go—a social dynamic is set
in motion. The backward culture knows it's low man and can't do
much about it."

"But in time . . ."

"Yes. In time the culture would assert itself. Or would it? We would
have to give more than material goods. Attitudes and outlooks go with
the use of things, whole sciences and technologies, everything that we
are. Right now we're not in the business of guiding planetary histories.

Usually it's best to avoid contact with young or backward cultures. Let them rise and bud away from their planetary surface by themselves."

"But we're related to these people, Frank."

The voice at the other end sighed. "That's why we permitted contact here, knowing that there would not be too much shock. We can leave some help, most of it in the form of usable information that will help later on. But listen—if you take Anulka you'll leave behind a lot of resentment."

"She wants me, Frank."

"Does she? Or escape from her life? Think again. She would become someone else if you extended her life and gave her an education. You would be her exemplar, teaching her to stand without you. After a quarter of a century she might understand enough to dislike your having made a project of her."

"What else can I do?"

"Well, consider that there is already at work on Lea a native dynamic of scarcity and intelligent response to problems—a human creativity that will one day create its own better circumstances."

"Or perish. You're saying it's good for them."

"Intelligence needs challenges. If you do things for a child, you make it weak, denying it the chance to grow by coming to grips with its environment in a give-and-take."

"Does it have to be a struggle?"

"It's all we know. John, if you want to stay and can get others to help you, we'll equip a base with all you need for a major project. We're not dogmatic. You might succeed—but it must be what you want, really want after careful thought. Or if you want to spend a lifetime with Anulka, we'll take her in, if that's what you decide. But do you see that Anulka is the large problem written small?"

"Blakfar is yourself along a different road."

"I know, I know—do you suppose I haven't thought about it?" Blackfriar was silent for a moment. "Consider: we have a free society, but

we can't say what each individual should do with personal freedom or
that each individual will be a success. The same goes for societies. Ignorance, incompetence, frustration, and helplessness—these are basics that
could only be eliminated by an omnipotent planner. Then you would no
longer have intelligent beings as we know them, finite and imperfect, or
a universe in process. The problems we've solved in our way of life are
old ones, easily recognized. What do we contribute to the future? We
reproduce our framework of freedom, a social container that guarantees
the material support of free life. We can expect certain duties from our
citizens, but it is not our business to dictate anything else."

"What do you think I should do, Frank?"

"Choose among your alternatives."

"Don't avoid my question."

"After all I've said, you want me to tell you what to do. I won't do
that. Go ahead, build a world-saving project here, build a macroworld
to circle Lea as a guardian of development. As a private citizen I have
the option to join your project, but as a planner I must remain neutral.
As a planner I don't try to mold the creative impulses of macroworlders, as the planetary civilizations of earth tried to do with each
new generation. My job is to preserve the frame, guarding it from
destruction. One day you will become a planner, but it will not be for
yourself, but to keep macroworlders free within their context, because
only that context makes macrolife work. My foresight and that of the
other planners must not strait-jacket the future. Foresight must always
limit itself to making creative novelty possible, to keep things open.
You seem to want an authoritarian context. . . ."

"Frank, these people are us, not some alien hominid culture!"

"As it happens, an alien species might have been exterminated
when the colony starship first appeared over Lea. From examining the
ship, we know that its weapons systems were powerful enough to clear
whole areas of life. Faced with nowhere to go, the colonists might have
committed genocide."

"That was a long time ago, if it happened. I want to help these people, Frank."

Blackfriar answered after a longer silence. "The reality would fall far short of your ideals for a long time. Doing good has no end."

"Maybe the new world would back me?"

"Ask them. There is one thing I could approve, though."

"What is it?"

"The village population is so small that we could remove them and distribute them here and on the new world. We would be saving the lives of countless unborn. A large planetary population will suffer extraordinary numbers of dead from natural catastrophes —earthquakes, electrical storms, floods, tornadoes, high winds, diseases. Actual figures from old earth are appalling. Sooner or later planet dwellers develop a crude technical civilization that kills even more people, and finally limits to growth lead to a final conflict. If the culture is lucky, it creates space settlements, opens the resources of its sunspace, and takes the pressure off the natural environment."

"All roads lead to us—that's what you're saying."

"It does become a life-and-death choice, a matter of demonstrable history. Villages and cities were rudimentary forms of macrolife, where people gathered to defy the authority of nature's gods. Commerce, art, science, and technology were born in urban areas, and it was there that human intelligence saw that the world might be remade. An old earth writer once said that the book of life is nothing more than man's war with nature, the battle between jungle and village. We say that the book of macrolife is the conflict between macroforms and natural planets. But the difference is that we don't want a conflict. We want to be free of the claims of planet dwellers, to develop in our own way. We don't want to be philanthropists or destroyers of natural worlds, which belong to their peoples, human or alien."

"How often have we observed all this to be true? Only on old earth and a few colonies. Have we seen an alien culture, macroform or planetbound?"

"No. But the view is built on the fact of diminishing energy and resources on planets. The culture must leave the surface or die, even if its macrolife does not become mobile, as we have done, but circles its sun."

"Could we take the entire village off Lea?"

"It would be your project. I think you could handle it with a minimum of help, because you won't get much interest, I think. How many are there?"

"About two hundred people." Suddenly John felt hopeful.

"We could isolate that number easily," Blackfriar said, "give them a small town in the core, something like what they have now."

He remembered flying in the green hollow, soaring alone, wondering about planets and suns and surfaces that curved the other way.

"What do you think?" Blackfriar asked.

"I don't know. I'll call you again after I think about it some more. Thanks for talking, Frank."

"Don't wait too long, and come back for a medical as often as you can."

"I feel fine."

Blackfriar broke the link.

Alone again, John sat back and took a deep breath. He thought of a small boy hiking around the hollow, lying in the tall grass next to a stream that emptied into a lake in the sky. Sita Kagami used to swim in the lake on the days he hiked to the shore, and he would wait for her to come out of the water so that he could see how beautiful she was in the nude. She would leave the water and lie down on the grass without paying attention to him. He had been five and she six, and he had been in love with her for a long while. Where was she now? Probably helping to build the new world. Where was his childhood exemplar, Nyl Tassos the biologist, who designed butterflies and nursed them into life? He had stopped seeing him after Margaret had come for him and he had made friends with Rob Wheeler. Why had Tassos decided to reproduce a Bulero? Was his sense of aesthetics outraged by the lack of a living example? John tried to think back to his earliest memories and startled himself again with the fact of self-awareness.

He looked up through the canopy. A cloud now covered the visible peak, suggesting a moored skyship. He leaned back and closed his eyes. *Anulka, Anulka,* he called within himself, *why could you not have been what I wanted?* She came up to him again in the pale realm of memory and put her arms around his neck, pulling his lips to hers. Then she pushed him backward onto the soft mat and fell on top of him, laughing at his look of surprise. Her mother's cabin smelled of old wood and human sweat, and the only light came through an open square in the roof. They struggled for a time with their clothes. The smell of her had been strange for a moment, but her smile renewed his desire. Free of their clothes, he rolled on top of her. She was pliant as he entered her, and she locked her legs around his waist and held him. Her eyes were closed as he worked with her. He looked around at the bare earth, the mud in the walls, the bits of bark still clinging to the crudely cut logs. Near the back wall, a small crablike creature was crawling into a hole. He closed his eyes and held Anulka fiercely. A bit of evening air coming in from above had stirred on his bare back. . . .

He opened his eyes and sat up in the flitter. Above, he saw the cloud pushing off from the peak with a new wind. The afternoon eclipse was in progress. He raised the canopy and heard the world whispering angrily at the loss of light. The breeze fluttered the leaves, adding a rustle to the whisper, and the smells of living and dying things seemed suddenly to be the signs of madness. John climbed from the flitter and started down the path toward the rock that overlooked the village.

Coming out of the trees, he scrambled up the incline and stepped back onto the outcropping, knowing full well that he was avoiding a return to the village. As he crept to the edge, he saw thick smoke coming up from the settlement. Far-off cries struggled to be heard as the wind whipped the smoke and hid his view of the dirt center.

Turning, he made his way to the path and ran downhill, knowing that it would be at least fifteen minutes before he reached the village on the winding trail; but he decided against returning to the flitter, which would have put him into the village in minutes if he had been in the clearing.

Fear stiffened his running. Had one of the houses caught fire? Which house was burning? The world melted away as he thought of losing Anulka, and distance became the only reality.

Finally he was running across level ground toward the trees and rocks. Branches brushed against him and he burst into the village. Horsemen were setting torches to dwellings. Others were sacking the smokehouse and food stores. Loud cries mingled with the roar of fire. The raiders were large, bearded plainsmen clad in thick animal skins. A group of nervous horses was churning up a dust cloud, as the men loaded the animals with spoils. The midafternoon suns, just coming out of eclipse, cast yellow beams through the dust.

John heard a horse grunt and watched as the rider and animal came toward him. The mounted invader was swinging a long piece of leather with rocks tied to the ends. The whistling stones caught John in the chest, throwing him on his back. Stunned, he watched a number of riders dismount to kick in the door of a cabin where several villagers were making a stand.

Struggling to his feet, John staggered through the dust toward his own cabin. His chest ached as he breathed; he tasted blood and spat it out. As he circled around the horses, he saw Anulka run out, clutching her ripped body shirt. A man rushed out after her, swinging a club.

John tripped over a stone and fell on his face. Blood and dust mixed in his mouth. When he looked up, the bearlike figure was clubbing Anulka across the back of her head as she attempted to crawl away on her belly. The man dropped the club and drew his knife. John tried to call out, but the man turned her over and cut her throat.

John strove to get up, but his hands failed and he fell forward. The pain in his chest was molten metal slipping into his stomach. He was lying with his back against the sky and the mass of the entire planet came into his open arms, crushing him into oblivion as he tried to embrace it.

When he opened his eyes, the pain in his chest and stomach was duller, and he knew that the shock of the blow had been worse than the actual damage. He was still lying face down in the dust. Turning his head to rest on one cheek, he saw Anulka. The village seemed peaceful, except for the settling dust and the crackle of burning logs; then he noticed the smell of burning flesh mixing with that of charred wood.

Suddenly he felt whip blows on his back. He turned over and saw Anulka's mother, a bloodied specter raising a wooden rod to strike him. Her lips were shut tight; her face was bruised and covered with dust. Every other blow missed and struck the ground next to him. "What are you doing?" he managed to whisper. She raised the stick again and collapsed onto him. For a moment he watched her face; her eyes were wide open and bloodshot, filled with reproach. Her lips moved but no sound came out; in a moment she was looking past him into some horrible abyss. A bit of saliva ran from her mouth into the dirt as he pushed her away.

He lay back and stared at the sky, trying to forget the old woman's face, the terrible sense of loss he had seen in it. All her past was gone, and all her future. She would never see Anulka's children; a passing of eternity would not be enough to change the fact. Home had always existed for him, and there were others elsewhere in the galaxy. He imagined what it would be like if even one macroworld died.

After a while he sat up and looked toward Anulka. She lay dead in the warm afternoon, sunlight bright on her bloody head. He could just see the red wound under her chin. There was a pool of drying blood next to her skull.

"John!" a voice shouted, breaking.

He turned and saw Tomas Blakfar writhing on the ground a dozen meters away. John climbed to his feet and staggered toward him, falling on his knees next to the old man.

"You should have been here to protect her," Blakfar whispered loudly. "You could have helped with your flier." The old man coughed. John noticed wounds in his chest and head. Blakfar was lying in his own blood, much of it already soaked up by the dusty ground.

"I'll get the flitter and take you to one of the med units at the mining sites."

"I'll be dead before you get back."

"I'll try anyway."

Blakfar grabbed his wrist.

"I'm going, lie still," John said. He felt tears pushing out of his eyes, more for Blakfar than for Anulka. The realization surprised him, making him angry.

"Don't let me die alone," Blakfar said, gasping.

"I won't, I won't."

"Save some of the children . . . if they live."

"I will, I will," John said, looking around.

The old man closed his eyes as John held his hand. There was still a pulse, but he had lost consciousness.

John forced himself to stand up. If he could reach the flitter, there might still be time to save Blakfar's life. He looked to Anulka, knowing that he could not approach her body; if her eyes were open, he would never be able to forget them.

He lifted the flitter out of the clearing. Somehow his body was still running up the long trail, which seemed to grow longer with each stride he took. He felt that his heart would burst before he reached the clearing. The pain in his chest and stomach was coming back, pouring now into his arms and legs; at any moment the molten liquid would solidify, freezing his motion.

He swooped down toward the village, bringing the craft to a hover over the circle of rocks, then setting down near Blakfar.

Climbing out quickly, he reached the old man and felt his pulse. The hand was cold, but there was still a pulse. Blakfar opened his eyes as the pulse died and the head fell sideways. John noticed the caked blood in the old man's hair.

John rushed back to the flitter and climbed inside. Clumsily he thumbed Frank Blackfriar's channel.

There was no answer.

He tried Miklos.

"Yes?" a voice asked after a few moments.

John opened his mouth to speak, but his throat was so dry that nothing came out. He swallowed hard and tried again.

"Miklos—there's been a massacre here. I think most of the village is dead. Can we get a freezer down here fast?"

"For how many, John?"

"Two people," he said, feeling the injustice immediately.

"If they have massive head wounds of any kind, we won't do it."

"Why not?"

"Too hard to repair. They come out different people and with too many functional problems. We couldn't get anyone there in less than two hours anyway. Are they dead now?"

"Yes," John said, the anger rising inside him.

"Forget it."

"Damn you, get them over here!"

"John, it's too late. We can't get approval fast enough. There are head wounds, right?"

"We can worry about that later." Time was running away from him and there was nothing he could do to grasp it.

"Come home," Miklos said softly.

John broke off the link. He looked out through the canopy at the burning buildings, most of them smoldering now, hiding the bodies among the charred timbers. Blakfar and Anulka seemed lonely lying so far apart in the bright sunlight.

Suddenly he reached for the manual stick and lifted the flitter straight up for a thousand feet, shrinking the village to a messy patch of stones, smoke, and barren ground surrounded by greenery.

He looked around, hoping for a glimpse of the retreating raiders. Beyond the green edge he saw the plain where the horsemen were certain to emerge. Dropping the craft to treetop level, he moved quickly toward the open country.

His thoughts raced, a thousand whispering voices merging into a babble. Then he was over the plain, an endless desolation of flat grassland stretching skyward, stirred into waves by a dry wind. He stopped his forward rush, turned the craft around, and settled on the grass.

Resting his face in his hands, he leaned forward, watching the treeline. He closed his eyes for a moment. The voices became sparks of light in his brain, threatening to coalesce into an angry mass of power.

He sat up. The horses were out of the trees, hoofs flying as the riders forced the animals forward. Together men and beasts made a larger creature, a giant insect body of brown and black dotted with human faces.

He waited until they were well into the open. Lifting the flitter, he moved it forward at a height of two meters, aiming for the center of the multilegged monster, flattening the grass before him as he increased speed.

The riders were clearly visible now, bearded men in thick animal skins driving their horses mercilessly. The tethered packhorses were overloaded with stolen provisions.

They're not human, John thought. *I'm killing a dangerous animal.* At two hundred kilometers per hour, he had enough speed to cut through the center without slowing. He gripped the stick with both hands as the craft closed. *What am I doing?* He wanted to close his eyes, but the skin of his face and scalp seemed to be stretched tightly around his skull, forcing his eyes to stay open. Faces filled his view, white patches with eyes, attached to a moving mass of flesh. He felt a thud, and another, and two more before he was rushing at the trees. Suddenly he felt the lash marks Anulka's mother had left on his back. Pulling the stick back, he climbed above the forest and circled for another run. The creature had split in two, leaving the center to riderless horses; mercifully, the ocean of grass had swallowed the disfigured dead.

Enough. He aimed for the riders at his right, accelerating until speed pulled clear perception into a blur at his sides. His heart was a cold, beating stone as he sped forward to shatter flesh. He looked up beyond the trees, farther to the lower hills, past the treeline to the mountain ridges, toward wall after wall of rock and snow; and it seemed that no amount of force would ever be enough to carry a man over the top. Two thuds registered as constrictions in his stomach. He pulled the stick back, circled again over the trees, and drifted back toward the riders.

The scattered survivors were moving slowly. John dropped down and flitted after a group of three still heading due east. *Enough, leave them.* He let the craft strike two blows in one sweep and turned his head in time to see the third steed stumble and throw the rider forward. The figure hit the ground and lay still, becoming small as the flitter rushed away.

He circled for a closer look. The man was crawling as John landed a dozen meters away. Raising the canopy, he climbed out into a dry wind and heard labored breathing. He walked up to the figure and stopped. The man fell from all fours onto his side and stared at him. It was Jerad.

"I did not want her killed!" He held his hand out to keep John away. "I did not know there would be so much killing. I could not stop it."

"You led them here to take our food!"

"They took me in when I had no place to go."

"The whole village!" John heard himself shout over the wind. Jerad rolled over onto his back. His brown eyes stared upward, tear-filled from dust and pain. "You could have left them their lives. It would have cost you nothing to do that!"

"It was a favor, they said, to kill them after we took the food. The village would not get through the winter."

"I would have gotten them through!" John shouted.

Jerad was silent, looking at the sky. John stepped up to his head and kicked it as if it were a ball, feeling the temple give way. Jerad's mouth opened and his throat gurgled. John kicked again.

He looked east and saw horses on the horizon. The riderless beasts were following the survivors. The suns started their late afternoon eclipse, fading one of his two shadows from the ground. He coughed from the dust in his throat, then turned and walked back to the flitter. He climbed under the canopy, shutting out the wind, leaving only the small voices in his head.

At twilight the twin suns pulled at each other with arms of fire. The world's deep blue was filling with stars; the reds and yellows of the sinking suns made a fresh wound in the western sky, spilling a bloody light onto the blue-white glacier below the peaks.

Anulka, Anulka, he called down into his bottomless, newly opened self, *I killed you. My coming made Jerad an exile. I caused his bitterness and your death, and I killed him and so many others I never knew. . . .*

He had come here hoping to be helpful. The village was avenged—except there was no village now, no community that he might have raised into something better.

Fire-linked, the suns touched the mountains, settling entwined into the quenching cold of snow and stone. In a moment the primaries were only a wash of light behind the range, leaving the sky to the growing light of the great cluster.

The night brightened and began to burn, hurling spears of starlight through the flitter's canopy.

Blakfar, Anulka, forgive me.

Are you leaving us? the small voices asked.

Yes, John said silently, looking up into the cold starlight.

And suddenly he was alone again. The voices were still, as if they had forgiven him; he lifted his hands to his face and wept.

20. Home

He was asleep on the rock, on a patch of soft moss; the warming sun filtered through his eyelids as the noon eclipse ended. The wind was gentle, cooling him just enough for comfort. He opened his eyes, remembering that Anulka was dead and he had come home. The silence was perfect in the apartment he had shared with Margaret. His eyes followed the ceiling as it curved gently down into a wall. Daylight spilled into the room through the one-way window at his right. Lea was far away as he floated in the room's blue hues. The reduced gravity of the bed, the lack of blankets and clothing, seemed strange, but his sleep had been deep and long, giving the kind of rest he had been without for months.

No one had come to see him since his return, and he did not want to see anyone. He stretched and thought of the Humanity II intelligences, who knew everything that had ever been known. He thought of Wheeler, whose link-extended mind roamed through a universe of superconducting patterns. Would life be so much different with a link? Would he be able to pass the tests of health and sanity to be granted a license? How much of humankind's collective wisdom would it take to teach him to live with murder? The pressure of the question forced him to consider alternatives. He had been living only a small part of human life, the life that had been the rule in the past, the life that can be only one thing at a time, that moves outward to grasp all things and fails, craving infinity as it falls back into finitude. The mode of consciousness bestowed by the link was also power over the limits of one's self, Wheeler had once told him; through it a macroworlder was also every human being who had ever recorded a feeling, thought, or discovery. One could never think all the information in the memory bank all at once, but it was available as one desired it, keeping faith with the past. In a sense it was no different from biological memory, which also had to be summoned a piece at a time; and like individual memory, the link formed a perceived background, tacitly altering one's sense of identity. The link made an individual a full citizen, a complete participant; to use the link critically was all of education. *I've been alone for so long, I don't want to be myself any more.* The thought of Lea tightened his stomach. His body moved with the memory of death, twitching as he saw himself breaking the bodies of the horsemen, faceless except for Jerad, all forever dead.

He had thrown his clothes from Lea into the recycler, where nothing was wasted. Hands had stitched the garments together with bone needle and leather thread, hands now still beneath the ground. The clothes had seemed such pitiable things lying on the floor of the bathroom.

He got up from the bed and went to the window. From the first floor, he could see people walking among the trees. The widely spaced columns stood like sentries over the scene, hundred-story pillars holding the levels apart as far as the eye could see. Irregularly shaped daylight screens covered the sky, looking like clouds of bright white light. The blue sky itself, the underside of the next level, seemed very near when he looked at it, but the light screens appeared to be portals into an infinity of white space. All this, he thought, is also the work of human hands, fingers and thumb made powerful by the brain's dreams.

He remembered that he had promised himself that he would never come back to this apartment, that he would never see Margaret again. *Anulka, you might have liked it here. I would have brought you.* He knew that it would have taken her a long time to adjust, to learn, and by then they might not have been together; but he was thinking of how it would have been for her, and her alone, and it would have been better than dying.

Suddenly he remembered his dream. He was with Jerad on the glacier, rolling down toward the edge with his hands around the other's throat. The sky looked as if someone had painted it a shade of blue too dark; the mountains looked too sharp, as if focused through a distorting lens. Jerad's neck was hot in his hands, the blood pulsing desperately into the dirtworlder's head. John squeezed harder as Jerad held him in a hug. Over and over they turned on the hard-pack ice, and still the final swift drop into a crevass did not come. *I wanted to kill him. I would have left him on the glacier to die. I wanted to kill him, but I wanted him to take me with him.* He thought of his boot and Jerad's head.

"Hello."

John turned around at the sound of Margaret's voice. She was standing in the bedroom doorway with both hands in the pockets of her short coveralls. He struggled against his own reaction, but he was glad to see her.

"You'll have to talk to someone sooner or later," she said.

"I didn't want to see anyone," he mumbled lamely, feeling that he would not have the strength to resist her presence.

"Miklos checked the village and took care of the dead. We have a pretty good idea of what happened, Rob, Frank, and myself."

She came into the room and sat down on the edge of the bed. "The planet hardened your body. You look coarser, older, too lean for a stocky person."

"I became a murderer down there."

She was silent for a moment. "It won't settle you to hear me, I know, but please listen."

He sat down next to her and sighed nervously, feeling himself tremble. She touched the small of his back reassuringly.

"I've been a menace," he said. He turned and looked at her, noticing that she still wore her hair in a bundle at the back. "I—I caused everything that happened down there—the bad feelings between Jerad and the village, the raid."

"Listen," she said. "The raiders destroyed the village, not you. How else could you have judged them except in their own way?"

"But I went down there to help, don't you see?"

"The raiders might have died in the winter except for the stolen food."

"But they didn't have to kill so much."

"The village would have starved without its food stores."

"I didn't have to kill so many."

"You were angry, unprepared. You're not responsible for the killing they did, only for your own, and that only in part. Why do you think you went to Lea?"

John shrugged. "I don't think I know anymore. I wanted it very much—to see something different, I guess."

"You felt it was important, and later you wanted to help change what you saw. A similar historical experience motivated the founders of macrolife. Many of us have agonized about earth's scattered colonies. We know they're isolated and backward. Humankind is a collection of fragments right now—those who are planetbound because they have no choice and maybe a dozen macroworlds like us."

"I know all that. What's your point?"

"Simply this: We're following our own path and maybe we're not wise enough or powerful enough to help."

"And we tend to discount the possibility of a successful civilization existing on a planet—that's really what is behind our reluctance to help."

"That's true. We haven't seen much to change our minds. That's the way cultures seem to grow. Earlier social forms are—well, earlier. A child is not an adult. A collection of dust in space will not necessarily become a star."

"But all we've seen is the overspill from a ruined solar system," John said. "What about alien cultures? Maybe others have done well with planets."

"Possibly, but only by turning their world into a garden through a return from space-based industry. Even so, they would have to limit their world's population, while offworld population would be growing without check, because it could do so without much trouble."

"You're assuming that any advancing culture will develop macroforms."

"It's not the terrible thing you seem to feel it is. Planets are geothermal bombs, plates of mud and rock floating on a molten core—all of it left over from objects that were not big enough to become stars. The surfaces are dangerous beyond anything you have seen, killing a myriad intelligent beings across the course of historical time. Resources are scarce, the level of industrialization limited by the capacity of the planet to absorb heat. Ecobiological concerns slow the pace of technical evolution, effectively preventing the emergence of an efficient technology and economics that would exist to serve humane aspirations. A culture moves off its planet in order to take chains off the human spirit."

John shrugged again. "How can I argue with any of this? I don't think I ever did, yet all that seems good is forever fleeing from my grasp."

"You went to Lea to learn. You wouldn't have had to go if you knew what you would find."

He knew everything she would say. You have to risk being wrong to have a chance at being right. We grow by taking positions for keeps and acting on them until we succeed or fail. It's a well-known theorem that error is more valuable than success, because error teaches you something new, while success teaches you only to repeat it. Success is a rut, error an exploration into the unknown. Humanity II practices this method systematically; but human minds are better at it, since they produce the most fruitful errors and are more creative as a result. . . .

"I'm a murderer, don't you see?"

"What happened was not premeditated killing, but more like warfare."

"What will happen to me?"

"We have no legal agreements with Lea—there is no government there."

"That's a real help."

Margaret sighed. He almost cringed at her show of impatience. "I know you don't like my being explicit because it does little for your feelings, but it's important to offer your feelings a strong alternative. Look—murder is generally wrong, but a general injunction against murder, or killing, has no force or meaning unless it can be applied in a variety of differing, even exclusive circumstances. Killing for profit is murder. Killing in self-defense is not murder. It's a strict application of the rule against murder, because not to defend yourself would mean that you acquiesce in your own murder. Your own life comes before the attacker's, since he initiated the situation and is responsible for it. Therefore, if you kill him you are *obeying* the rule against killing, because you are preventing your own murder and possibly the murder of others. The death of your attacker is incidental and entirely his fault."

"What about suicide?"

"Suicide is entirely your own business, even if you get someone else to do it for you. Defense during an invasion is also not murder. The attackers are responsible for their own deaths."

"And what of punishment?"

"We would never execute an imprisoned criminal. You know that. Your pursuit of the raiders came about as the result of their destruction of the village, which you could not control. Make no mistake, they were responsible for your rage, which was justified. Think of other villages you might have saved by your killings."

"But Jerad would not have encouraged them."

"They might have come anyway, as they had in the past. And Jerad is responsible for his own choices, not you."

John felt the tears behind his eyes. "But I didn't have to kill so many —they had no chance against me." Margaret's analysis seemed too easy.

"You used the tools at your disposal, the flitter. But all this is hindsight. Did you think at the time, or did you simply do it?"

"I wanted to do it after I saw Anulka die."

"You simply reacted." She sat closer to him and put her arm around his bare shoulders. "You were defending the one you loved, on a world where there is no law. Your outrage and punishment of the guilty was probably the only lawlike action against the raiders in centuries."

"I might have just knocked them off their horses. . . . I forgot the horses."

"What would you have done with the killers? They're too short-lived to change."

"Jerad might have understood. Now he's dead forever."

"The thing to do is to recognize that the situation was very bad from the start and go on from that."

He turned and looked into Margaret's eyes. "Thanks for trying to help, but it's no good right now, no good at all. The thought of living with this, especially when I can't get rid of it, scares me. I feel dirty and can't get clean."

"The memory could be removed, but whatever would be left would be false, unless we took it all. You might think Anulka still lived. Memories are related and you would become curious about the blanks."

I might have saved a few of the children, he thought, *if I had taken them away earlier.*

"No," he said.

"You see, you do value what has happened."

"I don't have the right to forget."

"Exactly what the value of it is for you will become clearer in time. I can't make you accept all I've said, but I think you will find your way to it."

"I disliked you, Margaret."

"I know, and I don't blame you."

"That makes me feel worse."

She leaned over and kissed him. "Maybe I can try a little harder. Welcome home."

But as he looked at Margaret and tried to hold himself together, the thought of Anulka filled him again. Blakfar's dying pulse beat was once more in his hand. His mouth was dry. He could not see the end of living with what had happened.

"Come in, come in," Blackfriar said. Tomas Blakfar's tones rose up out of memory as John walked into the office and sat down in front of the old teak desk. The official setting reminded him again that he passed in and out of Frank's awareness with hundreds of other matters.

"We're leaving this system. We've been in motion since this morning."

"No," John said, startled inwardly.

"We're going to see what happened to the solar system. Our new mobile is coming with us, at least that far. Later they'll decide to do as they please." Blackfriar leaned back in his chair and scratched the unchanging black stubble on his scalp. "What are you going to do?" Blackfriar always managed to sound genuinely interested.

"I don't believe that it has all happened. The last month I've been going around feeling that everything is terribly wrong. I hear sounds, normal sounds, but I interpret them as if I were still on Lea's surface."

"Don't worry, you'll get used to being home. How do you feel about linking?"

Smoke rose from the village, dirtying the sky. Run; get there quickly. . . .

"I'm sorry, Frank."

"What about linking—how are the exams going?"

"They say I'm fine. I don't know—do you honestly think it will help me?"

"Yes, I do. For one thing, you would not be locked up so much in yourself. You would share more. You would be able to compare your own mind with others and with the independent intelligence that is Humanity II. You would see precedent for your own problems on a large scale. Your own finitude and isolation would not be as great as it is now. But before you get your license, I would like you to go look at the work of Richard Bulero."

"You're so sure they'll grant me a license. Why Richard Bulero?"

"You'll see why when you read what he said."

"You're trying to appeal to my pride."

"Not entirely. Biologically, Richard was your nephew, Sam Bulero's brother's son. If he were alive now, Sam would be your social father and twin brother. My point is that you may find a kindred mind."

"I'll take a look, Frank. Don't push me."

"Good enough."

John felt the anger coming up in himself and fought to control it. Frank seemed so calm, so trusting. John tried to imagine Blackfriar killing someone with a club or a knife. He saw a small patch of dusty ground and Anulka falling forward, toppled by the crushing blow from behind.

Taking a deep breath, he asked, "Why don't we have more murderers? Where are our wars, Frank, why are we so special?"

"You seem sorry to find us peaceful."

"Well?"

"We have killing, mental illness . . ."

"I know, but why nothing on a large scale—what we find in earth's history or the lawlessness on Lea?"

"As a matter of fact," Blackfriar said, "we have just gone through the equivalent of a war, loss of population and all. When the quarrels reached a high point a few years ago, there was nothing to do but prepare for reproducing. When I say quarrels, I mean severe internal strife. It's usually our signal that we've exceeded our optimum size and should reproduce."

"You sound like you're trying to blame me for not being interested."

"You're right," Blackfriar said, raising his voice. "The right is yours to be a recluse, but I don't like it. It's about time I told you that you've been an ostrich. You've gone through the whole romantic malady, including the bleeding concern with anything and everything outside your own culture."

"An ostrich—what's that?"

"A goddam bird, hides its head in the sand."

"Goddam?"

"Let me get back to my point, please?"

"Go ahead."

"Even though we've institutionalized rebellion and made the process productive, we are still skeptical about unmodified human nature, though not cynical. Thus what would be a disruption of most past societies is made to work for us. Procedural revolution makes it possible for us to absorb new approaches without undue harm to the previous society, which remains intact, minus its defectors. What I'm describing is not simple. There's a whole new world next to ours, with enough potential surface area inside to equal the surface of an earth-sized planet. Within the next few years, half our population may switch over to it. Don't think there is no bitterness. No one has suggested we abandon the general guidelines of macrolife, but one day that may happen, I'm afraid."

"Why haven't we fallen apart, Frank, like the culture on Lea? Where's our corruption? Surely we don't just depend on people to be good?"

"Not completely. Think of it this way. Planetary problems arise from economic scarcity and the misuse of political power, either from greed or from the love of power itself. On planets a small class overproduces wealth through support of research and development, after stealing the wealth from human labor, from human and animal muscle in the beginning. Then the power of this class declines, since power can no longer be bought with wealth alone, but also with ability. Finally, physical wealth is abundant enough for everyone. So where anyone of ability can rise, the system remains creative. We don't depend on people to be good. Our society understands the causes of disorder, and our structure is such that those causes can be utilized. We haven't tamed human nature or even modified it very much yet. We've channeled it. There's nothing mysterious about our way. We've still got problems, but they're *our* problems, belonging to *our* way of life. For us, mental illness arises from envy of others' abilities, from status, when people compare their achievements."

"You make it sound simple."

"It's very complex if you take the time to look closely. Our youth are the barbarians. Our long-lived provide stability and a radical long view of things. The long-lived and Humanity II are the living commitment to macrolife. We don't interfere with either group."

"What am I?"

"An eccentric rebel. I thought you might leave us for a dirtworld. We have our failures."

"I've never heard you talk so hard, Frank."

"I must. This is your chance to try again and I must present the alternatives strongly. A man named Freud once said that a society of love is possible if there is some external group to hate. In a sense that is what we've got. We hate the past, we hate the circumstances that so deformed the human spirit, even though those same circumstances gave birth to human intelligence."

"Dirtworlds."

"Yes. The coming to consciousness is a terrible process, proof enough of the mindlessness of nature, which must cull consciousness in such a bloody way. Energy-poor, physically in danger from other life, diseased, and subject to natural catastrophe, intelligence endures long enough to escape, to give itself a chance at a high-energy existence which is safe and creative, making a mature, long-term culture possible. In the long run nothing can succeed, nothing is absolutely safe, of course. There is no deathless fortress in which we may live forever."

"I feel sorry for the humanity on natural worlds," John said.

"But those worlds are necessary," Blackfriar said. "We try to hold an attitude of empathy without altruism. Granted, this is an ambivalent attitude. Should we go around saving worlds? Wouldn't they resent us? Life is isolated in nature, ghettoized to develop individually. The size of the universe serves this kind of quarantine perfectly. Interstellar travel is difficult, and that's a good thing."

"But all the planets we've known are only scattered earth colonies,

Frank. We've seen no others, no originals that should be left to grow in their own way, only our own bits and pieces left at different points in history."

"That makes no difference. The horrible irony is that a culture has to grow away from its planet, not be torn away, regardless of its origin, regardless of its conditions. The damage and dislocation would be enormous if we came in and began to plan for them."

"It couldn't be worse than leaving them alone to stumble around in the dark."

"You really don't give them much credit. But yes, to help is about as bad as not to help. You're thinking that we could alleviate physical suffering. That's true, but there would be other scars. It's a matter of readiness. Look at the old United States. Human potential was recognized, but with little regulation. There was coercion through policed laws, but no genuine social persuasion through environmental incentives. The price in waste and disorder of natural and human resources was enormous. The finitude of the economic pie ensured that only a few could grow into their potential. It was a large number, true, but most people had no economic freedom, and they were not ready for it when it came. People worked hard to maintain a highly inconsistent physical affluence, frustrating their inner potentials. Tom Paine's comment, that we have been given the power to begin the world all over again, is truest of macrolife."

"Maybe earth would have succeeded if the disaster had not happened."

Blackfriar was quiet for a moment. "We would have grown away from earth more slowly, perhaps."

"I think maybe we should gather our own."

"You'd have to use force—most would not want to leave the settled worlds."

John was silent. He was not a doer or a thinker. His limits were suddenly very clear to him, as was the alternative. The glimpse was a shock. "I'm curious about earth," he said to break the silence.

"So are many of us. We're going back because enough pressure was brought to bear. That's all we really are—an economic base supporting a clearinghouse for pressures which grow into projects. As nature once prepared us for making a living and reproducing, so a life of affluence and practical immortality must be structured to encourage individual and social projects. These become our life. Without them we become severely demoralized."

"Have we been successful, Frank?"

"Not entirely. As a democracy we are a means for reconciling human differences. That's all democracy needs to be—a framework in which people can disagree without disaster. Beyond that we process information in our knowledge industries, and they are our ultimate authorities. There is no democracy in submitting to them, except that they are open to all. As I've said, on the human level we have envy, influence-seeking, some murder, personal cruelties—but generally we have cooperation rather than competition, achievement rather than aggression. We attack each other through status and personal style, but there is no economic greed. The major tragedy is the individual's too-frequent inability to find satisfying work. When his or her abilities are ordinary, there is little to do except find amusement or appreciate the achievements of others. There are still too many suicides. We seem to need a further development of the individual. There seems to be an insufficiency to life that is unconquerable."

"I'm just a simpleton," John said.

"The one thing we can't do for you is what you must do for yourself. Every generation must rebuild the world in its own mind to feel truly at home in it. This involves reevaluation of the past, a recap of social history as the process of birth recaps biological history. Any strong attempt to impose a view from outside may lead to a closed mental set and a closed society when such overimpressed individuals proliferate."

"You think I would have been a tyrant on Lea."

"Even if you were good about it. Unless you had brought all the resources of a world to reclaim the planet, you would have been very frustrated working within severe limits. You would have had to educate Leans offplanet, then send them back to help—a project for a century. It could still be done—just organize the interest. There will be time."

"I want to see earth," John said.

Frank continued: "When a primitive culture is not permitted to come up by itself, or to rise to a previous height after decline, then all the courage and cleverness of intelligent beings is preempted, coopted by the superior helper. Maybe exchanges on the interstellar level should occur only among equals."

"You've made your points. I still think it's a cruel view of history."

"The truth is not always kind."

John sat up erect. "But look—there's so little of earth-derived humanity scattered. I still think we could gather it together."

Blackfriar coughed and scratched his head. "Wheeler has talked about it. Still, the changes for many of the people on these worlds would be too much."

John sat forward in his chair. "We could gather them on one world, maybe Lea, as a transition area. That wouldn't be so bad a change. We could help them if they were all in one place."

"You'd have to force most of them to leave." Blackfriar rubbed his chin. "Wherever they are is home to them."

"If we told them what we were doing . . . Why do you have to make so many difficulties, Frank?"

Blackfriar looked directly at him. "I think you would spend a century just to prove me wrong, but I also think you'd end up showing that the obstacles are even bigger than we imagine. Again, this is not to say you should not try, but there's the other thing you haven't considered at all."

"What's that?"

"Missionaries give up the further life of their own culture, their own origins. They go native, but not all the way. It's not possible to do so completely. It's exile. You'll find that no matter how long you live, there will always be one more thing to do, one more matter to set right."

"You don't really believe I should even try, do you? It's just your way of covering both sides of the debate."

"Intelligence is hardy. It gets use out of itself through the struggle with problems and should not be denied this satisfaction. As a macroworlder, you are like the grown son who wants to reeducate his parents or the parent who will not let the child be itself. Or take me— I keep poking my nose into your life, yet you must live your own life. I can't do it for you."

"I shouldn't have gone to Lea."

"But you should have. Maybe you'll find a way to do what you want, and we'll all learn from you. At least you're not playing with a trivial problem, as many I know are doing at your age."

John felt exhausted, beaten, but some of his uneasiness seemed to be gone. "I think I'll go check up on Richard Bulero," he said, "but I doubt it will help me."

"You may be right," Blackfriar said. "Not all problems have answers."

As he got up to leave, John noticed a change in Frank's expression, and he felt suddenly that he didn't know Blackfriar at all.

In the apartment's library niche, John called up Richard Bulero's major work, *The Sociology of Macrolife*. The desk screen showed a small biographical note:

RICHARD BULERO (2001–2045)
Political philosopher and sociologist. The major theoretician of Macrolife after Dandridge Cole and Gerard K. O'Neill. Student of his uncle, the minor twentieth-century philosopher of science, Samuel Bulero. Died with Orton Blackfriar and Margot Toren in a freak explosion during construction of the second macroworld at Centauri.

The frame changed, giving titles of biographies, a complete list of works, and reference codes for information about Janet Marquand Bulero, Jack Bulero, and dozens of related historical persons.

John passed on to the work itself, planning to skip forward to get a good general impression before considering a closer study.

Document A-2050
Manuscript—IBM Bookface typescript
Posthumous publication, Asterome 2050 AD
THE SOCIOLOGY OF MACROLIFE
by Richard Bulero

He had not expected to see the original document. The typescript seemed strangely immediate and real on the bright screen. The past was there, reaching out to claim him. He started to read, and the words seemed to speak in his mind as if they were his own thoughts.

INTRODUCTION

The central political fact of Macrolife is that power exists solely for maintaining the economic framework that makes freedom possible; economic management and political authority are limited to enhancing creative and constructive opportunities within the social container. These powers of government and the physical structures are the social container, the basic features that must be preserved when the society reproduces, regardless of what other styles the social organism may develop. An attack on these essential features of Macrolife from outside poses no moral problems, since the defense of genuinely free institutions is always justified. The only forbidden freedom is the freedom to

jeopardize   the   framework.   All   other   serious
challenges to society are given a clear procedure by which they may become influential.

John touched the control surface and the screen blurred, becoming
clear again about a third of the way through the introduction.

A   society   of   unlimited   economic   capacity
might still go wrong internally; this may happen
as the result of a variety of mental frustrations
and pressures. How, then, do we deal with the
darker side of human nature? By giving the individual   a   generous   share   of   power   within   the
society, beyond the economic essentials. Dissi-
dents are free to leave at any time. They can
settle on any number of natural worlds . . .

How much choice had there been in the village? There was little
freedom to be found outside the largess of macrolife. What freedom
was there to be gained by choosing to live outside? He was not free to
choose to live outside.

. . . or, after suitable planning by the Projex
Council, they can start the construction of a new
container, which will hold the kind of society
that pleases them. To date, this open-ended
society has been possible because it restricts
power to economic management, the policing of the
various civil liberties, and the planning of creative projects (reproduction of Macrolife being
the most important such project). Stricter forms
are possible for Macrolife, but these would limit
the very creative possibilities for human ambition and desire, both intellectual and aesthetic, that prompted the creation of Macrolife.

John skipped forward a few pages, admiring the thousand-year-old English.

> The city was the first form of Macrolife, an organized way of life that looked to interests beyond agriculture, to science and art; but the finitude of planetary resources doomed the city. Macrolife offered a unique extension of human community concepts, a redemption of urban civilization, the city-state, as well as the saving of various aspects of rural life. . . .
>
> An observer raised in the restrictive conditions of a natural world, where resources are scarce and the power of the necessary few frustrates the yearnings of the many, might ask: What compels the Macroworlders to be true to their design? What prevents the fatal abuse of power? Human conduct is, after all, a fallible thing. Our answer is that we live without scarcity, without the need to represent valuable work and resources with equally scarce precious metals or a limited currency supply. Negatively stated, greed is satisfied; powerful ambitions are satisfied. Whoever wants power can have it; we rotate responsibilities among the citizens, making power an obligation, not the end of life. . . .

But I'm a failure, John thought. *I couldn't even do something small right. I was too selfish to succeed.*

> All status comes from achievements; rebels learn this quickly enough and have to put up or shut up. The acts of a successful, strongly cooperative ego, are effective because it looks beyond itself; the ineffective ego is concerned with itself, and fails to the extent that it misperceives what is not itself. Our wealth makes conscience, goodwill and personal development

possible, where before it was the luxury of the
secure minority, which often pointed to the lack
of these qualities in the majority as a reason
for keeping it down. (The minority could do
little else in any case, short of abolishing itself, and with it the means of passing beyond
agriculture and primitive technology).

"You should take more of an interest in history," Margaret had told
him a long time ago. "The only sense of identity I see in you is the
physical one, in the care you take with sports. Our citizens are brought
up like kings, but that doesn't mean you have to be as silly as kings
were." He had not understood. "If you knew history, you'd be angry at
what I said, but then I wouldn't have had to say it."

"There's no reason I have to do anything I don't want to," he had
told her. "I mind my own business and leave everyone alone."

"You're too much of a loner, and you don't know what you're
missing."

"Stop picking at me."

And yet, human perversity will remain. Perfection is not possible, or desirable. The universe seems to be made for the conscious intelligence which is lacking, and which strives to
remedy this by gaining in knowledge, experience,
pleasure, and insight, but not to the point of
perfection or certainty. This universe is not exhaustible, as if by design, since the alternatives (stricter determinism or greater chaos) do
not seem to be desirable, even though the universe may be moving toward one or the other, away
from the optimum balance between a severe limi-
tation of freedom and its augmentation.

We are not concerned with becoming angels, or
anything much beyond a hyperpersonal, coopera-
tive humanity. The solution of secondary prob-

lems, the classical difficulties of administra-
tion and distribution, does not lead us to claim
a final solution to the difficult problems
involving the intractable aspects of human
nature. Human plasticity is a genetic heritage.
It is an array of general potentials. Aggression
is one of them, but it may appear in a variety
of forms; all of them are socially elicited, in
worthwhile or in damaging modes. Our environments will be designed to elicit the constructive potentials of those tendencies which make
aggression possible.

A few pages later, he picked up the growing boldness of the words:

Civilization is a harnessing of reason, feelings, and imagination to practicality. Nature is
modified by social life, using the tools of language and information; social life is modified
through material organization; when these activities have been successful, it remains to modify
human nature and the physical form of the body.

Suddenly John realized that Richard Bulero had written all this
when Asterome was little more than a hollow rock. Hindsight made
all the ideas familiar, but for Richard Bulero these words had been the
instrument of foresight.

The technological environments of Macrolife
will attain the complexity of nature, becoming
"second nature" as they become homeostatic,
self-regulating, more a living organism than a
machine. Nature seems unmachinelike only because
its error-evolved adaptive systems work at
smaller, in-depth scales; they are subtle, made
of soft materials, and super-redundant (for a
reliable efficiency). . . .

Government must be like a natural environment—supportive, an antagonist at times, a realm which provides basics, like earth, air, fire, and water—within which individuals may flourish. . . .

Economics is the way in which a civilization uses energy, how it stores, transfers and records the use of energy in the form of individual access and credit. . . .

The problem is not economics, or social structure, entirely—primarily it is the problem of human nature, a nature that cannot be confined, only educated and persuaded. . . .

Human history is the battle of the cortex against the older, impulsive, instinctual layers of the brain; the cortex has an ally, however, in certain areas of feeling, those portions that give rise to feelings of sympathy for those of our own kind, making their welfare the same as our own. This sense by which we blur our individualities, by which we share and overcome our separation, is the basis for a sound naturalistic ethics, one that may extend even to other forms of intelligence.

A human being is a multicellular organism, a form of macrolife, the step beyond unicellular life; society is a form of macrolife, the step beyond the individual human, the superman; the superman need not be an individual, as Cole says—an individual society may be the superman. . . .

We are building a society that augments its individuals. Specialization, the management of automatic details in the logistics of life-sup-

port, library storage and retrieval systems—
these custodial tasks are carried out by artificial intelligences operating below the surface
of the social structure, much as portions of the
brain carry out automatic functions without the
intervention of human consciousness. In the
human brain, we will retain unspecialized
skills—the capacity to see wholes, to see the
relationships among entire blocks of information, to generalize, to create new wholes in all
the modes of human creative activity, from the
arts to the sciences. No matter how much we may
change through genetic creativity, all such
changes will have to be introduced around the
central core of unspecialized human plasticity;
bioengineering for specialized functions would
fragment us psychologically.

It seemed strange to see these old words reaching forward into
their future, his present. Would they move past him into some further
vision? He read on.

The size of the human brain can be increased;
but the brain's capacity can also be extended
through symbiosis with artificial intelligence,
either in reversible or irreversible modes. The
mental tools that we think with will certainly
grow, and they will drive the human brain to grow
in outlook and sophistication, as once the
simple tools of knife, hammer, and wheel helped
create a new life. Biological modifications are
simply part of a two-way process, by which
humankind creates cultural environments and is
then affected by them, only to see the possibility of a still further development.

John skipped a few pages of detailed example.

By the late twentieth century, the expansion
of the physical brain had leveled off, while
artificial intelligence was still growing by a
factor of 10 every 7 years. Our infant Humanity
II intelligence is not a personality as we understand it in ourselves. It is growing in consciousness, perhaps even in curiosity, but it is
without a localized ego, lacks ambition and
will; it is not anyone in the specific sense.
Biological intelligent self-consciousness, by
contrast, is a declaration of independence from
nature's blind sleep; it is nature coming awake.
The individual ego sometimes feels itself to be
a bit of something general become specific and
defined, sharpened and directed by a yearning
will. The symbiosis of these two kinds of intelligence will make Macrolife the wisest and most
knowledgeable society in history. No experience
will be lost to it; no individual will be without
the benefit of its cumulative effort and common
inheritance; no one will have to start from
scratch. Perhaps this reconstruction of human
existence will do something to relieve the sense
of doomed finitude, of smallness, so common in
perceptive minds.

Each citizen will have the benefit of a
quality-controlled birth (rather than the reproductive roulette of past ages), the benefits of a
limited population, educational techniques, the
vistas of an ongoing exploration of nature, access
to the necessities; the life problem will be one
of further growth, what to do with one's indefinitely long life. Ours will be an uncoercive plu-
ralism, providing both stability and novelty.

John ran the pages forward, looking for more about the Humanity
II intelligences.

Humanity II is the child of our fleshy intelligence. As I write, humankind is still dominant, the teacher requiring service in return for programming and improvements; but one day these children of ours will develop on their own, coalescing into bundles of individual personality within the system, perhaps acquiring equal say in the further development of Macrolife. Perhaps they will be our successors; at the least they will become our companions, inhabiting a universe psychologically coextensive with our own. The great convergence of intelligence in nature will certainly ignore evolutionary origins, be they biological or nonbiological, humanlike or alien.

John turned to the concluding pages of the introduction:

The confrontation of science and older cultures posed difficult questions of personal and social identity, calling into doubt the age-long affirmations of ethnic and regional humanity. A nonsimplistic scientific solution to the problem of culture-bound man called for a highly fluid and critical personal and social identity, one that would be open to growth not through the assumed posture of educated sufficiency, but through the homeostasis of egoless error recognition. For example, indefinite life span will lead to complete changes in an individual much in the way that cultures have changed over the ages. A person would be led on by the logic of newly acquired knowledge and understanding, as well as by the interests of his creativity and curiosity. In past cultures, this kind of activity would have been pursued in bits and pieces between the physical chores of staying alive, if at all, or passed across a few generations of workers, as in the cumulative effort of the sciences. This new freedom is what at bottom threatened culture-bound man, preserver of the past, national man, clinger to distinctive markings—the fear that little may remain of an overrated past, that identity may shift and transform itself with the emergence of genuinely new things.

Macrolife will seek a balance between stability and novelty, between the stay-at-home safety that so often leads to decadence, and adventurism, which may lead to disaster. Our adventurism, however, will take the form of investment in the activities of intelligence, in scientific innovation, in the mobility that will ensure survival when stars and planets die, a mobility that will give us a chance at discovering the nature of the universe, not as a curiosity for a few, but as the interest of all our citizens. Such a future for Macrolife seems pleasing, good and noble, reconciling as best as can be expected the futures of desire and fate.

In all this, in all the changes that might be possible for us in the transformation of material things, and ourselves, the present form of Macrolife is only a beginning, a suitable jumping-off point, a place free of the distractions and dangers so consistently active in our planetary past. Planets may not be fit places for a rational culture, because intelligence is at first incapable of thinking in terms large enough for the solution of its problems; and when it can do so, it no longer has need of planets.

These are the problems I have set to explore in this book. In the solution to these classic difficulties lies the fulfillment of the dream of space exploration, its true human significance, as a larger arena for growth, for social experimentation, and as the vantage point from which to view the prospects for continued survival.

John turned the page and examined the contents page:

Contents

He touched the plate gently and let the pages pass by at a slow pace. The work became technical for long stretches. Speeding up the pace, John turned to the last pages. This was not just a large work of three thousand pages; this was the complete constitution of his world, the background of his life. *This is the source of my very thoughts. I was brought up hearing variations on what is in this work.* The echoes seemed like a song now, the song of home, once far away, now growing closer.

The last page faded. As he moved to get up, John saw a miniature holo of a man appear on the desk.

"Hello. My name is Richard Bulero. I've been asked to add a personal note to my work, though I don't know what else the careful student might wish to know."

John sat down again, passing his hand casually through the recorded image. The screen flashed an instruction:

THIS IMAGE MAY BE PROJECTED IN FULL LIFE SIZE,
OR IN COMPACT FORM.

The screen went dark as the image of Richard Bulero strolled back and forth across the desktop. John could see that his light brown hair was slightly streaked with gray. The man was not very tall, but he seemed tall in his lean catlike grace. He stopped and rubbed his chin, looking out across time.

"This is how we saw things at the beginning," Richard Bulero said. "I hope it is how you see macrolife. I wrote the work you have been studying, but thousands of people did the work for it. In a sense, all of earth's humanity helped to create macrolife." He paused for a moment. "No doubt many things are different in your time. Whether I was too optimistic is for you to decide. I hope that you are examining what I wrote in an open society, not in secret. How I envy what must be available to you in your library terminals." He paused again before continuing. "My desire was to dream the future at a time when humanity had all but destroyed itself in the solar system. What more can I add to what you must know in your time? I hope that we have not confined your ambitions by our mistakes. I hope that macrolife lives by the words of Thomas Jefferson, who asked in 1801: 'What more is necessary to make us a happy and prosperous people? Still one more thing—a wise and frugal government, which shall restrain men from injuring one another, shall leave them otherwise free to regulate their own pursuits of industry and improvement, and shall not take from the mouth of labor the bread it has earned. This is the sum of good government.' This last part applies to us, I hope, only in the sense that our governments to come must not take away, either through accident or through perverse design, the freedom that the historical labor of humanity has created for us. I hope you are alive in a society that does not take away, but receives the creativity and goodwill of its people. I'm reminded of one further point. Human history is driven by basic developments which are too often misunderstood. I'll assume for the moment that macrolife, even in your time, is no exception. The most misunderstood basic development is the notion of an elite and its function. Our great talents never divide people into higher and lower, into winners and losers. The function of ability is to work in the company of normal people, those who consume and need skills and abilities, those who can appreciate and understand, but perhaps not originate, and with whom the talented share a common humanity. I wonder if it would be too much to hope that all our citizens might one day be high achievers and that what would pass for talented in the earlier society would be merely normal in the later one. Elites should be the first trickle in a direction that greater numbers may later follow. The function of the strong is to help the weak, the knowledgeable to spread knowledge. The writer writes for those who don't, the singer sings to nonsingers. Elitism, I feel, is the disease of those envious individuals of middle abilities who cannot rise higher, so they settle for the power of their prestige. They have fallen in love with the true half of a half-truth. They do not look outward to humanity, they look down, and fail truly to share. They hate those below them and envy those above. We can discourage these tendencies in our children in a thousand subtle ways, teaching them to hold one another accountable according to their best tendencies, their most generous feelings. These are in fact as real as any imaginable external moral standards, because they can be elicited from the array of potentials in our biological nature, as surely as the harsher inheritance that we carry from evolution's struggle. The ideals of macrolife must live in each individual consciousness as nothing has ever lived before. Macrolife must not exist in the economic externals alone, though they are equally important. Macrolife will be the test of an energy-rich civilization. Are you surviving without the whip of scarcity? Are the internal pressures of human nature stronger than the rational cortex? That's all I can add for now. Good-bye."

The image winked out. The screen lit up for a moment with a few bibliographical reference numbers, among them a list of the works of Samuel Bulero and the biological studies of Margot Toren, and then the lights went on in the cubicle.

This, John thought, was how it had looked at the beginning. He was struck by how much of this spirit was still alive. It was strong in Frank, in Margaret, in Rob Wheeler, in the builders of the new mobile. He had not seen it dying in anyone except himself.

He thought of the link. For Margaret, Rob, and Frank, the link provided a long cultural memory, while he was limited to what he could look up and the memories of a couple of decades. The historical amnesia of new generations was not a problem for them. For them, macrolife wasn't any one thing. It was a stand against death, ignorance, and forgetfulness, against chaos, against all the forces that tear down and destroy. Suddenly he felt the continuing patience of macrolife, holding together everything that he had known. Blackfriar, Margaret, and Rob were for macrolife because it stood against the death of individuals, the death of societies, the passing of knowledge and awareness, the death of love, appreciation, and joy, the death of species and stars in the flux of time. On planets death walks into every heart, poisoning the future with the promise of ruin. The young glimpse death as a far-off destroyer, rushing slowly toward them, then falling upon them sooner than expected. Despair and anxiety are death's left and right hands, winning death's battles for it. On planets the living are dead before they die, and death the victor, when it calls, comes upon itself. Richard Bulero's thoughts spoke across the ages, saying, "We have survived the solar system. Our social form will give us the necessary permanence, flexibility, and mobility to avoid most endings. Time will give us the patient accumulation of knowledge, to know ourselves and the universe better. We will endure."

Suddenly John realized that he was living only a small part of himself and that he wanted to be like everyone else at home: to know as they knew, to feel as they felt, to love as they loved; but the feeling passed, as if something were trying to steal it from him.

John leaned over the tablescreen and watched the three-hundred-ten-kilometer companion world suspended in space below them.

"All basic systems are now operational," Rob said as he sat in front of the screen at John's right. "Most of the population has moved in."

Around them, all twenty-five of the observatory's screens were on, showing the panorama of the Praesepe cluster as the two macroworlds moved away, accelerating toward light speed. Lea's twins were still bright, soon to be lost among the bright swarm.

"Are you feeling better?" Wheeler asked.

"I'm looking forward to link citizenship," John said. There was no point in mentioning his feelings until he had decided what to think about his stay on Lea, about home, about himself.

He was looking at the companion world. The idea of a gravitic field pushing all that mass was strange, even after he had used one so often in the flitter. He thought of a massive fish swimming in water and a grav generator making waves to push against the curvature of space-time.

"One day," Wheeler said, "we won't need this kind of running start. We'll be able to switch in the stardrive as soon as we're reasonably clear of a sun. Converting to tachyon structure is costly enough by itself."

"How long before we approach light speed?"

"Three months. Actually, we could switch to tachyon tunneling at half light, as long as our direction was properly set for the jump to sol. The margin for error is great—it's like stabbing a needle through a bunched-up fabric, hoping to hit the buttonhole. Fortunately, we always come out near point fifty c, so it's not long to our destination, our time."

There were a number of complementary theories, John knew. It had been called the tachyon tunneling effect, the tachyon quantum jump, and others. The tachyon universe had been described as having a highly variable spatial curvature.

"The tachyon universe," Wheeler was saying, "is, well, to be very picturesque, pasted against ours, on the other side, to continue the metaphor, and that's why our space is elastic to the degree that it is. Tachyon space-time can be stretched or compressed, practically speaking, from the point of view of our consciousness, to a higher degree than our space-time's usual malleability."

"What's our usual?"

"You know—as light speed is approached, experienced time drops toward zero, mass increases toward infinity. All the extremes demanded by theory never occur, of course, but these extremes do serve as barriers of a sort between universes, frontiers between different sets of physical order. Dimensional theory allows for paper-thin universes to be piled up one on top of the other. Universes may interpenetrate one another, yet be unknown to the inhabitants of each. I won't even start on time branching or time travel."

"Finish with jumps first."

"I think the best way to think of jumps is to imagine that we jump onto a supralight speed wave moving toward a far shore. We need initial speed and the tachyon switchover to get on. The wave then carries us toward that shore, which may be roughly congruent with our destination star in our original space-time. We come off by changing back to the tardyon slower-than-light wave structure while continuing to move, much as a person would have to keep running in his direction of travel when jumping off a slow-moving vehicle. Once we're off, we can slow down. Tardyon and tachyon structures are only relative terms. We don't feel much difference while we're one or the other."

"We don't know much, do we?" John said.

"It lacks complete elegance, but the unwieldy description of what happens will disappear as we learn more. My dream is to have a drive that does not take us out of our frame of experience at all, or as little as possible."

"What would that be?" John asked, knowing that he was using the discussion to distract himself, but another part of him found itself absorbed in the concepts.

"A direct control of the plasticity of space around the vehicle—altering the curvature of space directly without leaving our universe. Of course, if such a way to high transoptic speeds were possible, there would be some distortion of stars in the visual field, but we could correct for that. Navigation would be more accurate because we would still have some kind of information from our own realm to interpret."

"But what about the mass-speed-time relationships?"

"They would not be affected, because we would not really be exceeding light speed or moving at all as an accelerating object upon which a force is exerted. We would be moving the space around the ship, in a sense. Mass would not approach infinity, time would not contract in relation to anywhere else, and we would not drain the energy of the universe as we became more and more massive near c. Only distance would be reduced. We would be a little universe all our own, moving like a ghost through the normal universe."

"Why don't we run into a star when we come out of jump? And why don't we feel anything different when we're tachyons?"

"It's luck, the vastness of space, which makes it a low risk of hitting a sun or planet, or the fact that given the nature of the gravitational force involved, attractive and repulsive, it is just not possible to come out in a sun or even close to any material body with a deep gravity well."

"I don't understand that—but what about not feeling tachyonic?"

Rob shrugged. "We don't because the tach universe is self-consistent in physical structure, like our own. Equivalent physical structures replace our own. How would we compare? All realities are observer-oriented. Maybe if half of you were tachyons, half tardyons, you'd feel the difference, but not when you're fully one or the other." Rob smiled.

"I think I see."

John was silent. He turned his chair in a circle and looked out through all the screens. He was standing on an open platform in space, and the splendor made him feel like a localized bundle of awareness, the result of something that had fallen in on itself, become small and individual, full of pain and longing for a larger state.

"Rob, tell me something."

"What?" Wheeler turned toward him. Half his face was shadowed.

"Do you tire of your work, of all this? You've been at it so long."

"There's too much to do, practical and theoretical, and I've yet to have a chance at the crucial experiments and observations."

"That's all that bothers you?"

Wheeler laughed, and for a moment starlight was reflected in his eyes. "I wish I knew more. There is so much that is not in the link storage. I wish I could plan ambitious projects, but we're not ready for some of them."

"Like what?"

"A time travel device, for example—it can be built. We've known that since Tipler's work on earth in the 1970s. The device would be tens of kilometers in size, requiring dense materials."

"What else would you do?"

"Close approach to a black hole. It's almost certain there's a giant black hole at the galactic center."

"What would these projects tell us?"

"If we knew that, then we would not have to do them. These two would tell us a lot about what kind of universe we live in—not just our local universe, but maybe something about the larger reality. And we would learn experimentally, as a matter of measured experience."

John was silent for a moment. "Rob, does the universe die?"

"We think it does."

"How long?" The question seemed strange, almost as if he were asking about his own life.

"Anywhere from a hundred billion to a trillion years before the final collapse into a universal black hole. A long time ago we thought the time would be much shorter, about eighty billion years."

No conscious being could ever exhaust that amount of time, John thought, wondering about those final moments when nature would lose its self-sufficiency, its seeming lack of contingence, and slip away, to die as individual creatures had died for so long within it. He wondered if personal death was a slipping away into a greater self-sufficiency, into something godlike.

"Then what?" he asked.

"The gravitational force becomes dominant, pushing everything toward zero volume and infinite density. Since this is impossible, there is nothing left but to expand. It's really more complex than that. The explosion may push into a new space, creating a white hole, a new big bang. The new universe may have different physical laws each time, different constants and experiential properties. The model seems cyclical, but probably isn't. It's an oscillating model, and steady state in a sense, too."

"It's cyclical in the sense that there are a series of universes, but they are not repetitive, they're individual."

"That's right. I hope it's true. It would be another support for the idea that physical determinism is just strong enough to give us things like deductive explanations and weak enough to give us genuine novelty and the freedom to choose among alternatives."

What happened on Lea is the bottom of my past. I can't see beyond its horizon, either to what I was or what I might be, and I don't like what I am now.

The vastness of space-time on the screens was a beckoning puzzle, and he was an enigma within the puzzle. John took a deep breath. There would never be a solution to himself, at least not the kind of solution that might exist for the puzzle of nature. Only what he was to become had any chance of making sense.

21. The Jump

One month later, the mobiles passed one-third of light speed. The twin suns of Lea faded from the aft view, to be replaced by a growing circle of darkness that slowly ate the Praesepe group. Gradually the two stars had changed from yellow to orange, red to a deep coal red, before winking out; all light rushing after the macroworlds was being stretched into the infrared wavelengths that were invisible to the unmodified human eye, but still visible to the navigational scanners.

John watched the darkness that had swallowed Lea's suns and was now devouring the universe behind him. He had come into the observatory once a day for the last month, dividing his time between link training, the library terminal, and watching the progress of acceleration. Sometimes Rob sat with him in the screen room, but much of the time John was alone while Wheeler went about his work.

Sol lay 150 parsecs ahead, in a region of sparsely scattered yellow stars; but with increasing speed the light waves were shortened into invisibility as they piled head-on into the macroworlds. Sol turned yellow green, full green, and violet before the contracting wavelengths became ultraviolet and visible only to the navigational sensors. The area of sol became a black disk, expanding to meet the darkness behind them.

As the two worlds continued accelerating toward .90 of light speed, the two black disks covered more of the sky, until only a band of stars was left between what appeared to be two empty hemispheres. On the sol side, the bow of stars was banded with violet, blue, and green; yellow lay in the center of the ring; on the Praesepe side, the bands were orange and red, fading into the infrared hemisphere at whose center lay Lea's suns.

The great curtain of colors hanging in space grew narrower, leaving at last only the thin band of yellow stars at the starbow's center. John almost expected that the two hemispheres would meet to cover the remaining stars of the visible universe; but gradually the hemisphere ahead reached its farthest extent and started to recede, as if pushed back by the still expanding hemisphere behind the macroworlds. The ring of yellow stars moved forward, surrounding their invisible destination as if to mark it.

It's not worth living when so much is hidden, John thought as he looked out at the darkened universe. But a braver logic spoke within him. *We are splinters, angles of perception and awareness, and we would cease to be individuals if our personal limits were opened to infinity, if we became omniscient. We would become a different kind of being; individuality would lose its meaning. We float as isolated points in a plenum of the unknown. The points grow toward each other as best they can, achieving only an imperfect acquaintance, but they cannot merge.* Suddenly the potential openness of his life stirred within him, drawing him on again. The darkness ahead was a field of possibility, the darkness behind a black lake of things forever lost. He would have the link, the larger identity needed for endless life, the knowledge and outlook of selves which had passed through the life of worlds before him, leaving their best. The larger grasp of things would surely dispel the sense of smallness and inadequacy into which he had fallen.

Wheeler came in from the outer workroom and sat down next to him. "A few minutes now and we'll be ready for the jump. I'm told that this time we won't feel quite so disoriented."

On the screen in front of John, the companion world shimmered in its field. There was no sense of motion, except for a fleeting sensation born of knowing.

"Thirty seconds," Wheeler said.

Suddenly John felt as if he were falling, as if he could now feel their enormous velocity. On the screens around them, reality had been turned off. The band of yellow stars was gone; the black hemispheres were gone. Fore and aft, above and below, space was gray. The companion world was only a dim geometrical outline in the field. The gray itself was of varying intensity and texture. It seemed to be filled with short pinbursts of light, millions of them occurring with increasing frequency until they seemed like glittering sands.

"What are they?"

"We can't be certain," Wheeler said. "We might be passing through what may be solid matter elsewhere."

The pinbursts merged and the gray otherspace became a shade lighter, an infinite fog that flashed as if from a distant lightning storm. Abruptly it became a flat expanse near the bottom of the screens. The macroworlds seemed to be sliding forward on a hard gray surface.

"Sometimes it looks as if it had a curve to it," Wheeler said, "and we're going over the top."

"How much longer?"

"One or two ship hours. We can't come out too near to sol. We have to give ourselves enough space in which to decelerate. It would be best if we could enter tachyon space at point zero five light speed and come out the same."

"Rob, tell me something. Do you have doubts about our way of life?"

"Of course I do."

"What will become of us?"

"We're infants, groping our way from one set of goals to another. We seem to be fairly sure that we don't want to go back to the cradle of natural worlds. That's all I can say we are for now. Later, when macrolife has existed for a long time, I suspect we may no longer be human, as we know it now, as the natural worlders know it. If you and I exist then, we may be startled to recall that we were once as we are now."

"You think we will be alive, you and I? What will we be?"

"You see, John, it's hard to think past a century, even if you know that your life span is indefinite. A thousand years will bring conscious modifications, biological and mental. We have no idea yet how alien cultures may affect us."

"If there are any."

"They are there, I'm certain of it."

"If we can reach them."

"We will."

John thought of how he would forget Anulka. Entire lifetimes would disappear into the abyss of his personal future. Suddenly he wanted to be there, aged and changed beyond imagining, so that the pain of memory would be lifted. Yet a part of him was pledged never to forget.

"Rob, what do you feel most clearly?"

"I live," Wheeler said, "because the whole world lives, because the universe is both unbearable and absorbing, curious and sublime, and suspiciously *right* in the way it is. That is the most curious thing about it, and that's what I feel most."

"And that is what sustains you?"

"Yes, and other things. You asked about the big ones."

"Aren't there any other big things?"

"Love and friendship. Love becomes very private after a century. It has a chance to succeed, to come and go without the threat of death, because it has time. I've not seen Olivia for two decades, but both of us know that we will be together again."

When they had been in the jumpspace for two hours, there was a sudden dizzying instant of falling.

"We're coming out," Rob said.

John expected to see the band of yellow stars reappear, dividing the universe again into two black hemispheres; but the gray remained, glistening occasionally.

"What's wrong?" John asked.

"I don't know."

"We're not coming out."

"We'll overshoot sol," Wheeler said.

The bursts of light grew brighter, as if a vast fire were kindling outside.

"What if we don't come out?" John asked, imagining endless life without stars, without natural worlds, without young intelligences dreaming of spaces beyond their sky; that would not be a universe he would want to live in.

Stars faded in, recreating the universe.

"They're not distorted," Wheeler said. "We're well below five percent of light speed, but the drive still creaks."

The new world was still with them, motionless on the screen. John remembered his anticipation during the approach to Lea, the endless waiting to see the planet. Suddenly he understood that home's ties with earth, with natural worlds, had been the real motive, or a good part of the reason, for coming into the Lean system. Aimless wandering after material resources and knowledge had not been enough; lifeless solar systems, chosen at random, would have served as well; but only contact with other humanities would bring the special rewards of looking into a true mirror.

There would be less delay here. In a few minutes of scanning it would be known whether the home sunspace contained any activity or not, if earth was alive or just another wayside world.

22. Earth Again

The two macroworlds were decelerating toward earth's orbit at an angle of thirty degrees to the sun's equator. Sol lay at the bottom of the screen. John turned his chair around and looked back toward Praesepe, now 155 parsecs away, more than five hundred years in the past if measured by light's slow crawl. He had outrun the light that had left Lea's sun five centuries before Anulka's birth. He was looking toward the edge of the galaxy. Taurus, Orion, Cancer, and Gemini stood on the backdrop of intergalactic darkness, dominating the screens. Praesepe was a swarm of bright insects frozen in flight by the perspective of immensity.

He turned again to look at their destination. Sunspaces are whirlpools of matter, he thought. Sol's whirlpool is two trillion kilometers in diameter. A cloud of hydrogen collapses to form a protostar, and gravitational compression kindles the star's thermonuclear furnace. Two hundred billion such furnaces of pulsating plasma circle the galactic center, he thought, but we were born here.

"The sun seems normal," Wheeler said. "There's no sign of the anomaly. Are you going up into the hollow to watch with everyone else on the big sunscreen?"

"I prefer the observatory," John said. "I like the small room you've given me; I like the dining area and the atmosphere of work going on."

"John, I like to share what I do, but you're using the observatory to escape. You've been avoiding everyone except me."

"I'm also interested in what you do here, I really am."

"As long as you see what you're doing." Wheeler sat at the table-screen in the center of the room. John could see only his back as they spoke.

"It's what I want for now." He thought of the future again, when macrolife would be vastly changed. *Anulka, Anulka, where are you? All this immensity has got to be capable of throwing up your life again.* He knew that it was a stupid wish and that the life so ordered would never be the person he had known; but his mind persisted in projecting itself to the extremes of time and space, like a madman searching through a room for something he had lost. He could not control his dreams, his most secret wishes, which seized upon little bits of detail, always to enlarge them out of all proportion.

"There was human life here," John said. "On Mars and in the Jovian system, wasn't it?" Wheeler was a dark shape peering down into the tablescreen.

"We'll know in a matter of hours if anything survives," he said. "We're listening for any kind of noise. Frank will cut in to tell us if we pick up anything. I don't hear any radio. . . ." There was a tremor in Rob's voice, as if he was suddenly afraid, or suspicious.

"What is it, Rob?" John stood up and walked over to look at Rob's screen.

"Just a thought."

Wheeler switched to a view of the hollow, throwing a bright afternoon light into the dark observatory. John looked into the space of green land curving around the disk of light which now showed the smaller, brightly yellow disk of sol. More than a million people were in the hollow, milling around the lake, walking down paths and sitting by streams, filling up the resorts and ordering lunch in the outdoor cafés, reclining in the meadows and lounging on park benches, stopping occasionally to look up at the sunscreen, where the sun of earth was rising again. All were waiting for sight of earth, for the first glimpse of the world that had produced their ancestors, even if that earth turned out to be a dead world, an empty shell washed up on this shore of space-time.

"Look at them," Wheeler said. "Our birthplace is a spectacle for them. They're afraid of the sun, of any sun. So many are superstitious about suns and planets, especially the oldest, those over a few centuries old."

"Are you afraid?"

"I once was. I hate death but no longer fear it. My work gets on in a body of individuals, none of whom is indispensable except in a personal way."

"I've never heard you speak so critically."

"We need shaking up," Wheeler said. "I've heard some of the reactions to your stay on Lea, and they're all pretty narrow opinions. We're too detached from the grosser forms of pain and unhappiness which you've seen. Many of our people are quietly bored. They stop living. They either take their own lives or they just stop."

"Stop?"

"They give up and die with nothing wrong. I guess a perverse form of natural selection will leave us those who can take on an indefinitely long life, but I sometimes wonder. We don't live the fully engaged lives of planet dwellers, but we're not free of natural worlds, either. We always return to sunspaces—to reproduce, to gather resources, or to spy on lives harder than our own. Maybe we should not look back, not even in our thoughts. If we could become what we are completely, irreversibly, then there would be no danger of internal collapse from being part one thing and part another."

"But, Rob," John said, "I've begun to hope."

"The vision of the founders is not present equally in all our people. History is not an unbroken memory, despite the link. And even if memory were continuous in all individuals, human beings would not all be happy and accepting. Universal linking is like what the desire for universal literacy once was, but when it comes, it will bring problems of a new order. We have to permit the life that wishes to do nothing, the life that is weak and fails, as well as the life that is complaining and ambitious. Some links are being used as a drug, a source of entertainment, to support a purely aesthetic life, in the way alcohol and drugs were used by the middle classes on earth."

"Middle classes?"

"An economic designation. They were not as rich as the rich and very rich, but they were far from poor. Life was decent in physical terms. Of course, if the whole world had been middle class or rich, then things would have been different. But the entitled rich were above the middle class, and the poor made it feel guilty. Many of the problems of middle-class life were mental—problems of value and justice, self-development. How much time to devote to making a living and how much to leisure, and what to do with leisure. All that we can ever do, I think, is offer individuals a choice of opportunities. But individuals still have to make those opportunities work for them, and there can be no guarantees of success. Macroworlders know that natural worlds are what the old poor once were, but we're not sure that there is anyone better off than we are. We have not been around long enough to meet an alien culture."

As he listened, John realized that Rob, Blackfriar, and Margaret were aware of the conversations he had held with each of them. The link enabled them to compare notes, reinforce points made by the others, and continually follow up lines of discussion. They were his family, he realized, playing the roles they might have played if he had been born on a planet.

"There were earth cultures twice as old as we are," Wheeler was saying, "but they survived through rigidity and dogma."

John thought again of the humanity scattered within the 200-parsec radius of the solar system, most of it poor and unable to move to a high-energy civilization. Macrolife was growing, but no planet could join its circle unless it worked its way up.

"You think I was heading for the role of messiah on Lea?" John asked.

"Of course, and you would have had to take over the planet to make things work."

"But would that have been a good or bad thing?"

"I wish it were that simple a question," Wheeler said as he turned around in his chair. John backed up and sat down again. "What I've tried to say is that there are two kinds of macroworlders: the spoiled and the self-critical—those who are arrogant and feel naturally entitled to our way of life and those who see it for what it is, a high point of development which is nevertheless not absolutely beyond the problems of the past. In time we must come to help natural worlds, but in ways that will not be destructive."

"Is that possible?"

"We'll have to see, and there will be mistakes. You've been asking a lot of questions. You've struggled to affirm your own world. Keep that, but think of helping others also. The time may come when your experience on Lea will be very valuable."

"Rob, is the boarding and sacking story true? What happened there?"

"It's true enough. The planetbound population of the Tau Ceti IV colony became very resentful of the macroworld in its sky, which was recruiting young people very rapidly. There was an attack against the half-built world in 2331. Most of the new population was slaughtered, with the unfortunate result that most of the skilled scientific elite died, leaving no teachers. The few surviving macroworlders built the starship that we found circling Lea. They were too proud to resettle among the people of Tau Ceti after their families and friends were killed. On Lea we saw that all the old problems followed them into Praesepe, as well as new difficulties that were born along the way. We'll never know everything that happened on Lea, except that a technical civilization died there. Maybe a native one also."

"How soon before we cross the orbit of earth?"

"Within a week."

John sighed.

"Summarize," Rob said. "I want to see how you've put it all together."

"In the one view, we should leave planets alone. Natural worlders resent us, even though some would join us. We can't give help to different groups on planets because this would only create strife—clan against clan, nation against nation. So the only way that would work would require a team to impose order. But this would involve us in police guardian activities for every human colony world, and such an empire would distract us from developing our own civilization."

"Have you considered that such an empire might be a good thing? Maybe it would be part of our own development, not just a side activity."

"You're just trying to confuse me. Let me finish. Involvement would prevent us from working upward from *our* level of problems, *our* plateau of difficulties. We would become a parent civilization, forever looking backward to the nursery worlds. We're too busy to do that. Maybe one day, when macrolife is more numerous, we can close out the remaining planetary cultures by giving them a leg up."

"It changes them to know about us," Wheeler said, "and it changes us whenever we are confronted by them, as you have been. It can't be helped, even with all the best intentions on both sides. Miklos has been on all the human settlement worlds. He's never forgotten. He'll never tell you what help he's given and how ineffective his efforts had been. Maybe someday you will build worlds that will specialize in natural planets."

"I don't like what I did on Lea."

"Face the fact that humankind is not wholly rational and may never be. We have tried to rise above the animal without embracing the amorality of the intellect. But just because we can see beyond the slime a ways does not mean we have left it behind. Only the fact that exceptional individuals are born with a fair degree of regularity gives me hope."

"Is it a matter of biology?" John asked.

"Partly. The interplay of complexities is another reason we shy away from meddling. The array of genetic potential is difficult to develop effectively without being coercive. Persuasion is not enough. Too often cultures have merely punished older, previously acceptable forms of behavior. Biology is necessary but not sufficient. A creative social form is sufficient, given the biology, but it must be coupled with a creative psychology, one which develops individuals without tyrannizing them or fostering dependency. In both psychology and biology we must never be happy with what is, but must ask what should be and what we want to be. Now we've managed to channel our irrational impulses, controlling the gross forms of envy, fear, hatred, and destructiveness. But we still have fools and egomaniacs, as well as people who aspire to ideals and behave humanely. Our laws stand above us and resolve our differences, but these laws are still made to work through human beings. I think it's the long-lived among us, those who taught Humanity II, who are responsible for the continuity of our laws and practices. Yet we may decline in time, and to prevent that we may need the natural worlds again—we may need their view of us, their novelty, just as we need the rationality of Humanity II."

"So what do you recommend?" John asked, glimpsing how much there was still to discover in his own world.

"Build yourself. Start inside and work outward to a concern for others. You'll link, then you'll serve as exemplar while completing parallel specializations. The questions and problems will still be there when you come to them again."

"But planets are suffering now."

"You're not ready—it's not in your power. Don't you see that?" Wheeler's voice was harsh for the moment.

John felt like a child hoping that it was within the power of his parents to help him get what he wanted. He had recited his lessons correctly, and his parents had told him that it was impossible to do what he wanted. John felt betrayed. Something in the back of his mind had imagined a gathering of macroworlds to eliminate all the plight and poverty in the universe.

"What is the new mobile interested in?"

"Perfecting materials synthesis, improving our stardrive, exploration. They want to go off toward the central regions of the galaxy, where there may be a high incidence of advanced technical civilizations."

"They want to find the rich class," John said. "Maybe they'll find natural world cultures of a high order."

"Possibly."

"It would be quite a surprise for us to find an advanced planetbound civilization," John said.

"If a culture is advanced, it can leave the planet, even though it may not wish to do so. I'll withhold my opinion, but it's hard to get around the indication that planetbound cultures die very quickly or leave the planet. The limits of a planet demand that a culture leave before natural resources are gone."

"Planets can be moved."

"That's another form of macrolife, but no one we know has done that kind of thing."

Suddenly John felt himself rushing toward the secret image of Anulka that he had buried within himself. He was nothing without her. She had taken everything from him. Margaret had tried to help, but the feeling was still as strong as ever. It came upon him at odd moments, mixing with his most rational thoughts, bending him to its will. He had lived for Anulka on Lea. He had dreamed of helping her people, but in reality it had all been to impress her. He had forgotten to live for himself. After months of trying to understand himself, he did not know what he was waiting for. The people in the hollow were waiting to see old earth, to see sol grow large on the sunscreen. They wanted to be frightened and awed. He was waiting for his thoughts to resolve themselves into a set of balanced feelings about his life, if thoughts could flow into feelings.

He wanted to banish the squalor he knew existed on planets. A tyranny prevented his wishes from coming true, the tyranny of space-time that imprisoned intelligences in small, ineffectual bodies and condemned them to death.

Sensing his mood, Rob said, "I know. We can do so much, we can travel so far. It's hard for our young to realize that we cannot do everything. I was devastated by this fact once, and I think I am still living life as if it could be overcome one day."

"I'm going to get some sleep," John said, rising. "Wake me if anything important happens."

The face of earth was gray. A ragged flash of lightning turned the planet into a devil's mask. John felt cold as he fell behind the shuttlecraft and watched it disappear into the brown and gray swirl of clouds. The cabin lights brightened, pulling him back into his body.

A dust storm raged outside. The cabin was a cozy enclave, but he felt helpless. He wanted to strip the dust away and strew the planet with sunlight, bringing it back to life.

The shuttle burst out of a low cloud front, a thousand feet over a desolate landscape. A faint sun rolled in the rusty clouds. The land was without trees or grass. A grainy sand blew in the ceaseless wind, creating flats and dunes, with only an occasional shaft of sunlight to brighten the day. The wind was wailing as it had for centuries now, wiping away the last traces of humankind from the planet.

The shuttle dropped low over the desert and drifted forward, its light beams searching the ground. The screen showed a gully of red clay, where a trickle of water ran.

Shapes appeared ahead, a column of crablike masses moving toward him. The shuttle was over them in a moment, and John saw the hole in the earth from which they were emerging. In a world without oceans, these creatures were masters of the sandy wilderness. . . .

He was outside the craft, watching it hover above the creatures, a hardshelled invader made of metal, with beams of light for legs. . . .

He opened his eyes, remembering the room Rob had given him in the observatory area. It was little more than a place to sleep—a screen, a bed with g-controls, a small library-link desk—but he was glad to find himself in it.

Closing his eyes, he tried to see the desert of his dream. Somewhere on that ruined earth there had been a valley, the place where his grandfathers had lived and died. Samuel Bulero's father and mother were his parents also, dead for more than a thousand years.

When he opened his eyes again, the left corner of his screen was on, showing Wheeler's white-haired head.

"You're awake," Rob said. "Come out here."

"What is it?"

"You'll have to come out and see this."

The earth was a small green disk on the central screen. Around the planet's magnified image hung a hundred or more motes of light, brilliant diamonds catching the sunlight. The moon seemed to belong to the swarm, but its light was duller.

"What are they?" John asked as he sat down next to Wheeler.

Blackfriar's face cut into the bottom-left-hand corner of the screen. "We've got a message on tachyon band, Rob. They don't use radio or laser, so we didn't hear anything when we came in."

"What are they?" John asked again.

Blackfriar squinted at him. "Hello, John."

"They're communities, like us," Wheeler said, "in permanent positions around earth."

"The biggest is some fifty kilometers across," Blackfriar said.

"What about the anomaly?" John asked.

"It has receded," Wheeler said. "There's no sign of any disturbance. What does the message say, Frank?"

"They demand that we identify ourselves and order us to take up a sun orbit just inside earth's, a million miles forward of its position. They're very suspicious of us."

"But who are they?" John asked. "Where did they come from?"

"They're the descendants of earth," Wheeler said, "the same as we are. Sol did not die. They have rebuilt and progressed."

"They have a stay-at-home form of macrolife," Blackfriar said. "I wouldn't have guessed it, yet it's an obvious development."

John had been looking at the earth without noticing what was different about it.

"Rob, Frank—look. The earth is green!" The earth was alive. It had not died here in the stellar desert where the suns thinned out toward the galaxy's edge. He yearned suddenly. As he looked at the earth and its glowing children, he questioned why he so often thought of the end of the universe, the end that was implicit in the fact of gravity. As long as earth's orbital motion staved off its fall into the sun, as long as the motion of suns delayed their collapse into their galactic centers, so long would a universe of lighted spaces prevail against death's in-pulling, and there would be time for every kind of life.

"The earth is green," he said again.

"Let's hope they're friendly," Blackfriar said. "We've never dealt with an equal who might have the ability to destroy us."

"You mean weapons?" John asked.

"It's not impossible," Blackfriar said. "We've come into their space suddenly, without warning. It's too late to turn back."

"We could intercept or deflect any hostile object," John said.

"Not at point-blank range. There are weapons powerful enough to destroy us." Blackfriar was silent for a moment. "They're calling again. I'll get back to you later." His face faded from the screen, leaving the earth and its firefly companions to dominate the screen.

"What do you think, Rob?"

"This is a new situation for us."

23. Cities of the Sun

Within a week the two mobiles settled into their assigned positions sunward and ahead of earth. The earth-moon system and its companions now filled the rear screens in the observatory. More than a thousand worldlets cupped the earth in a porous half-shell that caught the sun's streaming energy. The moon was a dull pearl floating near the rim.

A delegation would be arriving to discuss the renewal of contact between earth and her prodigals. John wondered what, if anything, would be decided. For the last two weeks he had felt more at peace with himself. Margaret had come to see him in his room, and they had talked—about the link, about Anulka, about the effect that earth's recovery was having on the population. They had made love, but it was filled with friendly feelings and laughter more than with desire. As he sat alone one day in the observatory, he realized that he was recovering, that he was changing. His youth was coming to an end, he told himself, even though he knew that others might feel the same way at five times his age.

The meeting would be witnessed in every assembly watch. Although he was too young to be directly involved in the negotiations, he was experiencing apprehension. The orders given out by earth to the arriving worlds had conveyed an impression of resentment. John felt a vague guilt about returning to the solar system, but he told himself that it was the result of earth's reception. Blackfriar and Wheeler had been too busy to talk to him during the weeks following the arrival, and this added to his uneasiness. He had begun to suspect that something hidden was going on. "Almost everyone on our two worlds is waiting with you," Margaret had said, "so be patient."

John walked into the outer workroom. He went over to Wheeler's desk and sat down, his mind wandering. He would give anything to be suddenly Rob's age, to look back to this time as a faraway moment of growth and discovery. Facing the desk space were four old library screens, the controls on hold, set to recall the reference material Rob had been studying. John reached out to the touch plate and the screen at his right lit up:

A. Forward Time Travel Procedures to Verify Cosmological Models

1. Near light-speed passage
2. Black Hole ergosphere passage
3. Tipler 2-way time machine
   (construction of large rotating cylinder of dense matter)

B. Comments

1. Only (3) above offers a method that would not be psychologically ruinous to most human subjects, as they are now constituted, although unusual individuals may be able to adjust to (1) and (2).
2. See Feinberg, Ettinger, Haldane on the sanity and outlook of long-lived individuals.

C. Cosmological Models of Current Interest

A list appeared, but John turned off the screen. He looked at the wall clock and saw that it was almost time for assembly. A sick feeling came into his stomach, as if the world had dropped away below him. He went out into the hallway.

The auditorium was five hundred meters back from Wheeler's research center. John enjoyed the walk, grateful for the release of tension; it reminded him of Lea. Suddenly he was remembering the small, pleasant things of his life on the planet. He paused a moment, then walked through as the door slid open.

It was a small auditorium, with seats for a few hundred people. Most of the researchers had already arrived—astronomers, physicists, mathematicians, cosmologists—all of them from Wheeler's science sections in world forwards; all of them were over a hundred years old. John felt out of place, but Rob was already waving him to an empty seat in the second row. John walked down the aisle, then three seats across, and sat down next to Wheeler.

"I thought you'd gone to your room to watch," Wheeler said.

"I decided to have people around."

"You'll be more alert here."

John turned to look behind him and recognized Tassos the biologist, his childhood exemplar.

"Hello, John," Tassos said softly.

John tensed. The suddenness of the reunion was like an assault; he was not ready to see Tassos again. The man was unchanged. His hair was still gray, his brown eyes still kindly. He hunched more than sat in his seat. John smiled and turned away.

Assembly watch was something he remembered always doing, from primary to continuing school, first with Tassos, then with Margaret, later alone. He had broken the habit while on Lea, though he might have kept up through the flitter link. Now he felt all the old feelings returning as he looked up at the screen.

"The earth is not happy about our being here," Wheeler said.

"Have they said anything?"

"Think how you would feel if an economic and military power entered your stable and prosperous system. As a leader you would have to be skeptical."

"But we're no danger to them."

"They have to be convinced."

Suddenly John knew that part of his uneasiness came from the fear that earth might be a danger to them.

On the screen, Frank Blackfriar was sitting down opposite three delegates from earth. The round table was of teak from earth's forests. The room was a simple conference chamber on level thirty.

The delegates introduced themselves.

"I am Drisa Haldane. My associates are Melcia Chin and Reger Huw. On behalf of our people and government, I welcome you to our sunspace. Please bear in mind that you are subject to our laws and customs until you leave."

"Of course," Blackfriar said, but the tone of uneasiness had been set. "Is there a limit to how long we may stay?"

"What are your plans?"

"The potential for exchange of news and information is to our mutual advantage. We have been away for almost ten centuries."

There was an awkward silence before Drisa Haldane replied.

"We would not wish for you to stay indefinitely."

"Perhaps you would suggest an acceptable stay," Blackfriar said.

Drisa Haldane's short hair was a bright red, and she seemed rather small behind the table. She was leaning forward, profile to the screen; it was a strong profile, perfectly matched to her manner. Reger Huw was a tall, thin man with sandy hair and a weak chin; he sat with his arms folded across his chest. Melcia Chin was a stocky woman with straight black hair down to her shoulders. She sat with her hands on the table, her lips pressed tightly together.

"We would prefer an early departure," Drisa Haldane said.

"I don't understand," Blackfriar said quickly.

"You are not owed an explanation."

"Everything seems to be well here, and we don't pose you any threat."

"Councilman Blackfriar, we do not wish to be unfriendly, but since you press me . . ." She paused. "I have examined the circumstances of your leaving the solar system. Your way of life has grown and prospered and so has ours. You cannot have claims here."

"You misunderstand," Blackfriar said. "We shall not interfere in your internal affairs. We produce all we need, and we're curious only for news and knowledge. Surely you feel the same way? We're not exactly strangers."

"Are you planning a legal or a moral claim to be here, to return?"

"None at all."

Haldane looked at her two companions briefly. It seemed that her composure had weakened.

"You must do as we ask," she said.

Blackfriar was looking directly at her. "What is wrong? Can we help?"

"You must leave at once."

"And if we don't?"

"Are you threatening us?"

"Not at all."

"Then you will leave."

"To set your mind at ease, let me assure you that we are not a belligerent people."

"Neither are we—but you and I do not really know that, do we?"

"Nothing about this situation requires the use of force," Blackfriar said.

"Yes, of course."

"I don't understand your eagerness to have us leave."

"Must we give you a reason?"

"You do not have to—we respect your sovereignty. My aim is to persuade you to share some history and knowledge with us. I repeat: much time has elapsed, but we are not strangers. We may have a lot to give each other."

Drisa Haldane looked to her companions. "Just a moment, Councilman Blackfriar." She leaned toward them for a consultation. After a few moments of whispering, she retured her gaze to Blackfriar and said, "Are you empowered to speak for your government and all your people, here and now?"

"Of course. They're all watching this meeting."

"Very well, then." She folded her hands on the table. "Since it is clear to me that this is not a matter that either of our peoples would use force to resolve, I will tell you why we are reluctant for you to stay." She patently did not like what she was saying. "You will stay anyway, it seems, so we have no choice but to tell you in good faith, requesting that you honor our way of handling what is about to take place. We have spent years in preparation, so you must pledge not to interfere. You may observe, no more."

"Observe what? How can we pledge anything about something we know nothing about?"

"I do not find your attitude reassuring."

"I beg your pardon," Blackfriar said.

"In a moment you will understand why I am being circumspect."

"I think I know," Wheeler whispered. The assembly was perfectly still.

Melcia Chin spoke next. "You must remain bystanders," she said in a low voice, "to a meeting that will take place shortly with an alien emissary. In fact, we almost mistook you for that emissary."

"Your presence is already a risk," Reger Huw said, "since this culture restricts its contacts to a circle of eligible civilizations. Your arrival may have changed our status."

"How do you mean?" Blackfriar asked.

"They may not come," Drisa Haldane said. "You might have sent a message instead of behaving as if solar space was still yours."

"But we are the same people," Blackfriar said. "You cannot deny it."

"Matters of origin are trivial differences," she said.

"I can see that you were not planning to tell us, were you?"

Drisa Haldane rose abruptly. "I am not aware of any obligation to have done so. This is our project, one for which we have spent many years preparing. Doubtless, you have also considered the problem of alien civilizations. If you believe with us that intelligence is the most precious aspect of reality, then you must see the implications of contacting alternate humanities. Intelligences vaster than our own, or simply different, may help us see ourselves with an increased objectivity, help us check the validity of our systems of knowledge. . . . I don't have to go on."

Blackfriar nodded. "Of course. We will be bystanders."

Drisa Haldane sat down.

"But can I ask that if you see fit, you may share your findings?" Blackfriar asked in a softer voice.

"If the situation permits, in the long run."

"I'm convinced that you are probably better able to handle such a contact, given all your preparation," Blackfriar said.

"Is she telling the truth?" John whispered to Wheeler.

Rob shrugged, but did not answer.

"Could you tell us what happened after the anomaly receded?" Blackfriar asked.

"Certainly. A century after Asterome's departure, the disturbance fell back to the confines of earth and disappeared within the next half century. In the second century, we came sunward from Mars and the Jovian system. We found the earth a desert, but growing back. Some of us resettled the earth. Others live in the habitats you see around the planet."

"Have there been other departures from the solar system?"

"Once every few decades, but we never hear from them. You were the first to leave and the first to return."

"I take it that you do not approve of mobiles?"

"Many of us do not, though we see that it must be permitted. I feel that interstellar communication has the greatest potential."

"You consider information to be superior to firsthand experience," Blackfriar said.

"What is experience without the proper background of information and theory against which to view it? In any case, mobility, like the old idea of colonizing earthlike planets, is immature and uncreative. While it may be necessary to escape a sun or local disaster, colonization ignores the fact that a habitable planet belongs to the life that exists there or will develop on it. Mobile macroforms go in search of what they already possess—the environment of their own consciousness and culture."

"But you don't know what we have seen and learned," Blackfriar said.

"We probably know as much," she said. "As to what you have seen, that's an aesthetic matter, for adventurous types. To be useful, wide experience must be interpreted properly, not simply savored. Intensive development and creativity is superior to looking for what may lie over the next hill." John found himself liking Drisa Haldane.

"How can one help not interpreting?" Blackfriar asked.

"Mobility is not an absolute necessity."

"The aliens—why are they coming physically?"

"It's their choice, as it has been ours, to release those among them who wish to travel."

"Do you have a fix on their home system?"

"No, just the mobile," she said.

"Don't you mistrust them?"

"They have nothing to gain by deceiving us."

"Are you certain?"

"As certain as we are of your peaceful intentions."

"Do you know what they are like?"

"Physiologically, they stem from birdlike forms rather than from apes. We've exchanged DNA information and built up a common language. That took two centuries. In some ways, they seem more familiar to us than you do."

"Earth has grown up," Wheeler said softly. "She makes me feel like a roving wild man."

"She doesn't miss a chance to dig at us," John acknowledged.

"How much time do we have?" Blackfriar asked.

"They can arrive at any time. That is why we were anxious for an understanding as soon as possible."

"You will have our interested cooperation," Blackfriar said.

"We have an agreement, then?"

"We have an agreement."

"What do you think, Rob?" John asked.

"It's earth's project, not ours. Whatever happens will be their responsibility. It's certainly not worth taking weapons out of mothballs over. I suppose we'll stand by and see what these alien geese are like."

"Geese?"

"An old earth bird. I suppose it's no more ridiculous than apes."

"Rob, do you think we can arrange for me to go down to earth?"

"I don't see why not."

"I want to visit the place where the Bulero name came from."

"Want some company?"

"I don't mind," John said as he stood up to leave. Most of the others were still seated, watching the concluding formalities of the first session between Blackfriar and the delegation from earth. Wheeler rose and walked out with him.

At the entrance, Wheeler punched his opinion of the meeting into the Humanity II terminal.

"How do you think the opinion will run?" John asked.

"They'll go along with Frank's, I think. What would you vote?"

"There's not much to do except wait and see."

24. The Alien

There's no one here, John thought as he stood on the mountainside. Earthquakes had enlarged the Andes valley, and only the character of the peaks was unchanged. The receding anomaly had left a nearly barren soil, but everywhere a green moss was struggling to clothe the rocks. He had almost expected a house, or the remains of one; a thousand years was not so long as to have left nothing. He looked around, hoping for a glimpse of some object, a scrap of worked stone or metal, anything to suggest more than a past of natural forces, but there was nothing. He was as much a stranger here as he had been on Lea.

He turned and looked up at the sun hovering over the stony masses behind him, setting in a dark blue sky that was readying itself for the transparency of night. Snow glistened on the peaks, blood red from the sunlight, almost purple in the lower shadows. A slight wind carried the mountain cold to his face.

Human settlements still existed on the planet, fed by the occasional return of small groups. For this portion of humanity, he had learned, significant change was a fearful thing. The prevailing trends in the suncup worlds toward modifications of the human body, artificial intelligence links, increased mental capacity, and indefinite life span, were uncertain innovations that were preparing humankind for some further struggle, as yet unnamed, and the results might still be catastrophic and irreversible. The returnees wanted no part of such uncertainties; for them the earth still breathed and would be reclaimed by those who still wanted it, loved it with an intensity that was at least as strong as the desire to turn away from natural worlds completely. "It's superstition mixed with old instincts," Margaret had commented. "The returnees have no desire to become anything more than their biological past. These few will return to the womb of earth, but unless they shackle their children's minds with custom and law, the next generation will explode outward again, looking to the suncup habitats, as rural sons and daughters once looked to the cities. The stubborn minority on earth may remain for a long time. Perhaps the old tropism will never die away."

John walked up toward his flitter, stepping carefully among the small rocks. The quiet of the peaks was complete; silent before the agony of time, they would never be roused into speech.

He was drawn to the local macroworlders as he learned more about them. By denying themselves mobility, they had retained a better hold on the past, a sense of identity which contributed greatly to the pragmatic courage and personal energy he had seen among them. Earth, their place of origin, was a daily reality for them, to be treasured even though they did not live on it; sunspace was home, to be filled up with human communities as once the floating continents of earth had been built up with towns and cities linked by a planetary system of roads and communications.

The difference between the returnees and the space dwellers was that the local macroworlders were collectively up to something, while the returnees had no desire to be up to anything. The earth would support them; it was a good place for small communities of people who had made their peace with the universe. Sunspace and beyond was the perfect environment for the open-ended city-state. On earth such states had once emerged only to war with one another as soon as they had impinged on one another's territory; for the surface of earth was finite, its riches limited, its support of life a passing gift. Such conditions were intolerable for a civilization which saw itself as an ongoing project, that set its goals to be a growth of knowledge and ability; any claims to perfection and completeness, claims that meant a small, static existence of changeless outlook and custom, were seen as death. "Dogma always goes hand in hand with a lack of growth, both in knowledge and in technical ability, while growth must always accompany democratic ideals of improvement and innovations," Rob had said before John's departure for earth. "You will see that earth is a dead end. Their greatest crime will be their effort to stifle the minds of their children with an aesthetic certainty, denying them the right to explore and come of age as you have done."

He climbed inside the flitter and leaned back in the seat, closing his eyes. *"John, this is Yevetha Li-Alin," Margaret said. "Yevetha, this is John Bulero, your new examplar." She's skeptical, John thought, looking into her golden brown eyes. Her short hair was sandy blonde. She was willowy and long-legged. "You'll have to work hard to convince me you're worth listening to," she said. "What does being a little more than twice my age give you? Margaret, can't you find me someone older?"* She might have been one of the children from the village on Lea, grown now and climbing from one new awareness to another, if he had thought to save even one. He thought of their small broken bodies.

He opened his eyes and sat up. The shadow of the peaks swept across the valley in front of him, signaling that the sun had slipped down behind the mountains at his back.

He looked up through the canopy, wondering what it would be like when he got his full link—not the detachable trainer he had been given recently, but the permanent implant that would be under the direct control of his will. He might now be opening his mind to feel the life of his world in the sky as it looked down on the earth, think as Rob thought, with all the hoarded knowledge of macrolife as support, see what all the best who had ever lived had seen. This would give him what he hoped for—self-knowledge joined to human will, carried forward by the pressure of the past; this would be for him, as it had been for countless others, the end of forgetfulness, the end of the amnesia of generations, the discontinuity of knowledge and experience that had toppled civilization so many times, throwing up again and again the old, wearisome problems. All his dissatisfaction lay in his isolation from this vast stream of human effort; all hope for him lay in his now following that flow of creativity, wherever it might lead. It didn't matter now, he thought, because he had taken the right road, and once understanding takes hold of knowledge, all roads become the same road.

Yet something of him still held back, bidding him to return to earth, remake it, turn his back on the stars, the intruding stars that were now beginning to pierce the veil of day above him. There seemed to be no remedy for the emptiness between them. He felt again the hunger to see all creation from outside, as he had seen the dying embers of a night fire on Lea, with the darkness pressing in around him. *There is an insufficiency to life that is unconquerable.*

He noticed a light moving high above the valley. The flier descended and set down a hundred meters below him on the hillside.

John climbed out and started down the hill. A figure appeared as he neared the object. He heard a few words. The emerging passenger was speaking to someone inside.

John waited in the twilight. The figure noticed him and came up the hill.

"You're Drisa Haldane," he said in surprise. She wore a gray tunic, gray pants, and dark boots.

"You're from the mobile," she said. "What are you doing here?" She looked past him to the flitter. "You're alone?"

"Yes."

"Why have you come to this barren place?"

"Why have you followed me?" John asked. "I'm not anyone important."

"Are you looking for something?"

"I have permission to be here." He took a step toward her and looked directly into her eyes.

"I know that."

He noted how delicate her features were—a small nose, pale skin, hollow cheeks, and narrow lips. Her eyes seemed larger than he remembered. Her gaze did not break as she looked back at him.

"I was born here," he said.

"You're a millennium old?" she asked, tilting her head.

"No, my . . . family was born here." The thought seemed strange, as if he were lying. "I'm a clone of Samuel Bulero."

"You've come here out of sentiment."

"You seem relieved," he said. "You expected something devious?"

"I did from a Bulero."

He wondered if she had come to look him over out of personal curiosity or official suspicion.

"I'm sorry," she added quickly. "That was a rude thing to say."

He took a few cautious steps toward her, until they were standing face to face. She did not seem to mind.

"You see," he said, "we're not just strangers from the stars. We both come from the same place, originally."

"Of course. I was born in the Ceres hollow, grew up on Mars, then came sunward to the ring," she said more expansively, then, abruptly, "I'll leave you to your sightseeing."

"Drisa Haldane," he said as she started toward her flitter.

She turned suddenly. "Yes?"

"I would like to meet you again."

She smiled, turned again, and went quickly to her flitter. In a moment she was a faint star fleeing from the earth, and he wondered whether he had actually spoken to her.

He approached his flitter, knowing that it would be very hard to see her again. As he climbed inside, he tried to recall the color of her eyes.

A call lit up the touch plate. Instead of opening the audio, he picked up the trainer and pressed the clinging chip to his temple.

"This is Rob, John," a voice said within him.

"Yes?" he answered silently, feeling the multitude of listeners.

"The alien has entered the solar system. It's coming fast, John, a matter of hours. What's surprising is the thing's size. Take a look."

Some of the brighter stars were already blazing in the darkening sky. As John looked up through the canopy, another picture superimposed itself on the sky, a dark shape moving through space, obscuring stars, growing larger.

"It's at least twice the size of Mars," Rob said. "Next to it our two worlds and the sun cities will be specks. Their control of gravity and inertia must be very fluid to permit the movement of such a large body."

"I wonder why they need to move around at all," John said, feeling uneasy.

"They're up to something more than a simple meeting," Rob said. "I'm guessing, of course, but like any advanced culture, I think they must have projects that draw the abilities of their people. Apparently they think humanity worth contacting."

"Let's hope we can understand them, or they us."

"Drisa says she does."

"Do you feel uneasy, Rob?"

"Yes, I do."

There was a short silence. "I'm coming home now," John said. Half rising from his seat, he looked around at the now darkened valley of his ancestors, sat back again and commanded the craft to lift.

"Forward cradle 233."

The flitter pulled itself to a hundred kilometers above the earth, revealing a planet of broken gray-brown desert marked with patches of greenery. Large rocky islands sat in the sparkling Atlantic. The sunlight danced like diamonds on the polar caps. The flitter gained speed, shrinking the earth behind him.

Ahead were the twin home worlds. Behind him the space habitats glittered, cupping the earth and catching the sunlight. Somewhere in the night, something from beyond was moving toward the home fire. Anxieties like his own were probably rare; but then he reminded himself of the distrust shown his two worlds upon their return, and he resented the fact that so much less inhospitality was being shown toward the alien.

The two macroworlds were now visible ovals. The flitter turned left to approach home from the forwards.

"*They're here*," the link whispered.

He looked around through the canopy and saw the dark shape, larger than Luna, obscuring the stars behind the egg shapes of home. The object was not reflecting any light.

"Rob!" he shouted inwardly. A sudden fear clutched at his insides, as if something from deep within him had escaped to become real outside, forcing him to face it.

"We know, we know," Rob said.

The flitter raced toward the forward cradles. Suddenly the planet-sized globe brightened, as if signaling, dwarfing the two macroworlds in the foreground. Soon the alien took up the whole sky; but as John rushed toward home, the macroworld grew to blot out the visitor.

He floated into the open cradle, and the locks closed behind him. The flitter settled in, but he did not get out immediately. Responding to his curiosity, the link gave him a 360-degree view of the scene outside, turning for an image of earth's cup, his own companion world nearby, settling finally on the visitor, which was larger than all the spaceborne structures combined.

"They have perfect control," Rob said. "I can't detect any significant gravitational effect from their presence that might be harmful to us or to earth."

"Polite," John said.

"Just a minute. Something's happening."

"What is it, Rob?"

"Our artificial intelligences are chattering away, exchanging information at a fantastic rate, and we can't stop it. Drisa reports the same thing. The process is running like a chain reaction. Wait a moment. . . ."

John heard a high-pitched sound.

"I don't like it," Rob said faintly, as if an ocean of sound were swallowing him. John thought he heard a titanic whispering; there seemed to be laughter in it, or was it joy? A great night tide was washing in, another going out.

"There, it's over," Rob said. A great silence seemed to surround Wheeler's thoughts. "Here's something from Drisa. The aliens claim to have just given us information on how to build better drive systems, complete matter-synthesis capability, and their entire cultural history—as gifts of friendship." Rob almost laughed inside him. "I guess they can't be all bad."

"If it's true," John said.

"Drisa says that it's like an exchange of biological information during reproduction, but on a large scale, between three cultural organisms."

Suddenly John perceived a fact about the alien. The information seemed almost a memory, though he knew that he had just received it. The alien was not a complete stranger. It was carrying two earth-born macroworlds within its structure, bringing them back to sunspace as part of its contact project. The first contact had been made by a mobile a long time ago, so this could no longer be earth's exclusive project.

The alien spoke:

"*We invite you to join our circle of civilizations. The primary consideration for us is the fact that you have achieved organic and artificial intelligence interfaces. This frees you, to a large degree, from old instinctual patterns of motivation, the behavioral forms created in the competitive evolutionary process. Your interfaces are still another example of critical mind freeing itself from the unproductive aspects of instinctual mind.*"

An image appeared:

Bony, birdlike bipeds with large eyes, ancient and reptilian-looking shapes, their limbs bent into a strange posture, joints thorny and skeletal. . . .

As he held the image in his mind, John realized that it revealed very little; the words said more, conveying a greater sense of the culture's inner life and direction. Their words communicated everything, overriding body language and other deep-seated reactions in him; and he knew that this was quite deliberate. He was in the presence of advanced minds, ones that could rise above the irrational structures of brain and body, conveying the degree of their victory of the rational cortex to others without triggering fears and prejudices.

"How then do you deal with younger forms of life?" Rob asked.

"*We do not deal with them at all, but we are aware of their existence; youth is the source of new things in the universe, and worth watching for its fresh approaches to the tragedies and joys of life, even if never contacted. Since we have no problems of energy or resources, our only activity is to set goals worth accomplishing. We found your mobile worlds very promising, having developed this freedom ourselves. There are other circles of macrolife in the universe; one of our aims is to search for them, in order to compare systems of knowledge and experience. Decide amongst yourselves which of you will join us. We will not intrude on your interfaces until you let us know.*"

"They'll probably invite some exchange of population," John said.

"Perhaps. The exchange has given them more than our genetic code. They have enough to grow human individuals for themselves, to see how they will develop in that culture. Maybe they've done it already—we're not the first humankind they've contacted. I wonder how the two other macroworlds have developed."

Doubts came into his mind again, like vermin hunting for his hopes; for a terrifying instant he felt that all the pain of her death would flood back into him. It was incredible that Anulka was dead, infinitely cruel and inexplicable. The structure of her body was dissolving into chaos. What was the inner necessity of irreversible processes? Material things ran down, while minds grew in complex reference and internal resonance. *I did not know her*, he admitted, *I pitied her. I have not yet known another as another needs to be known, as I need to be known.* Pity for the suffering of natural worlds had distracted him, mixing with his real needs, luring him toward the solution of problems he did not yet understand.

He tore the training disk from his temple and attached it to its place on the control panel. Then he climbed out of the flitter; his footsteps echoed in the cradle chamber as he walked to the exit.

The door slid open and he stepped into the corridor of the engineering level. The wide passage was empty of vehicles. He looked right and left. The overhead lights stretched to the vanishing point, curving around the world's forwards. Across from him, the elevator doors were closed. He stood perfectly still, wondering about the endless oblivion of death, the many-legged insect horror that might come rushing toward him at any moment. A small failure within his body might kill him in an instant, despite his indefinite life span. He was still finite and mortal. Macrolife had not crushed death; it had only pushed it out of immediate sight.

He turned right and started to walk down the endless passageway. Was there any doubt, still, where his loyalty lay? People had been killed on a world where intelligence was a small, powerless force, enclosed on all sides by a killing nature, a cruel and squalid process of life clinging to the outside of a planetary surface. The village had been an agricultural community trying to throw off hunting and gathering, while the nomads had persisted in treating the village as just another wild animal to hunt for food. *I'm for macrolife because it is against death,* he thought. *Macrolife is the fulfillment of the hopes of all who have died before me. At last we are free of nature's agriculture of death. City life is finally free of the countryside. As long as there are raw materials, we can exist forever.*

The passageway was restful as he walked. The solar system, he realized, had drawn its children back for a purpose. Old ghosts were being laid to rest; the future was opening up again. In a thousand years, he would still be young, still starting out. Large, impersonal thoughts came into him again. What was this universe, this enveloping reality that made him doubt and hunger and desire? Would he always live without knowing? He stopped and closed his eyes, trying to see forward to ages of greater knowing, willing himself to move ahead into those times, to feel what they held. If he wearied of long life, a thousand, ten thousand, half a million years hence, there would be ways to advance into futurity more quickly. He felt impatient. The limits around him were there as firmly as death had once been. Although home had given a better life to generations, something was still missing. The little voices within him would not be still. He had been born too early, ages before macrolife became more than the uneasy cooperation of its individuals. He had waited most of his early life to see a planet, a local space bathed in the natural light of its sun; but despite the beauties he had seen, the experience had left him with bitterness and pity, and sorrow over the loss that he could not replace or forget easily. Having been born on a world moving in space, he had developed the expectation of arriving at a destination; yet all worlds moved in space, and such motion was incidental to life.

He opened his eyes and continued walking, knowing that he could continue down the passage for hundreds of kilometers without stopping. The thought calmed him, and he knew what he had to do.

25. Crossroads

Human thoughts were everywhere, as numerous as the people he saw in public places, surrounding him with welcome and reassurance. A week after attaining full link, he was still practicing the self-control that would ensure his privacy; separateness of mental space was a right that each citizen knew how to enforce at will. During the first month, he was not always happy about shutting himself up in his own skull; the time off was necessary, but he did not like it. He would send his mind into the information labyrinth of Humanity II, there to be guided by the various servants, who would appear in his field of vision as human personalities, real in every sense except that they could not be touched; they could be called upon to explain visual or written information, to give an audiovisual overview of public activities throughout the home biosphere. They also provided a continuous feedback of medical intelligence from each citizen's body, warning and prescribing as necessary.

Occasionally he would call up the image of Richard Bulero, who would appear full-size and respond to questions; the answers, of course, were only extrapolations made by Humanity II, based on everything that remained of Richard's views. John's biological nephew lived, in a sense, as animated information within macrolife's system of technology for transmitting basic cultural structure. Richard had been prophetic, John learned, about the link system: "The link will not be telepathy, but a direct line into the sensory and speech centers of the brain, perhaps in time using neutrino and tachyon beams as carriers, instead of lasers and radio. Individuals will still have to listen and speak to one another, but the ease of access among individuals, as well as to library information services, will be efficient and convenient, making possible a higher degree of personal growth and democratic participation for everyone. The promise of link implants in creating a cohesive social structure for macrolife cannot be underestimated. Not only will the links between persons be strengthened, enabling them to individuate themselves and to share a common culture to a degree previously impossible, but the sense of historical continuity, educational heritage, and direction will be enhanced." Richard had not foreseen the large-scale use of information imprinting, especially in languages and musical structure, or the link's use in sleep control, psychosomatic direction of the body's self-maintenance programs, the formation of dyads and triads of friends and lovers, the triggering of special brain functions in mathematics and long-term concentration. A whole inner space was opening up its vistas to him.

John found himself alternating between the larger extension of his awareness and the local mental space of his previous self. He had found that he could represent humankind's organized knowledge as a seemingly endless plain of growing things; he would rush across this forest, overcome by the sheer magnitude of stored treasures, dipping into the greenery to sample information. There was a poetry in mind's origins, which expressed itself in these visualizations—a nostalgia for the warm forests and teeming oceans of sunspaces, drawing him with a silent, reconciling music, which he knew to be the song of the brain's oldest regions. "The rational cortex," Richard said, "is the new kid on the block, presuming on the older wisdom of instinct and impulse. Well-dressed, clean, mannerly, the cortex becomes the natural target for the mind's ruffians, who always taunt and bully someone who is not like them. So the older brain bullies the more refined cortex, as well as seducing it with nostalgia, the siren song of a simpler, less conscious existence."

The link enabled him to observe the developing relationship with earth and with the visiting alien. There was discussion of taking the new mobile to the center of the galaxy, to study the core dynamics and to make contact with a number of fast-developing cultures which had recently attained tachyon signaling capability. His own world was considering staying in the solar system for a time, to develop various projects with Drisa's government; among these new undertakings would be the building of mobiles for the restless factions among the solarites.

Drisa wanted the sunward peoples to expand into the asteroid belt, to develop it into mobile and sun-orbit communities. The flying mountains were already settled by a large contingent of industrial workers, the descendants of Martians and Ganymedians; they provided much of the solar system's raw materials. Drisa herself was from Ceres, the largest asteroid, so it was not surprising that she should support the expansion into her native region.

He had not seen her since their meeting on earth; the thought of seeing her again filled him with hope. He was glad that his world was staying, even if that was not a venturesome choice. Drisa represented something completely new for him; Anulka stood for the kind of human past he wanted to forget for a while; Margaret was an unchanging present, giving security and understanding. Of course, Drisa might not like him at all. He wondered what he could do to catch her interest. His image of her was that of a strong woman with a controlled sense of humor. He thought of her body, as it might be; he saw her red hair, her breasts and supple belly. What color were her eyes? Would she be what he imagined, or would she disappoint him?

The world's past was vital again, the present a crossroads of potentialities. For a moment he saw the first three decades of his life as a set of problems, to be understood and put away after he had confronted them. He felt the changelessness of macrolife in himself, its openness, its strength and weakness; there would always be danger in openness, the chance of failing. It seemed that he was condemned to live a contradiction, to be himself and to change, to be permanent yet fluid. The secure world of his childhood was gone; the home biosphere had reproduced and returned to earth; and strangers had come from the stars to offer choices. Life seemed too large suddenly, too complex, making him apprehensive that he would lose himself in it. He longed for the simplicity of Lea, with all its discomforts and dangers; but the longing died as he understood the cause of his lapse. It would happen less frequently as he changed. He perceived the strength of macrolife within; it had always been there, when he had been doubting or accepting.

He did not regret his stay on Lea; he had seen through the eyes of two realms. Home was new to him again; beneath its surface lay a greater world of memory and understanding, an inner world of sympathetic mentors who ruled a universe of information, where he might quiet his hunger to know as he prepared for greater life.

Faraway thoughts drifted around him as he rested in the apartment, quiet, impenetrable clouds of consciousness moving through the mental space of the world surrounding him. There was comfort in the sensation of so many other thoughts; he watched them billow and change shape as their thinkers responded to the universe. The apartment no longer seemed unpleasant. It was his and Yevetha's now.

He sat up. Someone was coming toward the bedroom, a person without a link, probably Yevetha.

The lights brightened into an orange-yellow glow.

"Hello," Drisa Haldane said. "I'm sorry to break in on your rest, but I wanted our talk to be private." She paused. "You're a disturbing person. . . . It was something about you in the valley, maybe the history of the Bulero name."

"What is it?" John was too surprised to look directly at her.

"Perhaps I owe you this visit, since you took such a clear interest. Please don't protest. I'm a trained diplomat and three times your age. I'm not flattering myself."

"No, please go on."

"I'll be leaving soon with a diplomatic and scientific mission to the alien's home system, as part of an exchange delegation."

"I thought you didn't approve of interstellar wandering."

"I don't, but this is too important to pass up, so my personal views don't count. I prefer cultures that grow internally at a rate greater than that of mere physical expansion. I know that you'll be staying, so I wanted to see you before I go."

"I don't understand, but you're welcome, of course."

"Don't you see?"

"What?"

"I want you to know something about me as I am."

"You're really leaving?"

"Yes. I can see your disappointment, but you can't come with me. I've come to teach you a lesson, because I like you. In a century you might very well become an extraordinary person, and an equal."

"What are you talking about?"

He looked directly at her, slowly realizing his mistake. He did not really know her. "I wanted you," he said. "You attracted me."

She took off her tunic and pants, revealing a pale white skin, rounded hips, and small breasts; her red pubis was aglow in the light. She came toward him and his feelings raced, shutting out the link community, shrinking him back into the borders of his own skin as he gazed into her hazel eyes, imprisoning him in the place where he had first grown into awareness. He wanted her, as he had wanted Anulka.

"You don't have to delude yourself," she said as she leaned over him. "The past moves us all and does not have to be thwarted. If you can learn to give without losing yourself, then you'll know how to live across the centuries."

Three kilometers beyond the observatory, he came to a door off the passageway. It opened, and closed when he was inside. "I'm here, Rob," he said within himself as he looked around in the dark. "What do you want to show me?"

His eyes adjusted, and he saw that he was standing on a catwalk. He stepped to the railing and looked out into a seemingly endless space. Suddenly the dark vault burst into light, revealing a model of the galaxy, a titanic three-dimensional projection hanging in the night. The image was steady, as if it were made of glass. He was looking across the top of the lens toward the core, where the globular clusters were concentrations of fireflies floating over the enigmatic center. Streamers of gas laced the great spiral arms of the starry maelstrom.

He walked left on the catwalk, realizing that the chamber was at least five kilometers across. As he peered toward the center of the 100,000 light-years of stars, the image turned and he was looking down at the spiral. "The model can be turned, enlarged, or made smaller," Rob said through the link, "and specific areas can be enlarged as needed. It's only a general map, and only the well-known stars are accurately placed. Unknown regions appear as a wash of light, with only a suggestion of individual stars. What do you think?"

John knew that he did not have to voice his approval. As he tried to look beyond the galaxy, the model shrank, giving him a good view of the Magellanic Clouds, Andromeda and Fornax, the Leo galaxies, Sculptor, and beyond to the local region of the metagalaxy. One day macrolife would have a map of that larger structure; but for the moment this map was a step toward his wish of standing outside nature. On the scale of the cosmos, macrolife was a new kind of cell, the result of things growing upward from the infinitesimal into life, then into organized life and intelligent life, followed by social aggregates of intelligent lives, upward into visible masses within the galaxies, exchanging information between the giant cells, to become . . . what?

"Let me show you something else," Rob said within him.

A portion of the Milky Way grew large suddenly, and John saw red lines linking more than a hundred stars. "These," Rob continued, "are the stars to which the alien belongs. They lie about twenty thousand light-years toward the hub from us. What you see is their tachyon communications net. It has linked their culture for half a million years. The alien who came to contact us is a youngster, scarcely twice as old as we are. The solar system will become part of their net. They talk of developing a galaxy-wide net, then an intergalactic net, perhaps even a rapid-transit system following the routes of their communications beams."

"Rob, the systems in this net—are any planetary civilizations?"

"Some are. Others have industrialized their systems and live in potential mobiles, like Drisa's people. Some move around as we do— our visitor, for example."

John remembered something Richard Bulero had said. *"The history of macrolife will not always be the history of humankind."* He leaned on the rail and thought again of all the human lives before the beginning of his own. They were all with him, still standing against oblivion. *Nature enveloped us,* he thought; *now we are its custodians, carrying it with us wherever we go, whatever we do. What nature was to life, macrolife is to intelligent life.* Beyond the biospheres of planets, a greater nature was coming into being, one that thought and knew itself. Macrolife was the brain and nervous system of something being born all over the galaxy, converging out of the initial diversity of living things as surely as the dust and gas had come together to form stars, yet sustaining within convergence an infinity of change and difference. If the earth had been an infinite flat surface, people would have moved away from one another in an endless flow of groups, diverging continuously, growing unique and powerful, and having no chance to exchange cultural achievements with other groups when stagnation set in. *Macrolife is still diverging,* he thought. *Convergence will begin when macrolife increases in numbers, when new communications and transport systems become available on a large scale.* A day would come when the model before him would be dotted with macrolife, inhabiting the spaces between the stars, clustering around stars, and moving out into the greater darkness like seeds thrown off by the living galaxies, in a vast explosion of intelligent life. Macroworlds would grow to be millions of kilometers in diameter, enclosing entire sunspaces; others would be smaller, clustering in geometrical shapes like the molecules of life. Natural worlds

would continue to be the nurseries of intelligent life; there life would still grow violently, furiously, sweeping through evolution's biological storms, throwing up into consciousness series after series of viable intelligences; there, he knew, the gathering of knowledge would never be the prime concern of life. For a moment his mind started to rage against this cruel reality; that it should be so, that planets should be such festering wounds on the starry face of nature, was intolerable; that so much courage was demanded of life on planets, and with so little reward for individuals, was the ultimate tragedy, a cruelty that might almost have been planned by some universal demon. Now he knew why the marks of a mature culture had to be knowledge and permanence, cooperation and love—above all, a treasuring of all intelligent consciousness; the creation of such a civilization was a task denied to nature. Having provided the compost heap of necessary conditions, nature was content to do no more. Natural selection was at an end; the natural selection of mind's endurance was beginning. There would come a time when he would no longer be able to look back.

He looked into the darkness around the model. Macrolife was the place from which to ask all questions. Would the universe expand forever, destroying all intelligence as all matter reached thermal equilibrium? Would the cosmos collapse into a point of infinite density, crushing the varied intelligences within it? Was there anything beyond the darkness?

He thought of Yevetha and Drisa. He would have to see Yevetha as she was, taking her welfare as his own while remembering that she was different from him. Drisa had taught him that, by showing herself to him as she was—beyond his immediate understanding—and as he had wanted her to be; she had suggested that his yearnings were a young love affair with the universe, not a mature struggle with the tyranny of space and time. Was she right? Had she been amusing herself with him, trying to confuse him? Would he change so much in time to come? A defiant part of him said no; he would love her and Anulka, and everything else around him, as he pleased; while another part of him said yes, and it seemed like death.

He looked at the model for a long time, losing himself in its details as he drew out of himself, becoming old and impersonal, viewing the myriad stars with a kind of love that he had not known before; doubts came in to camp at his center, making him feel fluid, as if at any moment he would dissolve and re-form into someone or something else. The pain of life's passing was a feverish night pressing in around him, filling his mind with fear; but as he fixed his eyes on the glowing model, its stately beauty lent him peace, subduing for him the unassailable quality of all things.

He was about to leave when he came upon himself in his most secret thoughts. He saw what he had been, a being from the past, as man had been before, unchanged, unawakened from nature's sleep, blind to what he could become. He had traveled backward in time, drawn by the freshness of rivers, oceans, and forests, into the older regions of his own mind, seeking the viewpoint of an unknown self— a proud self, outraged by death, yet ready to give death. He looked into himself now, at this beast crouched in something like a deep forest surrounded by mountains, and it looked up at him, unrepentant, unafraid; and he knew that he would see this nursery self become the smallest part of him as it receded into the deepest recesses of his structure. Would it become nothing, he wondered, or would it reawaken someday in all its florid, romantic yearning?

John turned and walked slowly out of the darkness, as if from a holy place.

III. THE DREAM OF TIME

Our galaxy is now in the brief springtime of its life—a springtime made glorious by such brilliant blue-white stars as Vega and Sirius, and, on a more humble scale, our own Sun. Not until these have flamed through their incandescent youth, in a few fleeting billions of years, will the real history of the universe begin.

It will be a history illuminated only by the reds and infrareds of dully glowing stars that would be almost invisible to our eyes; yet the somber hues of that all-but-eternal universe may be full of color and beauty to whatever strange beings have adapted to it. They will know that before them lie, not the millions of years in which we measure eras of geology, nor the billions of years which span the past lives of the stars, but years to be counted literally in trillions.

They will have time enough, in those endless aeons, to attempt all things, and to gather all knowledge. They will not be like gods, because no gods imagined by our minds have ever possessed the powers they will command. But for all that, they may envy us, basking in the bright afterglow of Creation; for we knew the universe when it was young.

—ARTHUR C. CLARKE,
"The Long Twilight,"
Profiles of the Future, 1973

The history of macrolife will not always be the history of humankind. Intelligence is certainly not limited to humanoid forms, or to the chemistry of carbon; other forms will also develop technical civilizations capable of using the energy of their suns on a large scale; for the idea of independence from the chemical-energy-based ecologies of natural planets will surely flow out of alien imaginations, among other things, as it did from our own.

We can expect to alter our bodies as we expand our minds to deal with immortality, with the extended projection of unique personalities across time; we will still call ourselves humankind, but that word will stand for the universality of intelligence in nature, and not for appearances.

—RICHARD BULERO ET AL.,
The History of Macrolife, 10th ed.,
Revised and Updated, vol. 10,
"Projections and Notes," Sol, 3025
(See also vol. 11, "Posthumous Fragments")

We are poor and forgotten
When night falls.
Night after night
Diminishes us toward death,
While by day the smiles of women
Convince us of immortality.
The self is a trap
To escape.

—RICHARD BULERO
(poem found written in the margin of his major work)

There are two kinds of critics of any possibility; those who wait and see, and those who try to kill an idea in advance; at every crossroad, each forward-looking soul is opposed by a thousand guardians of the past.

—RICHARD BULERO
(aphorism in the margin of the last page of his major work)

Then the Old man of the Earth stooped over the floor of the cave, raised a huge stone from it, and left it leaning. It disclosed a great hole.

"That is the way," he said.
"But there are no stairs!"
"You must throw yourself in. There is no other way."
                                        —GEORGE MacDONALD,
                                          The Golden Key

Under my face a steady rivulet of blood was enlarging to a
bright red pool on the sidewalk. It was then, as I peered near-
sightedly at my ebbing substance there in the brilliant sun-
shine, that a surprising thing happened. . . . I lifted a wet
hand out of this welter and murmured in compassionate con-
cern, "Oh, don't go. I'm sorry. I've done for you."

The words were . . . inside and spoken to no one but a
part of myself. I was quite sane, only it was an oddly
detached sanity, for I was addressing blood cells, phagocytes,
platelets, all the crawling, living, independent wonder that
had been part of me and now, through my folly and lack of
care, were dying like beached fish on the hot pavement. A
great wave of passionate contrition, even of adoration, swept
through my mind, a sensation of love on a cosmic scale, for
mark that this experience was, in its way, as vast a catas-
trophe as would be that of a galaxy consciously suffering
through the loss of its solar systems.

                                        —LOREN EISELEY,
                                    The Unexpected Universe,
                                    "The Inner Galaxy," 1969

i

::*Know separateness again*::

He swam in a midnight sea. Something was preparing him for a return to individual consciousness.

"*What has happened?*" John asked of the thing that cared for him. "*What . . . am I?*"

::*You have been separated from another condition*::

"*Why?*"

::*Partially because we could not prevent it, partially because something of you wished it once, and because you may be needed*::

"*I don't understand.*"

::*Know: Macrolife has endured for a hundred billion years. Maroworlds ranging in size from one hundred kilometers to millions of kilometers remain in a universe where star formation has all but ended. Macrolife is the only remaining civilization*::

So much time, he thought, trying to feel where it had passed within him.

::*No time has passed for you. Your present, narrowed awareness has not experienced it*::

He tried to open his eyes.

::See: *The star is a hot blue-white dwarf. The material that was its planets and smaller bodies is gone. Gathered closely around the dwarf, you see thousands of macroworlds of differing sizes, forming a complex even-sided triangular solid, five million kilometers on each side, created for use in gathering the energy of the star until the very end. These worlds are populated in small part by derivations from the humanity you knew, but mostly by the progeny from myriad unions between intelligent species, including the children of organic intelligence, both open-ended and deductive minds. No stars are visible in the sky, as your eyes once saw them. All the remaining suns in the universe are too faint to be seen, except at the closest distances, and often only from inside their shell of worlds. Near us in the darkness, there is only one faint red-normal star, whose slow use of energy may continue for thousands of billions of years, if the universe continues to expand forever::*

"Will it expand forever? What is known?"

::*The galaxies long ago reached their farthest point and are hurtling back toward the center. More and more stars are collapsing into darkness, as are the galactic cores, creating an increasing number of intermittent quasars. Other stars are black dwarfs, their particles resting in the lowest energy states. Radiant energy is slowing its streaming, as the second law of thermodynamics nears its final physical proof. In time, all remaining galactic material will exist as galactic-core black holes, and these will eventually coalesce into the final collapsar::*

The voice became silent inside him, sensing his need to consider; for a time he was alone, a gathering of scattered thoughts in a dark place. Gradually his self-awareness improved, but he still half felt that he was someone else; at any moment the closeness with himself would fade, and he would wake up into another identity. . . .

He opened his eyes to an almost substantial darkness, a shroud thrown over all that was once open and alive with light, concealing the laughter of colors, the longing in distant vistas, the grace of movement.

Slowly the universe became a room filled with shadows and faint lanterns.

::Soon you will see as we do, throughout the spectrum::

It's so late, he thought, so very late. *"From where have I come to this place?"*

::You have come out of us . . . as we fragment. You will understand this later. It is possible that something may be gained by restoring your individuality::

The darkness receded as his eyes adapted. He saw a red glow near the edges of his vision. Gradually it became a bright orange, filling the room, leaving only a faint violet near the curved corners of the floor and ceiling. His vision took in one hundred eighty degrees and was clear right out to the edges. Slowly he moved an arm and floated into position to face the floor.

The floor darkened, revealing a night dotted sparsely with deposits of dully glowing stars, reds and infrareds now visible to his eyes. As he watched, the sky seemed to acquire a glow, as if a distant daylight were spilling in from over the edge of the universe.

::The background temperature of the universe is increasing from continued contraction::

Something drifted into the room. He turned left to face it. The being floating over the translucent floor was vaguely humanoid. Its head was perfectly round and hairless. The body was long and thin, golden-skinned, ending in a tail-like appendage; graceful arms ended in delicate six-fingered hands. The eyes were large black ovals with multiple pupils.

The view below changed to reveal a faint white sun surrounded by a shell of globes.

"John Bulero," the being next to him seemed to say, "I am as you are, but from a time past your origins. We are both restored to an extreme condition of individuality, to the state that preceded what we became later, you and I. The aggregate is all memory and will instruct us as needed."

::A thousand worlds around this star::

John Bulero. The name and gender were somehow his, yet both were strange possessions. Suddenly he thought of bright stars, wondering if home still existed. *::Parts of the home you knew exist within this one, unused memories near the center::* The information was provided without intrusion, gently, with a feeling for his need to reclaim the past.

A portion of the floor became a portal. He was suddenly enveloped in a glowing transparent bubble and carried downward. The thoughts of the alien humanoid reached after him. "Farewell. I hope you find what you need." Then he was moving into an endless passageway. A dull white glow erased all comparisons from his field of vision, producing for brief moments the sensation of rushing at a blank wall.

::You can see into the infrared and beyond, as well as below the ultra-violet::

As the bubble carried him forward, he watched the dull warmth of the walls, the hot fog of his own breath billowing out of his body to fill the red-orange shell of force; he looked at his hands, at the white glow of his naked body, feeling that the form was not his own, that it was an imaginary thing.

Abruptly the bubble flew out of the passage into a large space lined with a desolate landscape, and he knew that he was seeing what was left of the green hollow of home, as he would have imagined it would look after so much time. The hills, lakes, and vegetation were gone, leaving only a layer of fine dust and scattered rocks, a desert of gray and white. Sharp regret filled him as he surveyed the ruins of the place where he had once floated on wings.

The bubble stopped in the center. The sunscreen was a black disk before him, a broken window letting in the cold of space; for a moment he saw darkness rolling in like fog, but the vision vanished as his expectation changed.

An image appeared on the sunscreen. He was looking at a red dwarf, a small sun struggling to maintain its brightness; as he looked, he saw its companion, a dull brown-red existing at the edge of darkness. Then, as his eyes adjusted, he saw that both stars were enveloped in a tenuous haze of heat. Slowly, strange colors floated up out of the penumbras, colors that were not reds, yellows, or oranges, but hues lying between and beyond, somber shades that made him see intense differences and mixtures that he could not name; at one moment he saw only subtle tints; at the next, new brightenings.

::*There are more than two hundred colors in the full spectrum of a sun, from birth to death*::

As his eyes drank in the quanta of radiation emanating from the two stars, he noticed the dark mass of macrolife encircling the dwarfs in a thin ring.

He looked around him. The light crowding into the dust bowl interior through the sunscreen cast an oppressive red twilight across the desert. It's so late, he thought again, so very late. For a moment his orientation shifted, and he was looking down at the sunscreen, a black lake where all the bright stars had been drowned, their fiery glories choked in the deep.

He wondered what lifetimes had gone by, what worlds had lived and died. Why had he been reanimated in this dreamlike form? He felt that he was himself, but he also had the sensation of physical detachment, as if he were both in his body and elsewhere. Why had they not re-created his self from later ages? To this self, waking up in smallness, the life of the universe was past. What had he lived through in the ages following macrolife's first return to the solar system? Had he lived a life, or had it been a dream? The crimson-hued stars around him were capable of lasting longer than the lifetime of reality, misers slowly using their energy across trillions of years still to come, lighting a perpetual evening that refused to become midnight. There were things to be learned on this shore of dying suns, things that he could not learn in any other time. He remembered his curiosity about the ultimate fate of nature, his longing to pass forward through time, becoming timeless in the crossing. The intelligences of this time had surely gathered all knowledge and would tell him what he wanted to know; for he was kin to them, having come out of them, and they would not refuse his plea.

"*What will happen?*" he asked. "*Can the end be overcome?*"

::*We do not know. Our task is to decide what we will do about it*::

The end would be nearby in time, he realized, as they measured time, having experienced billions of years of consciousness.

"*How near is it?*" He could almost feel it pressing in around him, a shadow cast across the universe from a not too distant future.

::*Think and see*::

The sunscreen went black, swallowing the view of huddling fireflies frozen around the faint unmoving fires; thoughts and images filled his mind, unfolding the history of macrolife that he had missed.

ii

Thoughts flowed swiftly. Memory, conscience, planner, and crossroads for all intelligences within its realm, the aggregate's images of macrolife moved like a singing river, its source small and all but impossible, its main flow an inexorable rush across time, its emptying a humiliation before an infinite ocean. It was this humiliation, John sensed, that was intolerable to the vast mind of macrolife; it had not dreamed the dream of time only to die. Its fear became his fear, the terror of something large that had been made small again. He listened and watched.

::Arising from a liquid environment, intelligent life lived on the land masses of natural worlds, then left its cradles in mobile environments, at first using these small designs to move from one planet to another; but in time the designs grew larger, until it became possible to plan complete new environments to fit the needs of sentient beings::

John saw shapes appearing in hundreds of thousands of sunspaces; dead worlds were torn apart by the laser-directed energy of suns. The resulting materials were being used to build a variety of habitats: spheres, tubes, domed-over bowls, egg shapes, clusters of spheres and cylinders, honeycombed asteroids, clear blisters a hundred kilometers across; rings of habitats encircled suns, drinking in the radiant energy.

::These habitats became the containers of further cultural and biological development, consciously directed, replacing endosomatic evolutionary natural selection. The form of macrolife that was known to you began as the child of earth's planetary civilization. The first forms were highly organized land and sea communities; later forms included bases on other planets, as well as an endless series of spacegoing research stations that were capable of reaching any point in the solar system. Asterome, a hollowed-out mass of ore, became the first large

space home to leave sunspace, following the brief decline of civilization in that system. Asterome grew quickly, level after level, until it became a true example of macrolife, a mobile world independent of planetary circumstances::

John saw Asterome entering and leaving a hundred sunspaces, gathering resources, searching for intelligent life; he saw Asterome growing in the light of earthlike suns, double suns, green, red, and white trisystems, giant red suns and blue dwarfs; he saw Asterome's rocky surface acquire a shell, then another, and half a hundred others, until it became the size he remembered.

::Powered by hydrogen fusion, mini black holes, and occasional accumulations of radiant energy, free of a past ruled by scarcity, macrolife reproduced itself more than a hundred times in the following millennium. Later, the development of materials synthesis made macrolife almost completely independent of agriculture and planetary systems.

::Earth-derived macroforms, like so many of different origin, dispersed into the galaxy, living for their own interests and curiosities, largely ignoring natural worlds as being unfit for viable civilizations. Macrolife's versatility naturally fostered this attitude; being a society that could easily meet the needs of its citizens, it permitted them to live as they pleased, supplying wealth and power beyond the needs of any individual. Most interests were permitted within the social container; only its destruction was absolutely forbidden. Macrolife fulfilled the needs of beings in search of knowledge and novelty, the miraculous and infinite, while giving safety and adventure::

"How many were failures?" John asked.

::A large number. Not every world was able to isolate and preserve its most progressive and creative elements. In time these worlds destroyed themselves; but the macrolife that remained became the ultimate polis, a means for assimilating the past, utilizing the variety and rebelliousness of the present as a way to further growth and innovation. Thus macrolife secured its own future, and continues to exist::

John saw empty shells floating in the cold of interstellar space, armadas of dead shapes circling suns whose generous outpouring of energy now fled wasted into the dark abyss, past hearts and minds which had been unable to strike a balance between beast and angel.

::*Inevitably, earth-derived macrolife came into contact with alien macroforms, resulting in hybrid societies, joining cultures and technologies, as well as genetic heritages through biological engineering*::

John saw brightly lit interiors filled with graceful living shapes. The humanoid form was present in shades of brown, gold, black, and white; four-legged beings with heavy brows and finely muscled arms strolled together with birdlike figures; water-filled macroforms supported swimming minds of vast size and profound capabilities; zero-g worlds were filled with floating creatures who seemed busy and sympathetic.

::*Within the first million years, the galaxy came to be dominated by the mobile life-form, swarming in numbers greater than the concentration of stars in some sectors. Raw materials for growth, in the form of gas, dust, debris, and dead worlds, were everywhere, although some planetary cultures sought to restrict the gathering of resources within the confines of their solar systems; however, there were too few powerful cultures that were still ruled by scarcity to pose a serious problem in such confrontations*::

Suddenly it seemed to John that he was *remembering* the history of macrolife. Then he understood; he had been part of that history, and it was only his extreme individual self of the moment which could not remember; his wider self had never forgotten.

::*Macrolife became the galaxy's urban life. Planets became the countryside, with the difference that macrolife was independent of rural support. Each macroworld was different, developing along its own lines, reproducing to create individual children, growing against the common history of the societal framework, whose stability contained all change. In your history, only the Greek city-states had aspired to such a project, and failed for lack of material success.*

::*Special relationships arose between some macroworlds and star systems. Many of these contacts were friendly, others hostile, with blame on both sides. Scores of sun systems, once they had developed a workable form of in-system space*

travel, sought to detain visiting macroforms in order to obtain technical and sci-
entific stores; others sought to seize the starfolk's knowledge of immortality or
learn the legendary recipes for perfect nutrition. Early macroworlders regarded
flesh-eaters with contempt, while planet dwellers regarded the starfolk as can-
nibals, because their foods were identical to their bodily proteins. On more than
one occasion, a planetary system managed to destroy a macroworld; reprisals
against natural worlds became more common as rising civilizations became
aware of the circles of intelligent life existing on the galactic scale. The cry went
out that macrolife was an infestation, a despoiler of sun systems. The only solu-
tion to this hostility was to bring new cultures into the galactic community as
soon as they advanced to a certain level, while taking care to leave those in the
nursery state isolated::

"*What level was that?*" John asked.

::The level at which they could communicate a complaint, thus illustrating
the old principle that the surest way to close the gap between a scarcity-ruled
civilization and one ruled by affluence is to call attention to the gap. A gap
communicated spurs its own closing. Of course, a Type I civilization is one that
can use the power of a whole planet to signal its complaint, so it is already on
its way to solving its scarcity problems, before moving to Type II, which can use
a typical sun for its activities: one such activity is talking to distant equals.
Well-disguised observers often visited nursery worlds, not so much to report on
what was happening as to gain personal experience of life in the universe. This
was an effort to avoid the trained incapacity of specialization so often developed
by Type I and II civilizations, the result of isolation from the harsher aspects of
life, producing a deadening of personal resourcefulness. Later, when contact was
made with previously visited worlds, the results of observation and covert influ-
ence served to form a bond between the cultures.

::In time, many natural planets transformed the materials of their sun sys-
tems into macroforms. Some launched their planets away from their suns, taking
on the attitudes of macrolife, joining in the vast tide of states; others remained
in their sunspaces. Gradually the internal environments of macrolife discarded
the gravity-oriented systems of natural worlds. At first, zero-g had been used as

an industrial convenience, and for recreation; but as it became less necessary to visit natural worlds directly, many worlds changed over to zero-g interiors. A variety of intelligences adapted to life in these flexible, three-dimensional conditions; for these beings, visits to gravity environments were possible only through the use of exoskeletons to support their frail bodies, or in g-screened flitters. Eventually, the very atmospheres of zero-g worlds became mediums from which nutrients could be drawn directly; internally, macrolife became simpler.

::Macrolife permeated the galaxy, having come out of the smallest lifeforms, each unit of life growing to become the unit for the next: first the endless series of cells, then organisms in great variety; then intelligent organisms; societies of intelligent organisms, rising and falling as better methods of organization were tried; finally, the first multiorganismic forms capable of freeing themselves from the limits of planetary existence.

::After filling whole galaxies, macrolife exploded outward into the metagalaxy, there to meet others like itself, combining, consolidating, transforming itself. Five million years after the birth of macrolife, all conflict with natural worlds ceased; most planetary civilizations had either destroyed themselves or become part of macrolife, mobile and sunspace-bound.

::Eons passed. The new countryside being created by the birth of new suns and planets gave rise to new intelligence, which grew toward maturity unaware of our macrolife; these youths emerged into their galaxies with their own macroforms. For one thing is clear about all intelligence: however limited it may be in its origins, it sets no limits for itself in space-time. Mind sets about transforming itself into whatever form is necessary for the attainment of its desires, even if certain attainments can be possessed only in a world of dreams; in those cases, minds dream, living in synthetic realities tended by servant creations, and this form of mind dies when its suns die, unaware of the end.

::Across billions of years, macrolife became layered according to its time of origin, marked by the birth of new stars. The youngest would often initiate the boldest new projects after learning of the existence of the great circle of civilizations around them. Sometimes it took a long time for a younger group of cultures to learn of the existence of older forms::

"*Who are the oldest?*" John asked.

::*We are nearly certain that we know every one, but there may be older Type III forms hidden from us. Our greatest concern now is to continue our system of conscious organization against entropy, to find a way to outlast the decline of nature. We have unified the universe with our communications and transit web, enabling us to go wherever our worlds exist to receive us; because of this, the mobility of macrolife is no longer as important as it was once. Suns and black holes continue to provide all the power we need, as we prepare to suffer the ruin of nature, the end that will make all the epochs of our labor useless, unless we can survive. We have rediscovered the presence of death.*

::*But if we can perceive the nature of the problem, if we can make use of what we know of the nature of the universe, knowledge gained through billions of years of comparing universe models against the evidence of observation and experiment, then perhaps we may succeed::*

"*Where in the universe are we?*" John asked.

::*We are gathered around a dwarf sun that wanders above the plane of a darkening galaxy, the galaxy you once knew::*

The black mirror of the sunscreen revealed a plain of white stars, dull red coals, and massive clouds of gas. He was looking toward the galactic center from above. A strange brightness seemed to be hidden at the galactic core, a glowing fire covered by clouds. The small star, around which this group of macroworlds huddled, might have been an old bridge star to the Magellanic Clouds or a waif torn loose from one of the great globular clusters.

::*The galaxies rotate slowly now, and more mass is swallowed by the growing black hole at each center as rotation slows. In the times since you lived as a simple individual, we have had experience with three kinds of singularities: star-sized black holes; galaxy-core black holes; and the very small black holes that we create for our power generators, the kind that were once part of a younger universe. Some two billion years ahead in time lies the black hole of the universe. As time goes forward, more and more black holes, star-sized and galaxy-core sized, will form with increasing frequency, prefiguring the uni-*

versal collapse into infinite density and zero volume. Infinite density and zero volume being obvious impossibilities, the collapsed matter of our universe will disappear from the space-time we know; space will close up as it becomes infinitely curved in the vicinity of the titanic black hole's mass::

"*What happens then?*" John asked, feeling again that he was asking the question of another part of himself.

::Then all the energy of our universe tunnels out into a new space; the universe is wound up in a quantum fireball, expansion begins, entropy decreases. This is possible, we believe, because universes swim in an infinite superspace, each cosmos expanding and contracting in its season. Imagine that in superspace our universe leaves a mark, a point, and a track; the track grows longer and shorter as it expands and contracts; each collapse into a black hole means there will be a white hole reemergence. In the case of smaller black holes, reemergence may be elsewhere in the same universe, or not at all if the quantum conditions are wrong, leaving a dense mass and a region of curved space, and only the possibility of a white hole. Each emergent universe may be different; its life cycle may be longer or shorter; the final expansion may be larger or smaller; the mass of particles may vary; there may be more disorder, more energy than matter, or the reverse; there may be a difference in the way that the monoforce breaks up into the other forces.

::Each of the universes in superspace has gone through an indefinite number of births and deaths. We may be the first intelligence to think of surviving the end of our cycle. We have an idea of how this may be done::

"*By reaching across superspace to a younger locality?*" John asked.

::No, although that is a consideration. Unfortunately, we have no knowledge of the topology of superspace; there would be no way to know which direction to take, even if superspace could be entered directly. There is another way, however, one based on direct physical observations::

Another configuration of macroworlds appeared on the sunscreen, a ring of faint globes circling a dark center. As John watched, one world left its position near the black hole and began to move away. For the first time in his conversation with the aggregate, John sensed an emotion, a feeling of cold dismay; it passed into him suddenly, filling him up as if it was his own. The globe was moving rapidly away from its companions now. Abruptly it exploded into brightness and died.

"What happened?"

::That world has chosen to die::

"But why?"

::Death has been unknown to us, except by choice; now we are rediscovering it. That world saw nothing more to learn in the continuing slow decline of our universe, one that will fade across a finite time toward a fiery end. Our crisis, John Bulero, is that we have nothing to hope for::

"But you suggested that there was a solution." The dismay had settled inside him like a massive stone; he felt regret bleeding into him as he waited for the answer.

::There is a way, perhaps, to survive. The giant black hole at the center of our galaxy is rotating. Above the event horizon, which is the point of no return for anything approaching the singularity at sublight speeds, there is an area called the ergosphere, where the surface of the collapsar seems to hover forever. There time stands still. We know because we have stayed in this area for brief periods of time, comparing the passage of time there with time outside. Short periods of time in the ergosphere are large periods of time outside. By circling the singularity within the ergosphere, we can move forward in time at a rapid rate::

"When do we come out of the ergosphere?"

::If we stay in the ergosphere long enough, the time line will link directly to the final black hole of the universe, as all the black holes merge. Then we will be circling within the ergosphere of that giant collapsar; and from there we might be able to pass into the next cycle of nature by moving through the neutral area near the singularity's equator::

"Neutral area?"

::A navigable aperture in a spinning singularity where centrifugal forces balance the crushing effects of gravitational collapse. We need this area because we do not know whether our translight drives or protective fields will function in the singularity::

"*What happens then?*"

::*As we circle the galactic-core hole, we must move away when it begins to acquire other black holes during the universal collapse; we must do this to maintain a position in the ergosphere of the universal black hole. This will take a lot of power, possibly all the power we have, which is another reason we must have a neutral passage, an added safety in case our drives and protective fields are without power.*

::*Finally, only the last singularity will remain in the universe, carrying us in its very large ergosphere. Collapse will continue toward infinite density in zero volume, until the gravitational radius is reached, pulling us toward the center of the singularity in a matter of seconds; but the contraction will not continue to infinite density; long before the universe becomes very small, quantum effects will come into play, preventing ultimate collapse. At a certain radius from the center, expansion into new space will begin, carrying us with it, behind the white hole outstream. Black holes, you see, are passages into the future, white holes the outstream from the past. If the electric charge and mass of a black hole are sufficiently large, as they will be in the case of a galaxy core and the universal black hole, conditions should be normal for us inside the charged fields of our worlds; it might even be possible to protect ourselves by turning on our translight drives.*

::*As we emerge into the newly expanding space, the time of the new universe will become our own; the aperture will close behind us as the mass of the new universe disperses in the fireball ahead, freeing again the curvature of space. The passage will close much as the place where a straw pushes through a bubble in the process of formation closes after the input of gas is finished. Thus the configuration of complex information that is macrolife, its internal systems of power and consciousness, will survive the ruin of nature::*

The aggregate was silent for a moment, as if the effort of conveying the magnitude of this project had been too much. All space-time would be in anguished convulsion during the final part of the process; all form would be wiped from the face of nature; all phenomena would perish as macrolife struggled against dissolution, against the crushing hand of death, which it had not known since the universe was young.

"Why are worlds dying when there is an answer?" John asked.

::It may be a false answer. To begin with, it would take all our energy to maintain and adjust our position within the galactic core hole's ergosphere; energy expenditure would increase as we passed farther into futurity. We will need reserves to maintain our various protective fields against the possible effects of the white hole outstream, as well as against the density and temperature of the new universe in its early stages; we may need to use our tachyon tunneling drives for brief moments, to pass by the effects at the birth of the next cycle; this last may not be necessary, as the expansion might proceed with us at its outer edge. Still, there may be unforeseen dangers. What you must understand is that the price of using all our resources and energy on such a venture has created for us what may be an insurmountable crisis::

"Is there a choice?"

::Death by choice, or death by fate::

"But wouldn't it be better to die trying, to risk everything on even the smallest hope for success?"

::Now you know why your extreme individuality has been returned. Our mind is too conscious of difficulties and possible failure, too unused to death, to develop the impetus to risk everything. Caution is the first principle of practical reason, which is finite, dealing with the definable and known. Under the pressure of time and death, you have reappeared to stand apart from our large individuality. Macrolife began to fragment into blocks of worlds, then into single worlds; you are one of the first individuals to reappear inside a single unit. We are forced . . . I am forced to interpret this as a survival response. You, and others like you, will try to save yourselves, as you must, in the manner of younger intelligences, and you may save macrolife::

"Then . . . my body has not persisted from before." Suddenly John was afraid, as he confronted the thought that he was not himself, that something large had been dreaming him.

::You have been retrieved from past information; your bodily form, such as it is, has been visualized to be as it was. What you are now remembers the past,

even if what you are now is a duplication of an earlier self, an exact copy in everything except that it is a copy. Perhaps you are still your original pattern of complex awareness; I do not know, but that is not the central consideration. You might think it cruel to be brought back to such extreme finitude, to be small and powerless in your self; but I assure you that we may follow your will, because small, narrowly focused systems of past intelligent life were capable of what seem to us now as blind decisions of transcendent potential. What is convincing about this view is the fact that you were not called up entirely through our choice; you have been thrown up at a time when incapacity before death fragments macrolife::

In the aggregate's containing silence, John wondered about the limits to the size of intelligence. After a point, the parts of a vast mind might begin to separate, as the being broke up into simpler components. . . .

::This is happening because we are again faced with the possibility of death. Many worlds have already fallen into forgetfulness, with no center of general remembrance; they no longer know who or what they are, and live as dreams in the self-maintaining structure, which provides objects for perception in an energy environment. In time we may disintegrate into billions of individual entities as the galactic core holes coalesce and natural history accelerates toward its point of quantum uncertainty::

"Who are you?" John asked.

::I am one of the larger centers, a hyperpersonal aggregate of historical individuals. As I acquired facets, I grew more complex, containing whole worlds of awareness. Only a little while ago . . . I was larger. I know what is happening, having served those who have fallen away. You were part of me, and now you know also::

The aggregate sensed his confusion.

::Think of minds, individual bodies, both physical constructs and beings of force, pure patterns of energy. Imagine a vast system of minds within one macroworld, sustained by a central source of energy. Individuals are facets, but they enter into larger, linked unions, which become permanent, evolving into

still greater minds as they join with other macroworlds in a conscious design.
Imagine large biological masses, teeming with mind-linked individuals, cells of
life as large as entire sunspaces::

He thought of warm lighted spaces, where the cold darkness was
only a distant thought; where the eye saw bright violets, blues, greens,
and yellows, warm orange, and little else; where the universe was new.
All gone, all lost because he had forgotten. Countless joys and
tragedies flying up like sparks, discovering one another, loving, hating,
passing. . . .

He remembered wanting to witness final things.

Before him now lay the abyss separating all consciousness from the
end of time. Macrolife's spontaneous response to the problem of survival was a process of fragmentation, a narrowing of perception in the
manner of the ancients who had put blinders on horses before leading
them through danger. Isolated centers of consciousness would revert to
local control; blind to billions of years of critical doubt, these centers
of mind would lead. Alone in a midnight universe of dying worlds, he
knew what had to be done. He did not want to die; therefore, any
choice was better than waiting for the final darkness. . . .

"Is there anyone else like me?" he asked. *"Has anyone else reawakened?"*

The screen showed another sudden star, another world dying after
a final moment of light.

::There is::

iii

The bubble moved, carrying him out of the desolate hollow into a passageway, away from the once green place where he had played as a child, where the sunlight of a hundred different suns had streamed in to fill the garden-forest space, playing like liquid on the leaves and grass. He remembered well-lighted urban levels, stylish living complexes, environments created by the loving will and dedicated intelligence of a powerful people; he remembered a civilization created in a period of crisis, when only the new and the best had been sufficient to decide whether the life of earth would continue or be spilled back into evolution's echoing cauldron of screams.

::*You will meet someone like yourself*;:

The bubble shot out into darkness; his eyes adjusted and he saw a glowing white floor. The bubble floated forward across the limitless surface. John peered ahead, trying to penetrate the blackness, but there was nothing except the warm glow of the endless floor.

Gradually he began to see something. At first it appeared to be a mound with a gray peak, shimmering so far away that all the bubble's forward motion could not make it larger; then it began to look like a raised platform, a dais, or a huge bed. Something like a human figure sat in a black, almost invisible chair. The light from the glowing floor threw shadows into the figure's face, giving it the appearance of an eyeless mask looking upward.

Suddenly the bubble was gone from around him, and he was standing on the floor near the edge of the platform. As he looked up at the shape on the dais, John became aware of gravity. He observed his bare feet pressing against the lighted floor; it seemed that the ethereal light was passing into his legs and body, illuminating him from within.

::He is in a chair, to make a familiar image for you::

"Who are you?" John asked the figure.

There was no answer. The face was still searching the obscurity overhead. The eyes were dark hollows. There was no billowing of breath from the mouth. The body was covered by a seamless garment.

The floor darkened until there was only enough light to illuminate the figure, now seemingly floating in the darkness.

A distantly familiar voice answered him at last.

"I am like yourself. I lived in the time that you remember, in the memory that has been restored to you. Our origins were the same, but I have forgotten millions of lifetimes. What I am now is not the individual facet of macrolife to which you have returned. I have fallen back, but not to your state. I am as different from you as you are from the single cell that began your life. Yet once I knew you. . . ."

John almost knew the voice. "I did know you. Who were you?"

"Searching through stored knowledge and experience, I find that I knew you—only that, nothing more. I cannot remember as you remember. . . ."

"But tell me who you are!" The face was looking at him, eyes now clearly visible, large inhuman eyes. Someone was alive in those eyes, struggling to reach him, a lost friend swimming upward through cold, deep waters.

"Who are you?" John asked again.

He saw white lips part to answer; a hand raised itself and fell; the lips closed to complete a stony expression of failure.

John walked forward and stopped at the edge of the platform. For the first time now, he noticed the figure's size. The person in the chair was at least fifteen feet tall, sitting down. Looking up into the darkened face, John asked again: "Can you tell me who you are?"

"I was, in part, Blackfriar. Do you know me?" The words came painfully, as if they were being ripped out.

As the words spoke within him, John Bulero knew that something more than his old friend was speaking, and Blackfriar was the least part of it; the words were being pulled out of archaic substrata, sources so old that they could not be drawn upon with any sympathy or recognition. As he continued to watch the colossal face, feelings of recognition wrenched him. "Frank," he cried out. "It's me! Frank, why are you here, like this?"

The face looked into the oblivion overhead. "I don't know," it said. "I think . . . I have come here to die."

The sadness in the voice brought panic into John. "Frank—remember Lea? Remember the three centuries that followed? Remember when we left the galaxy, remember how we made nothing of the distance to Andromeda?"

The stone face looked down at him, and through him.

"Frank—try and remember when it was not so dark, when everything was young and bright." John felt himself grow more desperate, almost as if he were watching another person, until the panic inside him broke out in a reproach. "Why did you have to be here!" he shouted.

"I don't know," the great shape repeated. "I don't know."

::*Like yourself, he has become an isolated center of consciousness, falling back into this state from a greater state. You are the most isolated form, remembering life as it was before you were even one millennium old; he is an aggregate of individual centers, perhaps including others that were once known to you. His confusion is great as he tries to meet your demands. Now you see why something must be done quickly, why you must lead before we disintegrate into powerless, suffering forms, incapable of understanding our own instrumentalities. This is why we have arranged this meeting, visualizing it as best we could. Do you understand?*::

All of time is dead and gone. The thought was a cold, desolate wind. He wanted to weep, but the grip of sudden loneliness froze the reaction in him, suspending him in a barren silence, naked before his own scrutiny. . . .

A part of him took satisfaction in the understanding of space-time that he now possessed. Once he might have given anything to be here, to see and know what would happen at the end. He thought of the thousands of lives that he had certainly lived before the universe had reached its noon, and the millions that must have followed in the long afternoon and early evening. How often had be been cloned; how many destinies had his mind-body pattern followed? How long had he been an individual before macrolife took the next step upward in organization?

He thought of Anulka; her shadow and that of her murderer came into him, threatening to kill all sense of renewal and hope. Like the universe around him, those two persons, and countless others, would never come again.

Anulka stood before him, dressed as he had last seen her.

"John," she said.

Something—within him—was holding her back. Then he realized that she was a creation—too lovely to be the reality. The aggregate could not call up the original because all that was left of her was a memory, an idealization which responded to his moods. He remembered his anger toward her, and she tensed visibly; he recalled her strong arms and intense kisses, and she softened; he thought of her disappointment, and her eyes became cold. She continued looking at him, as if she were trying to penetrate a barrier between them; in a moment she would succeed and he would hold her.

::*The matrix of information out of which she might have been recalled is random noise. All that exists of her now is information flowing in one direction, out of your memory. There is nothing of her outside of you that remembers the past::*

As he looked into the eyes of the image, he realized that he was looking into himself and that he was only a thought in some larger mind. *I think, I feel, the irreversible loss of her, and I know that I do so. What am I?*

She faded and he realized that the aggregate held others who were real, that the aggregate was a sum of continuing personalities. Who were they, besides Frank? He saw hierarchies, whole worlds contained in the lower reaches of the aggregate, minds living out entire sensory existences, bits of information unaware of the greater whole, as cells are oblivious of the body.

::No. They are aware of the larger complex, and may enter it at any time, though not as discrete configurations, and they may return to the smaller focus of intelligent awareness::

"Who else is there?"

Drisa Haldane appeared.

"Help us," she said.

He saw Margaret, Rob Wheeler, Yevetha, and hundreds of familiar faces. What lives had they lived? How much was there to remember?

"You must help," they said.

These shapes insisted, existing as independent realities, not just memories. He could feel their pleas reaching into him, pushing into his pride. He was to be the horse who would go forward because blinders prevented him from seeing the danger; his mind was too small to see all the difficulties of the survival project; his narrow focus was the scalpel that would cut away inertia and the fear of death. . . .

Where were his memories of the midtime? He must have seen the great central ages of the universe; yet it was exactly as if he had not seen them, as if he had been exiled to this place without ever having lived.

::Do you understand?::

I'm alive somewhere, he thought, alive but dying, and all this is a desperate dream, the only thing that I can throw against death. He saw his body lying in a field, under a bright sun that would burn for another billion years, as his eyes turned inward to a growing darkness.

"Where are my memories?"

::First, do you understand the danger, and what you must do?::

"Yes, but tell me—"

::Will you do what is necessary?::

"Yes, but please tell me—"

John waited, suddenly afraid that the complex personality had disintegrated into smaller components.

"Tell me!" John shouted. The darkness was an army of shadows assaulting him from every direction.

::*As an extreme individuality . . . you could not contain, or differentiate, the memories of even a hundred thousand years; you would have to change, following the path of renewal, much like the strategy of birth and death in the natural realm. After a millennium, you ceased to be the individual that you recall now; you chose to expand your personality, so that it might better deal with time. It was the common choice of that period; extended lifetime demanded that individuals expand their minds, in order to cope. Less complex individuals quickly ran out of creative resources; unable to sustain life interest, these limited entities chose death or forgetfulness. After the first millennium of your life, there is no John Bulero, as he is again now. You would have to reintegrate in order to regain the subjective experience of the times that followed, and then you would not be the personality that now asks to know::*

"Return to me what you can!"

::*There is almost nothing left::*

"I want what is mine!" He pictured an endless series of missing moments, dead within him, their time stolen and stored somewhere, deteriorating into a noisy chaos of information.

He reached out, longing, and saw:

The last planet; the final bit of debris was gone, used up in the building of interior living spaces. The sun was now enclosed in a porous shell of worlds, a small galaxy of intelligences drinking its radiant energy.

He was among them somewhere.

He saw Drisa and himself for a moment.

Macrolife exploded outward from thousands of worlds, striving, building, intruding. . . .

He felt its effort to fill the darkness. Its will was his will, but he could not find himself.

The home sunspace was dying:

He saw a bloating red sun and millions of worlds retreating from its vaporizing tide. . . .

The red giant collapsed into a white-hot star; the worlds crept in closer again.

Still, he could not find himself in the breathing membrane of life.

He listened, bloodying himself on oddly shaped memories as the aggregate labored to reconstruct a personal universe. Only shards remained, hints and images, facets of a titan's life. Slowly John realized that what he wanted was to fulfill the desire of something that was a shard; he was a broken piece which thought of itself as the whole; but he could no more grasp the whole than a single drop could be an ocean.

Ocean? Once there had been oceans, the warm places of origin, the wombs that came before the war of evolution. . . .

::There is no more. It has not survived::

As he looked up at Blackfriar again, John felt a quickening, as if he were about to return to a state of swifter rational processes, faster intuitions and comprehension, all fed by vast knowledge and experience; but he held back, content for the moment to know that his sudden regret and grief could be dissolved.

"I am sorry," Blackfriar said, "that I cannot remember, that I cannot be the person you knew. Yet . . . there is . . . about you . . . a certain familiarity. Wait! I think I remember . . . something. . . ."

John rushed to the edge of an abyss and looked across at his friend.

"Didn't we? Wasn't it . . . could we have done . . . whatever it was?"

"Go on!"

"I . . . can't. I? What am I?"

John's hope fell away into the darkness. "That's enough," he said. "You and I and countless others have been together throughout time. I understand that now." He felt in control again, knowing that the half-truth would have to be enough. The kinship he felt with the terrified being existing behind the mask of the giant was real, whoever he was.

::Think of how many will suffer, as time throws each into its abyss of individuality and helplessness::

"We need a new universe," John said, trying to fill the thought with the necessary urgency. "We must act."

iv

He sat in space, seemingly unprotected on all sides. Below him, the infrared galaxy was a swirl of ancient stars, a black floor patterned with white and dull red coals, except for the hidden center. He was looking toward the galactic black hole from the edge of a desert cut out of the center of the spiral, an emptiness twenty thousand light-years in radius, the intermediate result of the core hole's ravenous appetite.

::*This is what remains of a quasar. Billions of years ago, supermassive star clusters within this galaxy core collapsed into a giant black hole; an accretion sphere formed. Electromagnetic forces are greatly intensified in sun-sized objects when they are pulled into large gravitational fields. Vast amounts of energy are given off when these objects are accelerated to relativistic speeds by the giant black hole's attraction; gravitational force intensifies electromagnetic forces, which in turn create the field conditions for the acceleration of incoming objects. The resulting emission of energy, 10^{44} ergs per second, is what powered the quasars, making them visible from all points in the universe.*

::*But as the central region of this galaxy was hollowed out, not all its suns were destined to be eaten immediately, whole or piecemeal, as were those nearest the core. For a time, a core hole settles down in a desert of its own making, until a slowdown in galactic rotation brings more objects toward the center, thus permitting new accretion of matter to begin. The moribund quasar may even remain quiet long after star formation has ceased and most suns have left the main sequence of their lives. When the galaxies rush together and the core holes coalesce, a superquasar will form, giving off the energy gained from the accretion of all the remaining matter in our universe; but finally this quasar will also quiet itself, because not even its violence can halt the final collapse of nature. The last black hole will swallow the remaining material of the uni-*

357

verse; and since compression approaching infinite density in zero volume is not possible, quantum cosmology predicts that a passage into new space will be opened by the massive monoblock's intense field distortions, when all forces are again one force, permitting the outstream of expanding material in a fireball, a white hole depositing the basic materials of the new universe.

::The universal collapse will have the characteristics of every stellar object in nature. As the core holes coalesce, we will see aspects of a massive sun as it becomes a neutron star pulsar, quasar, black hole, followed by the expansion of the tunneling fireball::

A whirlpool into infinity, John thought as he looked into the galaxy's central darkness, except that infinity is not reached, the collapsing universe cannot squeeze itself into nothingness. He turned in space and looked at the gathering of macrolife behind him, millions of worlds readying to approach the ergosphere of the core hole, where time would slow for them and the line of experienced time would link the present to the time of final collapse.

Using the tachyon drive systems powered by the gravitational energy of small artificial black holes, the swarm of macroworlds would reach the ergosphere in less than an hour.

Move, he said inwardly, giving the command. For a moment he imagined that he could feel the forward motion across the core desert, but it was only the blinking of space-time as the drive stitched through the parsecs, folding up the continuum to the central black hole, shortening space at the level of quantum structure. The force bubble brightened around him, and he knew that all the energy of macrolife was being directed into protective fields and drives.

The worlds were moving in to form a network of points in the ergosphere, surrounding the titanic black hole with a porous shell. Once established, the shell would continue to rotate swiftly; all the power of each world would go into maintaining its position just above the event horizon, an ergosphere of consciousness creating a time machine out of itself, its instrumentalities and the core hole's immense gravitational field. Time would stand still within, as the dark universe outside rushed toward its end.

The view ahead was now one of complete darkness, a sudden wall in front of him; in another moment the wall seemed to be a floor only a few feet below; then he was looking up at an impenetrable ceiling. He was rushing across the face of this darkness, but there was no sign of motion. He had almost expected a reflection of some kind, as if the black lake that would soon swallow all creation were a mirror. The resolve to outlast a short-lived nature was now complete; it was too late to turn back.

He called up multiple rear and side views. His companions glowed red and white, as their energy sources strained to deliver the power that would maintain the worlds in their positions. He reached out and looked inside the nearest world, a hollow sphere almost a million kilometers across. Here beings of pure energy circled the small artificial sun, their social structure sustained by ageless instrumentalities attached to the inner surface. . . .

He withdrew when he heard the whispers, a rising chorus of comments and questions, increasing toward a critical mass of confusion. Thoughts radiating from every world assailed him as he tried to listen.

". . . How long, how long . . . ?"

". . . Who am I, what has happened . . . ?"

". . . Why are we like this, alone? Where are my hands and feet, why can't I see . . . ?"

". . . Will anyone speak to me? Please, someone. . . ."

". . . Is this a mistake . . . ?"

". . . Someone turn on the light. I only want to sleep. . . ."

". . . Wake me, wake me, will someone please wake me. . . ."

". . . I went to sleep and my life disappeared, all my youth, all the light . . . the light, where is the light . . . ?"

The pleas were all around him, an invisible mob pressing into his mind, crushing his thoughts.

"What is happening?" John asked.

::These within us have regained earlier states, extreme individuality, like you and Blackfriar. They are confused and lost, until—::

"Until what? Say it!" He was filling up with pity and sorrow. The suddenness of the feelings frightened him, making him fear that he would be torn apart.

". . . Help us, someone help us. . . ."

::Until . . .we can reintegrate them . . . after the end, if we survive::

". . . Aaaah!"

::It will grow worse near the end. This has been coming for a long time, since the rediscovery of death. The larger aggregates rule the smaller, ever since the largest fragmented::

He was in a dark room with a million people, and he had to calm them before they trampled him and one another to death in panic.

"Quiet!" he shouted, wishing that his mental shout might brighten into a light.

::It would be as if an individual organism from your time fell apart into single cells. In that sense all multiorganismic life is macrolife, except the single cell—::

"How many can we lose before a world becomes incoherent? How many worlds before all macrolife becomes incoherent?"

::Most of these we have already left behind. . . . In a sense we are already less, since each grouping in each galaxy exists for itself now. In every galaxy, only a million worlds may have reached the core, to make the final effort. Most have not. I can hear them dying in the galaxies, John Bulero, those who are readying to destroy themselves, and those who are fragmenting into unconscious states—and yes, I hear those who are doing as we are doing, even though they doubt. The waste, the terrible waste! John Bulero! Those of us who can still see a larger course, we must hold everything together, until—::

"What is it?"

::I have lost another part . . . of myself, a small part, but there will be other losses::

"I won't fail you! Can you go on?"

::Yes::

Then he reached out, and his consciousness passed through all the worlds of the ergosphere, a tachyon lash flashing from one container of consciousness to another. Now he felt the presence of those who were still strong and organized; he felt their excitement, expectation, subdued fear, their trust and understanding. Through them, he was macrolife, the sum of all intelligence in nature, now making a final stand against death. He was all consciousness and hope, gathered here from all space-time to strike back at the monstrous oblivion that had dogged all life since the beginning of time. Outside the ergosphere, beyond this shore of rebellion, the universe was dying. Outside, he knew, time was racing forward, minutes for millions of years; yet to those intelligences still outside, time dragged onward as slowly as ever; by now it was a universe strewn with dead worlds and insane mentalities.

He thought of a hydrogen gas cloud expanding after the birth of a universe: gravity, the force that will later collapse all space-time, is already at work, gathering gas into galaxies, forming stars in the spiral arms, lighting the fires that will, for a time, resist the force of gravitational collapse with the heat of thermonuclear expansion. A universe of stars and galaxies comes into being. Life arises, and one day startles itself with self-awareness, growing in knowledge and puzzlement, as if something had designed nature to be finally unknowable, even while providing an endless stream of knowable particulars. The mainspring of cosmic evolution is the energy released by gravitational collapse; it lights the stars and waits for their exhaustion; the end is present in the beginning. The drive behind conscious intelligence is the perpetual inability to complete its knowledge; futility fuels purpose. The inability of mind to overcome certain built-in obstacles is the main feature of existence. He wondered if it could ever be any other way, anywhere. What would an existence of perfect knowledge, translucent perception, and complete power mean? It seemed almost . . . if one were to design a universe . . . it would have to be partially opaque, incomplete, knowable to its intelligent life only in little pieces; it would make no sense to reveal everything at the beginning. Knowledge had to expand in the minds of observers as the universe expanded, only to collapse when the universe collapsed. The failure of knowledge lay in its impossible hope of completion, as universal physical collapse lay waiting in the heart of all matter; there could be no other state but incompleteness. All this would be true, he realized, even if they passed through the end of this cycle; a final, explanatory power would always be denied to systems of knowledge built by finite intelligence. Yet so much, he thought, is known. For a moment he wondered if anything could exist beyond the cycles of one universe; could there be any way to explore the possibility?

Desolation swept through him. Perhaps this kind of survival was impossible? Maybe a kind of natural selection was at work here also, and survival would go to those who understood the problem best; perhaps the life now remaining had waited too long? He looked into the darkness, the place where the whole frame of nature would be shattered and crushed, and he felt small. As nature had given birth to conscious intelligence, and to macrolife, so now macrolife held all that was left of living nature within itself. Throughout its rise, mind had been dominated by the god of nature, tormented by natural cruelties and dead ends; no amount of worship had done any good. Now nature's obstacles were back in full force.

A coldly impersonal resentment grew in him now, confirming his earlier resolve to endure and prevail. If the entropic decline of this cycle could be overcome, then the limiting god of nature could be defeated again and again. Surviving intelligences might continue to develop, even though they arose within the absurdities of scarcity and through the murder of other forms, growing into consciousness marked by a sense of expulsion, the residue of evolution's adaptive programs.

He saw himself playing in the green forest of the hollow. Yellow sunlight painted the moss-covered ground with slanting beams. He was ten years old again, only a moment ago, a strange creature in the dawn of time, knowing already that he would not have to die or grow old and useless. He could learn anything he wanted to know, as long as he devised the right questions. In school they taught only questions—all the old questions, all the newest questions, and the context of asking them. There were questions which had answers; some had more than one answer; others had no answer; and about still others it was not known whether they could have an answer or not.

The trees and moss in the curving hollow had no interest in questions or answers; the animals, preserved since the passing of earth, were easily satisfied here. The trees seemed to care only for the beauty of their proud stance; with the sunlight on it, the moss seemed to be dreaming. . . .

He wrenched himself forward across the eons to the present. A universe of intelligences stood at his shoulder, as well as a universe where every black hole had been still another leak in a sinking ship, as inevitable as each gray hair in a human head, prefiguring in miniature the fate of every atom in every star and stone. The time line of every piece of matter arched forward across time into the final black hole that was now forming.

As he strained to pierce the darkness, his eyes drank in a faint light. It became brighter, and he realized that he was seeing the growing glow of the titanic quasar forming at the end of time. All the remaining matter in the galaxies was falling into the black hole as it merged with one core hole after another. The universe was getting hotter and hotter; now, he knew, macrolife was leaving the ergosphere, pulling back to a safer distance until the quasar quieted itself for the last collapse.

The sky brightened with energy, became white, bathing the shrunken universe with radiation and heat, washing by the protective field of each macroworld like a tide around smooth stones. Then, in the rush of time, it was over; there was no matter left to be pulled into the center. The quasar was dead, unable to generate more power. . . .

John felt the worlds give in, permitting themselves to be pulled into the ergosphere of the last black hole, but no closer. All that had been was here now, rainbow and rose, mountain and cloud, all yearning and its denial, an individual universe of light and life that would never come again.

Although it seemed that an eternity was passing, he knew that only microseconds were going by as the singularity collapsed toward its gravitational radius, carrying in its ergosphere all that survived of macrolife as the galaxies were pushed together toward infinite compression. . . .

His limbs kicked involuntarily, remembering an ancient terror of being enclosed. . . .

Suddenly he felt as if a great weight had been lifted from him. The superdense mass had reached its greatest point of collapse, bending the curvature of space-time toward infinity, and had tunneled out as a white hole in new space. No one would ever see the expanding fireball; one does not witness one's birth, though there are sensations of pulling and pressing, then relief, to be remembered only in a rudimentary way.

The way was open, where the collapsing mass had tunneled through; but it would not remain open for long. His sensors reached out to the glowing points of his companion worlds, motionless candles in a still midnight; he watched them grow faint as they fell toward a common center and winked out one by one, pulled to the future from an ultimate past. Quickly he flashed through the worlds, looking out from each as they passed below the point of visibility and no electromagnetic radiation could reach him. The last world disappeared, denying him his final observation point.

All sense of forward motion ceased, and he wondered again if it would all be for nothing—billions, perhaps nearly a trillion years of life and continuous civilization, wasted in the last moments. . . .

::*There was no other way*:: the aggregate said out of its long silence.

How long, John wondered, how long this darkness?

::The question has no meaning::

He thought again of black holes from all the ages streaming forward into a bottomless black pool. The universe, the greater continuum of superspace, was filled with an infinity of smaller spaces, separated from each other by singularities. Smaller black holes, as well as the final one, were the means for covering infinite intervals of spacetime in small subjective times. He knew that they would emerge soon—but how long would it seem?

"How is our power?"

::Almost gone::

Flashes of light, starlike bits of energy, appeared in the darkness ahead, passing through him to be left behind. Then the darkness acquired a strange glow, dividing itself into concentric circles growing smaller and smaller to infinity. As he watched, he realized that a model was being created inside him, something that would help him grasp the reality of time acquiring the characterisitics of space, and space becoming like time.

::All black holes, at whatever time in the life of the universe they appear, are congruent in a higher space. Collapsar galaxies rushing together are already together at a future time; if time is space, one the other, then all space is one and all times meet. All dimensionality of one universe is a point in superspace, where a monistic infinity may be divided into distinct things, and these divided further without end, as long as the law of boundaries is observed. A universe of individualities emerges, creating consciousness out of complexities; and consciousness strives toward unity through a consolidation of values::

As he stared into the darkness, he imagined that he was swallowing an infinity of darkness, compressing it into a black rope as it rushed into him, filling him like a coiled snake. Macrolife, he realized, his worlds, would have created *one* new individual, if the universe had not ended; the end would have been the beginning. *I am macrolife,* he thought, *as much as any individual.*

As time swallowed itself around him, he saw a faint purple ahead, almost deep royal blue in places. A series of afterimages followed, reflections and mirror images traveling backward in time into his perceptual field, as if something had passed him, leaving a wake. At one moment it seemed as if the space of the tunnel had retained not only a full negative record of the great collapsing mass that had formed it, but also an image of the mass that had collapsed toward an impossible condition. While macrolife had circled the galactic core hole, the light of the universe had been a record of all the future, all the remaining future rushing in to end in a few moments of experienced time; all that energy, matter, and light that had fallen into the pit was now ahead of them; nothing was left behind; the future was everything.

What if we never come out, he thought, what if this collapsed space is looped into an infinite limbo? What if the white hole closes immediately after the outstream? Macrolife might never see the morning light of creation. . . .

Again he saw some vast, blurred image, as if something rushing ahead of them were leaving a trail. Then darkness returned for a long time, and with it came a complete hopelessness.

The hopelessness shattered into a million thoughts.

". . . We shall never come out . . ."

". . . We should have stayed in the past, where the end was still far off . . ."

". . . What shall we do . . . ?"

If we come out, John thought, it will be like regaining the past, except for whatever original features might exist in the new cycle of nature. He tried to shut out the continuing assault of doubts and reproaches being exchanged in the darkness. Was this the first time creation had come to an end? Was it the first time that all distinctions had been collapsed, only to be remade anew into a new variety? Perhaps this *was* the first time the universe had ended, and there would never be another. The idea was as frightening as the thought of a universe expanding into cold nothingness, never to be drawn back together, never to grow warm again. It was unthinkable that only nothingness lay ahead; as unthinkable as the idea of absolute zero, left without right, or a unique beginning to the cycles of expansion and contraction.

::It may be::

"I reject even the possibility," John said. "It is as impossible as the idea of absolute nothingness; something must always exist; to imagine otherwise is to fall into contradiction."

But how knowable would the new universe be? How long would it last? He imagined the births and deaths of the universe to be days and nights, or seasons; each season would be different, filled with unique details, never fully knowable. Surely something like this was true. All that macrolife had done, was now doing, had once been imagined; what was happening now, in this passage between universe cycles, past and future, was as much understood through intuition and imagination as through accumulated knowledge. His perception of what was happening was indirect, built up out of his own and the aggregate's visualizations; the predictions had been correct until now, leaving only the emergence into new space to be fulfilled. . . .

::The weight of all that is known is on the side of our success. Too much beauty lies behind our models, too much is explained, for it not to be true::

"But you still doubt?"

::Doubt is always necessary::

He stared into the darkness, doubting as fear crept into him.

"What will I see? What should I see? Tell me what to look for!"

::Look for the light of cooling hydrogen, as the fireball dissipates. Hydrogen forms after the outstream, when the temperature of the fireball drops low enough. We will see the light of heated hydrogen::

But only darkness still lay ahead.

A renewed babble went up around him, but he shut it out, subduing the thoughts as they lanced into him, blunting their penetration, beating them into a contained silence, cutting the lines of panic to reduce the danger of disintegration; at one moment he struck out with mercy, but in the next moment it felt like murder.

"Let it begin," he said to himself. "Let the light begin."

A chorus picked up his thought as if it were a prayer.

". . . Begin, begin, begin . . ."

". . . Let begin, let begin . . ."

". . . Light, light, light . . ."

". . . Begin the light, begin the light . . ."

". . . Let it begin," he said, joining in as he felt the yearning take hold of him, desire struggling against a fate that seemed determined to drown the last of intelligence, down, down, down, throwing it into a bottomless spatial deformity, into an oblivion without death.

"Let it begin," he said again, afraid that his fearfulness would cause a critical mass of doubt, leaving him to drift in darkness, alone in a sea of mad beings. "Let us live," he said, as the hope drained out of him.

U

::Light:: The very word seemed to glow as John peered ahead.

Slowly, the rich royal purple of hydrogen appeared as a distant patch, growing suddenly to cover half the field of vision; the mixture of helium's vivid spring green created areas of faint yellow. John heard a sound, something like the tinkling notes of a soft harpsichord playing a ghostly row. His awareness flashed through all the worlds, rushing backward from first to last, watching as a million macroforms spilled out into the deeply glowing gas that filled the new space. He could see them all ahead, floating aimlessly in what seemed to be a warm daylight sky, not very far away. Some of the worlds were empty of conscious life, he noted, dead husks thrown out of the cave of winter by the spring wind, too late to live again.

He was the last to come out of the cave. Behind him, the knothole in space would become a closing gravitational vortex, existing long enough to help form the metagalaxy, whose member galaxies would condense into stars as they flew apart. In a million years, individual stars would begin to shine, as gravity pulled the gas together. It would be enough, this cloud of light and gas, to provide them with a supply of energy and hope.

As he watched his worlds gathering into a giant sphere, John found himself at peace. Each world glowed as its supply of hydrogen and newly formed mini black holes was replenished from the warm universe. He thought of streetlights going on in an endless fog. . . .

The glow of this universe would fade one day, when its free electrons and protons combined to form transparent hydrogen.

Then he noticed another glow. It was coming from far away, and suddenly he saw that it was a transparent globe.

::A hundred million kilometers in radius::

As the object drew nearer, John became aware that it was filled with millions of glowing objects.

::Macrolife from before our cycle, surviving from the uncounted ruins of nature. We are not the first large units of intelligent awareness::

He should have expected it, especially when the stranger had passed them in the aperture; but the reality was still a surprise. This, John thought, was the Type III civilization which had not revealed itself, preferring to wait rather than influence youthful development. This was the first form of macrolife, surviving from some unimaginable past.

There was no need to speak. The elder form opened its shell, and the million worlds passed inside without ceremony. There would be survivors from every cycle; they had been expected.

vi

Macrolife waits in the morning light of creation, its millions of worlds forming a complex figure in the field of the giant sphere. Inside, the youngest macroforms are setting out their newest understanding of the glittering sequence through which their parent universe pulses as it lives and dies and is reborn in the fabric of eternity; reality has given up its elementary secrets, while leaving a deeper grain.

Morning will pass; birthing suns will build up the light for noon. But macrolife is already looking to a greater frame of activity, in which this universe is only one in an ocean of possibility. Macrolife plans to move across the time of this cycle, observing the growth of intelligent life, adding, if possible, to its knowledge and awareness, gathering new macrolife at the end, ultimately sweeping across future cycles in shortened subjective time, taking on hydrogen and quantum black holes at each birth and new intelligences at each maturity, drawn ever forward by the continuing novelty of universes.

An infinity of universes swim in superspace, all passing through their own cycles of birth and death; some are novel, others repetitious; some produce macrolife, others do not; still others are lifeless. In time, macrolife will attempt to reach out from its cycles to other space-time bubbles, perhaps even to past cycles, which leave their echoes in superspace, and might be reached. In all these ambitions, only the ultimate pattern of development is unknown, drawing macrolife toward some further transformation still beyond its view. There are times when the oldest macrolife senses that vaster intelligences are peering in at it from some great beyond. . . .

Within the youngest macroform, John Bulero is slowly fading; the usefulness of his will, its narrowly gauged impetus, is over. His finitude, his ancient human aches are passing into what seems a larger dream. He understands now that knowledge can never be final, even as it grows with the forward unfolding of the universes. His thirst to know, his hunger to see and experience, must be content with the finality of endlessness, with the wisdom that teaches the acceptance of the logic of infinity. The unraveling of the illusion of last things should be least attempted, says the logic of infinities; the darkness of unreality hides last things better than any real cloak.

Yet: why is there anything? Why do universes come into being? To what greater process do these brilliant sparks owe their existence? Where was the valley of his beginning? Why was it the cruelty of death that ensured their unique value? Were they truly unrepeatable? He would take these questions into the greater gauge of consciousness. Perhaps then he could accept the fact that decline and destruction served to create new things—new individuals, novel physical cycles, the kind of intense development that could not otherwise be sustained; even macrolife, continuous as it was with the old and new, depends on natural universes for a supply of new minds and for the means by which it can nurture its own creations. As John Bulero, he had paid the price in loss, to live toward the midnight, past the fleeting seconds where night turns into a glowing morning, leaving him with the ashes of memory. . . .

Quietly, John Bulero forgets himself; the universe is mysterious again, at the very moment when its violent processes have become comprehensible to him. All knowledge is suddenly old knowledge, no longer curious or a delight, simply old and repetitious; elsewhere lies knowledge that is curious and new, to be gathered by the hungry, for whom the mystery of existence must always be its greatest beauty. The open book gives reference on its last page to a further library. . . .

All that had pulled him down was gone.

Having survived into its first maturity, the youngest macrolife has learned a new patience with which to soothe its curiosity; and in that patience of endless knowing it has found its own enduring kind of beauty.

GENEALOGY OF MACROLIFE

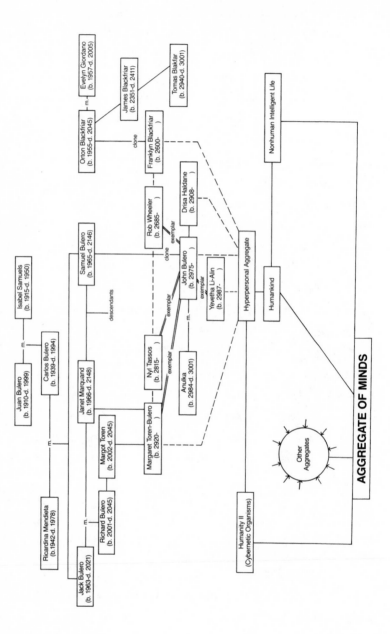

AGGREGATE OF MINDS

AFTERWORD TO THE FIRST EDITION

The physical concept of macrolife as a "societal container" is not the work of one person. Dandridge Cole originated the term "Macro Life," and described it in "The Ultimate Human Society" (1961). Konstantin Tsiolkovsky and J. D. Bernal had much earlier suggested this kind of space-colony concept, stressing the use of sunspace as an energy-rich environment for civilization. Artificial planets appeared in the works of Olaf Stapledon and others. The idea of self-contained space habitats as alternatives to natural worlds is also related to the "generation starship" idea, a kind of Noah's Ark for colonizing the stars.

I started with Cole's hollow asteroid and projected its development beyond this stage. I used an asteroid because it might be safer, providing shielding from solar radiation as well as natural resources. Gerard O'Neill's space cylinder, as well as other designs which assume construction from scratch, seem too precarious to me right now, but I may be wrong. O'Neill's approach to the space-habitat idea, however, strikes me as a thoroughly considered near-future vision. I suspect that space habitats will get built in just about every way they can be built.

I was also stimulated by Isaac Asimov's neglected version of long-term space-habitat development ("There's no Place Like Spome," 1965, reprinted in *Is Anyone There?* Doubleday, 1967), as well as by G.

Harry Stine's *The Third Industrial Revolution* (Putnam, 1975). Mr. Stine bears some responsibility for this novel's existence, because in 1961 he complained (in "Science Fiction Is Too Conservative," *Analog*) that concepts such as Cole's Macro Life were being ignored by science fiction authors and that most of the innovative speculation was going on outside SF. This is even more true today, I'm sorry to report. If he had mentioned Asimov's spomes, I wonder if the title on the cover of this novel might have been *Spomelife?*

The richness of the macrolife concept lies not only in its physical aspects, but in the psychosocial consequences for the idea of human society, in the ways that human experience might be affected and transformed into something else; this speculative richness is the province of the novelist. I am certain that I have not exhausted macrolife within the pages of one book.

I would like to thank those people who were directly helpful in the writing of this novel: Poul Anderson, Gregory Benford, Mark Olson, Pamela Sargent, Marjorie Horvitz (finest of copy editors), M. S. Wyeth Jr., and Stephen K. Roos (thoughtful, demanding editors both), Norbert Slepyan, Joseph Elder, William Pizante, Robert Neidorf, Robert L. Forward, Jack Dann; for their encouragement, Guy Streatfeild, John and Magda McHale.

Paolo Soleri's concept of "arcologies" (among them a spacegoing version) was partially responsible for my naming the first macroworld Asterome. Special thanks to "Rebus Heviwait" and "Emmanuel Lighthanger," whose enterprising book, *Projex* (Links Books, 1972), was invaluable. John McHale's classic *The Future of the Future* (Braziller, 1969) was also very helpful.

Of course, the people mentioned above had nothing to do with the changes I may have made in their speculations. All mistakes and misconceptions are mine.

DON'T READ THIS FIRST
AFTERWORD TO THE NEW EDITION

What can an author say about a novel he wrote in a bold mood of declamatory poetry over twenty-five years ago, a first novel that he dreamed about throughout his high school years and which finally came to him in handsome publication? Well, one can observe and measure the past, and be gratified that this novel received high praise from its many readers and continues to do so. At the end of his days, Isaac Asimov said to me, "These stories about macrolife will be your Foundation series. Don't neglect them!"

I was writing this book from about 1961 onward, struck by the social ideas of mobile habitats in the scientific/engineering work of Dandridge Cole and developing his vision not only in its engineering aspect but also in the philosophical view of mobile habitats as the ultimately flexible societal organism, capable of great divergent development. No work of fiction had taken the ideas as far as I did by 1979; one had to look to the nonfiction of J. D. Bernal, Konstantin Tsiolkovsky, and Isaac Asimov, to various suggestions in the works of Olaf Stapledon, and to Cole's brief works, not to stories and novels. But one thing was clear to me even as a teenager: I took the idea as a reality waiting to be realized.

The writing of my novel, which presents three visionary snapshots

377

in the life of mobile habitats and what they are *for*, swallowed my life for most of two decades. As Dante had been inspired by theological cosmologies to search out a context for human life, I was drawn to the deeper implications of space travel and to a critical reconsideration of a too easily accepted idea of settling the planets of other solar spaces. *Macrolife* also sang to me as a symphonic structure—a heroic first part, a slower middle movement, and a long visionary poem for the finale.

One criticism raised about the novel when it was first published claimed that it did not show "how we get from here to there." It was basically a dismissal of the utopian visionary ideals of the story, somehow forgetting that all of Part 1 presents catastrophe as the mid-wife of change, if not progress, as it has always been throughout human history, if one reads and remembers that the fall of every major civiliza-tion sows the seeds of the next. I would prefer that planetary disaster not be the midwife to the birth of macrolife; but it may in fact have to be so, whether it be ecological of our own making, cosmic (permitted by our own inaction), or sociopolitical. My contribution was in sug-gesting that a mobile civilization would not fail, at least not as easily as our planetary cultures have fallen, and perhaps not ever.

Ever is a cosmological word deeply rooted in our apprehensions about reality, because we still come and go too quickly. I was thinking of Robert A. Heinlein's Future History Chart, from which I fondly recall the entry for 2600 AD—"Civil Disorder, followed by the end of human adolescence, and the beginning of first mature culture." I also charted a future history, for use in writing the novel, on a white board in black marker; one day I will revise it.

Another notable misconception involved the scale of my mobiles. One reviewer asked why they were called macroworlds, since they were so "small," little realizing that length is not the same as volume and square surface area, which can yield an inner surface at least twice that of the Earth, as noted at the start of Part 2. One curiously derisive com-ment likened this novel to a famously difficult philosophical work, when in fact my novel's reading level has been measured as being that of midcollege. William Styron once said that a good novel should leave the reader slightly exhausted, and I say that a science fiction novel without actual thinking in it is not worthy of the name.

Much has been made of my Stapledonian influences. For sheer comprehensive vision, his body of work constitutes the single greatest achievement in science fiction's history. But the last lines of my novel answer Stapledon's *Last and First Men* and *Star Maker* by suggesting a music that will endure, one that does not come and go as in Stapledon's cosmic novels but contributes to a growing permanence and a net gain, as new macrolife comes into being with each new cycle of nature and becomes aware of macrolife sweeping across from previous cycles. If there is a physical forever to existence, then why not? Freeman Dyson has suggested an all-but-eternal survival of intelligent life through a thrifty, endless ratcheting down of energy use.

Clearly, *Macrolife* is a further development of the utopian novel, unnoticed despite some discussion of this in the novel itself that it is a "dynamic utopia," in H. G. Wells's discussions of the shift away from the "static" models that preceded him. So I have restored the novel's subtitle, *A Mobile Utopia*, and urge readers to keep in mind that there have been at least two meanings of the term *utopia* since the time of Wells, but too many still recall the static models of earlier writers.

Macrolife, although it can stand alone, is part of a broader canvas; between its three parts I have also set *Cave of Stars*, a darker, closer vision that still manages to oppose the darkness, despite the battering of our hopes in recent decades. Two published novelettes, which may yet grow to be parts of novels, deal with the conflict that the mobiles of "macrolife" have with settling nature's planets.

I still feel that the central conception is poorly understood, dragged down by weighty pasts, perhaps because it looks critically upon, and rejects, nearly all of science fiction's past visions about settling other worlds. I see this dialogue going on in my mosaic of stories and novels until the question is resolved—probably by the year 5000 in my fictional chronology. It may never be resolved in reality. The question may never even be tested, but I hope that this is merely short-sightedness. As one endures, we are weighed down by the spectacle of human quarrels, by the blindness of our swarm, by the realization that came to Napoleon that there was little he could do against privileged wealth and power, and maybe even less by the cat's cradles of familial knots.

Someone once said that there are no utopias that he would want to live in. I have always wanted to live in the macrolife culture and to continue learning throughout an indefinite life span, in epochs that would have their own emerging problems—but not those of the past. A room with heat, electric light, a television, and a library, not to mention online access to a library, would have been a utopian vision to Thomas Jefferson.

I now say, against a creeping darkness of doubt, that something like macrolife has to be the ultimate in social systems and in the survival of intelligent life, human life included. But even in the near term, across the next millennium, our failure to become a space-faring world may well be suicidal when we consider what we can do for our world from the high ground of the solar system: energy and resources, planetary management, and most important the ability to prevent the world-ending catastrophe of an asteroid strike. This last threat will happen; it is not a question of if but when. Today we are utterly helpless before such a danger and would know of it only when it was already happening.

But the deepest threat to our survival lives inside all of us. The powers of the Earth today took power from previous powers, with cultures overlaying previous ones by force, and the latest always fear innovation unless they control it, since innovation would rearrange the rule of the planet. The struggle over energy resources may yet plunge us into a new dark age, if not extinction, by our own hands. We have not gone out into the solar system, or raised up our poor and powerless, because that would also change too much for our existing powers, who do fear that more for the many means less for the few. Virgil wrote of the Romans, "To these I set no bounds in time or space/They shall rule forever," but today we are learning to reject a planetary minority as the Earth's master—and that is what the traditional masters fear most, that the future will not belong to their generations, to the devils they know within themselves. When confronted with the concept of space colonies in the second half of the twentieth century, politicians muttered, "Uh, we can't have that. It would change too much. And it's too expensive." Public interest waned by the mid-1980s, much as it had turned against space exploration in the early 1950s, until the political disaster of *Sputnik* in 1957 revived the idea, and I began to wonder what kind of planetary disaster would kick our world out of its cradle into genuine space-faring and world-building. The view of the Earth from the Moon gave us a sense of our world's fragility. It is in fact a space colony, a skylife conglomeration of materials held together by gravity, and far from safe.

The test of a utopia is its treatment of the individual. A dynamic utopia, one that responds to the external universe and to the inner life of its people, must safeguard both itself and the individual, with legal, fully usable safeguards for both. Olaf Stapledon held that a society must deserve its individuals *and* its individuals must deserve their society. That is the solution to the problem of the individual in society; it calls for responsibilities from both, so the solution is both profoundly conservative and radical at the same time, hinging on the *and* of that sentence being practiced. The economic social container has to be inviolate, since it supports all that is possible without determining its content; but the true test would come in its tolerance of dissident and departing individuals, something the Soviet Union and many other governments have not been able to tolerate consistently. "The State is for Individuals," Wells wrote in *A Modern Utopia*. "The law is for freedoms, the world is for experiment, experience, and change; these are the fundamental beliefs upon which a modern Utopia must go." These great words sound the very theme of science fiction as an exploratory fiction, as a freedom of inner exploration and self-programming that our world has hit upon to help it see ahead. Fictional and imaginative, but aspiring to reality. The words of a novel, however, cannot guarantee any future reality's success; therefore, one cannot make of macrolife a failure unless we go out and try it out.

Utopian ideas, whether of the static or dynamic kind, are usually confronted, often with derision, with the evidence of human nature, which, it is claimed, requires conflict inherited from the evolutionary mill. Few critics of utopias care to admit that we can in fact see beyond the dramatic imperfections of our given physiology, that we can to a large degree question our biological constraints, that these do not completely block our imaginative efforts to step back from our humanity and see possibilities in freer, economically liberated measures of man.

Great fear is made of the lockstep of impoverished utopias not worthy of the name; that is why this has been a term of derision. Yet utopias remain as the great empty space on our maps, reproaches to our acceptance of who we have been given to be by nature. They have threatened and beckoned with creative possibilities and shame the easy way with which so many of us have turned away from the effort. What we are has its own inertia and a self-serving way of rationalizing what should be questioned and perhaps even despised by a creative, adventurous spirit that has acquired enough plasticity and free will to make of itself its own project for the future. Our literatures, fictions all, have been a way of "distancing" ourselves from ourselves, of seeing, as the historian Giambattista Vico saw, that much of what we ascribe to human nature is more circumstance and culture than nature, much of it made by ourselves, and that what we have made in one way we might make in another. Vico was generous with his vision of human freedom, but despite the catastrophe of the twentieth century, our creative freedom to remake ourselves through a growing knowledge does in fact await us, even if we can take only small steps; but if we believe that we are ruled by unreachable inner forces that will only subvert all the promise of our science and technology, that the complexities of our short lives transcend our ability to understand and deal with them, then we are indeed lost. We do have the choice to reject this view, even if it may be true, and bring the battle to a test that will defeat the past and grow a new freedom.

"The Ultimate Human Society," as Dandridge Cole presented the idea, is perhaps misleading, since the concept of macrolife is *one* thing only in its economic and technological sense, but an endless series of opportunities for cultural ways to grow on the basic life-support model. What more could intelligent life ask for? All of our planetary societies have tended toward it, in every form of community from village to city. Dandridge Cole had it right, but his visionary successors, from Gerard K. O'Neill to many a science fiction writer, did not consider the idea's full implications. It is not all engineering, hardware, and "big dumb objects," but a waiting opportunity for a better human life. It has been my privilege to write novels searching out the human implications, as well as the implications for intelligent life, in the arena of the novel, which has traditionally been a central and complex court of human inquiry, and where so much of today's literature, in the words of Fred Hoyle, is myopic and shortsighted before the "golden chances" that wait for us and which we may lose. No planetary future for intelligent life is assured except through knowledge and action.

So I welcome this new edition of my early hopes, now darker, to confront my doubts. And I welcome the fact that this new edition comes from a publisher who has long stood for Enlightenment values, which for me have always lived at the heart of science fiction's loftier but too often commerce-crippled life. The best of science fiction has increased human awareness of the future tense for some two centuries now, but we must remind ourselves how new such an impulse is, as it struggles to grow in the human mind, which is still hobbled by our inheritance from a survivalist nature.

All literature, at whatever scale of observation, has been a stepback seeing effort; and we must take it as a sign of hope that we have any-thing like this ability, not only to look back but to gaze forward, and not just to see what is merely possible but even to make new things happen.

George Zebrowski
Delmar, New York
June 2005

About the Author

George Zebrowski's forty books include novels, short-fiction collections, anthologies, and a book of essays. His works have appeared in all the science fiction magazines, as well as in *Omni, Nature, Popular Computing*, and the *Bertrand Russell Society News*.

Arthur C. Clarke described *Macrolife* as "a worthy successor to Olaf Stapledon's *Star Maker*. It's been years since I was so impressed. One of the few books I intend to read again." *Library Journal* listed *Macrolife* as one of the one hundred best science fiction novels, and the Easton Press published it in its Masterpieces of Science Fiction series. *Cave of Stars*, a recent novel, also belongs to the *Macrolife* mosaic. Zebrowski's works have been translated into eight languages; his short fiction has been nominated for the Nebula Award and the Theodore Sturgeon Memorial Award. *Brute Orbits*, an uncompromising novel about a future penal system, was honored with the John W. Campbell Memorial Award for Best Novel of the Year in 1999.

About the Artist for the Interior Illustrations

Rick Sternbach has been a space and science fiction artist since the early 1970s, often combining both interests in a project. His clients include NASA, *Sky & Telescope*, Data Products, Random House, *Smithsonian*, *Analog*, *Astronomy*, the Planetary Society, and Time-Life Books. He is a founding member and fellow of the International Association of Astronomical Artists (IAAA), which was formed in 1981. He has written and illustrated articles on orbital transfer vehicles and interstellar flight for *Science Digest*. Beginning in the late 1970s Rick added film and television illustration and special effects to his background, with productions like *Star Trek: The Motion Picture*, *The Last Starfighter*, *Future Flight*, and *Cosmos*, for which he and other members of the astronomical art team received an Emmy Award, the first for visual effects. Rick also twice received the coveted Hugo Award for Best Professional Science Fiction Artist, in 1977 and 1978.

With the rebirth of *Star Trek*, beginning with *The Next Generation*, Rick was one of the first employees hired to update the Trek universe. He created new spacecraft, tricorders, phasers, and hundreds of other props and set pieces. Using pencil, pen, and computer, Rick added *Deep Space Nine* and *Voyager* to his spacecraft inventory and kept his hand in real space design with *Voyager*'s Ares IV Mars orbiter (blessed by planetary scientist Dr. Bruce Murray).

Rick contributed graphic designs for the *Star Trek: Nemesis* feature film, including the new Romulan bird of prey and Senate chamber floor. He also provided computer playback graphics and animation elements for Steven Soderbergh's *Solaris*.

About the Cover Illustrator

John Picacio is an award-winning illustrator who has illustrated covers for works by Harlan Ellison, Michael Moorcock, Robert Silverberg, Neil Gaiman, Joe R. Lansdale, Jeffrey Ford, Graham Joyce, Lucius Shepard, Charles De Lint, David Gemmell, Frederik Pohl, Hal Clement, and many, many more. In 1992 he earned a bachelor of architecture degree from the University of Texas at Austin. Four years later, he illustrated his first book, the Thirtieth Anniversary Edition of Michael Moorcock's *Behold the Man*. In May 2001 he chose a career in illustration over a career in architecture and devoted himself full time to the craft of illustration.

Since then, his client list has continued to grow, including companies such as Random House/Del Rey, HarperCollins/Eos, Roc Books, Tor Books, Pyr, Viking Children's Books, MonkeyBrain Books, Golden Gryphon Press, Earthling Publications, and *Realms of Fantasy Magazine*.

His illustrations have been selected numerous times for the *Spectrum Annual*, and in 2002 he received the International Horror Guild Award for Best Artist. In 2005 he won a Chesley Award for Best Paperback Cover Illustration. In addition, he is a two-time nominee for the World Fantasy Award in the Artist category and a 2005 Hugo nominee in the Best Professional Artist category.

He lives and works in San Antonio, Texas. For more info, see www.johnpicacio.com.